FUR

Fury features as the main character Newman, but is really the story of their colleague Philip Cardon and his agonized search for the men who killed his wife, Jean.

During his quest – from the Chichester creeks to Bavaria and Austria – Philip stumbles on Project Tidal Wave, a mysterious and vast plan to overwhelm Europe in the very near future. Tweed, suspecting catastrophe, follows Philip with his team, fearful for the safety of the lone hunter.

Who is the deadly woman assassin, Teardrop? Rosa Brandt, a strange veiled woman, together with vivacious Lisa Trent, financial analyst, and cool Jill Selborne, fashion reporter, all attract Tweed's attention. Paula Grey plays a more dominant part than ever before as Teardrop murders one informant after another.

What is the real role of Gabriel March Walvis, billionaire owner of a global communications system? From Munich to the underground salt mines on the Czech frontier, from grim Passau to ancient Salzburg – and back to Chichester – Paula Grey and Tweed's team fight to unravel the secret of Tidal Wave, the identity of Teardrop.

The author has woven into this remarkable novel the story of the extraordinary courage of his late wife Jane, who, out of consideration for her husband, concealed from him the fact that her remaining lifespan would be short. The emotional element is powerful and disturbing.

FURY

Colin Forbes

MACMILLAN

First published 1995 by Macmillan London
an imprint of Macmillan General Books
Cavaye Place London SW10 9PG
and Basingstoke

Associated companies throughout the world

ISBN 0–333–64197–3 Hardback
0–333–64414–X Airside Edition

Copyright © Colin Forbes 1995

The right of Colin Forbes to be identified as the
author of this work has been asserted by him in accordance
with the Copyright, Designs and Patents Act 1988.

All rights reserved. No reproduction, copy or transmission
of this publication may be made without written permission.
No paragraph of this publication may be reproduced, copied or
transmitted save with written permission or in accordance with
the provisions of the Copyright Act 1956 (as amended). Any
person who does any unauthorised act in relation to
this publication may be liable to criminal prosecution
and civil claims for damages.

1 3 5 7 9 8 6 4 2

A CIP catalogue record for this book is available from the British Library

Photoset by Parker Typesetting Service, Leicester
Printed and bound in Great Britain by
Mackays of Chatham plc, Chatham, Kent

AUTHOR'S NOTE

Like my previous books this novel is a thriller, a whodunnit and an adventure story.

Tweed, Paula Grey and Bob Newman feature as the main characters.

But, entwined in the plot, it is also a tribute to my late wife, Jane. A remarkable woman, I know I shall not meet her like again. The novel is a mix of fact and fiction. Some of the dialogue, certain of the incidents, are authentic and happened in real life.

All the characters portrayed – with the exception of Jean and Philip Cardon – are creatures of the author's imagination and bear no relationship to any living person. All residences and companies are non-existent.

IN MEMORIAM

FOR JANE

who always cared

Prologue

'She's dead. She died at 5.12 p.m. I'm going to find the people who murdered her . . .' said Philip Cardon.

The atmosphere in the corridor of the Nuffield Hospital was unbearable. Tweed and Paula had just arrived. Too late. Philip Cardon's wife, Jean, had died a few minutes earlier.

It was the calm lifeless tone in which Cardon spoke that scared Paula. He stood very still, quite erect. They were alone in the corridor. A nursing sister had appeared and then vanished quickly. Cardon continued, his blue-grey eyes cold – continued in the same remorseless tone.

'They had her linked up to a machine that registers the pulse rate. Your pulse rates are ninety to the minute. I watched the screen on the machine. She was sleeping peacefully – they had treated her intravenously with diamorphine to eliminate the pain. Earlier the rate was registered at ninety, then eighty, then it climbed back to ninety. Suddenly it dropped to forty. The sister glanced at me. I saw her do that out of the corner of my eye. At 5.12 the screen went blank. No pulse rate. I couldn't believe it.'

'Philip . . .' Paula began.

Tweed silenced her with a gesture. Behind the glazed look in Cardon's eyes he detected a terrible fury. He tried to think of words to say but they choked inside him. No words could comfort Cardon now. He had loved his wife: she had loved him. It had been the

1

perfect partnership, a rare phenomenon. Cardon was speaking again in that dreadful monotone.

'They took me into another room. I knew why. They don't waste time. They had phoned the undertaker. He arrived quickly. I heard the lift coming up, stop. They were wheeling her away in a trolley. For ever. I shall never see her again. I'm going home now to our flat. No one will be allowed to view her again. She will be cremated, as she wanted. Burnt to dust and ashes. I'm going home now to London,' he repeated.

'You shouldn't drive,' Paula protested. 'Not in your present state . . .'

Again Tweed silenced her with a gesture. Cardon, of medium height and build, clean shaven and with a high colour, opened his hand. Paula fought back tears as she saw what he was holding. Jean's engagement ring, her wedding ring.

'That's all that will be left of her,' Cardon remarked. 'I'm sorry you had a wasted journey.'

'Oh, for God's sake . . .' Paula began.

Tweed's hand gripped her arm, silenced her for the third time. He was still watching Cardon, who nodded at them and walked away towards the exit. He was moving on automatic pilot. Tweed pursed his lips. For once in his life he felt completely helpless. Paula swung on her heel and watched Cardon's back retreating with a slow deliberate tread. His lack of emotion was even more heart-rending than if he had broken down.

'We should have said something,' she snapped in her misery.

'And risked saying the wrong thing,' Tweed told her. 'So many people do that in a situation like this. They don't know what to say, so they come out with something absurd.'

He followed Paula who walked to a window on the first floor overlooking the car park. They watched in silence as

2

Cardon appeared below, unlocked the Mercedes 280E Bob Newman had loaned him. They went on staring down. Cardon closed the door, settled himself behind the wheel, sat quite still and then lit a cigarette.

'Both of them,' Paula recalled, 'had cut down their smoking to four cigarettes a day for a year. Jean found it most difficult, she told me, but she did it. She had such a strong character, such a remarkable intellect. I suppose someone should inform that strange firm she was working for.'

'In due course,' Tweed replied. 'We'll have to take over all the beastly arrangements.'

'I think he's going now. Murdered. And so horribly.'

Cardon had turned on the ignition. The car moved, a skilful U-turn, exited from the car park, turned slowly, approached the road beyond the hospital. Paula watched anxiously, scared that Cardon wouldn't be driving safely. She let out a sigh of relief as he paused to look both ways, then swung left which would take him on the direct route to London. He vanished from sight. Intuitively Tweed sensed the reason for her anxiety.

'Don't worry about Philip. He goes ice cold in a crisis.'

'Where do you think he's going?'

'He told you. Back to the flat in London he shared with Jean.'

'They were so close,' Paula whispered, and Tweed had the impression she was talking to herself. 'It was an ideal marriage, so rare nowadays.' She sank into a seat by the corridor wall and buried her face in her hands. She was crying quietly. Tweed grasped her shoulder.

'What are you thinking about now?'

She removed her hands, exposed her tear-stained face and gazed up at Tweed in sheer misery.

'How it started before Jean spent her last six days on earth in her room in this place. That horrible phone call Philip had at Park Crescent. An unknown man's voice.

3

The few words he said to Philip. *"If you want to find what's left of your wife try Amber Cottage on the road to West Wittering south of Chichester..."'*

Tweed and Paula had been in the same office when the call had come through. Philip had put down the phone, turned to face them with an expression like stone and repeated the words.

Bob Newman had told Philip to take his Mercedes 280E parked outside. Philip had driven out of London and once on the country road to Chichester had rammed his foot down on the accelerator. Behind him in an Escort, Tweed driving and Paula by his side, they had followed Cardon, eventually climbing the winding road over the South Downs, cresting the summit and seeing in the clear November afternoon light a vast panorama. The flatlands below the Downs stretching out towards the distant sea, the tiny spike which was the spire of Chichester Cathedral, silver streaks which were the labyrinth of creeks south of the city.

It was Paula who had spotted the thatched building well back from the Wittering road which was Amber Cottage. She had used her horn to bring back Philip, who had driven past it.

'I'll go in first,' Tweed had suggested.

Unusually he was holding a Walther 9mm automatic in his right hand. Tweed rarely carried a firearm. Paula gripped the .32 Browning automatic she had slipped out of the special pocket in her shoulder-bag. Cardon, holding no weapon, had pushed them aside, running up the mossy path leading to the front door. It opened when he rammed up the latch and he darted inside into the musty gloom. They found her inside a downstairs bedroom at the back.

Jean Cardon was lying on a pillow, waving both arms in

a strange way – as though pushing something away. She was fully dressed.

'Can't breathe,' she gasped. 'It's awful. Feels like an iron band tight across my chest . . .'

Which wasn't a surprising statement. Philip found a flexible band of hard metal pressed into her chest. Jean was fighting for breath.

'My glasses . . .' she gasped.

Paula retrieved them off the planked floor. They were unbroken. Tenderly, Cardon had eased her into a sitting position. Paula started to put the glasses back on to Jean's nose but she grasped them herself, looped them behind her ears and blinked. Then she groaned with pain.

Cardon's expression was murderous. Behind her back the band had an adjustable screw to loosen or tighten the fiendish instrument. He unscrewed it, eased it away from her body. She collapsed back on to the pillow.

'Can't breathe . . . it's horrible . . .'

When Jean was able to speak coherently she insisted on being moved to the Nuffield Hospital on the edge of the town in Surrey where the Cardons had a house. The top consultant who attended her, a friend of Tweed's, warned Philip as soon as tests had been made.

'There is very little left of her lungs, but she may just be treatable. I am hoping so . . .'

In the beginning Jean seemed on the verge of recovery. At the consultant's suggestion Philip made arrangements for round-the-clock nursing help at their Surrey home during her recuperation. On the fourth evening Philip had dinner with Jean in her room at the hospital. They drank a bottle of champagne and Jean seemed perfectly normal.

Tweed and Paula had very little sleep during those nights. He sent two key members of his SIS team to Chichester to find out who owned Amber Cottage. The isolated dwelling had been rented over the phone by a man who gave his name as Martin West. The rent for the first three months had been paid in cash by a woman who called at the estate agent's office. He could only give a poor description of the mysterious woman.

On the fifth day there was a sudden rapid deterioration in Jean's condition. She was in great pain and suffered bouts of major agitation. The consultant was so disturbed he prescribed diamorphine fed into her system intra-venously. Milder pain-killers had not worked but now she lapsed into a deep sleep. She never woke up.

Cardon was in her room when she was linked up to the machine that registered her pulse rate.

'Your normal pulse rate is ninety to the minute,' a sister told Philip.

Like a man hypnotized Philip watched the figures regis-tering on the machine. Early on the sixth evening the reading dropped to forty. The sister on duty bit her lip, glanced at Philip. His eyes were still glued to the screen when it suddenly went blank. No pulse rate. He felt as though he had been hit by a sledgehammer. Tweed and Paula arrived back a few minutes after the undertaker had removed her.

That was when Philip Cardon uttered the grim words: 'I'm going to find the people who murdered her . . .'

A few moments before Paula had left the window after watching Cardon drive off in the Mercedes, before she had broken down, she noticed something.

Cardon's car had disappeared from sight when a motor cyclist left the car park and took the route Cardon had followed. It was a powerful machine and the rider was clad in a black leather jacket and leggings. Impossible to see his face – the visor was dropped over it from the heavy-duty helmet and goggles he wore. A despatch rider who had delivered urgently required drugs to the hospital, she assumed.

Philip Cardon did not make the same assumption. He looked in his rear-view mirror as he turned on to the M25. He studied the motor cyclist for a short time and then concentrated on his driving.

'If you're what I think you are, laddie, then I welcome your company,' he said aloud. 'If you stay with me you may not welcome mine before the night is out.'

Getting close to six o'clock in the November evening it was pitch dark and a stream of headlights crawled towards him in the opposite lanes. He had glanced in the mirror five times as he approached Putney, making good time with light traffic in his direction.

On all five occasions he had still seen the same motor cyclist no more than one vehicle behind him. When he turned down into the South Ken streets he would know for sure.

'Looks like you and I are going to have a chat – and that won't be friendly,' he said aloud again. 'At least I know I'm talking to myself,' he went on. 'And with Jean gone for ever I'll be doing a lot of that, I suspect. In the house and at the flat. God, they'll seem empty. And now, chum, we'll know whether you are tailing me . . .'

Five minutes later he had left the Cromwell Road behind, driving slowly along the crescent curving round one of the most prestigious addresses in London – The Boltons. The motor cyclist was still about twenty feet on his tail. Cardon performed the manoeuvre he'd worked out after driving along the Fulham Road and turning down the deserted side street towards where they lived.

'Where we live – lived,' he thought bitterly.

He slowed suddenly, swung out, catching the pursuer off guard. The side of the Mercedes kissed the machine, toppled it, hurling the rider into the road. Cardon was out of his car in seconds, grabbing hold of the sprawled motor

7

cyclist, hauling him into the entrance to his flat, stopping at the door of the stone flight of steps leading down into the basement, his hands squeezing the man's windpipe.

'You've got thirty seconds to live unless you talk,' Cardon said savagely. 'Who are you working for? Who is your boss?'

'Don't know. Can't breathe . . .'

'Neither could my wife before she was murdered.' He had relaxed his grip so his captive could reply. Now he increased the pressure using both thumbs. 'Name of your top man. Won't ask you again. It would be a pleasure to kill you.'

The motor cyclist had been beating at Cardon's body with his gloved hands but they were feeble blows. He was choking. In a desperate attempt to indicate he wanted to speak he jerked up one thumb in a conciliatory gesture. Cardon relaxed his grip for the second time.

'Martin . . .'

The motor cyclist gasped out the name. Cardon was aware another high-powered machine was cruising down the street from the direction he had driven. There was a loud explosion like a car backfiring. The Perspex visor drawn down over the captive's face crazed. A large hole appeared in the forehead of the captive. Despite Cardon's grip the man was jerked out of his hands, was hurled down the steps and tumbled into a pile of filled rubbish sacks awaiting collection.

Cardon hauled out his .38 Smith & Wesson revolver from his hip holster, ran back into the street gripping the weapon in both hands. He was too late: the second motor cyclist, the assassin, had zoomed away round a corner.

Cardon moved fast. He parked the Mercedes by the kerb, lifted the abandoned motor cycle, parked it by the opposite kerb a few yards down the street. There was

8

still no one about, no sign that anyone had heard or seen what had happened. And in the middle of London, he thought grimly.

Running down the basement steps he checked the crumpled man's pulse. Nothing. Which didn't surprise him. The force of the bullet to hurtle its target down the steps suggested a very powerful hand gun, probably a .45 Colt automatic. He stood for a moment looking down at the body after a swift and expert search. It was unlikely that anyone glancing into the basement would distinguish the corpse from the stuffed black sacks. The search had revealed nothing to identify the man. Again, no surprise.

'Philip, you'll have to wake up,' he said aloud. 'You did not spot the second tail. This must be some outfit. They rub out one of their own if they think there's any risk of him talking.'

He looked up at the three storeys above him. No sign of life. So far as he knew they were all away. Unfastening the security locks on the front door, he entered the narrow hall, closed the door, quietly unlocked the door to his ground-floor flat. He didn't want to enter – the place would seem so horribly empty. Dead.

Once inside, Cardon again moved quickly. He had a most distasteful task to perform. Jean had kept a diary each year and the diaries were kept in a Davenport, her own private world he had never before invaded. Like searching her handbag, he thought as he sat down on a chair, raised the lid, his hand hesitating before he picked up the current year's diary and swiftly began reading words he had never seen before. He talked out loud to himself as he read, sorting out recent events.

'They followed me from the Nuffield. One of them would probably have said he was a relative – or used some other lie – to confirm Jean was dead. The *bastards*!' He closed the diary. 'Well, Jean, I think I now know why the swine did what they did to you – and it's my bet you didn't talk.'

He stood up, collected all the diaries, slotted them inside an executive case. He closed the lid of the Davenport with tender care. 'I just don't know *who* is responsible, but I'm going to find out. At least I know where to start looking.'

Then, standing by this very personal piece of her property, her world, he broke, shouting at the top of his voice. A sound like a wolf howling broke out. 'Jean!' he called out in his anguish. He repeated the unearthly wolf-like howl, unaware until that moment that he was capable of uttering such an animal scream, followed again by her name. A part of his brain functioning normally counted how many times he called out. Twelve times before the tears came.

Gabriel March Walvis, the richest man in the world, sat comfortably in his leather armchair aboard his specially designed private jet waiting at Heathrow. It was a big armchair constructed to take his bulk. He had a large head and his face was fat, his cold eyes pouched in heavy lids. His thick lips pressed tightly, expressed his impatience at the delayed take-off. He was waiting for his messenger.

His dense grey hair drooped over his high forehead and his nose was short and fleshy. His ugly pudgy hands were clasped in his ample lap. He glanced down again at his Blancpain watch. The woman seated by his side made the mistake of trying to soothe him.

'Martin can't be much longer. Then we can leave at once for Munich . . .'

'When I want your comments I will request them. In the mean time perhaps you will make a great effort and keep quiet.'

Walvis had a soft voice. His tone was deceptively soft – more menacing because it managed to convey the utmost venom.

'I'm sorry. I made a mistake,' the woman said quickly.

'I notice many people make mistakes. The important thing in life is not to repeat them.'

The woman sighed with relief. In her thirties, she wore a dark cap with a black veil which covered the upper part of her face. Her two-piece suit was black and her knee-length coat was of the same colour. Rosa Brandt was Walvis's confidante, his most trusted assistant, but this did not always save her from his biting sarcasm.

'And you had better never go near Chichester again,' Walvis ordered. 'Ah, Heaven be praised, I believe Martin has at long last arrived.'

A jeep stopped at the foot of the staircase and a tall well-built man hurried aboard. Dark-haired, in his early forties, he was clean shaven and his plump face had a ruddy complexion. He rarely stopped smiling. He sat down opposite his chief and smiled at Walvis.

'Well?' the gross man demanded. 'Is the Cardon woman out of the picture? Permanently, I trust?'

'She died in the Nuffield Hospital earlier this evening. It is the end of the story.'

'Excellent!' Walvis smiled crookedly with pleasure. He turned to the woman with the veil. 'Kindly inform the pilot I wish to be airborne at the earliest moment it is possible to wake up the control tower. Tell them it is urgent.' He looked at Martin as she left her seat. 'We can relax now that small loophole has been closed.' He spoke as though a minor business problem had been solved to his satisfaction.

1

'I think we ought to visit Philip's house here,' Paula said. 'He gave me the key, said could I check to make sure the place was properly locked up. He also said Jean would want him to be careful. That was before they started the diamorphine, apparently.'

They were sitting in Tweed's Escort in the hospital car park. Tweed had a faraway look and Paula thought maybe he hadn't heard what she'd said, but she was wrong.

'I'm sure Philip locked up the house – working on automatic pilot before he returned to resume his death watch.'

'What a horrible phrase,' Paula protested. Normally she had the experience to stand up to anything, but she had liked Jean.

'It was a bit too graphic. Sorry if I upset you.' Tweed's tone changed, became businesslike. 'I agree we ought to check their house here – but for a different reason. I'm convinced Jean was kidnapped, then tortured inside that cottage near Wittering, because someone thought she knew something very dangerous. Now how could she have acquired that kind of information?'

'No idea. She did work for that small outfit that collected information about a company's financial status and stability. They had some surprisingly important clients. Reed & Roebuck was the name of her outfit.'

'And didn't she keep meticulous diaries?'

'She was meticulous in everything she did. And yes, she

13

did keep a diary every year. I saw her writing in it in her study when I was down here to bring something to Philip.'

'We *are* going to check that house,' Tweed decided. 'You can guide me there? Good. Let's get moving. I want to get back to town to see Philip. I didn't like the look in his eye just before he left. It was an expression of sheer ferocity. He could do something silly . . .'

With their trained skills Paula and Tweed swiftly searched the Cardons' house on the edge of the countryside. Paula took a deep breath before entering Jean's work study on the ground floor. She felt she was desecrating the dead.

'Can't find any diaries,' Tweed reported half an hour later. 'She must have kept them at the London flat. They're not in here, I suppose?'

'No. I've drawn a blank. Something else I must check – where she keeps her underclothes. That's a place where a woman hides things.'

'I checked in their bedroom. Quickly, I admit. I didn't like handling her personal things.'

'I'm going to double-check,' Paula insisted.

Again she found it distasteful rifling carefully through Jean's drawers in the bedroom. The underclothes were so neatly arranged, so spotless, as though brand new. She shook her head as she came downstairs to where Tweed was waiting impatiently in the large living-room.

'Time to go,' Tweed snapped, checking his watch.

'I just want to look at something in her study before we leave. It's a beautiful piece of unfinished embroidery – it must be the last piece of work she was creating. It's folded up.'

'I still say time to go . . .'

Tweed was talking to himself. Paula had disappeared into the study through the double doors leading off the living-room. She picked up the sheaf of embroidery, carried it into the living-room.

14

'This is a large project. Let's spread it out on the drum table, see how far she'd got with it.'

'Why? It's only going to be upsetting.'

Ignoring Tweed, Paula carefully unfolded a large piece of white linen divided into panels. The meticulous attention to detail was shown by the fact that dark thread had been used to divide it up into centimetre squares over the unfinished area. The work had been executed with brightly coloured threads and was a map with houses, horse riders, golfers and other activities.

'It's so beautiful,' Paula whispered.

'I agree,' Tweed commented, impressed as he stooped to examine the extraordinary detail. 'It's a map of Europe including Britain. Only half-finished – she was obviously going to complete southern Europe. What's the matter?'

'There are tiny dark crosses on the map. You can easily miss them.'

'I did,' Tweed admitted. 'Where are they?'

'There's one here,' Paula said, pointing at one section. 'That's strange – it's west of Chichester at the edge of the creek opposite the lovely village of Bosham. There's a whole labyrinth of creeks and channels snaking inland from the sea. Look, there's another cross here over Munich, in Germany. And another over Passau, the port on the Danube near Austria. And then a final one to the north of Passau on the border of Czechoslovakia.'

'The Czech Republic, you mean,' Tweed corrected. He rubbed his glasses on his handkerchief and peered more closely. 'That Czech one appears to be in the middle of nowhere. That's wild lonely country out there – on the way to the East.'

Paula straightened up. She took great trouble to refold the large embroidery as she had found it. Then she looked at Tweed.

'Something tells me this is very important. Jean was very clever. If she wanted to record strategic locations

15

where better to hide them than in a complex piece of embroidery? Jean has a collection of cardboard-backed envelopes in a drawer. I'm going to put the folded embroidery in one of them so we can take it with us back to Park Crescent. I think Philip will be very interested in this.'

'Just supposing we can find Philip,' Tweed commented.

Paula was unusually quiet while Tweed drove them back to London. She sat staring ahead, not seeing the traffic, gloved hands clasped tightly in her lap.

'Where are we going first?' she asked eventually.

'To their flat. The diaries must be there. I think they could give us vital clues. I'm particularly interested in that outfit Jean worked for – Reed & Roebuck. But mainly I want to talk seriously to Philip, to find out what he intends to do. He's in no mental state to investigate who was responsible for Jean's murder – to say nothing of the horrific torture which was inflicted on her.'

'I've just remembered something,' Paula said. 'About a year ago Jean was nearly killed late at night in the Fulham Road by a hit-and-run driver. She wasn't seriously hurt but she spent a couple of days in hospital. Philip later told me that when he visited her lying in bed she made a strange remark. She said, "*When I get out of here we're going to live a normal life.*" He briefly thought it was odd but then our work plunged him into a period of frenetic activity.'

'That's the first time I've heard about her saying that. It *is* a very odd remark – was . . .'

They lapsed into silence and it was ten o'clock at night when Tweed parked behind Bob Newman's Mercedes still parked by the kerb. He glanced up and down the deserted street and approached the front door to the

16

building where Philip had a flat. Suddenly he grasped
Paula's arm, pushing her back.

'What is it?' Paula whispered.

'The front door is open.'

His gun was in his hand as he took several paces forward. With his other hand he took a pencil torch from a
pocket, focused it on the door. He switched it off and
again glanced up and down the street.

'What is it now?' Paula asked.

'Forced entry. Someone has used a special tool to deal
with both locks – they left scratches. You'd better wait
here while I check Philip's flat. I just hope he's here.'

'And all right,' Paula added. 'And I am coming with
you,' she said firmly, the Browning in her right hand.

'I'm giving you a direct order to stay here.'

Tweed's tone was unusually harsh. He entered the
hallway, which was lit by a chandelier, listened. He had
acute hearing but the building was dead silent, a silence
he didn't like. He paused again a few paces from Philip's
flat. The door was a quarter open. Oh, my God, what
am I going to find inside? he wondered.

He pushed open the door into the lobby slowly. It
moved silently on well-oiled hinges. Far too much
silence. He pushed the door flat against the wall in case
there was someone behind it, switched on his pencil
torch. Gloom met him. No lights on anywhere and the
beam of his torch showed all the doors were open – to
the bathroom, the bedroom, the large living-cum-dining-
room beyond. He moved forward slowly, first
illuminating the bathroom, then the bedroom, then
stood at the entrance to the spacious living-room with a
kitchenette perched above it in a side-wall alcove. Two
steps led up to it. All the curtains had been closed over
the wide bay windows, as in the bedroom. He sighed,
went back to Paula.

'Is Philip all right?' she whispered.

17

'Philip, thank God, isn't here. But you'd better come and see what the state of the place is.'

'Maybe first you'd better see what's down those basement steps. I risked aiming my own torch down. Something terrible has happened . . .'

He followed her down the worn stone steps and looked at the body crumpled among sacks bursting with household rubbish. By the light of Paula's torch he examined the corpse, checked the pockets without moving the position of the body. He straightened up, sucked in breath between his teeth.

'A motor cyclist with no identity papers, nothing to say who he was.'

'I saw a motor cyclist leave the Nuffield soon after Philip drove away from the car park. Do you think Philip had to shoot him?'

'No. Wrong calibre of bullet. Size of that hole in the centre of his forehead indicates a very heavy hand gun – a .45 would be my guess. Philip carries a .38 Smith & Wesson. Something very strange happened here. Come inside.'

Paula followed him and he borrowed her more powerful torch. When he shone it into the living-room she gritted her teeth. The room had been ransacked. Drawers pulled out, contents emptied on to the floor, cupboards open, more contents swept on to the fitted carpet. The fabric of upholstered sofas and armchairs had been ripped open. The chairs had been up-ended and left in that grotesque position. Chaos. A sideboard opened, bottles flung out, some rolled underneath the furniture which had contained them.

'Couldn't we switch on some lights after I've closed the lobby door?' Paula suggested.

'No lights. Not with that body lying down in the basement. But close the main lobby door. I think all this happened after Cardon went off somewhere.'

18

'Where could he have gone?'

'Lord knows. Let's hope he left a clue behind. I can detect a faint aroma of smoke.' While Paula went to shut the lobby door Tweed moved the torch beam slowly round the room. 'He's started to smoke again in a big way,' he told her when she came back.

'How do you know he's smoking? I can smell it, too, but the thugs who took this place apart may have done so.'

To demonstrate his point he focused the torch on a large crystal-glass ashtray. In it were five cigarettes, each stubbed after being half-smoked. A packet of Silk Cut lay next to the ashtray. Tweed elevated the torch, aimed it at the interior of an old-fashioned roller-top desk. The outer wrapping of a carton of Silk Cut cigarettes was screwed up into a tight ball.

'Philip must have put all ten packs in a case,' he said.

'The thugs who took this place apart may have taken them,' Paula objected.

'And then screwed up the outer wrapping into a nice neat ball? I think not. That has all the hallmarks of Philip. We must search this place for clues as to where he went. I'm getting more and more worried about the idea that he is following a lead to the murderers of his wife. Better call Park Crescent, ask Monica to contact Butler or Pete Nield. If she gets one of them quickly she's to ask him to drive here – but to park his car further down the road. He's to call this number first. No reply and he heads for SIS headquarters.'

In the glow of the torchlight Paula studied Tweed, whose tone was grim. Of medium height and uncertain age, he was clean shaven and stared into the distance through his horn-rim glasses. He was the man people pass in a street without noticing – a trait which had served him well in the dangerous work he undertook as Deputy Director of the SIS.

19

'Why do we need someone else so urgently?' she enquired.

'Because after we've finished here we're all driving down to Chichester and that labyrinth of creeks you mentioned. I want to check myself who rented Amber Cottage where poor Jean was found. Someone else knows that area well – so it's likely they have frequented it. Come on now, make that phone call, please. We're going to move fast when we leave here . . .'

Bob Newman arrived as they were completing a hopeless search of the flat by torchlight. So far it had seemed Philip had left no clue as to where he had vanished to.

Newman, who had been fully vetted and had worked with Tweed on many missions, was in his early forties. Several inches taller than Tweed, he was well built, clean shaven and with a strong nose and jaw. He also had great reserves of energy and vast experience as a foreign correspondent, famous the world over for his reports from trouble spots. Since writing his international bestseller, *Kruger: The Computer That Failed*, he had financial independence for life.

Paula had told Monica during her phone call what had happened and she had passed the grim news on to Newman.

'I'm terribly sorry to hear what happened to Jean. It sounds fiendish. Philip must be devastated, poleaxed.'

'Devastated, yes – poleaxed, no,' Tweed corrected him. 'Which is what is worrying the hell out of us . . .' He explained the situation in a few words. 'So it's vital we trace Philip's whereabouts. He could have flown off into the wide blue yonder—'

'Looks as though he did,' Paula interjected. 'See what I've just found.'

She held up an airline timetable she had found under a

pile of papers swept on to the floor. It was folded open at a certain section. Tweed examined it by the light of his torch.

'Can't we switch on a few lights?' Newman protested. 'It's going to be quicker than reading by Braille.'

'No,' Tweed snapped. 'There happens to be the corpse of a motor cyclist shot through the forehead dumped among the rubbish sacks in the outside basement . . .'

He explained what had happened soon after their arrival, giving Paula credit for the grisly discovery. Newman stroked his chin as he listened.

'That explains the motor cycle propped against the kerb on the other side of the street. Should I check it out, even move it further down?'

'No!' Tweed was still unusually edgy. 'When we're well clear of London I shall have to call New Scotland Yard to report the presence of the body. As luck would have it, they'll tell my old sparring partner, Chief Inspector Roy Buchanan, to take over the case. With Philip disappearing you can imagine the conclusion he'll jump to. I wouldn't blame him. Now, Paula, this timetable?'

'You'll see it's open at a section that has flights for Rio in Brazil. Why would he go there?'

'If he did,' Tweed commented sceptically. 'Philip would foresee we'd try to trace him. This could be a red herring. Hold the torch so I can go through every page . . .'

Starting at the beginning Tweed slowly turned the pages as Paula raised her eyebrows at Newman, as much as to say *I find a clue and he won't believe it.*

'Hold the torch a little closer, please.'

Tweed had paused halfway through the timetable. He held it closer to the torch, grunted with satisfaction.

'Philip was in a hurry. He wouldn't normally make such a mistake. And he'd be in an agitated state.'

'I don't see anything,' Paula objected.

'A minute quantity of ash – cigarette ash – caught in the

21

centre fold. He was smoking like mad when he looked up these flights to this particular destination.'

'Where to?' Paula pressed, annoyed. 'Don't be so tantalizing.'

'Munich, in Bavaria. One of the locations you cleverly spotted was marked with a tiny cross on that embroidery Jean was working on – the map of Europe.'

The controller on duty at Munich Airport watched the plane descending, making a perfect landing on the runway. He turned to his assistant who was being trained.

'That's one of the strangest machines in the world. And one of the most expensive. They say Walvis paid Boeing a billion dollars to produce his designer aircraft.'

'What's so special about it?' his assistant asked.

'It looks like a normal outsize private jet. Actually it is a combined land- and seaplane. Concealed in the fuselage and wings are huge floats that can be lowered like any undercarriage. That machine can land on water in rough weather. I wonder what Walvis is coming back for this time?'

Aboard the luxuriously appointed aircraft Gabriel March Walvis shifted his bulk in his swivel armchair as he peered out of the window. Beside him the woman in black with the veil looked across at Martin but kept quiet. Martin could make the mistake of speaking before he was spoken to, and he did.

'I've arranged for the stretch Mercedes to meet us. But I still think a Rolls-Royce would be more suitable.' He was smiling, showing his perfect white teeth, when Walvis moved one thick lip over the other and half-closed his pouched eyelids as he stared at the other man.

'You are a complete and utter bloody fool,' he remarked mildly. 'I wonder why I should renew your contract of service . . .'

He paused and Martin's smile vanished. He swallowed hard and cursed himself for opening his mouth. The ending of a contract of service meant another kind of contract would be taken out – to remove him from the face of the Earth.

'You see, dear boy,' Walvis continued in the same soft tone, 'Germany is full of black stretch limos with tinted glass. No one knows who is inside such a vehicle – especially as I have an arrangement with Munich to change my registration plates frequently. A Rolls-Royce would identify me at once.' He changed the topic without warning, a tactic which disconcerted his subordinates. 'Martin, did you remember to leave someone in Chichester just in case a busybody starts nosing round after the unfortunate experience suffered by Jean Cardon?'

'Yes, sir.' Martin brightened up. 'Leo Kahn is staying at a Chichester hotel. Under another name, of course. And he speaks better English than I do.'

'I should hope so,' Walvis sneered. He turned his huge head to gaze at the woman in black. 'Rosa, we are driving up to the castle in the mountains. Double-check the security on the staff when we arrive – they will all have to be dispensed with in good time, of course. As soon as we arrive we will take Project Tidal Wave one step further. Soon the whole of Europe will be overwhelmed – including Britain. Decadence will receive its due . . .'

'It will be done,' Rosa assured him. 'It will be my pleasure.'

2

Tweed and Paula drove to SIS headquarters at Park Crescent in his Ford Escort used by Newman earlier. Newman followed them in his Mercedes 280E through the dark deserted streets of the city. It was very late when they arrived and their building was ablaze with lights.

On the way Paula had sat quiet for a while, a prey to her thoughts. She made the comment near Baker Street.

'We never found Jean's diaries. You think the people who broke in took them?'

'No. I'm convinced Philip got there first, found them, skipped through them and found something that sent him rushing off to Munich. The trouble is he's left us in the dark. Munich is a big city – we wouldn't know where to start looking.'

'Why do you really think Jean was tortured in that cottage and murdered?'

'At an educated guess, she stumbled on something so vital to a large organization they tried to find out what she knew, killed her in the process.'

'You'd have thought she'd have told her husband about it. But then Philip would have come straight to you. Why didn't she tell Philip?'

'Here again I'm guessing, but as you know Philip has been immersed completely in his job for the past year. Jean was a very strong character. I think she didn't want to distract him, maybe cause him to make a mistake. She knew his missions were dangerous.'

'That's tragic. She must have locked it up inside her-

24

self. What was she waiting for?'

'I've a horrible feeling she knew she was under sentence of death and just hoped she could last out until she told us when we were less busy. Or maybe she felt she hadn't got to the bottom of her discovery and squirrelled away trying to build up a complete picture.'

'She must have found out a lot – those location crosses on her embroidery cover a wide sweep of Europe. And why did you talk about a large organization being involved?'

'They moved so quickly. That takes a lot of people – and highly trained people, including a professional assassin. The killer who executed the motor cyclist outside Philip's flat. All this happened as soon as Jean had died. Also they must have tracked us from Amber Cottage when we followed the ambulance to the Nuffield. Come to think of it there was a helicopter that kept appearing while we drove north. A large organization to track us the way they did – and speed of movement to follow Philip to his flat.'

'Wouldn't Philip have spotted a tail at that hour of the night? It was dark and there'd be very little traffic.'

'I think he *did* spot the motor cyclist,' Tweed told her. 'Then trapped him outside his flat, not knowing there was a second motor cyclist tracking the first one. All of which again suggests a highly professional organization.'

He parked by the kerb as Newman pulled up behind them. Getting out of the car the icy temperature of a late November night froze his face. He glanced round but no one else was in sight.

'Nippy,' Paula said, clutching her collar to her neck. 'But it is November 29.'

'A date Philip will never forget,' Tweed said as they went up the steps. 'And for a long time he's going to hate Mondays . . .'

Inside Tweed's first-floor office, which had a view of

25

Regent's Park in daylight, several people were assembled. Monica, his faithful assistant, a woman of uncertain age who wore her grey hair in a bun, looked up from her desk with a sad expression. Tweed realized she had been crying.

'What ghastly news. I'm so upset. Jean Cardon was such a remarkable woman and so intelligent and shrewd. She always had a kind word for me when she came here.'

'I appreciate you're upset,' Tweed said briskly. 'But we've got to pull out all the stops now: Philip has gone missing. He won't be available to attend the inevitable inquest on Jean's death – and that will look suspicious. Plus the fact that there's a dead body in his basement. Monica, I want to know all about the outfit Jean worked for – Reed & Roebuck. They have offices in Covent Garden.'

'Specifically what am I looking for?'

Monica had pulled herself together, her pen poised over her notepad. Tweed hung his overcoat on a wooden stand, sat behind his desk, nodded to Harry Butler and Pete Nield, who sat perched on Paula's desk. He began rapping out orders.

'Who controls this outfit? Is it independent – or owned by some other organization? Find out what clients they had – and who was being investigated over the past year. We must be ruthless – use any devious or underhand method to get the data. Hint to anyone reluctant to talk that they might be involved in two murder cases. Tell them we're Special Branch – that always puts the wind up most people. Use Gilbert Hartland – he's a professional tracer of company activities.'

'So we'll be using a rival tracer to dig out any secrets Reed & Roebuck might want to conceal?' queried Monica.

'Use a thief to catch a thief, to coin a cliché.'

'I can start now – I know Hartland works through the

night.' Monica's expression was grim. 'He often rings people at a late hour when their morale is low. He'll be expensive.'

'Spare no cost. You may be up all night. I'm sorry about that,' Tweed replied. 'But I want results yesterday.'

'Where do we fit in on this operation?' asked Butler.

Harry Butler and Pete Nield often worked as a team and could practically read each other's mind. Butler was well built, in his thirties, dressed casually and wore a shabby windcheater and dark grey slacks. He was practically invisible in the shadows of the night. Clean shaven, his hair was dark and thick. He was a formidable opponent in combat.

His partner Pete Nield was a contrast in every way. Slim, with black hair and a neat moustache, he was a snappy dresser and was clad in a blue business suit. His movements were swift and he spoke fluently, unlike Butler who used words as though they were costing him money. Tweed addressed both of them.

'You're coming with us to Chichester and the creeks south of the town. We're going to turn over the whole area because that's where Jean was originally found in a cottage on the Wittering road.'

'Turn it over looking for what precisely?' pressed Nield.

'First who rented this Amber Cottage where Jean was held. Second is there anyone in the neighbourhood who wields a lot of power – real power.'

'When do we start looking?' Nield pressed again.

Tweed checked his watch. 'It's nearly 1.30 a.m. We'll all drive down there through the night.' He looked at Monica. 'We need two hotels in Chichester as bases. Paula, Bob and I will stay at one. Harry and Pete at another – if you can phone soon and book rooms.'

'I'll have to locate two hotels – shouldn't take long . . .'

'I can give you two,' interjected Bob Newman for the

27

first time. He had been standing behind Paula's desk as she sat in her chair and rifled through a drawer. 'One is the Dolphin and Anchor. Faces the cathedral. The other is The Ship Hotel . . .'

'How far apart?' rapped out Tweed.

'A ten-minute walk down North Street from the Dolphin to The Ship. Five minutes the way I move. Won't it seem funny our arriving in the early hours, might arouse some comment?'

'Monica tells them in both cases we're businessmen on our way to attend a seminar which starts with an American working breakfast.' His face expressed distaste. 'A disgusting and futile American idea – as though people are alert on such an occasion. But it will be convincing . . .'

As he spoke Monica had looked up phone numbers in her library of reference books and was already dialling a number. Paula had hauled out an Ordnance Survey map and waved it in the air. Tweed was talking again to Monica.

'I've had another thought. Book for three people at The Ship Hotel. Then call Marler at his flat, tell him to get over here with his case and that it's operational.'

'So, we're bringing up the big guns,' Nield commented humorously.

Marler was the deadliest marksman with a rifle in the whole of Western Europe. He was also a loner by nature. Paula was opening up her map, spreading it out on her desk while Newman, Butler and Nield gathered round her.

'I knew I'd got it,' she said triumphantly. 'Map of Sussex. Now here is Chichester. But look at the maze of creeks and channels snaking in and out further south – the sea surges in from this opening on the coast at East Head . . .'

'I know the area,' Newman commented. 'There's a load

28

of money down there. Marinas berthing luxury yachts costing a bomb – two bombs. The biggest one in Britain is at Chichester Yacht Basin, which is actually several miles south of the city—'

'Just shut up for a moment, Bob,' Paula rapped at him. 'I know the area too. As you see,' she said, explaining to Butler and Nield, 'there are four main channels east of Hayling Island – Emsworth, then further east Thorney and Chichester and Bosham. It's the last one – Bosham Channel – I'm interested in, which I think is important . . .'

She explained quickly her discovery of the crosses hidden inside the last piece of embroidery Jean had worked on. Her finger stabbed at a point on the south side of a creek flowing into Bosham Channel which terminated in a dead end.

'Jean had marked something just opposite the beautiful village of Bosham. On the far side of the creek. You have to watch the high tide – it sweeps in without warning and a soggy marsh is suddenly deep in sea water. It floods some of the roads. But I'm confident I can identify what Jean marked with one of her crosses when we get down there.'

'I'd like to have seen those so-called crosses,' Newman remarked sceptically.

While they had been studying the map, Tweed had joined them, staring down with his hands in his jacket pockets, his thumbs perched on the outside of the pockets. Monica had been frenetically active on the phone. She put it down finally with an air of triumph.

'All fixed up. Rooms booked. They're expecting you at both hotels. A night porter will let you in. Marler will arrive here in his car any moment now.'

'As soon as he does we leave immediately,' Tweed ordered. He went to a cupboard where packed cases were kept ready for instant departure. Handing one to

29

Paula, he lifted out his own suitcase, looked at Nield and Butler. Nield forestalled his question.

'Harry and I automatically put cases in our cars when Monica phoned. What about you, Bob? I suppose you'll want to borrow my toothbrush and shaving kit tomorrow morning.'

'You suppose wrong,' Newman informed him. 'I brought my own case after Monica called me. What about weapons?' he queried with Tweed.

'We all go armed. I have a nasty idea we're up against some no-holds-barred characters. Monica, when you have some data on Reed & Roebuck call me at this Dolphin Hotel. You can be devious about anything dangerous you discover.'

'You think I will discover something dangerous?' Monica asked.

'It was dangerous – and then lethal – to poor Jean,' Tweed reminded her.

3

At three o'clock in the morning on a bitterly cold night – it was November 30 – Leo Kahn strolled down North Street in Chichester. He had been summoned from Munich by an urgent phone call from Martin. For once Martin had not been smiling his false *bonhomie* when he met Kahn at Heathrow Airport.

'Your instructions are explicit and must be carried out very precisely. Otherwise the consequences could be very grave. And get a decent haircut tomorrow morning.'

'What are the instructions?' Kahn had asked him quietly.

'If you will just listen I will give them to you. Concentrate your mind, Kahn. You hire a car and drive down to Chichester in the south near the coast. I have a map here which shows you the route . . .'

'I do know where Chichester is,' Kahn said unwisely.

'All right, you've spent time in England before and you speak English better than I do,' Martin remarked with biting sarcasm. 'Now shut up and listen. A room has been booked for you at the Dolphin and Anchor Hotel – in the usual pseudonym you use when you are here, Leopold Winter. You brought all the papers I told you to?'

'The forged passport, driving licence—'

'I don't want a list,' Martin had snapped. 'A plain "yes" would have done. A woman called Jean Cardon was found at a remote dwelling called Amber Cottage and has since died. I have marked the location of Amber Cottage on the map. I want to know details of any civilian who goes near that place. But be careful – the police will probably be keeping it under surveillance.'

'I would have assumed that,' Kahn replied mildly.

Martin always found Kahn's presence unsettling. He was dangerous and you never knew what he was thinking. Several inches shorter than the tall Martin he had a bony squarish face with high cheekbones. His build was slight but Martin knew this lean and hungry-looking man possessed enormous strength with the ability to kill people in many ingenious ways. Kahn had watched Martin through his wide-rimmed spectacles without blinking once. The truth was that even though passengers were swirling round them in the airport concourse Martin was frightened by the little man. He went on speaking rapidly.

'It's just possible that certain people – civilians – will arrive in Chichester asking questions about Amber Cottage. If they do, identify them and report back to me.

31

They'd probably stay at one of the hotels.'

'If they seem to know too much should I deal with them?' Kahn enquired politely.

'You can't have any weapons – coming through airport security,' Martin objected.

'You can buy a weapon at a hardware shop. A screw-driver will kill a man – or a woman – as effectively as a knife.'

Martin suppressed a shudder. He glanced round to make sure no one was taking any notice of them and had decided to get away from Kahn immediately.

'Make a balls-up and you'll be for it,' he blustered.

'I thought you knew my track record,' Kahn had reminded him.

'You know what is required. Give it a week. No results and you return to Munich. Keep me informed by phone at regular intervals.'

Having made this feeble attempt to assert his authority Martin had walked away. Kahn was recalling this amusing encounter as he continued his stroll down the deserted Chichester street. He had explained to the receptionist that he often took a walk in the middle of the night as he suffered from insomnia. He was, in fact, checking to see if there were any late arrivals at the two main hotels – the Dolphin – and The Ship at the far end of North Street.

Even though Leopold Winter was not his real name neither was Leopold Kahn, a fact unknown to Walvis, his ultimate employer. Kahn was a member of the notorious Chechen Mafia in Russia. He had been ordered – and had carried out this order with superb skill – to infiltrate Walvis's enormous international communications syndicate.

It was four o'clock in the morning when Tweed, Paula and Newman arrived at the Dolphin and Anchor. The night porter let them in after they had left Newman's

Mercedes in the private car park at the rear of the ancient hotel.

Tweed was registering when Newman glanced at the man who sat slumped in a chair in the lobby. What caught his attention was the haircut that stretched low down across his forehead like a crude fringe.

The little man was dressed in a shabby suit and perched on his straight nose was a pair of wide-rimmed spectacles. Behind the lenses the eyes were closed. As he registered, Newman spoke to the porter in a whisper.

'Is that chap slumped in the chair drunk?'

'Oh no, sir,' the porter replied in a shocked whisper. 'He's a guest. Suffers from insomnia and roams the streets to tire himself out. He's asleep now . . .'

As Tweed, carrying his own case, made his way up a narrow staircase he followed Paula. Newman brought up the rear carrying Paula's bag as well as his own. He glanced suddenly at the little man in the chair. Behind the lenses he glimpsed the glitter of pale eyes. He made his comment as they assembled briefly in Tweed's spacious room which overlooked the Cathedral opposite.

'That odd cove in the lobby. He was watching us. Asleep, my foot. Something disturbing about him.'

'Imagination runs riot at this hour,' Tweed responded dismissively. 'Now, we'll only get four hours' sleep. I want to see all of us down at breakfast at eight a.m.'

'Eight o'clock!' protested Newman. 'Hardly worth going to bed.'

'I can easily get by on four hours and I'm older,' Tweed told him.

'And I'm anxious to drive down to Bosham,' Paula remarked. 'I do want to identify whatever Jean marked with a cross on her embroidery.' She had a dig at Newman. 'Since you've seen the embroidery on our way down you must agree I may be on to something.'

'Maybe yes, maybe no,' Newman grumbled. 'At least

you have it safely in your bag. I think one day Philip will want to frame that unfinished work – to go with the other framed embroideries we saw in the house.'

'Poor Philip,' Paula replied as they left Tweed to go to their own rooms. 'I wonder where he is now. I hope to God he's all right.'

International & Cosmopolitan Universal Communications have their European headquarters at Maximilianstrasse 2001, Munich. Control of operations in Europe from London to the Urals in Russia . . .

It was this note, written in Jean's bold hand in her diary, that had taken Philip Cardon to the chief city of Bavaria.

Arriving at Munich Airport, which is about an hour's drive from the city, he hired a BMW and drove through the night across open flat countryside stretching away into the distance on both sides in the moonlight. Within ten minutes he knew he was being followed by two men in a grey Volvo station wagon. He began talking to himself.

'No one followed me from my flat. No one followed me on to the aircraft. That means someone has incredible surveillance on Munich Airport. That someone is worried. So he's arranged for any Englishman who arrives to be tracked. I must have come to the right place . . .'

He made no attempt to shake off the tail. The objective now was to establish a secure base for himself. Cardon knew exactly how he would achieve this. Like all senior SIS staff he kept a large sum of money in 1,000-franc Swiss banknotes, ready to take off in an emergency anywhere in the world.

His mind went back to Chichester and the awful denouement at the Nuffield. Chichester was an ancient city with some of the finest Georgian buildings in existence. A contrast to the rococo elegance of Munich, he

34

thought, as he entered one of Germany's most beautiful cities.

As he drove slowly along the ruler-straight Maximilianstrasse the grey Volvo was still in sight in his rear-view mirror. He smiled grimly.

'You two hacks are going to report a load of codswallop to your boss.'

Pulling in off the street at the small crescent-shaped drive in front of the five-star Four Seasons Hotel, he got out as a commissionaire opened his door, refused the offer to carry his case.

'I'll be staying here for a few days. Philip Cardon . . .' He spelt out the name, continuing to speak in fluent German. 'Park my car for me, please. We'll get a mechanic to look at it in the morning. It drives erratically,' he lied.

Just before he entered the large reception area he saw out of the corner of his eye the Volvo pull in further down the street. He booked a large double room at the rear of the hotel, took his suitcase upstairs, again refusing the aid of a porter.

Once inside the luxuriously appointed room with a sitting area he unlocked his large case. Inside rested a smaller case perched on top of neatly folded clothes. He took out the clothes from the larger case, distributed them in drawers and wardrobes. He was careful to put a sponge bag in the marble bathroom, extracted toothbrush, toothpaste, razor and shaving brush and arranged them on a glass shelf. The room now had all the appearance that he was occupying it. He next phoned the concierge, speaking in English.

'I need a small Mercedes. Now. Send the papers up to my room. The car is to be parked in the Marstallstrasse – the little street running alongside the hotel. I want to meet someone privately.'

'Certainly, sir,' the concierge replied. 'I will call you back in five minutes . . .'

'Just send up the papers – and park the car while I'm dealing with them. Then send up the keys. I'm in a great rush. My companion will expect to find me waiting there . . .'

Philip smiled bitterly to himself. He knew the concierge would assume he was secretly meeting a woman, someone else's wife. Fifteen minutes later, with the keys in one hand and his smaller case in the other, he stepped out of the lift into the vast entrance area, which was also a lounge. It was milling with German men and women, all tarted up. Arriving for some party. He'd got lucky.

He edged his way round the outside of the crowd furthest away from the long reception counter. He wore a shabby dark coat, and a black beret rammed well down over his thick brown hair transformed his appearance.

Emerging on to Maximilianstrasse, he did not glance back to where the Volvo had parked. Walking in the opposite direction along the wide street, lined with the most expensive shops in the world, he turned down the side-street. A small red Mercedes was waiting by the kerb.

Philip drove to his next objective by a devious route, almost completing a circle, emerging back on to Maximilianstrasse past the opposite side of the Four Seasons. Swinging right on to the main street he passed the Volvo still parked by the kerb. In the front sat two stocky individuals, one of them smoking a cigar.

'You'll get through several cigars before the night is out,' Philip said to himself.

He drove on, then turned left into the Old Town. The tall buildings, many ochre-washed, of Maximilianstrasse were replaced by ancient stone buildings, some with large stone balcony rooms on the first floor bulging over the street. He parked in front of the Platzl Hotel, an old white-painted edifice with a pointed gable at its summit above the sixth floor. Again he booked a room, insisted

36

on carrying his own case, and went through the same procedure he'd adopted at the Four Seasons, spreading the contents of his smaller case so the room looked occupied. This was his real base, hidden away in the maze of the Old Town.

Before leaving the room he slid open a secret compartment in the base of his case, took out a slim leather pouch which contained some very special tools. Then, donning his sheepskin, he left the hotel. He passed a bar and wondered for a brief moment whether to have one drink.

He dismissed the idea immediately. Both Jean and he had been moderate drinkers of white wine. I could just as much consume alcohol now as I could jump off Tower Bridge, he thought. Maybe, after all, it would have been better if he had jumped off Tower Bridge.

No! He had a job to do. He was on his way to the headquarters of International & Cosmopolitan Universal Communications at the address Jean had noted down in her diary. He was going to break in to the place.

Gabriel March Walvis stirred restlessly inside the rear of the stretch Mercedes which was speeding along the autobahn carrying them to the castle in the mountains whose jagged peaks loomed ahead. Rosa, the woman in the black coat beside him, waited for him to speak. Walvis stared at Martin who sat on a flap seat facing him.

'Well, have we been followed from the airport?' he rasped.

'No, sir,' Martin assured him with a broad smile. 'We have not. I would bet my life on it.'

'You may be doing just that.' Walvis's overlapping eyelids twitched irritably. 'And you arranged to have our watchers on duty at the airport? To follow any Englishmen who disembarked from a regular flight from London?'

'Ten men were given the task, working in pairs, each pair with its own transport.' The telephone attached next to Martin beeped and he answered it in German. Walvis, ever suspicious, crouched forward, eyes twitching as he tried to grasp what was happening. Martin ended the conversation, replaced the phone and showed all his teeth in a grin. He always welcomed the opportunity to flatter his boss, and laid it on with a trowel, unaware that Walvis read him like a book and was contemptuous.

'You were so right earlier on to reinforce the security at HQ with two guards. An Englishman called Cardon came off a flight from London and is staying at the Four Seasons Hotel.'

'Reinforce the place with more guards. Wait . . .' Martin was reaching for the phone. 'First order the driver to turn round and drive back to headquarters in Munich at once.' He settled back in his seat. 'We had that meal on the way up here so we are in good form to confront whatever menace faces us. Now, get on with it.'

'We are not going on to the castle, then?' ventured Rosa.

'Your powers of deduction are indeed remarkable. I had never any intention of going there. I wanted to see if we were being followed. I seem to have to think about everything for myself. Let me ponder.'

Rosa sighed inwardly. She knew Walvis was paranoid about being followed, that he saw spies everywhere. Which was strange, she thought. Walvis was the richest man on earth but he had never been photographed. Here again he had shown his great cunning.

In the past he had arranged for four men of varying appearance to impersonate him, staying at top hotels and registering in the name of Gabriel March Walvis. The result was that floating round in the world's press there were four conflicting pictures of the billionaire – and not one of them remotely resembled his real appearance.

38

'I have a sixth sense which tells me we are going to trap an intruder at headquarters,' Walvis observed, and smiled with cruel satisfaction at the prospect.

On the same night at the Dolphin and Anchor Hotel in far-away Chichester Tweed, fully dressed, was walking down the staircase into the entrance lobby. He had his excuse ready if he encountered the night porter. He'd say he was very thirsty and ask for a bottle of mineral water.

The outer doors were all closed and the lobby was deserted except for one man. Leo Kahn sat very upright in his chair, reading a newspaper. Important to keep up with the news of what was happening in England – it would help his cover.

He had not heard Tweed's stealthy approach down the carpeted steps and could no longer pretend he was asleep. He had already checked the hotel register in the porter's absence. The three guests who arrived so early in the morning were Tweed, Newman and Paula Grey. The names meant nothing to him.

'Good morning,' Tweed addressed the little man. 'Still up? You won't get much sleep.'

'I do not need the sleep,' Kahn replied, studying Tweed with his blank eyes behind the outsize spectacles. 'Why are you not asleep?'

'Because I need some mineral water. Have you come from a long way to stay here?' he enquired off-handedly.

'From London.' Kahn's tone was abrupt suddenly. He disliked people who asked questions. An unpleasant English habit. The chat, it was called. He prepared to continue reading his paper.

'You are here on business?' Tweed persisted. 'Or, I hope, for a holiday?'

'I never take the holidays,' Kahn replied, modifying his tone. It had been a mistake to show hostility and he felt

39

nervous of this man whose eyes never left him. It was almost like an interrogation.

'Oh, you should,' Tweed babbled on. 'Take a holiday – it freshens you up for the pressures of business life. I like to guess people's professions. You are an accountant?'

Kahn stared again at Tweed from under his crude fringe of hair. His whole body had stiffened and Tweed sensed the tension emanating from the strange little man. There was something very odd here.

Out of the corner of his eye Tweed had seen Newman appear silently on the landing at the top of the staircase. Newman, also fully dressed, unable to sleep, had heard Tweed's door open in the room next to his own. He had quietly followed his chief and now he stood motionless, one hand inside his jacket, gripping the .38 Smith & Wesson in his hip holster.

'No, I am not an accountant,' Kahn said eventually.

Tweed lapsed into silence, waiting. His eyes were fixed on Kahn's. He remained silent and the pressure on Kahn grew, the pressure to say something. It was a tactic Tweed had used many times before during an interrogation. A battle of wills. The hard lines of Kahn's cheekbones seemed to grow even more prominent.

'I am a researcher,' he said after a long pause.

'Now that's an interesting occupation,' Tweed said amiably. 'What sort of research do you engage in?'

'Scientific,' Kahn replied quickly, having foreseen the possible question. 'I am writing a book. It will take the long time.'

'I'm sure it will.' The night porter had just returned. 'I have enjoyed our little chat,' Tweed went on with disarming pleasantness. 'I hope you will get some sleep later. Good night – or rather, good morning . . .'

Newman had disappeared from the landing before the night porter came into view. When Tweed carried his

40

litre bottle of mineral water up to the first floor he found Newman waiting beyond the fire door.

'I don't like it,' Newman said. 'I don't like him. He knows we're here.'

'But presumably he doesn't know about the presence at The Ship of Marler, Butler and Nield. They must have arrived there about the same time we walked in here.'

'They did. Marler phoned me briefly just before I left my room to follow you.'

'So Mr Leopold Winter knows about us but not about them. Which could be a great advantage.'

'How do you know his name?' Newman asked.

'I asked the porter to open the bottle for me. While he was doing this I glanced at the hotel register – which had been examined by someone else, I suspect. It was turned round at an angle towards the guests' side of the counter. Leopold Winter was the name before we registered.'

'You deliberately went back down into the lobby to have a closer look at him? I thought so. Why?'

'His appearance. The facial structure suggests Mittel–Europa, maybe even Slavic. His English is good but not perfect. And even pretending to be asleep when we arrived I detected tension in the way he held himself. In the morning, if Winter is having breakfast, leave the room and hurry down to The Ship. I want our three back-ups to have Mr Leopold Winter's exact description . . .'

There was not a single other human being in sight as Philip Cardon approached Maximilianstrasse 2001. The Volvo had disappeared. He walked slowly. The address he was targeting was a tall ten-storey building near where Maximilianstrasse crossed the ring-road. Grille gates, closed, protected the entrance to an arcade.

Philip already had in his hands the tools he expected he would need. Standing by the grille gate he slowly lit a

41

cigarette to give him a reason for pausing. And Jean and I were down to four a day, he thought grimly. Well, the count is climbing and I don't care. He squirted a colourless liquid over an electrical connection that controlled the alarm system. The liquid congealed, sealing off the main connection.

Philip had to fiddle with two complex locks, using two different tools. He had unfastened both locks, relieved that no car had passed along the street, no pedestrian had appeared. It was a bitter cold November night, he'd removed his gloves to carry out his delicate tasks, his hands were frozen to the bone.

He slid back one of the gates, the motion which would have activated the alarm, closed it behind him and walked into the gloom of the arcade. Philip was very alert now, ice cold in temperament as well as in body. He ducked under two sensors he spotted attached to window frames. A third one was so low down he slithered under the beam, sprawled out on the marble floor.

Behind the windows he had a faint view of giant aerial dishes. Double doors, solid bronze without a window, faced him at the end of the arcade. He dismantled another alarm, blessing the expert training in the latest guard devices he had experienced at the large remote mansion outside Send in Surrey. The doors gave him little trouble and then he was inside the fortress of International & Cosmopolitan Universal Communications.

'Just keep alert for more traps,' he told himself.

He waited until his eyes became accustomed to the darkness, then risked switching on a torch. Beside a bank of lifts a staircase climbed out of sight.

'The stairs,' he said to himself. 'The lifts probably have their own alarm systems. And don't be fooled by the quiet. There could be guards. Now locate the top man's office!'

He checked the time by his illuminated watch. 1.15 a.m.

* * *

42

In the back of the black limo Walvis checked the time. It was 12.30 a.m. They had entered the outskirts of Munich. Martin noticed the action and glanced at his own expensive timepiece, which recorded the moon phases and a lot of other useless information. He smiled broadly.

'12.30 a.m. Check?'

'For once that piece of junk is registering the right time,' Walvis commented. 'No traffic, so when do you calculate we'll reach headquarters?'

'Well before one o'clock,' Martin assured him. 'Then we can check out the whole building.'

4

Philip was inside the top man's quarters. At least he was confident he was there – the other executive offices on the tenth floor had solid oak doors. This one had bronze doors. Someone was fond of bronze. It was a curious layout: on either side of the bronze doors large windows of frosted glass faced the wide corridor beyond.

As with the other windows Philip had swiftly examined they were armoured glass. Someone was paranoid about his personal safety. A spacious marble bathroom and toilet led off the main office. Philip glanced inside, pursed his lips as he saw bronze taps, bronze shower rail.

'Get moving,' he said to himself. 'It's the main office you want to explore . . .'

His flashlight moved slowly over a rank of filing cabinets. All were locked and each had a card bearing letters: A–C, D–F, and so on. Faint illumination from the overhead corridor lights – which had been on – threw a glow into the room and helped his search. He checked his watch. 1.45 a.m.

Opening the double doors of a tall cupboard set into the wall he glanced inside. A deep cupboard, it was a wardrobe, and a collection of expensive clothes hung from another bronze rail. Vicuña coats, Burberry rain-coats, business suits, mostly in dark colours.

What struck Philip was the size of the garments. A very large man occupied this office. If only he could find a name. Later he'd open that first filing cabinet. He wore gloves and opened the drawers of a massive mahogany desk. The contents gave him no clues – notepads of top-quality paper with the company name embossed in bronze.

'Big man, you must have personal notepaper,' Philip said to himself as he expertly checked every drawer, careful not to disturb anything. He wanted to leave no traces of his search. He had closed the last drawer when he heard voices, footsteps approaching.

Philip moved to the side of the room close to the wardrobe. The voices came closer. One set of footsteps was padding heavily and with a deliberate tread on the marble-floored corridor. A huge silhouette appeared beyond the frosted glass, a massive figure with other silhouettes behind him.

Philip had taken the precaution of relocking the door of the office after entering the place. He thanked Heaven for his prudence but went ice-cold: he was trapped. The huge figure was making a clinking noise, selecting the right keys. Without pausing for a second Philip opened one of the wardrobe doors and slipped inside among the hanging coats. He pulled the door closed but, as he had noticed earlier, it had a tendency to open again a few inches.

'Don't do anything except keep still,' he said to himself.

44

Too late to try and close the wardrobe door properly – he could hear the outer door being opened. Lights were switched on. Through the narrow gap between the doors Philip had a limited view of the office beyond. Several men sounded to be entering. One man began talking in English, talking slowly with a throaty sound, a voice that emanated authority and grim command.

'There is someone inside the building, Martin. We found the alarm tampered with at the entrance and the grille was unlocked. At this time of night when we find the intruder we could smuggle the body out of the entrance and into the car on Maximilianstrasse. You have the hypodermic.'

'I always carry it,' a very different voice answered, a voice which suggested false *bonhomie* to Philip. The front man, probably, he thought to himself.

He was cursing himself for coming unarmed. Marler had on one occasion given him the addresses of various men in Europe who supplied weapons – for a price. And some were in Germany. Then Philip had a glimpse of the huge man he presumed wore the clothing he was pressed against. It was a brief snapshot vision because the man was glancing round and gazed at the wardrobe doors.

Philip saw a large head, thick shaggy grey hair, cold eyes twitching under overlapping flaps, fat fleshy skin, jowls and a thick neck. He guessed the shoulders must be exceptionally broad. He had the grim sensation this ugly brute was staring straight at him.

'That wardrobe door is open,' the pseudo-jovial voice remarked.

Philip tensed. The large-faced man was advancing towards him. He had another glimpse of a younger man, clean shaven and with a beet-red face.

'It's always coming open,' Throaty Voice said, a sinister voice. 'We'll have to get it fixed.'

Walvis stretched out a huge pudgy hand with short

stubby fingers and pushed the door closed until the latch clicked. Philip let out his breath slowly, pressed an ear as close to the door as he dared. The voices were muffled but he caught what was said.

'That guard outside the elevator on the fourth floor,' Walvis growled. 'He was fast asleep in his chair. You will immediately post him to Grafenau on the Czech border. The temperature drops to −40°C.' An unpleasant chuckle. 'That should keep the lazy bastard awake. Inform our Passau office immediately in the morning, Martin.'

'And transport Helmut direct to Grafenau?' Martin asked, anxious to carry out his chief's instructions perfectly.

'Surely that is the obvious way to proceed – should have been obvious to you. We will now assemble the other three guards and descend by the stairs, checking floor by floor. Someone is in this building.'

'That will take hours,' Martin pointed out.

'What a remarkable observation.'

'I was just thinking . . . that you might prefer to return to the limo and your apartment while I take charge of the search team,' Martin explained unctuously.

'Were you, indeed? I wish to be present when we locate the intruder and demonstrate to him the unwisdom of poking his nose into my affairs. Lucien here should be able to tell us who sent him, make him talk. Even if, Lucien,' he sneered, 'you were unsuccessful with Jean Cardon . . .'

Philip heard the outer door close and the locks being turned as he stood like a statue inside the wardrobe. A terrible fury was filling his mind. He struggled to control it. If he'd had a gun he'd have followed the men who had left the office and shot them all in the stomach. That

46

would have guaranteed they would have died slowly in agonizing pain.

Lucien . . . He now knew who had been responsible for torturing Jean at Amber Cottage. Sooner or later he would meet Lucien and exact a grim revenge.

'Get a grip on yourself,' he whispered. 'You have work to do.'

Gradually his fury came under control and his ice-cold resolve returned. The fact that it might be difficult to leave the building alive never occurred to him. *He would escape.*

He thought he'd allowed enough time to leave the wardrobe when he heard the door from the corridor being opened again, heard it close, followed by that elephantine pad of the big man's footsteps crossing his office to his desk. Again he moved his ear close to the door.

There was a faint clicking sound. The big man was dialling a number on the press-button phone on his desk. Philip was intrigued. What sort of a call was the giant making that he didn't want his subordinates to overhear? Throaty Voice began speaking.

'You know who this is speaking? Good. A journalist, Ziggy Palewski, is making a nuisance of himself. He plans to write a major article on my organization for *Der Spiegel*. Contact Teardrop – tell her to deal with this Palewski in her normal manner. Fifty thousand dollars is her fee? A lot of money. She won't bargain? Very well, put out the contract on Palewski. It is, of course, essential, that she – Teardrop – never has any hint of who gave the order. I rely on you to protect my interests. Yes, of course you will get your usual fee for making the arrangement. I am most surprised you asked the question. It is a gross impertinence, bearing in mind who you are talking to.' The voice rose to a vicious rasp. 'No apologies. Just do it.'

The phone was slammed down. The footsteps padded

47

back to the door, which was opened, closed, locked. Philip unlatched the cupboard door quietly, pushed it open, peered out. He was just in time to see the huge silhouette pass the frosted-glass window. As a silhouette the big man seemed even more menacing.

Ten minutes later Philip emerged from the cupboard, closing it behind him. Fortunately the light in the office had been switched off. Using his flashlight, he went to the steel filing cabinet with the card marked A–C.

He didn't even have to force it open. With one of the special keys fashioned in the Engine Room in the Park Crescent basement he simply unlocked it. He wore surgical gloves to examine the files. It was the Cs he was interested in.

With not much hope he checked the names on the tabs attached to the files. Even though he was looking for it he had a shock when he found a tab with the name Jean Cardon. He glanced through the papers inside quickly and had a pang when he saw a sheet of notepaper carrying Jean's distinctive handwriting.

'I certainly came to the right place, thanks to you, Jean,' he said in a low voice.

From a drawer in the large mahogany desk he took an empty cardboard-backed envelope he had discovered during his earlier search. The file fitted easily into this envelope. He stuffed it down the front of his shirt and behind his belt, checked to make sure it didn't cramp his movements. Now all he had to do was to get out of the place alive, evading the team which was searching for him.

Like most of Tweed's staff Philip had exceptional hearing. He stood by the closed bronze door, listening. Not a sound. They must be prowling round a lower floor. He needed some kind of weapon. During his first training course at the large mansion outside Send in Surrey his instructor had emphasized one point. 'In a tight situation, Cardon, there's always something which can be used as a weapon if you're unarmed. Just look around wherever you may be . . .'

Philip slowly surveyed the office. His eyes were becoming accustomed to the near darkness apart from the light glow from the corridor. On the large desk was a marble pen-and-ink set. Behind it rested an old-fashioned circular ruler made of ebony. He had donned his leather gloves and when he left the room he was holding the heavy ruler.

He made his way back cautiously down the staircase, pausing to listen at each corner. He had reached the eighth floor, was on the third step from the corridor, when the uniformed guard appeared round a corner. Both men were taken by surprise but Philip's reflexes were faster. As the guard reached for the gun in his leather holster Philip leapt down the last three steps, the ruler raised like a truncheon. He brought it down on the man's skull with all his force.

The guard grunted, was sagging when Philip grabbed hold of him, hauled him part way up the staircase. He dumped the unconscious guard against the side of the staircase, out of sight unless someone walked past and looked up. Within seconds he had unbuttoned the holster flap, hauled out the gun. A Walther 7.65mm automatic with a magazine capacity of eight rounds. His favourite hand gun.

He extracted the magazine, checked that it was full and rammed it back inside the butt. Now he felt less naked. He located the search team on the seventh floor, saw the man called Martin with the ruddy face disappearing inside an office. He listened briefly, moved noiselessly past the elevator bank and down on to the next flight. They had made one tactical mistake – omitting to leave a guard, gun

49

in hand, with his back to the wall so he could see up the first flight of this section of the staircase. Nice to know Throaty Voice's organization wasn't perfect.

He continued, proceeding with extreme caution, but had met no one, heard no sound as he reached the flight leading to the ground floor. Just a few more steps and he should have escaped from the building.

He peered round the corner on the bottom step, glancing swiftly in both directions. Nothing. No one. Odd. It seemed an obvious precaution to have a guard at the exit. He felt uneasy as he crossed towards the double doors exiting on the arcade. Some sixth sense, maybe he felt the current of air. He looked to his right and an Alsatian was airborne, teeth bared in a silent snarl as it aimed for his throat. Most men's reaction would have been to attempt to shoot the savage beast. Philip knew the sound of a shot being fired could doom his escape. Instinctively he struck at the Alsatian's head with all his force, bringing down the ebony ruler with such strength he felt the vibration up his arm.

The dog twisted sideways in midair, hit the floor with a thud, lay still. Five minutes later, after unlocking the door and the grille beyond – the alarm was still out of action – he was walking down the street, making his way back to the Hotel Platzl in the Old Town by a roundabout route.

It was still dark as he entered his bedroom, flopped on the edge of the bed. He reminded himself aloud of his next task.

'In the morning I must contact Bob Newman to find the whereabouts of this Ziggy Palewski. He knows more about reporters and magazine writers than anyone. And maybe he's heard of this mysterious woman Teardrop . . .'

5

Paula, Tweed and Newman were having breakfast in the large L-shaped dining-room at the Dolphin and Anchor. It was a frosty brilliant sunny morning. The windows looked out across the road to the great cathedral surrounded with spacious lawns. Paula nodded towards the windows.

'It was a heavy frost last night. Look at those lawns. They're the colour of crème de menthe. And I do feel surprisingly fresh, considering the lack of sleep.'

'Winter hasn't appeared yet,' said Newman. 'I hope he didn't skip breakfast. I want to get down to The Ship to warn the others, give them a description of the odd little man as you suggested.'

'Give him a few more minutes,' Tweed suggested.

A waiter stopped at their table. 'Mr Newman, please.'

'Yes. What is it?' Newman asked.

'A phone call for you. The gentleman didn't give any name but said it was urgent.'

'I'll take it in my room. Have the call transferred . . .'

Long experience had taught Newman to take unexpected calls in a place where he couldn't be overheard. Picking up the phone in his room he gave his name.

'Who is this?' he added.

'Philip here. Don't waste time asking where I am. I've a load of information. Some needs checking out but I'd like the answer to one question now. Ever heard of some freelance – I imagine – reporter called Ziggy Palewski? Shall I spell . . .'

51

'Not necessary. I've met him in Germany. Specializes in taking on dangerous assignments. Goes for the sensational story. He's a strange character but he knows his stuff . . .'

'OK, OK . . .' Philip sounded impatient, in a rush. 'And I'm phoning from my hotel room,' he added, warning Newman to be devious because the call went through the Platzl's operator. 'Where can I find him quickly? It could be a matter of life and death.'

'Munich. Can't give you an address – he flits about a lot for safety. But he frequently has coffee, sometimes lunch later, in a restaurant called Die Kulisse . . .' Newman spelt it out. That's on Maximilianstrasse, on the opposite side to the Four Seasons Hotel. A bit further down the street towards the River Isar. He's working on some major story?'

'You could say that. Next point. I think Tweed ought to check up on a monster outfit called International & Cosmopolitan Universal Communications. Don't ask me why. Just tell him.'

'Got it.'

Years of training had made Newman always carry a notebook and something to write with. Philip was talking again.

'This is tricky. Someone you ought to check out unless you've heard of them. A professional – you understand what I mean? Good. And it's a woman. Known as Teardrop. Ring any bells?'

'Weird name. No, I haven't. But we'll make enquiries. I have someone in mind who might know.'

He was thinking of Marler, the marksman. Marler had exterminated most of the top assassins in Europe. This sounded like a different kettle of fish altogether.

'Where are you, Philip? We need a number we can contact.'

'I'm not saying . . .'

'Come off it, Philip. Tweed is worried stiff about you. You owe it to him. And if we do dig up some vital data on the names you've given me surely you'll want to know. Otherwise you're walking in the dark – you're probably doing that anyway. Forget me. Think of Tweed – he'll need a number to pass on data. Think of Paula who's on edge about what might be happening to you.'

There was a pause. Newman was careful to keep quiet – he sensed Philip was under great tension, that any prodding would drive him back into his shell. His tone had had a grim bitter note. Philip replied.

'Take this down. 89. 23. 703–0. Just ask for me by name. If I'm out leave the message "Bob called urgently". I'll get back to you.'

'I need the country to get the prefix code.'

'Germany.'

'One more thing, I'm curious how you traced me here . . .'

'I phoned Monica a few minutes ago—'

The connection was broken. Germany had given Newman the clue. He knew 89 was the code number for Munich.

He returned to the dining-room, sat down between Tweed and Paula and reported the gist of the conversation. He had just completed his terse explanation when Paula touched his hand with her index finger.

'Don't look now. Winter has just walked in. Wait a minute . . . He's chosen a table at the upper level in the other arm of the L. Keep quiet everybody,' she continued in the same low tone . . . 'He's ordered a full English breakfast. Bacon and eggs, the lot.'

Newman waited a few minutes. He would have liked to light a cigarette but the dining-room was a no-smoking zone. Then he put a cigarette in his mouth, stood up without lighting it and walked out of the restaurant. In the lobby he paused to light the cigarette and put on his heavy

53

overcoat and gloves. He walked out into the glare of the sunlight.

He remembered Chichester had four main streets in the pedestrians-only centre. North Street, with The Ship at the far end. East Street, South Street and West Street, which ran alongside the Dolphin. It is one of the most attractive towns in Britain, he thought, as he turned left at the Cross. North Street was wide with a feeling of spaciousness. The architecture was Georgian and this end was lined with shops. The pavement was laid with ochre-coloured slabs, which added to the attraction. He passed The George, a promising-looking pub. He met Marler coming out of the entrance to The Ship, a brick-built edifice four storeys high, including elegant dormer windows in the roof.

'And I thought I was going to have a pleasant stroll up to the Dolphin and Anchor,' Marler drawled.

Slim, less heavily built than Newman, in his thirties, Marler was, as always, smartly dressed. He wore a thigh-length British warm, a scarlet cravat at his throat and a cynical expression. The two men were always sparring verbally but in a tight corner they would support each other at the risk of their lives.

'Then let's stroll that way,' Newman suggested. 'Maybe you need the exercise. I suspect you've put on a little weight,' he lied.

'You didn't come here just to admire me,' Marler responded as they walked slowly back up the street. 'What sort of emergency has arisen requiring my unique talents?'

'Why should there be an emergency?' Newman rapped back.

'Simple, my dear chap. If you'd merely wanted to check up on our safe arrival you'd have phoned. I'm all ears – and don't make the obvious wisecrack . . .'

Marler listened while Newman described Winter, gave

54

the reason for being uneasy about his presence. Then he told Marler about the phone call from Philip Cardon. Marler frowned.

'Teardrop? Haven't heard about this one. Odd name for a professional assassin. I'll make a few calls from a public phone box to Europe. Wonder if the lady's name has any significance?'

'How could it have?'

'An assassin's name is sometimes linked subtly with the killing technique. What's on the programme for today?'

'A frenzy of activity. Tweed wants to move very fast – now he knows Philip is prowling round Munich. Come to think of it, we'd better go back and collect Butler and Nield. The tasks Tweed has listed for today will keep us all in perpetual motion . . .'

'Did we hear our names called in vain?' a cultured voice said immediately behind them.

Newman swung round, recognizing Pete Nield's distinctive and clear manner of speaking. Almost on his heels were both Butler and Nield, who had moved close so silently neither Marler nor Newman had been aware of them.

Butler wore his usual shabby windcheater and corduroy trousers. Nield sported a smart blue business suit and a dark Burberry open down the front. He fingered his neat moustache and grinned.

'Just protecting your rear. We saw Marler slipping out on his own and decided to see what he was up to. And you two must have been deep in conversation. You're in a pincer movement. Look in front of you . . .'

Newman swung round again, annoyed that he'd been caught off guard. Coming down North Street towards them from the direction of the Dolphin were Tweed and Paula. Newman frowned as he watched their approach. He'd never seen Tweed moving so quickly. By his side Paula was stepping it out to keep up with him.

55

The sun reflected off her thick glossy black hair and outlined her strong features, her excellent bone structure, her determined but shapely chin. She wore a two-piece blue suit with her shoulder-bag swinging as she walked. Several men stared at her with interest as she passed them looking neither to right nor left.

In his clipped accent Marler was bringing Nield and Butler up to date with Newman's warning about Winter, his description, and Cardon's phone call from Munich. Paula alerted them as she arrived with Tweed.

'It's battle stations. Tweed is worried about Philip and we have to take Chichester apart. Starting now.'

'Everyone briefed on the latest developments?' Tweed began. 'Good. You'll be lucky to get anything to eat today. I've started the wheels moving already.'

'What does that mean – and this "taking Chichester apart"?' Newman enquired.

'For openers,' Paula explained, 'Tweed has just called Monica from a public phone box. She has to find out everything she can about International & Cosmopolitan Universal Communications. We've all heard vaguely about it but does anyone have a clue as to how this global organization works? What its objectives are? I personally haven't.'

'Join the club,' said Marler and lit a king-size cigarette he'd inserted into an ivory holder.

'The next thing,' Paula went on, 'is to tackle an estate agent – a local one – to try and find out who rented Amber Cottage. Also is there someone in that area who carries a lot of clout – money, power. We've found a likely estate agent in East Street near the Cross. The hotel receptionist recommended him to Tweed. We peered in and there's only one man inside. Beech and Bradstock is the name of the agent.'

'Enough talk,' Tweed interjected. 'We'll go there now. I want that estate agent in a nervous mood. We all go in

56

but you leave the talking to me.' During Paula's explanation he had stood with his hands in his raincoat pockets, rocking slowly back and forth on his heels, a rare sign of impatience.

'Then what are we waiting for?' Marler enquired.

'Mr Beech or Mr Bradstock?' Tweed asked the thin man alone inside the estate agent's office, his manner abrupt.

'Beech.' The agent, a weedy man with a foxy face, looked anxiously at the number of people in his office. Marler was leaning against a wall to one side where Beech had difficulty seeing him. 'What can I do for you? I fear there aren't enough chairs for all of you,' Beech said as he remained standing behind his desk.

'No cause to be frightened,' Butler growled.

'Why should I be frightened?' Beech blustered.

'Can't imagine,' replied Butler.

'Mr Beech,' Tweed went on, starting his psychological onslaught. 'We are interested in Amber Cottage on the way to West Wittering. Who owns the place?'

'Amber Cottage?' Beech's eyes flitted round the room, avoiding eye contact with any of his visitors. 'Perhaps I should warn you there was an unpleasant incident there recently.'

'Something that became a murder case,' Tweed snapped. 'You might like to know who you are dealing with.'

He produced a folder, opened it. The document was a forgery produced in the Engine Room at Park Crescent. Beech's eyes opened wider as he stared at the folder Tweed held on to.

'Special Branch. It's the first time I've ever met anyone from that organization.'

'So now you're meeting a whole delegation. Mr Beech, I really would like an answer to my question immediately if not sooner.'

57

'I was approached about two weeks ago along with a number of other agents. The local police have the matter in hand.'

'Don't try and evade me,' Tweed warned. 'You know what I asked. Now give me the answer. And did you handle the transaction?'

'As a matter of fact, I did. It was all most peculiar.'

'Peculiar in what way?' Tweed rapped back.

'I suppose the local police won't mind my telling you as you're Special Branch . . .'

'You suppose correctly. So start talking to me.'

Beech sat down in his chair so he could see Marler, whose almost statuesque stillness was getting on his nerves. Marler moved further along the wall, out of his line of vision. Beech steepled his fingers, spoke rapidly as though worried he would dry up altogether.

'Amber Cottage is handled by a most respectable lawyer with offices in The Pallants. That's a most picturesque area in the very heart of Chichester—'

'We do know where The Pallants are,' Newman said brusquely. 'Let's hurry it up, shall we?'

'This lawyer acts for a convent which owns Amber Cottage. The convent thought it was an investment for spare money in their coffers. On the way to the coast and—'

'Are you going to tell us who rented it?' Tweed demanded. 'And what was peculiar about what happened?'

'Well, I had a phone call from a man called Martin asking how much it would cost to rent the cottage for three months. I told him and he immediately accepted the price. He said someone would call later in the afternoon to pay all the rent in advance. That was when this strange woman came into the picture.'

'What strange woman?' Tweed probed.

'I had, of course, expected a cheque would be

58

delivered. Instead this woman turns up just before I'm going home – with an executive case. I had a fit when she opened it – the case was full of fifty-pound notes. She counted out the correct amount and demanded a receipt made out to Martin. The following morning I had the notes checked at the bank and, as I had thought, they were genuine. Most unusual.'

'What was strange about the woman?' Tweed persisted.

'She wore a black cap with a black veil which masked most of her face. She spoke very few words. I had an impression of sharp features but could never recognize her again.'

'Try and describe her in a little more detail,' Tweed said.

'She stood very erect, dressed in a black knee-length coat. She was slim, about five feet six tall. Oh, and she had a very expensive looking ring on her right hand – the third finger. Diamonds, I'd say, shaped into a design like a fox. Her hands were well-shaped, very white, but the fingers reminded me of talons. I thought I detected a trace of some foreign accent when she spoke her few words.'

Tweed was astonished. Beech's powers of observation were quite remarkable. He softened his tone.

'Another quite different question. In the general area of Amber Cottage – maybe miles away – I heard you had a very wealthy and powerful man living in this part of the world. I can't recall his name.'

There was a long pause. Everyone instinctively remained very still and quiet. Paula had an intuition that Beech was worried, was grappling with a decision which worried him considerably.

'Can't think of anyone fitting that description,' he said eventually.

'There's a lot of money at the giant marina called Chichester Harbour,' Paula mused. 'To say nothing of the district round Bosham. We do need your help, Mr Beech.

59

And this whole conversation is confidential. That's a promise.'

'You're interested in a very expensive property close to Bosham?' Beech suggested.

Tweed said nothing, leaving Paula to carry the ball – she seemed to be getting somewhere.

'We do have limitless resources,' Paula mused aloud again.

'There is one man – although I know very little about him. He has a very large property with extensive grounds facing Bosham across the creek.' He leaned forward as Paula opened her Ordnance Survey map. His finger stabbed an area that coincided almost exactly with the cross on Jean Cardon's embroidery. Tweed blinked, glanced at Paula as she glanced back at him. He hadn't put much faith in the crosses Paula had discovered. Now he was beginning to wonder as Beech leaned back and began speaking quietly.

'I've no idea of this man's name or his nationality. He owns this huge property facing across the creek to Bosham. It has a twelve-foot-high granite wall round it with the mansion and twenty acres of grounds inside. I gather he comes and goes like a migrating bird. He flies in abroad this huge aircraft which has floats. It lands further down, near the exit to the sea, then cruises up the creeks – it has to be high tide – and then a funny thing happens. It really is a weird machine.'

'Weird in what way?' Tweed urged.

'The normal plane has one undercarriage to lower its wheels. This job has two – one which lowers the floats, another which lowers ordinary wheels so he presumably can land at any airport in the world.'

'What happens when the tide goes out?' Newman intervened. 'I remember the creek facing Bosham becomes a marsh of mud.'

'True,' Beech agreed. 'It's an extraordinary machine. It

60

cruises up to opposite the mansion's waterfront, then lowers its wheels, raises its floats and enters the grounds up a huge ramp which is hydraulically extended to the water level. It then disappears behind the wall. The locals watch it, take pictures. It's one of the sights round here. Trouble is you never know when it will be coming in.'

'Surely there have been rumours as to the identity of the owner,' Tweed persisted.

'Search me. If there have been I've never heard them. The property was bought through one of the big London agents several years ago. A man called Gulliver signed the contract, handled completion. A pal of mine told me that – but he said he was convinced this Gulliver was a front man for someone who never appeared.'

'Just one more question and then we'll leave you in peace,' Tweed said amiably. 'What is the name of this property?'

'Cleaver Hall . . .'

6

They were driving out of Chichester along the Avenue de Chartres. Earlier, leaving the hotel's garage, they had proceeded along the other section of West Street which was not part of the pedestrians-only area. Paula had gazed out of her side window, admiring the Georgian doorways and windows.

She was seated alongside Newman, who was behind the wheel of his Mercedes. Tweed sat in the back, his eyes closed as he played back mentally the conversation with the estate agent, Beech.

61

Butler followed, driving Tweed's Ford Escort. Nield sat in the passenger seat. Marler drove behind them in a Ford Sierra. He kept glancing in his rear-view mirror.

'So we're heading for Bosham right away,' Paula confirmed as she studied her map, acting as navigator.

'I want to see this Cleaver Hall close up,' Tweed agreed. 'Then we'll drive into Bosham and get chatting with the inhabitants. The locals may know more than Beech realizes.'

'Well, it may be freezing cold but the air is marvellous,' Paula commented, then gave an instruction to Newman.

'The air won't be so marvellous when we get back to Park Crescent,' Tweed warned. 'On the phone Monica told me Chief Inspector Roy Buchanan is stirring up the pot to boiling point.'

'What's bothering him now?' Newman asked.

'The local police have been in touch with the Yard. Jean Cardon's death is being treated as a murder case. Which it is. But who should we get investigating it but our old friend Buchanan? He's found out that Philip has disappeared and he's treating him as number one suspect. The fact that he's gone abroad doesn't help.'

'He must be barmy,' Paula protested. 'It's obscene to suggest that Philip would have done that to his own wife.'

'You're underestimating Buchanan,' Tweed warned again. 'This is his ploy to smoke out Philip, to make him feel so appalled that he'll come forward to clear his name. Roy B. is ruthless in pursuit of his duty.'

'Do you think it will work if Philip ever hears about it?'

'No, I don't. Philip is in a terrible, controlled fury – I understand that. He's like a missile who's fired himself to find his target. What bothers me is he's on his own. I thought of something a few minutes ago . . .'

'At least we know he's in Munich,' Newman pointed out.

'That's what occurred to me. We have to move quickly . . .'

'I thought we were doing just that,' Paula joked, trying to lighten the conversation.

'Don't interrupt me again,' Tweed chided her. 'I was going to say, Paula, that when we find a public phone box I want you to phone Monica. Tell her Philip is in Munich. Tell her to start checking every hotel in that city to find out if Philip is registered in one of them. And if she does find a registration in his name tell her to continue to phone other hotels, five-star and downwards.'

'Why?' Newman asked as Paula gave him a fresh instruction to turn left. She had seen a signpost to Bosham leading off the A27 they were driving along towards Havant.

'Because,' Tweed explained waspishly, 'Philip employs the techniques I've taught him. When in trouble, book a room at one prominent hotel, then slip away and stay in a smaller place off the beaten track.'

'Understood,' replied Paula.

They were driving through flat countryside with ploughed fields on either side. To her right in the distance Paula could see the undulating curves of the South Downs, silhouetted against a duck-egg-blue sky. They turned down the side road. As soon as they were driving down a hedged road Marler's Sierra drew alongside. He waved them down, pulled ahead as Newman parked by the roadside, setting his hazard lights in action. Marler backed his Sierra close to Newman's car, jumped out with his usual agility. Behind the Mercedes Butler had already stopped and Nield came to join them. Tweed pressed the button that lowered his window.

'Trouble,' Marler announced jauntily, quite unperturbed. 'Basin Cut, as I've nicknamed him – your little

63

friend, Mr Winter – has been following us ever since we left the hotel. Show me where we're headed for and I'll sort him out while you drive on.'

Paula leapt out with her map, showed Marler the route they would follow to reach Bosham. Marler glanced at the map, photographing the complexities of the area in his mind.

'Got it. He won't be tracking us much longer.'

'No rough stuff,' Tweed warned.

'Rough stuff? Me?' Marler had an expression of schoolboyish innocence, his pink face expressing indignation. 'I'll just lead him astray. Fair enough?'

'Do it,' said Tweed and raised the window.

They left Marler behind in his car while Newman and Butler drove on out of sight. Whistling to himself, Marler sat in his car, watching his rear-view mirror. The silver Citroën with Winter at the wheel appeared round a distant bend behind him.

Marler had the engine going and began to crawl forward. It was a quiet road – they had seen no other traffic since leaving the A27. The Citroën slowed as Marler drove round a bend and a straight section of road stretched ahead.

'That will bother you more than somewhat, chum,' Marler said to himself. 'Two of the three cars have vanished. You'll be in a state of indecision.' He timed the manoeuvre carefully.

Without warning he slewed his car to the right, blocking the road. He was standing in the road, waving both arms, as Basin Cut slowed, stopped. Marler was whistling as he strode up to him. The eyes behind the wide-rimmed spectacles were hard and watchful. He lowered his window a few inches as Marler approached him.

'You are blocking the road. It is illegal, is it not?'

Winter's right hand was tucked inside his raincoat low

down. So he's armed, Marler thought. Bit of a giveaway. He smiled broadly.

'Sorry to bother you, old chap. But we're lost. Do you know the way to Bosham Hoe? We're trying to locate the ferry which takes you over to Itchenor.'

'That is where I am going also,' Winter said quickly in his flat voice. 'I do have a map but everything is most confusing.'

'Then let's have a look at your map,' Marler suggested at his most genial.

They studied the map together when Winter had lowered his window completely. The fact that his hand had emerged from under his raincoat told Marler the bluff was succeeding. He let Winter find Bosham Hoe.

'Jolly good. Let's hope my friends get there OK. They probably will. They have an excellent navigator.'

'Navigator?'

'Map-reader, my dear chap. I'll lead, you follow. It will be a jolly party . . .'

Marler maintained a reasonable speed until he reached Bosham Hoe. Winter had obediently stayed behind him. Marler suddenly realized Bosham Hoe was not open to the public – it was a private estate of fairly expensive houses.

With a good few thousand added to the prices for the view over the creek, he thought. Then in the bad weather they'll come to detest the view.

He prepared to lose Basin Cut. And sure enough he saw five 'For Sale' notices after turning a sharp bend to the right. He was now driving parallel to Chichester Channel a few hundred yards away to his left. Marler watched the Citroën moving at a sedate pace behind him. At one time, like Newman, Marler had been a racing driver. He turned another corner, knowing he was now driving parallel to Bosham Channel. Road ahead clear, still no sign of traffic, of human life.

He rammed his foot down on the accelerator. The Sierra shot forward like a rocket. The speedometer climbed. 50 m.p.h. 60 m.p.h. 70 m.p.h. . . .

'And this is illegal, is it not?' he said aloud, mimicking Winter's flat tone.

In the rear-view mirror the Citroën had faded to a silver dot. He swung round a bend and was alongside the creek facing Bosham. The tide was well in. He glanced across the water where the neat tower topped by an attractive steeple located the ancient church of Bosham. Ahead of him the water was across the road. He'd just passed a notice, *This Road Is Liable to Flooding*.

'It most certainly is,' Marler agreed.

He aquaplaned through the water, sending up great cloud-bursts of spray. Without pausing he reached the end of the creek and drove on, following a devious route back to Bosham village.

'With a bit of luck, Basin Cut, your radiator will end up flooded. Just supposing you've the guts to attempt the crossing . . .'

'Stop the car,' Tweed called out.

Newman slowed. Bosham village was about half a mile further on. At this point they were in the middle of a built-up area with a road leading off to the right sign-posted to Chichester. There was a triangle of grass where the three roads met and an inn sign reared up in the centre of the triangle. The Berkeley Arms.

'Bob,' Tweed continued, 'isn't that the pub you said you'd had lunch at several times when you were down here? Run by a nice woman who knows the area well?'

'That's the place.'

'Then I suggest we go there for drinks and you talk to the lady. Pity there isn't somewhere we could hide the cars in case Marler didn't shake off Mr Winter.'

'There is. We drive in through that entrance at the side and there's a car park at the back.'

'I know . . .' Paula was preparing to get out of the car. 'I've seen the phone box. I'll call Monica and ask her to phone the Munich hotels. I'll join you when I've made the call. If they've got shepherd's pie order that for me. This cold weather has given me an appetite.' She sighed.

'What's the matter?' Tweed asked.

'Just thinking of poor Philip. Wondering how he's getting on. He must feel very lonely . . .'

It was mid-morning in Munich but the main street in the city was quiet. Snowflakes were falling and already the pavements were treacherous with an embedded carpet of icy snow. The temperature was −10°C.

Philip had emerged from the Platzl, had then gone inside a confectioner's selling expensive chocolates. Looking out of the windows he could see no sign of any watchers. Instead of the dark shabby coat and the black beret he had worn to break into the building the previous night, he was clad in a beige military-style Aquascutum raincoat with wide lapels. He could have purchased it from any of the top-class shops selling British goods. He wore on his head a wide-brimmed Tyrolean hat and earlier he had bought a pair of German-made shoes.

He was on his way to the restaurant Newman had named. Die Kulisse. The place frequented by Ziggy Palewski, now the target of the assassin called Teardrop. He walked down the street, crossed a side road called Falkenbergstrasse, saw the name Die Kulisse.

Waiters were using long brushes to sweep snow off a canopy tilted over the pavement. As Philip approached they rolled it back under cover. He checked his watch as he entered after shaking snow off his raincoat and hat. How on earth was he going to identify Ziggy Palewski? He had

67

forgotten to ask Newman for a description.

A waitress came forward as he stood looking round. The centre of the spacious room was occupied by a three-sided bar with stools. Tables with chairs were arranged along the walls and the lighting was dim. Illumination was provided by round lamps like cyclists' helmets and the colour scheme was medium brown. A large espresso machine perched behind the bar made a snakelike hissing sound, something Philip had not heard since he was a boy.

The tall slim blonde waitress wore a frilly white blouse and a short skirt, displaying her excellent legs. She addressed him in German.

'Did you want a drink at the bar, coffee or a meal at a table?'

'I've got a problem,' Philip replied in the same language. 'A friend of mine asked me to meet one of his friends who patronizes this restaurant. I can't give you much of a description.'

He thought his explanation sounded feeble but he was at a loss to think up something better. She smiled.

'You're English, aren't you? Maybe we could talk in that language.'

So much for my hope of passing as a German, Philip thought. Maybe the disappointment showed in his expression because the waitress smiled warmly.

'Your German is very good. The only reason I detected a tiny hint of English accent was because I spent four years in your country. Now who could it be you wish to meet? As you see, there are very few customers – it is the weather. Bad for business. The man you are looking for must be a regular. There is only one here at the moment. That man sitting at the back by the wall smoking a cheroot.'

'Thank you. I'll try him. And I'd like a cup of coffee with a jug of cold milk.'

68

'At once, sir . . .'

As he drew nearer to the solitary individual Philip was struck by his unusual appearance. Gnomelike, he sat hunched over his coffee, watching Philip. Middle-aged, he had a striking face, a strong straight nose, prominent cheekbones, a dark moustache and a fringe beard.

It was the eyes under dark brows which most caught Philip's attention. Very still, they were shrewd but kindly. He sat with ash at the end of his cheroot as Philip stopped by his table. He had the feeling he was in the presence of a most unusual personality.

'My friend, Robert Newman, suggested I might find a friend here. Ziggy Palewski. I'm sorry if I'm interrupting your reverie.'

'Please be good enough to describe this Robert Newman . . .'

Philip described Newman in great detail. The gnome puffed at his cheroot after carefully tipping the ash into a glass tray. He nodded for Philip to sit down in the chair facing him.

'This Robert Newman is married?' he enquired.

'He was. His wife was murdered during the Cold War . . .'

The words were out of his mouth before he realized what he was going to say. Oh God, he thought – just like Jean. He had the dreadful feeling he was going to break down, to burst into tears. It hit you like this – the grief – at the moments when you were least prepared for it.

'I have upset you,' the man with the cheroot said. 'Have you suffered a similar bereavement?'

His English was excellent. Philip had a strong sense that this was a compassionate man. He decided to tell the truth.

'Yes. My own wife died on November 29. After torture. It was cold-blooded murder. How did you guess?'

'I detected the pain in your eyes. One more question.

69

Has this Robert Newman ever been an author?'

'Yes. He wrote a book called *Kruger: The Computer That Failed*.'

'You are looking for the people who murdered your wife?' The man puffed at his cheroot. 'You look like the sort of man who would do that.'

'I am doing just that,' Philip replied, unable to temper the vehemence of his statement. 'I don't even know who I'm talking to.'

'Oh, let me introduce myself. Ziggy Palewski. Freelance journalist – hack might be a better word. How can I help you?'

'I am Philip Cardon. I can help you. You have been targeted by a woman, an assassin called Teardrop. A contract has been put out on you.'

'Thank you for warning me. I rather expected something of the sort. Walvis doesn't approve of people who set out to investigate International & Cosmopolitan Universal Communications.'

'Walvis?'

'Yes. Possibly the most evil man in the world today. Gabriel March Walvis.' Palewski waved his cheroot as Philip sipped at the coffee brought earlier – the only brief break in their conversation. 'A most complex character, Walvis. Capable of great kindness – and the most abominable cruelty. He hates humanity, is planning to destroy Europe. While in Washington he was not accepted into the top circles, despite his power and wealth. Not the right background, it was thought. He became violently anti-American. He moved to Britain, tried to join some of the exclusive clubs – and was blackballed every time. Not the right sort of chap, I believe is the phrase. He became anti-British. They say he is very ugly and he is pathologically conscious of his repellent appearance. A very strange man indeed. Who is this Teardrop? An odd name.'

70

He enquired about the assassin who was going to kill him as though it was just one of those problems you come up against in life. Philip found himself admiring the man's intelligence, his strength of will, his self-detachment.

'I've no idea,' he replied. 'Except it is definitely a woman. Why she is called Teardrop Heaven alone knows.'

'Maybe Hell knows,' Palewski said with a sardonic smile.

'You haven't asked me how I know about this threat.'

'If you wanted me to know you would tell me. It might be better for your own safety if I don't know. Please excuse what I am going to say – it might well upset you.' Palewski spoke the next few sentences rapidly to avoid pain. 'You mentioned torture – if I were subjected to it I cannot guarantee I would not break and talk. What I don't know I can't tell.'

'What function does Walvis's organization perform?'

'Officially he is the world master of communications – his TV stations providing the world news first. His satellites cover the whole Earth. His computers store the greatest library of confidential information in existence. Including government secrets, the data to blackmail half the world's so-called leaders.'

'You said officially,' Philip pointed out.

'I suspect this image of his organization is a gigantic front for something quite different and more deadly. I need more time to penetrate his remarkable camouflage.'

'Camouflage?'

'The array of aerial dishes, computers, satellites orbiting in space – I'm convinced this equipment is a smokescreen for his real objective. Something quite different and terrifying. I have not completed my investigations yet so I will say no more.'

'You said earlier,' Philip recalled, 'that Walvis was capable of acts of great kindness. Something like that. It

71

doesn't fit the picture you have painted of this man.'

'Part of his complex character. We're all a mix. Walvis supports convents, the renovation of old buildings. He is agnostic but believes only religion can stabilize the world. A stern religion which will exert strong discipline. And now I must leave. My personal advice to you is to catch the first plane back to London. But I don't think you'll listen to me.'

'I'm afraid I won't . . .'

Palewski stood up, gave a warm smile, patted Philip on the shoulder but said nothing more. Philip watched the stooped gnome walking slowly away. He wondered if he would ever see him alive again.

7

Paula dashed out of the phone box, her call to Monica completed. She had seen Marler's Sierra approaching slowly. She waved madly, he pulled up alongside her.

'They're all in that pub over there, The Berkeley Arms. Drive into that gap to the left. It leads to a car park behind the place. Tweed wants all transport hidden.'

'Anything the lady says, but Winter is trapped by the tide on the road across the creek from Bosham . . .'

He joined the others after parking alongside the Mercedes. It was a typical pleasant English pub with a dark wood-raftered ceiling, a bar to his right as he entered and a small dining area to his left. They were all eating sausages and chips.

'I can recommend the sausages,' Tweed greeted him. 'I gather they're made by a local butcher the lady over there who runs this place has known for years. What about Winter?'

Marler ordered the same dish when the middle-aged woman came straight over from the bar to take his order. He gave a concise account of his encounter with Winter as soon as she disappeared into the kitchen.

'So he's marooned,' Tweed commented in the same quiet voice. He raised his tone as the woman returned. 'You were going to give us a description of this Gulliver.'

The woman glanced round before she replied. There was only one other customer, a man in a deerstalker hat who was out of earshot as he ate his meal. She lowered her voice.

'As I said before, I don't think you have a hope of buying Cleaver Hall. Gulliver, the land agent who looks after the place, only came in here once. He's short and plump with a fat face. About forty, I'd say. I didn't take to him – he has an oily manner. He wore gold-rimmed glasses, tinted. Never set eyes on him since. I'll let you get on with your meal while it's hot,' she said to Marler, having just placed his food in front of him. 'Anything to drink?'

'I can recommend the French dry white wine,' chimed in Paula.

'That will do me,' Marler agreed.

'Cleaver Hall,' Tweed told Marler, pushing his empty plate away, 'has an unsavoury reputation among the locals – not to say disturbing. The lady was reluctant to talk about it earlier.' He spoke louder. 'I wonder how high that tide will be today?'

Deerstalker, an elderly man with a lined face, had acute hearing. He swung round in his chair.

'We're in for a major tide today. Probably cause havoc. On top of that there's a south-westerly blowing and that magnifies the strength of the tide. I live in Surrey and have a small boat moored to a buoy. This time last year I came down to see how it was faring. I found the boat in someone's front garden. You ought to go down to Bosham and see something dramatic.'

'We might do just that,' Tweed replied.

Half an hour later their convoy of three cars was driving along a road with a mix of old and new houses. They were close to a corner when Tweed called out to Newman.

'Pull up, Bob. There's a nice-looking hotel on our right. It would make a good base, well out of the way if I want to leave watchers in Bosham . . .'

The Millstream Hotel. Two storeys high with walls white-washed. Paula accompanied Tweed as they crossed a small wooden bridge over a stream, walked down a path between trim lawns, entered a pleasant hall.

Tweed obtained a colour brochure from a woman who greeted them. She said they had plenty of accommodation available at this time of the year. Thanking her, Tweed returned with Paula to the Mercedes. He was giving the order to Newman before he'd closed the door.

'Make haste to Bosham. I want to clean up our visit here and get back to London pretty damned fast.'

Paula was surprised: Tweed rarely swore even mildly. And she sensed he had taken a major decision about their future movements.

'We'll use the car park,' Newman remarked. 'People park their cars on the road running below Bosham and alongside the creek. I've seen two of them stranded with the sea up to their gunwales . . . . . .'

Paula was fascinated by the car park leading off to the left just before they reached ancient Bosham. It had as many boats as cars stationed there – many large yachts perched high up on huge cradles. They were protected against the weather with large blue plastic sheets. The wind was rising and the rigging was twanging against the aluminium masts, reminding her of a glockenspiel.

'That sou'westerly is building up,' Newman observed as

he locked the car. 'This is going to be quite a diabolical high tide.'

'Is there a restaurant or café in Bosham?' asked Tweed. 'I want to talk to some more of the locals.'

'Place called the Bistro perched on the edge of this creek,' Newman told him. 'We could call in for a cup of coffee . . . Oh, my God! Look at that.'

Newman had stopped abruptly as they reached the end of the car park drive and could see down the short stretch of street to the creek. Paula joined him. The sea had advanced up a hill and was still coming in. She noticed the entrances to walled gardens had a foot-high stone barrier you had to step across to reach a pathway to one of the houses.

'I've never seen it like that,' Newman went on. 'To the right at the bottom of that hill there's a short section of road below the village. To the left you can normally drive round the curve and along the end of the creek to join the road on the opposite shore. We'd better hurry or we won't be able to enter the High Street . . .'

The first part of the narrow High Street was under water. They were about to hurry along it when Newman stopped. He'd caught a brilliant flash of sunlight in the upper floor of a large Georgian mansion behind a high stone wall on the opposite shore. Marler had seen it, too. Whipping out a monocular glass, he focused it rapidly.

'That great house is just about where Jean marked a cross on her embroidery,' Paula commented.

'Which will be Cleaver Hall,' Tweed said grimly. 'Are we under observation?'

'We are.' Marler slipped the glass back into his raincoat pocket. 'A man in the window with a pair of field-glasses.'

'How could they have known we'd be coming here?' Paula wondered.

'I can guess,' Marler said immediately. 'I noticed our

75

friend Winter had a mobile phone in his car. That chap has probably been checking everyone who enters Bosham for the past hour or so. Well, they know we're here.'

'Excellent,' responded Tweed.

His reaction was so surprising no one said anything while they followed Newman, keeping to the dry side of the narrow High Street. The cottages were ancient, often thatched, and a number had been converted into memento shops. They could see the famous church a short distance ahead when Newman led them inside the white-walled Bistro. There were quite a few people sitting at tables, consuming cakes, drinking tea or coffee. To the right was a small modern bar. A large well-built man greeted them and they ordered coffee.

Tweed was staring at a huge watertight door let into the far wall with a large wheel in its centre. It reminded him of a watertight door in a submarine. He gestured towards the door, looked at the proprietor.

'Is that a dummy or the real thing?'

'The real thing, sir. Tides like this one coming in can swamp the terrace outside and then rise up the wall.'

'I'm writing a book on unusual eating places,' Tweed lied. He went over to a window with the well-built man, peered out. Alarmingly high waves were coasting in, splashing over the edge of the terrace.

'In summer customers eat out there at tables,' the proprietor said, anxious to create a good impression.

'Could I just step out on that terrace for a few moments? This is a most unusual feature – and the view must be magnificent.'

'Certainly. I'll close the door while you're out there. Mind the wind. Signal when you want to come back . . .'

He swung the great wheel several times, hauled open the massive door just wide enough for Tweed to step out. There were other customers sitting at tables eating their meal but the Bistro was half empty.

Tweed stepped out and the wind hit him like a blow in the face. Behind him Marler and Paula followed with Newman. The door was closed behind them. Their raincoats flapped madly in the gale-force wind and surf from the incoming waves splashed their faces.

The view *was* magnificent. They looked a long distance down the creek to where it joined Bosham Channel. Boats moored to buoys were tossed into the air and one had capsized. Marler pressed his monocular glass to his eye and focused it on Cleaver Hall.

'Spyglass is still watching Bosham,' he said. 'Checking on everyone who enters, I think.'

He switched his glass to where a silver Citroën was parked alongside the granite wall surrounding Cleaver Hall. Winter was climbing up a rope ladder that had dropped down the side of the wall. At the top someone was peering over, watching his progress. The climber reached the top and disappeared. The rope ladder was hauled up out of sight. Marler lowered his glass, studied the Citroën – the sea had not yet reached it but was coming closer.

'Friend Winter panicked,' Marler commented. 'Must have used his mobile phone to ask Cleaver Hall for help. He's inside the property now.'

'And I think we ought to get back inside,' Paula warned, one hand clasping her skirt. 'Don't like the look of that giant wave approaching one little bit.'

She had just spoken when they heard the door being opened behind them. The proprietor called out urgently.

'Better get back in quick. A monster wave is coming . . .'

Tweed took one last glance at the green surf-tipped mountain of water and they all hurried inside. The door was slammed shut, the wheel closed. Seconds later there was a sound of heaving water breaking, the windows were masked with water, and when Tweed looked out again through the window he saw the terrace was flooded.

77

'Thank you,' he said. 'That terrace is a most unusual feature for summer visitors. Could we just have coffee? Unfortunately we've had lunch.'

'Certainly, sir . . .'

Tweed chose a large table in a corner away from the other customers. Butler and Nield had said nothing but they often waited for an instruction. Paula noticed Tweed's expression was thoughtful, almost grim. After coffee had arrived he turned to Marler, speaking quietly.

'I've had enough of this mob, whoever they may be. They murdered Jean Cardon, killed the motor cyclist outside Philip's London flat. We need information. If you get the chance to confront Winter again in a remote spot you are to put maximum pressure on him. Who he is working for is the key question. Don't be too gentle.'

'What has galvanized you?' Paula asked, then sipped coffee.

'Links are being formed in the chain. A man called Martin rents Amber Cottage. Beech, the agent, says a man called Gulliver, acting for someone else, buys Cleaver Hall. We've been followed by a foreigner called Winter – undoubtedly a phoney name. Now we see Winter disappearing inside Cleaver Hall. Yes, it's time we found out something more about who is running this outfit.'

'Everything to your satisfaction?' enquired the proprietor, who came to their table as Tweed finished speaking.

'Excellent coffee – most unusual in this country,' Tweed assured him. 'Oh, you might be able to help me. I am acting for a consortium interested in buying a property in this area. Cleaver Hall has caught my attention.'

'You're talking millions.'

'That's acceptable. I gather the place is run for its owner by a land agent called Gulliver. Do you know him?'

'Not really. He came in here twice for a drink. Sat out on the terrace with a pair of field-glasses.'

'What does this Gulliver look like? Could you describe him?'

'Tall and thin as a reed. In his thirties, I'd guess. Has a straggly ginger moustache. Made a fuss the second time about something being wrong with his drink. Never laid eyes on him since. His second visit would be about two months ago.'

'I gather some weird machine with floats arrives there occasionally. Any idea who's inside?'

'I have watched it through field-glasses,' the proprietor admitted. 'Has a huge cabin. You can't see who is on board – the windows have mirror glass you can't see through. Funny business all round, Cleaver Hall. Excuse me . . .'

Paula smiled wickedly as Newman twisted round in his chair. The new arrival was a very attractive slim blonde woman in her early thirties. She had whipped off her raincoat and was wearing a high-necked silk blouse which hugged her figure. Her long legs were clad in ski pants tucked into leather boots. She had blue eyes, a shapely nose and a good chin. As she ordered a drink she glanced over at Tweed's table.

'Right up your street, Bob,' Paula whispered.

'She's not bad,' Newman said a shade too airily.

'Come off it, you're smitten . . .'

The blonde woman looked round the room again, then carried her drink to an unoccupied table close to Tweed's. As she sat down she stared straight at Newman, who smiled back.

'Sorry to be so obvious,' she said, 'but aren't you Robert Newman, the foreign correspondent? I'm sure I've seen your picture in *Der Spiegel* and other papers.'

'You're right,' Newman admitted. 'I'm surprised you have recognized me – those pictures make me look like a gorilla.'

'Well, you certainly don't look like one in real life. I'm Lisa Trent.'

'Why don't you join us?' Newman responded, standing up to drag an empty chair from another table.

Trent looked at Tweed and Paula. She addressed the query to both of them.

'Do you mind? I don't want to intrude . . .'

'You're most welcome,' Tweed replied with an enthusiasm which surprised Paula.

'I apologize for bringing this thing with me.' She indicated the compact mobile phone she was carrying. 'So many people hate you using these instruments in public places and I sympathize. But I'm on call.'

'You sound like a doctor,' Newman suggested, leaning forward with a broad smile.

'Nothing like that, requiring brains and the ability to study like mad . . .'

Come off it, Paula thought cattily. You're loaded with intelligence and you've the poise of the devil.

'. . . I'm actually a researcher for financial consultants,' Trent went on. 'Please call me Lisa – it's pretty lonely round here. Not exactly a geriatric ward but heading in that direction.'

'Sounds a most unusual occupation,' Newman replied. His mind flashed back to Jean Cardon, who had held a similar post with Reed & Roebuck. 'What exactly do you have to do?' he went on.

'I'm given the name of a company someone is bothered about. I dig into their activities – try to contact the key people so I can draw up profiles on them. To put it bluntly, I'm on the lookout for conmen. I also read balance sheets, assuming that they've cooked the figures. Oh damn . . .'

Her little phone was bleeping. She said, 'Excuse me. I will keep this brief . . .'

Her end of the conversation was a succession of 'Yes'

80

and 'No'. Once she asked her caller to rephrase something so she could be sure she understood what he was driving at. 'Agreed,' she ended.

'I'm sorry about that,' she said to everyone. 'Would you believe it? I come down here to get away from the rat race – I'm staying at the Millstream Hotel – and now I have to drive back to London later this afternoon. And look forward to a boring dinner by myself.'

'So why not have dinner with me?' Newman suggested. 'I could take you to Brown's Hotel in Albemarle Street off Piccadilly – unless you'd prefer something more lively?'

'Brown's? Dreamy.' Lisa glanced at the ceiling as though gazing at heaven. 'I've had their famous tea there but dinner – never. The dining-room looks so comfortable.'

'Seven o'clock this evening suit you? I'll be waiting in the lobby at the Albemarle Street entrance.'

'Deal.'

Lisa leaned forward and shook hands with Newman. She looked at Tweed and made a moue.

'I do seem to have monopolized the conversation. I hope you don't think I'm awful.'

'I think I envy Bob his dining companion,' Tweed said gallantly.

Lisa clamped her full red lips together. She glanced at her watch, swallowed her drink of white wine, pushed her chair back. Tweed spoke without warning.

'In your profession I expect you've heard of a similar outfit, Reed & Roebuck?' Lisa shook her head. Tweed nodded.

Lisa frowned, glanced at Paula who was studying her with her head turned to one side. Lisa Trent had a beautiful bone structure, she had to admit to herself.

'Sorry, everyone, but I have to leave now. Packing to do, then a fast drive back to the great big roaring city of stress and struggle.'

81

'Seven at Brown's then, this evening,' Newman said, standing up as Lisa prepared to leave.

She moved with long strides as she left the Bistro. She radiated energy and *joie de vivre*. Tweed waited a few minutes and then went over to the window overlooking the terrace. The storm had subsided, the water was on its way out, exposing islands of marshy grass. He came back and told them what was happening.

'In that case,' Marler said, 'I think I'll love you and leave you. I might just get lucky with friend Winter . . .'

Halfway down the hill leading to the creek Marler waited in the Sierra. Hunched behind the wheel he watched the entrance to Cleaver Hall, a pair of immensely tall wrought-iron gates which were closed. Using his monocular glass, he focused it on the gates, saw behind them guards with savage-looking dogs patrolling the grounds.

'You've got something to hide, chum,' he said to himself.

A few minutes later he saw one of the gates swing open slowly of its own accord. They were electronically controlled. Winter, a tiny figure across the creek, walked out to his car. He was getting into his Citroën when Marler drove to his left round a wall through receding water.

He drove fast, reached the end of the creek, passed over a water-logged road and then stopped behind a tall clump of reeds which partially hid him from view. Winter drove along the road, vanished from sight as he proceeded towards a T-junction which would take him to Chichester. Marler had in his mind a mental picture of the complex area.

He drove on, turned left away from the creek along a country road with a few cottages and more modern houses at intervals. Within a couple of minutes both cars were in open country with no habitation in view along the otherwise deserted road.

Marler pressed his foot down, overtook Winter's car and slowed as he passed it. He signalled and then eased his car across the path of the Citroën, which was forced to stop. He was out of the Sierra in seconds, running to the driver's side of the Citroën. Winter again had his hand inside his raincoat as Marler gave the order through the open window.

'Take your hand out slowly with what you're holding or get a bullet.'

His Walther was aimed at Winter's head. The little man blenched, began to protest, then obeyed the order when he saw the expression on Marler's face. He was holding a knife, the type a butcher uses.

'Don't drop the knife,' Marler snapped. 'Keep hold of it and step out into the road slowly . . .'

Winter paused, his face ashen, then he opened the door, stepped out slowly, still holding the knife as Marler backed away, putting distance between them.

'Now shut the door with your other hand. That's fine. The next move is to drop the knife. Yes, *drop* it. So now we have a deadly weapon with your fingerprints on it. Anything ends your miserable existence and I can plead self-defence. No jury in this country will convict me. And the police will find out who you really are . . .'

Marler suddenly leapt forward, grasped Winter by his shirt collar and tie, bent him backwards over the bonnet of his car. A helpless man is a frightened man.

'Who is your boss? Who the hell are you working for?'

'Don't know . . .'

'That's a pity. Life can be so short . . .'

Marler rammed the barrel of the Walther under Winter's chin, pressed it hard into his neck, the nose of the gun pointed upwards. Winter was gurgling. Something about 'mercy'.

83

'No mercy,' Marler said in an unnerving calm tone. 'I hear your lot doesn't know the meaning of the word. You know something? I've forgotten its meaning too. When I press the trigger the bullet will go straight into your brain, will burst open the top of your rotten skull. For the last time – who is your boss?'

'Martin . . .' Winter was having trouble breathing. 'I'm telling you God's truth . . .'

'What does he look like?' Marler demanded, easing the pressure on Winter's neck so he could answer more easily. 'A clear description.'

'Only spoken to him over phones,' Winter gasped. 'Pull the trigger but . . . I've never met him.'

'Martin? Surname or Christian name?'

'Honestly . . . don't know. Never met him.'

'So how do you contact him? I need the number you use to report what you've found out about us. Don't say you don't know. Why commit suicide?'

Marler had removed the gun from Winter's neck but still held him bent over the bonnet. Winter reached up to rub his neck and winced. Sweat was pouring down his face and had misted up the wide-lensed spectacles. He gave Marler a number in fits and starts. The international code at the beginning told Marler which country Martin was based in at the moment.

Germany.

Walking away, Marler first recorded in his notebook the number he had memorized. 'Never rely on your memory' was a maxim Tweed had hammered into his team. Marler next leaned into Winter's car, grabbed hold of the ignition key after turning off the engine. He threw the key into a ditch full of mud by the roadside.

Taking out a handkerchief he bent down, picked up the knife by the blade. He held it up as Winter struggled to stand erect. Winter gazed at the blurred outline of Marler through his misted-up glasses.

'I need a doctor . . .'

'Call the NHS. Your car key is down inside that ditch. I'm taking this knife with your fingerprints on the handle in case we need evidence against you. Give my love to Martin . . .'

8

'That creek changes into a dangerous quagmire when the tide has gone out,' Newman commented, driving out of the car park.

'Mind you don't find yourself in a dangerous quagmire with the sexy Lisa Trent,' Paula teased him.

'That reminds me,' Newman replied. 'When we reach that telephone box near The Berkeley Arms could you call Monica again? I'll do it myself if you want . . .'

'Just tell me what you're after,' Paula said.

'I'd like Monica to run a check on Lisa Trent. She won't have much to go on but we know the type of firm she's working for.'

'That will be enough for Monica. She'll know just the right contact to get inside that sort of world. And I thought you were infatuated with her.'

'She's attractive,' Newman agreed. 'She may be all she says she is. But it was rather a coincidence the way she walked into the Bistro soon after we'd arrived.'

'That occurred to me,' Tweed remarked from the rear of the Mercedes. 'And another odd coincidence is that she should be working for the same kind of firm Jean was employed by. Odd she hasn't heard of Reed & Roebuck.'

'Unless,' Paula suggested, 'she has heard of them and

85

knows Jean worked for them and what happened to her. She might not want to get involved in talking about the outfit.'

'I think,' Tweed said with a note of deep satisfaction, 'more links in the chain are appearing. I sense the enemy is alerted to our presence.'

'Well, they will be after Marler has finished with the Winter character,' Newman said. 'Was that a wise move?'

'It was a deliberate move,' Tweed informed him. 'This lot likes keeping under cover, whoever they are. Look at the two wildly different descriptions we've been given of this land agent, Gulliver, who's supposed to run Cleaver Hall. A small, fat, plump-faced man back at The Berkeley Arms. Now at the Bistro he's tall, thin as a reed. So does Mr Gulliver exist? If so, what does he really look like? Then the mystery man at the top – he flies in aboard a land–sea aircraft which has windows with one-way glass, which is why the chap at the Bistro couldn't see inside.'

Newman had paused at the exit from the car park where he could turn left to the creek or right to The Berkeley Arms.

'So which way now?' he asked.

'Paula can call Monica later. Wait a minute while I have a word with Butler and Nield.'

'We should have a mobile phone like Lisa Trent,' Paula suggested as Tweed was getting out.

'I don't like them,' he told her. 'Nowadays calls can be intercepted . . .'

He climbed back into the car after only a minute's conversation with Butler and Nield.

'You have that cine-camera,' he said to Newman. 'Good. Turn left, drive round the creek, make a U-turn beyond Cleaver Hall, then drive back close to the gates but park by the wall. Then you get out with your camera and stand photographing the mansion through the bars of the gates. Butler and Nield will back you up if there's any rough stuff.'

'What's the idea of that?' Newman asked as he turned towards the creek.

'To light a fire – to smoke them out a bit. We are now launching an offensive against them. No holds barred . . .'

Tweed and Paula sat inside the Mercedes parked under the lee of the wall and now pointing back towards Bosham and Chichester. Paula looked back at Tweed and was struck by his grim expression.

'You're feeling pretty strongly about this, aren't you?'

'Jean Cardon was an exceptionally intelligent and clear-sighted woman. I liked her. But I also have to think of the purpose for the existence of the SIS. I suspect she found something very menacing during the course of her work. I want to know what it was. Bob is performing well . . .'

Newman, accompanied by Butler and Nield, who remained out of sight behind the wall a few paces behind him, had reached the gates. He raised the camera, focused it along the pebble drive, began to photo Cleaver Hall between two bars. An unpleasant-looking man with an athletic build appeared close to the gates. He was holding a savage Alsatian on a leash. He waved and shouted at the top of his nasal voice.

'Not permitted. Get to hell out of it or I'll set the dog on you.'

Behind the wall Butler took off a glove, slipped a pair of knuckledusters over his fingers. Nield picked up a large piece of driftwood shaped like a cudgel. Newman continued filming. The man behind the gates, clad in country clothes, advanced a few paces closer, his expression ugly.

'I've warned you once, you nosy bastard. It's illegal to

87

trespass on private property. All right, you asked for it . . .'

He released the leash and the Alsatian leapt forward, snarling viciously as it jumped up to the gate close to Newman. Calmly, Newman filmed the dog's vicious rush. Two more men appeared, one a short stocky man with a pear-shaped body and a beer belly protruding over his belt. His manner suggested he was the boss.

'If I open the gate the dog will have you for dinner.'

'If you open the gate and let the piece of scruff out it will have had its last dinner.'

Nield had appeared, brandishing his heavy club. He spoke in a mild tone, as though it was all in the day's work.

'And talking about illegality,' Newman hammered on, 'I would remind you it's an offence to have guard dogs running loose on public land, which is what I'm standing on. As for photography, your minion in the first-floor window is having a ball recording us with his cine-camera. Am I addressing Mr Gulliver?'

Something flickered in the piggy eyes of Pear Shape and Newman knew he had scored a bull – he had found the elusive land agent. Gulliver wore a sleeveless leather jacket and corduroy trousers tucked into gumboots. His black hair was brushed back over his dome-shaped head and he had an air of authority.

'Who are you?' he asked quietly.

'Robert Newman.'

'Oh, I see. The newspaper hack. Well, there's no kind of story for you here so push off before you have a nasty accident.'

'No story?' Newman's tone was incredulous. 'Cleaver Hall is guarded like Fort Knox – I can see steel mantraps half concealed in the grass. They're illegal too. A *Star Trek* plane lands here and it has one-way glass windows to conceal who is inside. We've linked you with the horrific murder that started at Amber Cottage. There's probably the biggest story of the decade behind these gates.'

'Try and write it and you won't last long enough to finish it.'

'That's a threat to commit grievous bodily harm,' said Nield. 'I'm a lawyer,' he bluffed.

Gulliver's fat, fleshy face was flushed. Newman had the impression he regretted losing his temper. He smiled, the smile of a man-eater.

'Why don't we talk this over like civilized human beings? The three of you come inside, have a drink with me. Krug champagne. Nothing but the best.'

'I'm declining the invitation,' Newman replied, raising his camera and filming Gulliver. 'Main reason is I don't see any civilized human beings on the other side of these gates.'

Gulliver's expression changed to one of the utmost malevolence. For a short man he could move quickly. He came forward, both hands clutching a steel bar.

'You'll receive so many writs your bloody stupid head will be spinning. That's for starters. From now on, watch it crossing roads. You may get killed by a hit-and-run driver.'

'You mean like Jean Cardon almost was about a year ago?' Newman asked coldly.

The effect on Gulliver was startling. Uncontrolled rage was mingled with confusion. He stepped back from the gate and his right hand whipped inside his sleeveless jacket. Butler already had his hand on his concealed Walther. The first man, who had appeared with the dog, grasped Gulliver by the arm, shaking his head as he spoke.

'Best to take it easy, sir . . .'

'Silly to lose your temper,' Nield chided him. 'That's schoolboy stuff.'

Newman turned on his heel, walked swiftly back to the

89

car hidden behind the wall. Butler kept an eye on Gulliver and then followed Nield to their Ford Escort behind the Mercedes. Newman revved up the engine, shot past the gates at speed, glancing to his right. Gulliver was tramping along the pebble drive towards the mansion, his wide shoulders heaving.

'Back to The Berkeley Arms so Paula can make her call to Monica,' Tweed ordered.

He listened while Newman reported the details of their encounter. He had a grim smile on his face when Paula looked back at him.

'You did well, Bob, very well,' Tweed commented. 'The first confrontation with the enemy went better than I dared hope.'

'How can you be sure we're talking about the enemy?' Paula asked.

'Because Gulliver in his rage made a fatal mistake. When Jean Cardon was mentioned by Bob, Gulliver's natural reaction should have been "Who the hell is Jean Cardon?" The fact that it wasn't shows he knows the name. We're now on the right track. We must identify the top man and turn on the pressure.'

'Marler's Sierra has caught up with Butler behind us,' Newman observed.

'I'll talk to him while Paula is calling Monica. What a marshy mess that creek is when the tide has gone out.'

Paula was staring at it as they drove round the end of the creek and headed back towards Bosham and the Chichester road. Islands of wet grass and reeds were scattered amid evil-looking mud with narrow channels of water running through it.

'I wouldn't like to fall in that,' she remarked.

'If you did you'd be sucked under,' Newman told her. 'I once saw a man topple out of his rowing boat. Luckily it wasn't far out and other fishermen organized a chain of boats. They had the devil of a job hauling him out – he

90

had been sucked down to the waist. They had to loop a rope round his waist and heave like blazes – he came out gradually from the ooze.'

Paula shuddered. In places the ooze had a sinister greenish tinge. The wind blew a strong smell of decaying vegetation into the car. It's best seen round here when the tide is in, she thought. They turned up the road past the car park, past the Millstream Hotel, then parked near The Berkeley Arms. Marler strolled up to the Mercedes whistling as Paula left to use the phone. He climbed in beside Tweed and told him about 'my brief meeting with Mr Winter' while Newman listened.

'Martin is becoming a regular feature of this mystery,' Tweed remarked. 'He is the man who rented Amber Cottage, which ties him in directly with Jean Cardon's murder. Now he's the chief who instructed Winter to follow us. Wish we knew whether it was a surname or a Christian name.'

'The trouble is,' Newman pointed out, 'it's a pretty common name. It might even be a pseudonym. Could he be the top man we're seeking?'

'I doubt it. "X", the top man, takes such trouble to remain in the background. At a wild guess Martin could be his deputy and confidant, the man who carries out the orders of "X". What I'm worried about now,' he explained, 'is that as soon as we get back to Park Crescent I'll have Chief Inspector Buchanan sitting in my lap. I'd bet a lot of money he already has a round-the-clock roster of officers from the Yard watching Park Crescent. There's so much I don't want him to know at this stage—'

He broke off as Paula ran back from the phone box. He could tell from her expression that she had news after talking to Monica.

'Tell all,' he said humorously as Paula slipped into the front passenger seat and closed the door.

'Monica has been fantastically busy. Up all night

91

phoning contacts. Now, Gilbert Hartland, the tracer, came across. Reed & Roebuck were bought out secretly yesterday by guess who.'

'No time for guessing games,' Tweed said sharply.

'By International & Cosmopolitan Universal Communications. Reed & Roebuck were a private company so the deal could be carried out in great secrecy. But Hartland found out.'

'A global mammoth begins to emerge from the fog,' Tweed commented. 'Does Monica know exactly what Reed & Roebuck did? The buyout must have taken place soon after Jean's death.'

'And that's another coincidence I don't swallow,' Paula continued. 'Someone is trying to cover their tracks.'

'A shrewd observation,' Tweed agreed. 'But *who*, for Heaven's sake?'

'Let me go on. Hartland has found out something else: the price International & Cosmopolitan paid for Reed & Roebuck was two million pounds – far in excess of its true worth – for an instantaneous deal. Hartland also knows Reed & Roebuck had their top researcher investigating International & Cosmopolitan. And who do you think the top researcher was? Jean Cardon.'

'Another link in the chain,' Tweed said almost to himself. 'But we have huge gaps in the chain which we must discover. Who was Reed & Roebuck's client? Who was Jean working for?'

'That's something Hartland didn't know. What he does know was that in the middle of the night vans turned up outside Reed & Roebuck's offices and removed all the records.'

'Then it's a dead end,' Newman said.

'Not quite,' Paula corrected him. 'Monica phoned among other people Tweed's friend in the City, Keith Kent, the stockbroker and financial consultant. He

92

wouldn't talk to her. Said he'd only talk to you, Tweed, face to face.'

'His information must be dynamite. I'll go and see him as soon as we return to London,' Tweed decided. 'What has Monica found out about International & Cosmopolitan?'

'Nothing much, I'm afraid. That organization seems to be shrouded in secrecy. None of the contacts she called could tell her anything. She found that strange. It is a privately owned company – even though it's a global giant. Hartland had no data. But when in desperation she called Keith Kent he went blank on her. She's sure he knows something.'

'Maybe he'll tell me,' said Tweed. 'I want to give Butler and Nield some instructions . . .'

He left the car and was away for several minutes. When he returned he seemed pleased with something. He sat very erect in the back of the car.

'Butler and Nield are staying down here to nose around the whole area. They'll move immediately from the Dolphin in Chichester to the Millstream Hotel just behind us. Winter won't know they're still here. I'm sure when he's recovered from Marler's little chat with him he'll check The Ship where they stayed last night.'

'Where to next?' Newman enquired. 'Don't forget I have a date at seven this evening with Lisa Trent.'

'If she bothers to turn up,' Paula teased him.

'Oh, she will turn up,' Tweed interjected. 'Marler, you follow us in the Sierra. We'll drive to the Dolphin, pay the bill, pack our things and head back fast to London.'

'When we get there,' Marler suggested, 'I may stop off at a phone box. There are three strange characters I want to talk to in their different European countries.'

'What about?' Paula asked.

'Nosy,' Marler chaffed her, already halfway out of the car. 'I'm determined to get some information about this

93

woman assassin. She could be dangerous. Teardrop.'

'Call me at Keith Kent's if you get something,' Tweed said. 'Paula and Newman can go back to Park Crescent but I want to evade Buchanan for a little longer.' He scribbled in his notebook, tore out the page. 'That is Keith's private number. My sixth sense tells me that the sooner we know about Teardrop the better . . .'

9

The attack came within minutes of their leaving behind The Berkeley Arms. Newman had turned up the lonely country road leading to the main Chichester highway. Marler was a few yards beyond their boot.

In his mirror Newman saw a huge covered truck appearing behind them. The vehicle was rocketing towards them at a murderous speed along the narrow road.

'These ruddy truck drivers think they own the world because of their size,' he snapped. 'Marler is waving at me. I wonder now—'

He never finished the sentence. To get out of the way of the hurtling juggernaut he had to move almost on to the grass verge. He couldn't see the driver high up in his cab – the windscreen was smeared with mud.

It roared past Marler who had also swerved on to the verge. Thundering forward, it towered over the Mercedes as it began to pass them. Newman noticed the driver was suddenly losing speed. A very odd way to drive.

The juggernaut swerved a few yards in front of New-man and they had a view of the rear. The cover was rolled back, exposing the inside. Newman had an impression of a squat figure in workman's clothes crouching down. The tailboard dropped.

'Hold tight everybody!' he shouted. 'I may turn without warning . . .'

The truck was a dozen yards ahead of them when sealed drums were pushed out on to the road by the crouching figure. Three metal drums which bounced and rolled towards them.

Newman turned his indicator to the right to alert Marler. As the drums continued to sweep towards them Newman swung his wheel over, crossed the grass verge, smashed his way through a five-barred gate into the field beyond – with Marler on his tail. Newman continued a short distance across a grassy field, then swung the car in a U-turn and found Marler alongside him. They all got out of their cars.

At that moment the drums exploded with a deafening roar. Flames soared high above the hedge alongside the road, a blazing inferno which singed the hedge and then set it alight.

As a cloud of black smoke rose, mingling with the flames, Newman sniffed the polluted air. The sou'westerly, still blowing strongly, had brought drifts of the smoke towards him.

'Petrol,' he said. 'Those drums were filled with petrol . . .'

'And,' drawled Marler, lighting a king-size, 'some kind of timer device which delayed the detonation until the truck was clear of the conflagration.'

Tweed stood with his hands thrust into the pockets of his Burberry, a typical stance. When he spoke, his tone was almost off-hand.

'Mr Gulliver really doesn't like us, does he.'

'I think it's going to rain, pour,' Paula said. 'Let's get back into the car . . .'

She had noticed ominous low black clouds brought swiftly overhead by the gale-force wind. Spots of rain as big as fifty-pence pieces were decorating the bonnet of the Mercedes. They had just got back inside their cars when the heavens opened up.

A cloudburst hammered the roof of the car, rain bounced up off the bonnet, the windscreen was almost opaque. Newman set the windscreen wipers going at top speed and the view cleared. No more flames. The hedge had stopped burning.

'That's a bit of luck,' Newman remarked. 'We'll be able to drive over the road in a minute. But how could they have organized that in such a short space of time?'

'It confirms what I suspected,' Tweed replied. 'We are up against a most powerful and widespread organization. As to the time element, don't forget Gulliver's henchman with the field-glasses on the first floor of Cleaver Hall saw us entering Bosham some time ago. Gulliver is a man prepared for all seasons.'

'And some pretty dirty ones,' Paula said vehemently.

They drove back over the smashed gate on to the road, which was flooded where the drums had exploded. Arriving at the Dolphin they wasted no time packing, paying the bill. As they descended with their cases into the lobby Marler returned from The Ship Hotel.

'No sign of bully boy Winter,' he remarked ironically. 'I think it will be a few days before he can hold his head upright.'

'Back to London,' Tweed ordered briskly. He looked at Marler. 'Don't forget to call me at Keith Kent's number if you get lucky.'

'In the lap of the gods,' Marler commented as they walked round the back to where Marler had also parked his car. 'Teardrop. A weird name . . .'

*   *   *

96

Keith Kent was a slim dark-haired man in his thirties, faultlessly dressed in an expensive grey business suit. Clean shaven, he had a pink face and looked very fit. His dark eyes were sharp and there was a trace of cynicism in his clipped way of talking.

Tweed knew he was a high-flyer who travelled all over the world. He had recently returned from São Paulo in Brazil. Tweed settled himself into a comfortable swivel chair as he faced Kent seated behind his own desk.

'Sorry I couldn't talk to Monica,' Kent began. 'Don't trust the phone and she was asking some tricky questions. You'll do the same, knowing you.'

'Marvellous view you have up here,' Tweed remarked, trying to ease the tension out of Kent.

The office in the City was on the fifteenth floor and had a panoramic sweep of the Thames between other high-rises. In the streets below the last office workers were on their way home and the City was going to sleep for the night.

'International & Cosmopolitan Universal Communications is the organization I'm interested in. You know about them, of course?'

Kent winced, pushed back his chair, went to the window and stared down. Then he opened a cupboard and took out a brand new thigh-length British warm. He spoke as he was putting it on.

'Don't wish to seem inhospitable but I think we ought to chat outside. No one much about down there now . . .'

Tweed was surprised. Surely Kent wasn't worried that his office was bugged? But it seemed that way. Perhaps he was wise – Kent had some dangerous secrets about many financial organizations and other companies in his head. They were just about to leave when the phone beeped.

'Damn!' said Kent. 'Who is it?' he demanded when he'd picked up the receiver. 'Oh, well yes, he is here. I'll

97

put him on.' He looked at Tweed. 'Some chap called Marler wants you. Urgently . . .'

'Wait a minute,' Tweed said to Marler.

He unscrewed the mouthpiece, examined it. No listening devices. He quickly screwed it back again.

'Just checking the phone, Marler. It's safe. Anything?'

'Chap in Belgium came up with the goods. Last one I called, of course. Teardrop exists, is one of the most successful assassins operating for years. No description of her. Has a diabolical technique . . .'

'Which is?'

'Come to that. In the past year she's eliminated no fewer than five top financial or political figures in Europe. Quite a range of targets. A very key Chechen Mafia boss in Moscow. In Budapest, a very brilliant financier who was getting Hungary back on its feet. In Prague the Czech chairman of a flourishing industrial company. In Germany – in Bonn – a very able behind-the-scenes advisor to the Chancellor. And in Paris the clever man expected to be appointed Chief of Police. A very active lady.'

'Why Teardrop? What diabolical technique?'

'No description, as I said, but she's very attractive – must be to get dates with such a variety of men. She often wears a black cap and a veil which conceals her face. A witness to the Paris killing swears she has red hair. Could be a wig, of course.'

'Why Teardrop?' Tweed persisted, still keeping his voice down so Kent, by the door, couldn't hear.

'Because of her technique. At some stage, say during a dinner in a public restaurant, she gets upset and starts to cry. As her companion tries to comfort her she produces a gun from under her napkin and fires a bullet into her target. A bullet tipped with cyanide. He jerks upright and she calls out that he's having a heart attack. In the confusion she disappears. No one hears the shot so she must

98

have a silencer on the gun. The crying – then the bullet. Hence Teardrop.'

'Sounds rather fiendish. I'll meet you at Park Crescent in about an hour from now. We must keep moving . . .'

At Brown's Hotel Newman was waiting in the lobby, checking his watch. Seven o'clock. At that moment Lisa Trent walked in. Newman whistled to himself. She wore a beige two-piece suit which looked Chanel and a tight white blouse which outlined her modest well-shaped breasts. Over her shoulder she carried a shoulder-bag, also beige in colour.

'Welcome. You're quite a picture,' Newman greeted her.

'Am I on time?' She checked a small diamond-encrusted watch and gave a wry smile. 'I hate women who turn up late for a date.'

'On the dot,' he assured her. 'Now shall we go in straight for dinner or have a drink in the bar first?'

'The bar would be lovely. Let's hope it's quiet. I've had one hell of a rush getting through work. Don't let's talk about that . . .'

Newman escorted her past the panelled lounges where the famous teas were served. The bar, on its own near the end of the corridor, *was* quiet. The only occupant was the bartender in the distance, polishing glasses.

'Let's sit here,' Lisa suggested, choosing a couch tucked away in a corner. 'Then if someone else arrives we'll still be on our own.'

'Champers? A glass?' Newman suggested as they sat close together on the couch. 'Get the evening off to a sparkling start.'

'Dreamy. Yes, please.'

While Newman was ordering she unfastened a flap of the shoulder-bag, took out a scrap of handkerchief and

99

mopped her forehead. The atmosphere in London was oppressive and there was the feel of a storm on the way.

'Do let's talk about your job,' Newman urged when the bartender had served them. 'I'm interested in everything you do.'

'Cheers!' she said, sipping her champagne. 'I know you used to be a reporter. I suppose old habits die hard – it sounds as though you're interviewing me. I live with a girl friend in a flat off Bond Street. As for my work, it's a mix of being a researcher, detective and conwoman.'

'Conwoman? That doesn't sound like you. It has a rather sinister ring to it.'

'Doesn't it?' She lifted a hand to push back a wave of blonde hair. 'I'm being very frank with you – I feel that I can trust you. Can I?'

'Try me,' Newman invited.

'If I want information from a man who is suspect and will be reluctant to talk I adopt one of several roles. Researcher for an outfit conducting business surveys. Representative of a security firm. Even a newspaper reporter. Right up your street,' she said wickedly.

'That should put anyone off you.'

'Not if I say my editor is reluctant to print the story because he's very unsure he has the facts right. The great thing is to get whoever I'm visiting talking. Oh, bartender, could I have a pack of menthol cigarettes?'

'Have to go out to get them. Another lady not unlike yourself asked me for the same thing an hour ago. I'll pop across the road and get you some. One pack? Take me five minutes . . .'

Lisa started blinking rapidly when they were alone. She felt her right eye and tears began to form, running down her cheek.

'What's wrong?' Newman asked.

'Sorry about this. One of my eyelashes has got into the eye . . .'

100

'Keep still.' Newman produced a clean handkerchief and twisted a corner. 'This won't hurt. I'll fish it out.' As he took hold of her chin with one hand Lisa's right hand slid inside her open shoulder-bag.

10

Tweed was walking along the canyons of the City with his companion. Keith Kent stepped it out briskly. Everything he did was fast, including his manner of speech, which had a cultured accent.

'International & Cosmopolitan,' Tweed began. 'I need to know who runs that mysterious organization.'

'Mysterious is the word. Considering it's global you'd think that would be public knowledge. It most certainly isn't. You ask the most dangerous questions. I hope you have a good reason for this enquiry. Personally, I would prefer we go into a decent pub and have a drink.'

'I have a good reason,' Tweed said in a chilly voice which made Kent glance at him. 'Confidentially, the wife of one of my best agents has been foully murdered – she was tortured before she died. In this country.'

'Sounds quite ghastly.' Suddenly Kent seemed concerned. 'Can you tell me who the victim was?'

'A remarkable lady called Jean Cardon. She worked for an outfit you must know. Reed & Roebuck.'

'I see.' Kent paused and Tweed was careful not to push him but he knew now he was talking to the right man. 'Reed & Roebuck was the best financial search agency in this country, if not in the world. It's just gone out of existence – bought out by Danubex for a sum of money that has made Roebuck, the owner, a millionaire overnight.'

'Danubex?'

'Yes. Not many people know International & Cosmopolitan has changed its name. My guess is because of its new focus on Eastern Europe – and Russia.'

'We're not back to the KGB, I hope,' Tweed remarked.

'No, we're not. Russia is one of the pawns now in this global game someone is playing. The Moscow Mafia is involved – but they don't realize they, too, are pawns. What I'm telling you could end me up on a mortuary slab.'

'Mind telling me how you dug up this information?'

'My contacts in Moscow – I was there recently, not out in São Paulo as people think. That's all I know. I was only given a fragment here, a fragment there.' Kent smiled. 'My best informant, believe it or not, was a Moscow call-girl. Very high class. I didn't avail myself of her services but I did pay her a thousand dollars. I need to know what to steer clear of.'

'So what is that?'

'From now on, Russia and the whole of Eastern Europe. I wouldn't be so lucky a second time. Even now I find myself looking over my shoulder. Here in London.' Keith sounded indignant.

'Don't panic,' Tweed warned. 'We've been followed by two men ever since we left your building.'

'I see. Who are they after? You or me?'

'Probably both of us. What we are going to do is to go into that pub near the Bank Underground station ahead. While I use the phone to fetch help you buy drinks and take them to a table with its back to the wall. They won't risk starting anything lethal in such a public place. Oh, don't go to the toilet while I'm using the phone.'

*   *   *

102

The pub was filling up. When Kent had ordered the drinks Tweed asked the barman for the phone and was directed to a booth in the corner. He stood facing outwards inside the box while he called Park Crescent. Monica sensed his urgency, said Newman was still not back in the office.

'This is a rescue mission . . . is Marler back? Good. Tell him to get that old London cab we bought, bring it round to the front . . . but first, is Marler with you? Put him on . . .'

Rescue mission. The phrase galvanized Monica. Marler came on the line within seconds after Monica had told him swiftly what Tweed wanted. He listened as Tweed gave his order.

'Pick up a friend and me urgently. We'll be standing outside the Green Dragon, a pub near Bank Under—'

'Know it. I'm on my way . . .'

Tweed put down the phone, saw the two heavily built pursuers enter the pub. Very white faces, cheekbones hard, prominent. Probably Slavs. He joined Kent at the corner table. Two glasses of beer were on the table.

'Help is on the way,' Tweed said. 'Our friends have just arrived.'

'Don't think I was very smart to talk to you. This is like being back in Moscow.'

'Keith, stop tapping your fingers on the table. Relax . . .'

'Relax! My God. All right, you got me into this so I suppose you'll get me out of it . . .'

Tweed had checked his watch under the table. The way Marler drove he reckoned the cab could arrive in ten minutes. The two Slav types seemed uncertain what to do. Eventually they went to the bar and ordered two vodka-and-limes.

'Time to go,' Tweed said suddenly. 'We hang about outside, chatting as though we're saying good night.'

103

'As long as it's not goodbye,' Kent remarked with a flash of his normal cynical humour.

Tweed took up a position closer to the Underground station, turned to look at Kent as he talked about nothing in particular. He was now facing the exit from the pub. The two Slavs came out and he stared straight at them. His visual confrontation seemed to disconcert them and again they appeared uncertain what to do next. They began conversing.

A police patrol car cruised slowly down the street and this increased their air of indecision. Tweed nodded to it.

'Bit of luck, Keith. That car coming along.'

'We'll need a lot of luck to get out of this. The few other people about are disappearing off the street – soon we'll be alone with that gentry . . .'

He had hardly finished his comment when a cab raced round the corner with Marler behind the wheel. For the sake of appearances Tweed held up his hand. The cab jolted to an emergency stop, Tweed opened the rear door and the two men dived inside.

Marler, wearing a shabby old blue jacket and an open-necked shirt, had the vehicle moving as Kent slammed the door shut. Tweed noticed Marler had a folded newspaper in his lap.

'What's under the paper?' he asked.

'A Walther automatic. Fully loaded. Back to Park Crescent?'

'Make it there fast,' Tweed called back. 'Watch those two thugs on the edge of the pavement.'

'Spotted them as I came round the corner. Here goes . . .'

One of the Slavs had stepped into the road to force Marler to stop. Marler accelerated, aiming straight for the Slav. The thug jumped backwards, fell heavily on to the pavement. Marler's cab vanished round another corner.

'Some people are lucky,' he called out to Tweed, 'Bob

104

Newman is chatting up his glamour bird while we charge round the town trying to stay alive . . .'

In the bar at Brown's Hotel Newman moved closer to Lisa as he searched for the errant eyelash. Her blonde hair touched the side of his face and the brief caress turned him on. He caught a faint whiff of expensive perfume.

'Can't see a lash,' he told her. 'If you'd keep still and stop fiddling in your shoulder-bag.'

'I'm searching for a tissue which might help.'

The tears were still spilling down her cheek and she was gazing into his eyes. He found their intense blue almost hypnotic. She moved closer, their bodies touched and then she remained still.

'Your menthol cigarettes, madame.'

It was the bartender, who had returned with astonishing speed. He stood watching them, noted the tears dripping.

'Nothing wrong, I hope, sir?'

'Just a lash in her eye.'

'Can be painful. I'll put the cigarettes on the bill.'

'Do that,' said Newman.

Lisa had relaxed, waved his handkerchief away. Then her shoulder-bag slipped open on to the floor, spilling out the contents. All the usual junk a woman carries in her bag, a man carries in his suit. She brought out a large tissue from a box, dabbed at her eye, then her face as Newman gathered everything up, slipped it all back neatly inside the shoulder-bag. She apologized for her clumsiness and thanked him for his help. She blinked her eye several times rapidly.

'Whatever it was I think it's gone. I do appreciate your help. Now, my tummy's rumbling. Any chance of dinner?'

105

'The table's waiting for us . . .'

They chatted easily over the starters, drinking Chablis and talking about their favourite places for a holiday. Soon Newman felt they had known each other for weeks rather than hours.

Lisa, he decided, was full of self-confidence without the hint of arrogance which successful businesswomen sometimes displayed. He waited until they had finished the main course of Dover sole and consumed a quantity of wine – Lisa kept up with him glass for glass. Then it seemed the right moment of mellowness for him to ask the question he'd been holding in reserve.

'I'm floating and enjoying every moment of this evening,' Lisa had just remarked.

'I recall back at the Bistro in Bosham,' he began, 'you said you worked for a financial consultant. As detective and conwoman. What firm do you work for?'

'You'll be shocked if I tell you. Let's not spoil this lovely dinner.'

'I'm unshockable. I could find out, you know, but I'd much sooner you told me. Test how hard-boiled I am,' he said with a grin.

'You have far too engaging a manner. I can see why you were such an outstanding foreign correspondent. Bet most of your informants were women.'

'A mix. You still haven't answered the question.'

'I hope you'll still like me.' She paused. 'I'm talking about Aspen & Schneider Associates.'

'I see.' Newman paused. 'Hardly consultants – they're the biggest investigators of a company's financial standing in the world. Based in New York.'

'You are shocked,' she accused. She fingered her diamond-encrusted wristwatch. 'But they pay well. I fly to New York quite often. Aboard Concorde. Now I have been switched to Europe. I still think you're shocked.'

'They have the reputation of being the most ruthless

106

and unscrupulous firm of their type in the world. They have a whole division of lawyers – to keep them just one step inside the law while they're probing a company. And it's not unusual for them to charge a client a fee of a million dollars – or more.'

'So you are shocked. You think I'll do anything to keep my big fat salary.'

'Well,' he grinned again, 'you said that, I didn't. So will you?'

'I do draw lines. They don't like it when I do but – at the risk of sounding immodest – I'm good enough at my job to make them not want to lose me.'

'The European assignment. Where will that take you to? I often go there myself so maybe we could meet up again.'

'I'd love that, Bob. My new assignment – the organization I have to investigate – is especially hairy.'

'I won't ask the organization's name, but if we're going to meet again I do need to know where to look for you.'

'I fly there tomorrow. Rush-rush. I'll be staying at the Four Seasons Hotel. Munich . . .'

11

A good seven inches of snow had fallen on Munich. It was the morning after Newman had dined with Lisa Trent. In the lobby of the Hotel Platzl Philip Cardon sat pretending to read a newspaper. He was worried.

He had withheld from Ziggy Palewski two vital pieces of information he had heard Walvis refer to while hidden in his office cupboard. Mentally he was carrying on a conversation with himself.

'Can I trust Palewski? I didn't tell him about Walvis's base at Passsau on the Danube. Weird place, Passau. It was known by Hitler in his youth. And what about the remote town of Grafenau? Walvis was sending the sleepy guard there as a punishment. A really strange location for a global company to be interested in. Stuck out in the wilds well north of Passau and close to the Czech border. Just off the main road from Munich to Prague.'

Philip decided the only solution was to call Newman again at his Beresford Road flat. He checked his watch. Time was one hour ahead in Germany. That meant eight in the morning in London. He left the hotel, clad in a sheepskin he had bought earlier, a Russian-style fur hat and fur gloves. It transformed his appearance.

He hailed a cab in Maximilianstrasse and told the driver to take him to the main post office. Hoping the foreign correspondent was at his flat he was relieved when the voice answered.

'Yes? Who is this? Who are you calling?'

'It's Philip. You do sound cautious. I have one vital question. Can I really trust Ziggy Palewski?'

'You found him?'

'Yes. Liked him. Now can I really . . .'

'You can totally trust him if you tell him what you are saying is off the record. But you must do that. He's a top-flight professional journalist. So everything he knows is grist to his mill. But if it's off the record it's sacred to Ziggy. Not to be used even if it means losing the scoop of the century. It's that reputation which makes people right at the top talk to him. Now, are you still obtainable at the same number you gave me yesterday?'

'For the moment, yes I am . . .'

'Wait a minute. For the moment? Tweed needs to know where he can contact you all the time. We know

108

how you feel, all of us are very conscious of that' – he thought he heard Philip swallow – 'but you might well need back-up – to do the job you want to do. We are finding out things you'd be interested to know – but I'm not telling you over the phone.'

'Thanks a lot . . .'

'Face to face I'll tell you everything. I'm pretty sure some of it would help you.'

'Understood. I have to go. Thanks for the info . . .'

There was a click. The line had gone dead before Newman could ask him more questions. He put down the phone and swore aloud. Checking his watch, he decided he'd have to skip breakfast. Tweed had called an urgent meeting to discuss all the data uncovered so far. He had the feeling Tweed was itching to get on to the Continent.

Gabriel March Walvis, dressed in a dark blue silk business suit, stared in the mirror. He had just shaved with his electric razor. His puffy, fleshy face in the magnifying mirror resembled a landscape of hills and gullies. Behind him Martin entered after knocking on the bathroom door and receiving permission to enter.

'We have found the Englishman, Cardon, registered at two different hotels,' Martin reported with a delighted grin. 'He came off a London flight yesterday soon after we left the airport, as I told you. Otto and Pierre followed him to the Four Seasons where he registered. When he had not appeared again they went inside . . .'

'You are babbling,' Walvis interjected after adjusting his floppy polka-dot bow-tie.

He had a vast wardrobe of clothes – including a fur-lined cape – and each day wore a different outfit. It was a tactic he adopted to avoid recognition.

Martin lost some of his ebullient manner. Walvis was in one of his ugly moods.

109

'To cut a long story short . . .'

'That would be a novelty for you. Proceed.'

'They began to check all other hotels in the vicinity. Cardon is also registered at the Platzl in the Old Town. They believe he is staying there. Before I came to tell you I personally checked the Comprehensive Index. He isn't recorded.'

The Index was a huge list of names of men and women all over the world. All were either potentially dangerous or useful to Walvis. Each name had a biography listing any vices – a married man with a mistress, a Minister with peculiar tastes in pleasure. Anything that would enable pressure to be exerted if necessary.

'Then that makes him someone who should be investigated. He could have been the intruder who broke into HQ last night. There is a coincidence in his arrival and that break-in which I find suggestive.'

Walvis struggled to pull on a check jacket which although outsize he could just squeeze his bulk into. Martin waited for an instruction he sensed was about to be given.

'Tell Otto and Pierre to kidnap this Philip Cardon and you then take him to Grafenau where we have excellent facilities for interrogation. After extracting all the information that can be squeezed out of him his body can be buried in one of the abandoned mine shafts.'

'You want me to accompany them?' Martin was unable to suppress his dismay.

Walvis turned round, his eyes twitching unpleasantly. He smiled at his deputy.

'You don't like the cold, do you, Martin?'

'Well, sir, if you really wish me to . . .'

'Tell Otto and Pierre to do the job on their own.' Walvis was amused at the relief which flooded Martin's face. 'I am interested as to how they were able to trace this Cardon. Hotels do not give out names of guests easily.'

110

'You will recall that Otto was thrown out of the Kriminalpolizei based at Wiesbaden. He managed to retain his police pass. He simply showed concierges the pass and they felt compelled to tell him what they knew, to show him their registers.'

'I thought so. Now order my breakfast. First a pint of prawns then bacon, three fried eggs and two sausages. You have seen Rosa's new friend, the little dog?'

'Yes, sir. I didn't know she liked dogs.'

'She doesn't. When I was visiting the Nymphenburg Palace I saw a woman with this dog – a wire-haired terrier – being dragged along, almost strangled on a tight leash. I sent my chauffeur to buy it from her for two thousand marks. I cannot bear cruelty to animals.'

Not for the first time Martin marvelled at the contradictions in Walvis's character. He had sent a woman to her death after torture and now he was bothered about the health of a mongrel dog. Walvis padded out of the bathroom across his bedroom into the luxurious apartment in the wealthy residential district beyond the bridge over the River Isar. Walvis had bought the adjoining apartment on the ground floor at great expense, had then had both apartments made into one.

Martin gave the order for breakfast to the housekeeper and then went out to find Otto and Pierre. That kind of order was always given verbally. 'Nothing on paper, no evidence,' was one of Walvis's favourite maxims.

After completing his call to Newman from the post office Philip headed for the exit. A hand grasped his arm and he stopped dead. He really must visit Marler's contact in Munich and obtain a weapon, maybe several.

'Don't look round,' a familiar voice said. 'We are being observed,' Ziggy Palewski continued, 'but for the moment we are concealed by the crowd.'

111

'Can we get rid of them?' Cardon asked coolly.

'Most easily. I have a grey BMW parked outside. It has a lucky charm dangling over the windscreen – a furry gnome. You walk outside, get immediately into the front passenger seat.'

'Will do. What about the watchers?'

'They will encounter interference from two sturdy German ladies with heavily laden shopping baskets. Please move now . . .'

After the steamy heat of the post office the bitter cold air hit Cardon. He walked carefully – ice coated the snow-layered pavements. To his right he saw the same Volvo that had followed him from the airport parked by the kerb. He turned left and was startled to see Palewski on the other side of the BMW unlocking it. The engine had started as he dived inside, slammed the door. The vehicle was moving.

Philip was impressed by the gnome's speed of movement – and by his sense of humour. To have as a mascot a miniature gnome suggested a man who could laugh at himself.

'Obvious question,' Philip said, 'but how did you know you could find me in the post office?'

'You are staying at the Platzl. I followed you yesterday.'

'I'm supposed to know when people are doing that.'

'I have practised the art for years. It helps me in my job. This morning I was parked out of sight near the exit from the Platzl, I saw you get into a taxi, then I simply followed you to the post office, knowing you were being tailed by two men who might not be good for your health.'

'I should have spotted them, too,' Philip said grimly.

'You had little chance of doing that. They stayed well behind my BMW. I fear you are a target. The normal technique would be to kill you with a hit-and-run driver.'

112

A hit-and-run driver... Philip choked with emotion. His mind flashed back to a year earlier. Jean had almost been killed by a hit-and-run driver in the Fulham Road.

She had managed to jump clear but had tripped on the kerb, her head crashing down on hard paving stones. For several days she was kept in hospital, suffering from concussion.

The emotion threatened to overwhelm him. He now felt so guilty. He was recalling what she had said to him when he had visited her in a private room at the hospital the day before her discharge. She had been lying down, her head on the pillow when he entered the room.

They had conversed for a few minutes. Then Jean, staring at the ceiling, had uttered the words which now came back to him and overwhelmed him completely with a terrible sense of self-guilt.

'We're going to live a normal life...'

At the time it had seemed a strange remark but then one of the sisters had come into the room to check her blood pressure. Shortly after returning to the house in Surrey Philip had become so inundated with the dangerous task Tweed had set him that he had never got round to asking her what she had meant.

Later, he decided not to question her. He had the strong feeling Jean didn't want him to recall what she had said. He turned away from Palewski as his eyes filled with tears. Oh, God! If only he had understood.

Jean had realized the hit-and-run driver was no accident, that the intention had been to kill her. Because she didn't want to worry him she had kept the knowledge to herself. Yes, that was what had happened. It was typical of her strength of character.

He hadn't had the insight to realize something was wrong. No, that wasn't quite true. In odd moments he had recalled the words, worried over them, but had known she wouldn't want him to say anything. So, with the knowledge that she was under sentence of death for a year, that she might die at any time, they *had* lived a normal life.

It had begun to snow as he gazed out of the window. His sensation of deep remorse was replaced by one of fury. He *would* stay alive long enough to hunt down the men responsible for that dreadful act at Amber Cottage – long enough to kill them slowly.

He took out a handkerchief, blew his nose several times, surreptitiously dabbed at his eyes. Palewski spoke in his gentle voice. 'Something I said has upset you.'

'I'm not used to the low temperatures. It makes my eyes water.' He changed the subject quickly, adopting the steel mask he had faced the world with since leaving the Nuffield. 'Are we still being followed?'

'No. They skidded when they started to move, nearly hit a van. One of the German shopping ladies I employed had waited outside when those two thugs went into the post office. She used her boot to kick slabs of ice under the front wheel. What are you going to do? You need back-up if you are going to survive.'

'People are on the way from London,' Philip lied.

'I hope you are telling me the truth. I have decided that Munich has become unhealthy for me. In any case I want to go to Salzburg. International & Cosmopolitan remotely control their traffic on the Danube from there – because Salzburg is not on the Danube.'

'Traffic? What traffic?'

'Barge traffic. Whole barge trains. Laden with the most modern weapons. Surface-to-air missile launchers – and the missiles. Of a very sophisticated type. They are bought from Moscow which has a flood of arms it doesn't want. But they do want the dollars that are paid for them. Enough weaponry is travelling on those barges to launch

114

a major war. Incidentally there is one fact which may be useful – it would certainly interest Robert Newman. Recently International & Cosmopolitan has changed its name secretly to Danubex. Suggestive. The Danube – Danubex.'

'Am I going to lose contact with you when you leave for Salzburg? I hope not.'

'That is the final piece of information I will give you. You can meet me at any day between ten and eleven in the morning in Salzburg at a first-floor – Stock 1 – eating-place called Café Sigrist. It is almost opposite ÖH – that probably means nothing to you.'

'ÖH is the locals' way of referring to the Hotel Öster-reicherischer Hof, one of the best hotels in the city over-looking the river Salzach. I do know Salzburg and I can find that café.'

'Excellent. I look forward to our possible meeting. If I am still alive I may have more news for you. At some earlier date your wife was nearly killed by a hit-and-run driver? Am I right?'

'Yes.'

'My apologies for reviving horrific memories. We are now approaching the main station. If you would take over my car and return it to this address – put it in the garage. I would be grateful. If Walvis's rats come sniffing round they will think I am still in Munich . . .'

Pausing by the kerb, Palewski wrote out an address in a notebook, drew a brief plan of the location, tore out the sheet, handed it to Philip with a slim black case.

'That is the electronic device which opens the garage door. When you have parked the car drop the device inside my letterbox in the hallway of the building . . .'

He drove on and soon the main railway station came into view. Very few people about – the snow was clearing the streets of Munich. Palewski was about to park by the entrance when a car overtook them, parked ahead of them. A grey Volvo.

'Don't back,' Philip ordered as Palewski prepared to reverse. 'I'll deal with them . . .'

'No . . .'

Philip was already out of the car. The fury which had taken hold of him since he had realized the significance of Jean's strange hospital remark was at a peak but he was ice cold. He had an irresistible urge to get to grips with the enemy.

One man sat in the back. The driver, with long dark hair, was still behind the wheel. Philip opened the rear door, smiled as he spoke swiftly in German.

'You wanted to have a chat with me?'

He had removed the glove from his left hand. The thug in the back looked startled, then slid his hand inside his jacket. He leered as he replied.

'It will be our pleasure but perhaps not—'

He never finished his sentence. The stiffened left edge of Philip's hand smashed into the man's larynx. He gulped horribly, sagged forward. The driver was turning when Philip grasped his long hair with his right gloved hand. He hauled the man's head back over the end of the seat.

'Name?' he demanded in German. 'Quick, or I'll kill you.'

'Otto. I am police . . .'

'Like hell you are . . .'

Philip pulled harder. Then without warning he slammed the man's head forward, the skull connecting with the steering-wheel. Otto lay still, slumped forward. Philip hauled him back again, unconscious, rested him against the seat as though asleep. The other man had keeled over on to the floor out of sight.

Philip closed the door, glanced round. No one to witness what had happened. He felt a little better.

Palewski was already climbing out of the car, carrying a case. He handed Philip the ignition key.

116

'When does your train leave?' Philip asked quickly.

'In about five minutes. The Salzburg Express . . .'

'Now you can board it and no one will know where you've disappeared to.'

'My eternal thanks. Such precision . . .'

'Go, go, go,' Philip ordered.

He was behind the wheel of Palewski's car before the owner had disappeared inside the great vault of the station. He had transport now and he was going to use it.

12

'I hear that no one has ever seen the owner of Cleaver Hall,' Pete Nield said.

He was inside a memento shop in Bosham's High Street and chatting to the woman who ran the place. Nield had an easy social personality which encouraged people to talk.

'No one has ever seen him. They don't know his name. Never comes into the village – so far as I know. But,' she continued, 'if he walked in here this morning how would I know it was him?'

Nield was aware their conversation was being overheard by another man peering at the huge collection, most of which was junk. He glanced at the listener. Tall, slim, he held himself erect and his stance suggested to Nield a military man.

'Well, thank you,' Nield said to the woman, carrying a packaged small wooden replica of Bosham Church. 'You can rest assured I don't own Cleaver Hall . . .'

Patiently, Nield had visited every shop, deliberately

117

posing the question in the same way during conversation. His psychological approach was that if someone had seen the owner, knew his name, they'd be only too anxious to impart unique information.

It was late in the afternoon and night was falling as he left the shop. Butler was elsewhere, exploring the locality round Cleaver Hall, checking its defences. It suited Nield to be on his own – Butler was a formidable ally but didn't excel socially.

'Excuse me,' the man behind him said in an upper-crust accent, 'but you seem very interested in Cleaver Hall. 'I've heard you ask the same question three times – twice on the front when you were chatting to fishermen. I'm David Sherwood, late of the SAS. Care for a drink at the Bistro?'

Nield studied Sherwood more closely. He had a hooked nose, alert eyes, a firm mouth and an air of command.

Clad in a riding habit, his jodhpurs were thrust into a pair of knee-length leather boots which gleamed like glass. His movements were easy and agile.

'SAS?' Nield queried cautiously. He was always on his guard if approached by a stranger. His first thought was that this was a prowler from the Hall, but Sherwood didn't seem the type who would be employed by Gulliver – in fact probably wouldn't touch Pear Shape with a bargepole. 'Thank you,' Nield said, 'be glad to join you.'

'Now that you've summed me up.' Sherwood, a handsome man with a neat brown moustache, smiled cynically. 'I'd say you've heard of the SAS – I was an officer. Came out and formed a security unit. Might tell you about that over our drinks. It concerns Cleaver Hall . . .'

The strong sou'westerly gale was still blowing and Nield was glad to get inside to the warmth of the Bistro. They sat with their whiskies at the same table Tweed and his team had occupied. Again there were few other customers and no one could hear their conversation.

118

'Cheers!' said Nield and waited for Sherwood to take the initiative.'

'I got the distinct impression,' Sherwood began, 'that your questions were not based on idle curiosity. Were they?' he asked brusquely.

'Tell me first about this security unit you formed.'

'Well, if you insist on my playing the opening shot. I'd been with a regular Army regiment before I was seconded to the SAS, of course. I then had two options when my SAS period ended. To leave the Army with a fat redundancy payment – or wait another year when there would have been a whole flock of army types thrown on the streets. I decided to jump the gun before that happened. With a partner – he put up most of the money – I established this specialized security outfit.'

'Specialized in what way?' Nield queried.

'We didn't have security trucks or move valuable cargoes – too much competition. I came up with the idea that we'd concentrate on securing stately homes, millionaires with houses in Belgravia. I invented some of the most sophisticated systems in the world. They worked, the firm's reputation spread. Then we were asked to secure Cleaver Hall. That was my great mistake.'

'Why a mistake?'

'You're good at asking questions but not so good at answering them,' Sherwood rapped back. He swallowed the rest of his whisky. 'Have another one?'

'We will. This time on me . . .'

While Nield was at the bar he was thinking furiously. He was good at assessing character and Sherwood sounded genuine. He decided to take a chance when the opportunity arose. Carrying the drinks back to the table he asked the question again.

'Why a mistake?'

'I didn't take to the land agent, Gulliver, from the start. A shrewd tyrant. Ran the place like a prison. Came to the

119

point where he tried to interfere once too often. I told him he could finish the job himself and we'd charge only for the work done. Didn't even consult Parker.'

'Parker?'

'My partner, who put up sixty per cent of the money to finance the venture. Gulliver asked me to wait and disappeared upstairs to a suite of rooms where the doors were always kept locked – presumably to consult his boss. Came down a bit later looking chastened. Crawled to me. Apologized in the most nauseating manner, begged me to finish the job. Well, he'd apologized and so I agreed.'

'I still don't understand the mistake,' Nield persisted.

'You talk like a man who is a trained interrogator. I don't think you trust me. Supposing I show you my SAS identity pass, which I pinched when I left the outfit?'

'It would help,' Nield admitted.

He looked at the folder. It gave his name, age – thirty-four – and rank. Captain. No SAS symbol, but a curious rubber stamp. Newman had once trained with the SAS to write a major article on their work. The experience had half-killed him but he'd completed the course. And he had once described just this type of pass. No photograph of the owner.

'Satisfied?' Sherwood snapped. 'Good. So who the hell are you? Not a normal civilian I'll be bound.'

Nield said nothing. He took out his forged Special Branch folder, handed it to his companion. Sherwood raised his thick eyebrows, handed back the folder.

'I see. So there is something funny about Cleaver Hall and its inhabitants.'

'We don't know yet. Finish your story.'

'We had completed the job. Gulliver paid up promptly. Two days later I had a phone call from abroad. It was Parker, telling me he'd sold the firm for a packet. My proportion of the deal he'd paid in to my bank. I was staggered when I checked the amount – five hundred thousand pounds. And while I remember it, there was a funny incident in this place a few days ago. A stunning blonde arrived at Cleaver Hall to interview the owner for some magazine. I gather she had to put up with an interview with Gulliver. When I saw her in here she pretended she didn't know me. Most odd.'

'Know her name?' Nield asked casually.

'Lisa Trent.'

'And any idea where Parker phoned you from abroad?'

'The Hotel Bayerischer Hof, a de-luxe job. I tried to get back to him several times but the concierge said he'd paid for his room for a week but hadn't been seen since the first night of his arrival. That bothers me. We were close friends. I'm going to find out what has happened to him.'

'Why should something have happened to him?'

Nield was now interrogating Sherwood. He knew that Tweed would want all the facts about this strange – and possibly sinister – event.

'Because,' Sherwood barked, then lowered his voice, 'his wife, Sandra, hasn't heard a word from him since he told her he had urgent business abroad.'

'Where is this Hotel Bayerischer Hof?' Nield enquired.

'In a city where there's a small English community. They may know something – Parker is very sociable and has contacts all over the continent. I'm flying out there myself to investigate.' He paused. 'At one time in the Army I was with Military Intelligence.'

'Which city are you talking about?' Nield demanded, a note of exasperation in his tone.

'Munich . . .'

Nield had persuaded Sherwood to wait at the Bistro and to drive back to London with him later. He went out into the blustery night and found Butler waiting for him at the car park.

121

'I've been taking a good look at Cleaver Hall,' Butler told him. 'The place is guarded like a fortress. An electrified wire spans the top of the walls – they must have switched off the power while Winter shinned up the rope ladder and over the top. At dusk the whole mansion is illuminated with arc lights. Guards in dark clothing patrol the grounds and the dogs are let loose. No way you can get inside that place. Gulliver accompanies the patrols at intervals, carrying what looked like a shotgun.'

'Tweed will be interested . . .'

'Something else,' Butler went on, in the longest report Nield had ever heard him make. 'Winter came back on foot, looking pretty groggy. Later drove down the drive with his neck bandaged. I was near the gates and heard Gulliver call out to him. "Get back to London as fast as you can. Then take the first flight to Munich. That's an order from the top which just came over the comsat."'

'So they communicate by satellite phones. Wasn't it dark by then? So how could you be sure it was Winter?'

'Because among other things they have a bloody great searchlight beamed down the drive. Saw Winter as clear as I can see you. They must have rescued the Citroën earlier. He was driving the same car. What do we do next?'

'Drive like blazes back to Park Crescent. We'll have someone with us – I'll bring him back in the Escort. On the way I'll stop at that phone near The Berkeley Arms – the one Paula used. I think Tweed may want advance warning of Winter's movements. He could be intercepted at Heathrow . . .'

122

13

'Philip Cardon is on the line,' Monica said to Tweed in his office. 'I managed to get him at the number Bob gave me . . .'

'Tweed here, Philip. I'm not asking you for any data you've unearthed – unless you want to tell me in a round-about way. This call is to tell you I'm sending a heavy team to Munich . . . Don't go! Hear me out! You will be in sole charge of the team. Everyone has agreed to take orders from you. They're in my office now. Bob, two men who work closely together—'

'You mean Harry and Pete?' Philip interjected.

Tweed noticed with alarm that Philip's normal amiable manner had changed. Those few words had been spoken in a cold tone with a hint of ferocity underlying it.

'That's right,' he went on quickly. 'And someone whose hobby is shooting ducks . . .'

'Is the duck shooter there? Could I speak to him *now*?'

'Yes. But please wait afterwards for me to come back on the line . . .'

'Will do. The duck shooter *now*!'

Tweed cupped his hand over the phone. He looked at Marler, who was among the assembled company in the crowded room.

'Philip wants to speak to you. Tell him what he wants to know. Don't argue with him – he's in a very tough mood.'

'Marler here, Philip. Shoot . . .'

'I need to know urgently where I can buy equipment – the type you use for your hobby.'

123

That meant illegal arms from an underground dealer. Marler saw Tweed nodding his head, urging him to co-operate with whatever Philip was demanding.

'Take this name and address down. Ready? Manfred Hellmann, Seestrasse 4500, Berg. It's a small resort south of Munich on the lake – the Starnberger See. Take Auto-bahn A95 from Munich on the way to Garmisch. Manfred lives in a bungalow, very de-luxe. To get his help give him my name and the code-word Valkyries. It will cost you a bomb, whatever you need.'

'I have plenty of funds. Brought the lot allocated to me. Thanks.'

The last word sounded very much like an afterthought. Philip sounded in a devil of a rush, Marler warned Tweed as he handed the phone back to him.

'We can only help you if you stay where you are until the team arrives, Philip. We're finding out what you're up against. I wouldn't tackle it myself on my own. I predict a tremendous firefight.'

'When are they coming? I'm not hanging round here much longer. Too dangerous.'

'They board the first direct flight to Munich tomorrow morning. No more flights tonight – Monica checked before she called you.'

'Who do you think I'm up against, then?' Philip asked in the same cold detached tone.

'You don't want me to give you the name on the phone – but it's global. I've been attacked personally out in the country, damn near killed.'

'By the same people?'

'I'm sure of it . . .'

'How can you be?'

Tweed changed tactics. His tone became authoritative and impatient.

'Would I make a statement like that if I didn't know what I was talking about? So don't start questioning my judgement. Just wait for twenty-four hours. And take care . . .'

Tweed put down the phone before Cardon could reply. Paula, seated behind her desk, looked startled.

'That was pretty rough, the way you spoke at the end and then slammed down the receiver on him.'

'Psychology,' observed Newman, perched on the edge of her desk. He looked down at her. 'Philip has been offered the earth by Tweed – total command of the operation. He is in a bitter mood but when he thinks it over he won't be able to let Tweed down.'

'I hope it works,' was Tweed's brief comment.

'Offered the earth – and the moon, too,' Marler drawled. 'It must have slipped my memory when I agreed he'd give me orders – not that he isn't capable of leadership of the first order.'

'I don't recall agreeing, either,' Newman said humorously.

'I had to anchor Philip until we reach him,' Tweed said. 'I sensed that he was on the verge of moving on somewhere else. He'll accept my authority when I arrive with you all.'

'Philip is capable of operating on his own,' commented Nield seated on a couch next to Butler. 'But I doubt he fully appreciates what he's going up against.'

'You're coming with us to Germany, then?' Paula checked with Tweed.

'Yes.' He looked at the other desk where his faithful assistant sat taking everything in. 'Monica has worked nonstop all night and through the day, so let's hear what she's found.'

'All roads lead to Munich,' Monica said.

'First,' she began, 'the pedigree of Gabriel March Walvis, mystery man. Age, unknown. Appearance – well, couriers have brought me three newspaper pictures and one

125

magazine photo of him. Care to take a look?'

They all gathered round her desk where she had spread out four pictures. Marler, who had been leaning against a wall, smoking his king-size, strolled over, looked at the display and whistled.

'Washington, London, Berlin, Moscow. They're all different people.'

'Exactly,' said Monica. 'And my bet is not one of them is the real Walvis. Make yourselves comfortable and I'll go on. Appearance, unknown. Country of origin, unknown. I checked three different sources. One said he was born in Prague, another London, the third Istanbul. But this is factual – through International & Cosmopolitan Universal Communications he controls the greatest network of newspapers, communications satellites and TV and radio stations in the world. He's even beaming news to China and has a dominant grip on the Pacific Rim . . .'

'Where did the money come from?' Newman asked. 'I suppose he's borrowed so much from forty or fifty banks they daren't withdraw the loans.'

'Wrong,' Monica snapped. 'Completely wrong, although it is what I expected until my money tracers began burrowing. *Walvis* controls the banks he deals with. He owns *them*.'

'Then he must have been born with a whacking great gold spoon in his mouth,' suggested Marler.

'Wrong again, although gold is the key. The most reliable rumour – still a rumour – is that he was born a peasant in Mittel-Europa, educated himself. Now, the nearest to fact. As a young man he did borrow money from a small bank. He invested it in a new Australian gold mine, Mount Isa. The shares soared from threepence each to ten thousand pounds. He'd bought a huge amount. He sold out near the top and then sold the shares short. He made a second colossal fortune when the shares nosedived and the bubble burst. At the end of that little investment Walvis

126

was the richest man in the world. That was the beginning.'

'Some beginning,' Newman commented. 'Why doesn't the whole world know about this? I didn't.'

'Because even then he was so secretive,' Monica explained. 'He used nominee names – six of them to conceal the sheer magnitude of his operation.'

'So how,' Paula, intrigued, chipped in, 'how did you find out, Monica?'

'By knowing the right money tracers in Australia. I called Sydney in the middle of the night here so it was daytime in Australia. Walvis then immediately bought the small bank he'd borrowed money from – again to cover his tracks. This job was like tracking a phantom. Four years ago he married a woman called Jill Selborne. She's English, in her thirties, and now lives in a flat over here in Half Moon Street. I can't make out whether they are separated or still together. I have her address . . .'

'Give it to me,' Newman requested, standing upright. 'I think I'll get a cab and see if she's in residence. A long shot, but it might come off. Any more data on this Jill?'

'None at all. Here's the address . . .'

Newman took the sheet of paper, tucked it in his pocket. He was putting on his trench coat when Tweed spoke.

'What do you hope to achieve by this evening call?'

'A woman who's been married to a man is likely to know more about him than anyone else. I'll be back here as soon as I can. Monica can bring me up to date later . . .'

As soon as he had left the room Monica continued with her report.

'Walvis not only owns this vast communications complex, which enables him to influence what the West thinks is solid news, but so often is Walvis's propaganda, he also controls a host of small banks all over the world – including in the Far East. Another pointer to his character – and his operational technique. He flits all over the world in *Pegasus V* – that's the state-of-the-art aircraft you probably

127

heard about down at Bosham, Tweed. The one with floats and also normal landing wheels. Recently he visited Russia, but not Moscow. He flew in *Pegasus* to Leningrad, landing on the Baltic. It's rumoured he was negotiating with the Russian Mafia. My informant also said that although they don't know it he has the Mafia there in his pocket. He used bribery on a grand scale.'

'Surely,' Paula interjected, 'this *Pegasus* machine is a giveaway. As soon as it appears anywhere it becomes known Walvis has arrived.'

'You underestimate his cunning. He frequently sends it on bogus flights. He's not on board and may be thousands of miles away.'

'Tricky sort of chap,' Marler commented. 'Any more little tricks up his sleeve?'

'One major thing. Despite his vast communications empire important instructions are never sent via this system. He favours verbal messages sent by motor cycle couriers. Then no clever hacker learns anything by breaking into his computers,' Monica concluded.

'Russia keeps cropping up,' Tweed remarked, 'but I do not think that is the answer. One huge fact stands out about Walvis in my mind.'

'Which is?' Paula enquired.

'It isn't money that drives Walvis on. It's the pursuit of unimaginable power to mould the future in the direction he wants it to take. An evil and incredibly dangerous man. Tell Bob about what he missed when he gets back, Monica. You've shut your notebook. Thanks.'

'I wonder how Bob will get on with the mysterious Jill Selborne,' Paula mused.

Newman pressed the bell on the first-floor landing of the address in Half Moon Street. He noted the heavy door had three locks, a Chubb, a Banham and a make he didn't recognize. It also had a fish-eye spyhole.

A glare light came on above his head and he was careful not to look at it – those ruddy things could blind you. Security was all very well but this set-up suggested to him a woman in fear of her life.

He heard the locks being unfastened. The door was then opened slowly about six inches on two heavy chains. He couldn't see clearly who was studying him but knew it was a woman.

'Yes?' a cultured feminine voice enquired.

'I'm Robert Newman. I'd like a few minutes with Jill Selborne. I can prove my identity . . .'

He was fishing out the press pass he had held on to when the voice spoke again. It had a seductive but not aggressive lilt.

'I recognized at once who you are. From pictures in old magazines. Why do you want to see Jill Selborne?'

'To ask her advice about a story I'd really sooner not write. Indirectly, it could involve her.'

'How intriguing, Mr Newman. Please wait a minute while I take off the chains.'

There was a pause after the door was closed again. Too long a pause and no sound of the chains being released. He wondered whether she had someone in the flat she didn't want him to see. Then the chains were removed and when the door was opened more lights had been put on inside the flat.

'Please come in. I am Jill Selborne . . .'

Newman was impressed. A striking woman with jet-black hair, Jill would be in her early thirties, he guessed. About five feet five inches tall, she wore a white two-piece suit and her generous mouth, full lipped, greeted him with a warm smile. After dealing with all the security, she escorted him into a small living-room where the floor-length curtains were closed.

'Please do sit down,' she invited, indicating an

armchair. 'I was just going to have a glass of white wine – Sancerre. Do join me.'

'That's very hospitable.' Newman smiled back at her. In the lobby she had taken his trench coat and hung it inside a cupboard with a door that stuck when closed. 'Yes, I think I could do with a glass.'

He was relieved when she brought two glasses and a bottle to a glass-topped table. He was ever on the alert for strangers who might dope his drink. During the few moments while she fetched the bottle and glasses from a cabinet he'd glanced swiftly round the room.

Protruding slightly from under a table draped with cloth that reached the carpet he saw the corner of a suitcase. The airline tag dangled but he couldn't read the name. So that was what she had been doing during the pause before she opened the door – hiding her suitcase.

As she filled the glasses she glanced up at him while she bent forward. Her dark eyes were very luminous and penetrating. Newman wasn't sure whether she was assessing him as a man or an opponent.

She sat on a couch on the far side of the table, arranged cushions behind her back and sat very upright. Looking at him directly again she raised her glass.

'Cheers!' She sipped her drink, put down the glass. 'So what do I owe the honour of a well-known foreign correspondent visiting me to?'

'Do I address you as Mrs Walvis?' he threw at her.

'Ah!' She smiled again and crossed her legs which were revealed by a slit in her white skirt. They were very shapely. 'The answer is no. "Miss Selborne" would be more correct, but sounds so formal. Call me Jill.'

'Bob,' Newman replied, returning her smile. 'I must have been misinformed, but I was told you were married to Walvis.'

'Tell me, Bob,' she parried, 'what is this story you said you'd prefer not to write?'

130

'*Der Spiegel* have pressed me for a long in-depth – awful word – article on Walvis,' he explained, making it up as he went along. 'I've almost stopped writing for the press now I don't need the money. Would you sooner that I forgot the whole thing? I'd have to mention you.'

'OK.' She twiddled the stem of her empty glass. 'Want a refill? No? Don't think I will either. One glass occasionally is usually my limit.' She paused. 'Yes, I was married to Walvis. In a way. At least that's what I thought was the case.'

'I'm not with you.'

'And I'm not surprised. I wasn't with it either. We were supposedly married in Slovenia, the northern province of what used to be Yugoslavia. Sorry . . .' The eyes glowed at him. 'You'd know where Slovenia is. Later I discovered the pastor who apparently married us was a conman. I could never be sure whether Gabriel knew but I walked. He didn't mind. He likes experiments.'

'Experiments?'

She chuckled ruefully. She had a soft persuasive voice.

'Yes, experiments. He acts frequently on whims – just to find out what something is like. Including marriage, I suspect. His mood can change ten times in a single day.'

'What does he look like?' Newman asked casually.

'That's forbidden.' She smiled again to take the sting out of her reply. 'When I said I was walking he gave me a very generous settlement. One condition was that I would never let anyone know what he looks like. I keep bargains.'

She suddenly refilled her glass, then gazed at her guest, still holding the bottle. When Newman shook his head she put down the bottle, lifted the glass and drained half the contents. Newman sensed she had suddenly become nervous. Was it his most recent reference to Walvis that had unnerved her?

131

'Forget his appearance. He controls a vast organization. Is very rich. You must have led the high life when you were with him.'

'You are going to write that damned article, aren't you?' she suddenly burst out.

'No, I've decided I definitely won't. Partly for your sake, partly because I wasn't keen on the idea in the first place.'

'So are you looking for a new girl friend?' she teased him.

'Always in the market. How are you going to spend the rest of your life? You're an attractive woman.'

'Thank you, Bob. I'm a journalist now – like you were but in a different field. You can keep this if you want to.'

She reached for her shoulder-bag on the couch, took out a card, handed it across the table to Newman. He read the wording. *Jill Selborne. Fashion consultant.* It also gave her Half Moon Street address and phone number. He thanked her, slipped it into his wallet. She had glanced at her watch.

'Think I've taken up enough of your time for one night,' Newman suggested. 'Maybe we could meet again?'

'That's a date I'll look forward to. I'll fetch your coat.'

While she was in the lobby and he heard the squeak of the cupboard door being opened he darted across to the table draped with cloth, pulled out the case, read the label, was back in his armchair when Jill returned with his coat. She insisted on helping him on with it and escorted him to the door. When she had dealt with all the locks and chains she turned to him, rose up on her heels and kissed him on the right cheek.

'You won't forget me, will you, Bob?'

'You can count on it,' he assured her.

He had mixed emotions as he took the stairs down to the ground floor. He was attracted to her. But the

Lufthansa label had been for a flight for the following morning. It was addressed to Jill Selborne, Hotel Bayerischer Hof, Munich.

14

Earlier in Tweed's office Nield had reported in detail his encounter with David Sherwood at the Bistro in Bosham. Tweed had listened, had heard that, after travelling up to London with Nield, Sherwood had said goodbye and told him he was staying at the Connaught.

Tweed had reacted immediately. Calling a friend at the Ministry of Defence he had checked up on Sherwood. After putting down the phone he looked at Nield.

'The MoD confirms every detail Sherwood told you about himself. Is it too late to get him over here tonight?'

'Shouldn't be,' Nield had said, fingering his moustache. 'Struck me as a late-night bird. Want me to call him?'

'Do it . . .'

Newman had left some time before to visit Jill Selborne. The only occupants of the office were Tweed, Paula, Monica, Marler and Nield when the phone rang fifteen minutes later. Monica took the call, spoke to George, the doorman guard, then looked at Tweed.

'Sherwood has arrived.'

'Wheel him up,' Tweed told her.

He stood up to shake hands with the tall, hook-nosed man who strode into the office with a bouncy tread. Fresh as a daisy, Nield thought to himself.

'Thank you for coming over at this hour, Captain Sherwood,' Tweed greeted the visitor. 'Sit down. Would you

133

like a cup of coffee – or something stronger? I'm Tweed.'

'Just slaked my thirst at the Connaught's bar,' said Sherwood, still standing. He looked over with interest at Paula.

'One of my right arms, Paula Grey,' Tweed introduced.

'Not often you get beauty combined with competence,' Sherwood remarked in a clipped tone as he shook her hand.

'Thank you,' Paula responded coolly. 'I'm not sure where you noticed competence. You've only just arrived.'

'Used to be my job – to weigh up people, men and women, in the first ninety seconds . . .'

He smiled at Monica, nodded to Nield, sat down, began talking almost without pause to Tweed.

'I was once with Military Intelligence before a spell with the Scots Guards, then the SAS mob. I like your cover. The General & Cumbria Assurance plate next to the front door – a long way from Special Branch.'

'It has its uses,' Tweed said briskly. 'Now, I gather from Nield you are worried about your partner, Parker – who sold out the security outfit overnight. Any idea who bought it?'

'Yes, some outfit I've never heard of. Reed & Roebuck.'

Paula dipped her head in case her expression betrayed she knew the name. Sherwood caught the movement out of the corner of his eye, whipped round in his chair to study her.

'The name strikes a chord?' he rapped at her.

She shook her head and Sherwood swung back to stare at Tweed. He read nothing in his host's face.

'What about you, Tweed. Ring any bells?'

'I've heard the name somewhere. Can't recall where. I don't think it was important. Why are you so determined to investigate Parker's disappearance? Maybe he's found a girl friend.'

134

'Not on! Thinks too much of his wife, Sandra. She's nearly going crazy with worry. He always rang her every night when he was off on one of his trips. Now this Hotel Bayerischer Hof says his room is still waiting for him. Hasn't seen him for five days. Not like Parker at all. I certainly hope something bad hasn't happened to him, or something very bad. I fear the worst. Still, Sandra must know – it's not knowing that is driving her up the proverbial wall. That's it. I'm catching a Lufthansa flight in the morning.'

'I could be flying to Munich myself tomorrow,' Tweed remarked. 'You'll be at the Bayerischer Hof if I want to contact you?'

'That's the form.' Sherwood leaned forward. 'Just what is going on – about Cleaver Hall and this Reed & Roebuck outfit? You're interested, I can tell.'

'It's probably nothing to do with my mission – just a case of crossed wires. Have a good flight.'

'And if you arrive in Munich tomorrow where will you be staying?' Sherwood enquired as he stood up, put on his British warm. 'Like to keep in touch.'

'Monica hasn't found a hotel yet,' Tweed lied, standing up. 'Thank you for coming in. Good luck in the search for Parker.'

'Play it close to the chest, don't you?'

On this note Sherwood left the office. Newman arrived back a few minutes later, listened as Tweed recalled his conversation with Sherwood.

'Captain David Sherwood bothers me, despite your MoD check,' Newman commented.

'Why?' asked Tweed.

'Three things, two of them coincidences. First he was working on installing security at Cleaver Hall when Lisa Trent arrives. The coincidences? He bumps into Pete Nield by chance – or so it would seem – in the Bistro at Bosham. Second, he'll be staying at the Bayerischer Hof

135

Hotel in Munich, which happens to be the same place Jill Selborne is arriving at tomorrow when she flies to Munich from Heathrow . . .'

'All roads lead to Munich,' Tweed said again. 'Monica, is it too late in the evening to check on two other people? Unless you need some sleep, in which case . . .'

'Sleep I can do without,' interjected the sturdy Monica. 'Once I get revved up I can go on and on. And it is not too late. Not even over here. Also don't forget the Pacific. People are waking up in the Far East – in San Francisco, eight hours behind us, they're eating lunch. The targets?'

'Jill Selborne, alleged fashion writer. Lisa Trent, alleged company investigator. Don't forget Lisa said she works for that notorious outfit, Aspen & Schneider.'

'Who have offices in New York, San Francisco, Tokyo, to mention only a few of their world-wide organization. As to Jill Selborne, I can name three women's magazines here and on the continent she writes for. But I will check her out further.'

'I wonder how Harry Butler is getting on,' mused Nield. 'Prowling round Heathrow – it's a big airport . . .'

Earlier in the evening, before leaving Bosham, Nield had called Tweed from the phone box near The Berkeley Arms. Tweed's instructions had been precise.

'Give this job to Harry. When you get back to London he's to proceed straight to Heathrow. I'll phone Jim Corcoran, ask him to give Harry full co-operation . . .'

When Butler had arrived at the airport he had parked his car and made straight for the office of the Chief of Airport Security, Jim Corcoran. He had given Corcoran a description of Winter, expected to arrive at Heathrow at any time.

'Hang about in my office,' Corcoran suggested. 'I can send in some filthy coffee. I'm going to patrol the

136

European reservation counters – you did say he'd be heading for Europe? Good . . .'

Corcoran, a tall, well-built man in his early forties with an outdoor look, had rushed back into his office an hour later.

'Harry, come with me. Move the feet . . .'

Reaching the concourse, he nodded towards the Lufthansa counter. Butler spotted the small slim figure of Winter immediately. Carrying a suitcase, he was just leaving the counter, moving slowly so as not to attract attention.

Corcoran darted over to the counter, had a word with the girl handling reservations, darted back to Butler.

'He booked a seat on the early flight to Munich tomorrow morning. But not as Winter – gave the name Leo Kahn . . .'

'Thanks, Jim. Don't want to lose this one. See you . . .'

Butler was just in time to follow Kahn aboard the airport bus which toured the hotels where passengers stayed overnight. Kahn alighted at the Penta Hotel, booked a room for the night. Butler waited until he had gone direct into the restaurant, still carrying his case.

'You must be hungry, mate, after your experiences today. Especially with Marler,' Butler said to himself.

He booked a room for himself, phoned Corcoran, asked him to book a seat for himself on the same flight, then called Tweed to keep him in the picture.

'Leo Kahn?' Tweed had repeated. 'This is getting more than suspicious. Yes, I'll send a courier to the Penta with the case we keep packed for you. Follow him to Munich. When you can, take your bag to the Four Seasons Hotel on Maximilianstrasse. Several of us will be staying there. Good work, Harry . . .'

*   *   *

137

It was ten o'clock at night when Tweed asked the kitchen staff in the basement to prepare a hot meal for them. Except for Butler, everyone was now assembled. Tweed told his team to relax while he briefly summed up the present situation, which was grim. At that moment the door burst open and Howard, Director of the SIS, made his grand entrance. Tweed pursed his lips.

'Having a jolly party, are we?' Howard began. 'Wish I could share the fun . . .'

'None of it is fun,' Paula snapped and wished she'd held her tongue.

Howard was six feet tall, beginning to put on weight – too many dinners at his club. Dressed in a new Chester Barrie suit from Harrods, a blue-striped shirt and the fad for a splashy tie in outrageous colours, he flicked an imaginary speck of dust off the sleeve of his chalk-striped suit. The Director had a full, pink face, an air of superiority, was clean shaven and spoke in an upper-crust accent.

'Trod on someone's toes, did I?' he went on. 'I'm just back from Washington. They do you rather well over in the US of A – providing you know the right people.'

'It does help to know the right people,' Nield commented ironically but with an expression of respect.

Marler had adopted his normal stance, leaning against a wall, smoking a king-size. Nield and Newman sat in armchairs while Monica huddled behind her desk, staring venomously at Howard's broad back. There was a heavy silence which Howard, not normally sensitive to atmospheres, felt was becoming uncomfortable. He stroked a hand over his glossy greying hair.

'I think I'll leave it to you, Tweed.' He folded his arms after shooting his cuffs, spoke in his most pompous manner. 'Rely on you to keep me in the picture later. Time I got home now.'

'Cynthia will be worrying about you,' Tweed said in his most innocent tone of voice.

138

This reference to his unloved – and unloving – wife was the last straw for Howard, as Tweed had hoped it would be. Nodding to everyone, Howard marched off, closing the door quietly.

'Is it still a cat-and-dog fight between Cynthia and Howard?' Paula enquired.

'I fear so. Now, let's get on before the meal arrives. Jean Cardon was brutally tortured and murdered. She worked for Reed & Roebuck. We can assume she found out something dangerous about Walvis, who found out what she had unearthed. Philip must have found her diaries and they had a clue that sent him haring off to Munich. Those diaries, which I'm sure he took with him, may have more vital data . . .'

'Couldn't this be speculation?' Paula queried.

'No! Because Walvis bought out Reed & Roebuck soon after Jean had died. I go down to Bosham, we make the acquaintance of Mr Gulliver. He likes us so much he sends a truck with explosive drums to wipe us out. Proof that we are on the right track.'

'Then, enter Lisa Trent,' interjected Paula with a wicked smile at Newman.

'I was coming to that. On the surface she is genuine – but we learn she is in the same line of business as Jean was, and denies ever hearing of Reed & Roebuck. Which puts a big question mark over her. Plus the fact *she* is on her way to Munich.'

'Enter Captain David Sherwood,' Newman remarked. 'The pattern repeats itself. His partner, Parker, sells out Reed & Roebuck to Walvis, then disappears . . .'

'Again Munich,' Tweed continued. He smiled at Newman. 'Enter Jill Selborne . . .'

'Who conceals from you the fact that she is flying off tomorrow. Where to? Again Munich. The concealment puts a question mark over her,' Paula pointed out.

'Don't forget an earlier entertainment,' Marler

139

recalled. 'Brother Winter – who later becomes Leo Kahn
– follows us from Chichester. Enter Martin, his boss . . .'

'And the telephone number to contact Martin you
squeezed out of him was Munich,' Newman reminded
him.

'Now listen to me, all of you,' Tweed ordered. His tone
ws grim, determined, and Paula recalled how rare was the
ferocious expression he displayed as he leaned forward.
He paused and a heavy silence descended. All eyes were
on him.

'We are all going to Munich,' Tweed rasped. 'This man
Walvis has enormous power so it's going to be a take no
prisoners battle. Trust no one, suspect everyone – and I
do mean everyone. With his vast money reserves he has
probably bought people very high up. What we are
looking for is a chink in his armour – and when we find it
we drive through it ruthlessly. I will not rest until Walvis
is wiped off the face of the Earth . . .'

15

The following morning, as various passengers flew to
Munich, some aboard Lufthansa, others via British Air-
ways, Philip Cardon was driving into the resort of Berg on
the Starnberger See. He was behind the wheel of the
BMW Ziggy Palewski had loaned him.

It had stopped snowing overnight and the air was crys-
tal clear, stimulating as wine. Driving down the main
highway, following Marler's instructions, in the distance
to the south he could see the sharp-edged silhouettes of
the snowbound Alps. Philip was hardly aware of any of

these factors which would normally have created a cheerful mood.

It was Thursday, but he was thinking of Monday. He knew he was going to dread Mondays for a long time to come. Jean had died in the Nuffield on a Monday. He glanced at his watch, calculating how many hours she had left to live on the fateful day. It was this distraction, the surge of emotion, which made him unaware he was being followed.

In a blue Audi, two cars behind him on the autobahn, Otto sat in the passenger seat – Otto, the ex-policeman he had knocked unconscious in the driver's seat outside Munich main station the previous day.

Earlier, in his office at the headquarters of Danubex – the new name on the entrance plate had appeared that morning – Walvis had been warned by a doctor. He indicated his patient who sat in a chair with bandages swathing his head.

'He has mild concussion – at least it appears to be mild. He must have plenty of rest and . . .'

'Otto looks perfectly all right to me,' Walvis had replied. 'He can speak normally. His brain is functioning. He is able to walk normally. You know the trouble with the medical profession?'

'I didn't come here to be insulted.'

Behind the doctor, a slim man of medium height, Martin winced. Walvis, sagged in his large swivel armchair, stood up and his great bulk loomed over the smaller man. His eyes were twitching and his thick lips had an ugly twist. He lisped when he spoke and Martin knew he was in a rage. His voice was deceptively soft.

'The trouble with the medical profession is they feel they have to find something wrong with a patient. Why? For one reason. To justify their huge inflated fees. I pay

141

you a fortune. You have taken bullets out of my staff . . .'

'Please, sir!' The doctor had become agitated. 'We are in the presence of a witness . . .'

'Interrupt me again and you will never cross a street without fear. Haven't you read about the number of people killed by hit-and-run drivers? Not that if that happens to you it will have anything to do with me. So many young macho drivers on the roads these days. What *were* you saying about insults?'

'A slip of the tongue . . . nothing personal . . . I do assure you it was nothing personal. I apologize most humbly for an unforgivable remark.'

The doctor was stuttering, trembling as Walvis stood so close he was almost touching the man. The large man thrust out his lower lip, staring malevolently at his victim. The doctor hastened to find the right words before he could leave.

'I think Otto is recovering very nicely . . .'

'*Recovering?*' Walvis repeated with deadly emphasis.

'I mean he has recovered. In a few days the bandage can be removed. I trust I can continue to be of service to you in the future . . .'

'That,' Walvis had concluded, turning away from him and padding over to the drinks cabinet, 'that is something I shall have to give my earnest consideration. I believe your absurdly large annual retainer is due in a few weeks. Of course, you need that to support your mistress in that flat in Schwabing. Goodbye, Doctor . . .'

After the medical man's departure Walvis had beckoned Martin to accompany him into an ante-room, closing the door so Otto could not hear.

'We need Otto to identify this Philip Cardon. You have men watching the Hotel Platzl? Good. Since Cardon, who attacked your team outside the main station yesterday, nearly killed Pierre we have to rely on Otto to point the finger.'

'I suppose the doctor has indeed exaggerated Otto's concussion,' Martin had ventured cautiously.

'As long as Otto lasts out long enough to finger this Cardon, I see no problem.' Walvis had swallowed half a glass of whisky. Irritation always upset him. 'So, you now take the team to watch the Platzl, relieving the men already there.'

'I'll leave at once,' Martin said quickly.

'You see, as regards Otto, we must get our priorities right,' Walvis had ended jovially, then giving a great belly laugh.

Philip jerked himself out of his black mood as he turned off the autobahn on to the slip road leading to Berg. He automatically glanced in his rear-view mirror once more. He frowned – despite his mind being caught up in powerful emotion he realized another part of his brain had stayed in gear and the blue Audi, now fifty yards behind him, seemed familiar. Surely he'd seen it several times earlier on the autobahn after leaving the suburbs of Munich behind?

'So we'd better test you, Mr Audi. First, let's slow everything down so I can get a gander inside you, see if the driver is someone I've spotted earlier during my Cook's tour of Munich . . .'

His manoeuvre caught the driver of the other vehicle off balance and the Audi came close. Close enough for Philip to see inside as the sun shone strongly. One glimpse of its occupants was enough. Front seat passenger with a bandaged head, the man whose head he'd hammered down on the steering-wheel outside Munich station. In the rear a very red-faced man was leaning forward, mouth open as he said something, exposing gleaming white teeth.

'You just made one big mistake, chum,' Philip said aloud.

143

He was developing a habit of talking to himself. Just so long as I *know* I'm doing it, he thought. He rammed his foot down, the map of the area he'd bought in a shop clear in his mind.

Keeping clear of the lake and Seestrasse he drove round a series of winding roads, having increased the gap between himself and the Audi to several hundred metres. Then he saw the police patrol car parked by the side of the road with *Polizei* inscribed across its rear. He pulled up alongside it, his window lowered, and called out to the officer in the passenger seat in German.

'I'm English. Chap in the rear of the blue Audi that will appear behind me in a minute tried to sell me heroin. Told him to leave me alone, jumped in my car and he's followed me. Please don't ask me to stay as a witness. My father's been involved in a car accident, may be dying. I'm rushing to the hospital . . .'

'You know it was heroin?' asked the burly uniformed officer as he climbed out of his car.

'Never saw it. Wouldn't know the stuff if I did. But that's what he said he was selling. Please,' he said again, 'I must reach the hospital before it's too late.'

The officer waved him on and in his rear-view mirror Philip saw him taking his pistol out of his holster. The officer stood in the road, flagging down the Audi.

'Chum, that should give you something to think about,' Philip said as he disappeared round a corner and headed back towards Seestrasse 4500 and Manfred Hellmann, supplier of arms to known customers. For a price.

Philip soon realized that Berg was a resort for the rich, the very rich. The land which sloped down towards the lake was dotted with stylish properties – bungalows and two-storey houses – with generous grounds laid out with lawns and trees.

144

He got lost and pulled up outside a large chalet-type hotel with twin roofs. Park Hotel. The receptionist guided him to Seestrasse which was only a short distance away. Philip found himself very close to the large lake which he knew stretched many kilometres to the south towards the Alps.

Seestrasse 4500 was a long way along the road, past more luxurious houses. At that time of the year the place seemed deserted but the snow was melting. He caught brief views of the calm blue lake, glittering like mercury where the sun reflected off it.

Philip was not sure what he was expecting Hellmann's property to be like but it exceeded any expectations he might have had. A very large red-tiled bungalow with a long frontage, standing well back from the road behind a sloping lawn where the snow had melted. He turned up the curving drive, parked close to steps up to a terrace spanning the whole frontage. The windows had curtains closed across them as though no one was in residence.

'Here's hoping,' Philip thought as he climbed out, locked the car and ran up the steps.

The front door was a great heavy wooden slab decorated with brass studs. A fish-eye spyhole was set into the centre and he noticed under the eaves cameras aimed at the entrance. He pressed the bell and waited, staring at the speakphone grille in the whitewashed stone wall.

'Identify yourself,' a soft voice ordered in German.

'I'm looking for Manfred Hellmann,' Philip said stubbornly.

'Identify yourself,' the voice repeated.

'I'm Philip Cardon. I was sent here by someone who is an old friend of Mr Hellmann's. Marler, from London.'

There was no response and for a few moments Philip thought he wasn't going to be admitted. Then the heavy door swung open very slowly and silently. It had to be operated with an electronic mechanism. Sure enough, as the man who had spoken came into view he was holding a small black case in his large hand.

'Please come inside and we may talk further. I presume you were not followed?'

'Yes, I was,' Philip replied, deciding to tell the truth after his first impression of the German. 'But I shook them off. They're being interrogated several miles away by a police patrol car officer who thinks they may be heroin dealers.'

'Why?' asked the German, who was now speaking in English.

'You are Manfred Hellmann?' Philip checked.

'I am . . .'

Whatever picture Philip had conjured up in his mind of Hellmann's appearance, the reality was very different. Six feet tall, in his fifties, with a high forehead and thick fair hair, he wore a heavy white polo-necked sweater, white slacks and a blue blazer with gold buttons. He reminded Philip of a yachtsman and gave the impression of being a sporty type as he watched his visitor with quizzical amusement.

'Why?' he repeated. 'Why does the patrol car officer think your pursuers may be heroin dealers?'

Philip explained briefly the trick he had played on the pursuers in the blue Audi. Hellmann threw back his head and roared with laughter. He seemed to Philip too amiable and good natured to be a secret arms dealer.

'Who were these men who followed you?'

'No idea,' Philip said automatically.

Hellmann's manner changed. He folded his arms, stared at Philip with a hard expression, spoke abruptly.

'Is this all you have to tell me about this man – Marler, did you say he was called?'

'He also said I should say "Valkyries" to you . . .'

'Splendid!' Hellmann was welcoming again. 'Now we can do business, but first let me show you something.'

146

He put an arm round Cardon's shoulders, guided him to a small staircase at the side of the hall, removed his arm and mounted it to a large circular window. He beckoned Philip to join him.

The view from the porthole was spectacular. It looked down on the lake over other rooftops and the water spread out to the far shore. In the middle of the lake a huge aircraft floated, moored to a buoy. A large dinghy powered by an outboard was just leaving the aircraft, heading for the shore. It was crammed with men.

'Have you heard of a man called Gabriel March Walvis?' Hellmann enquired.

'Yes, I have.' Philip decided it was time to be frank – up to a point – with his host. 'I think it was Walvis's men who came after me in that Audi.'

'And lost you,' Hellmann observed. 'Did you see in the car a very red-faced man with white teeth like a shark's?'

'Yes, I did.'

'That would be Walvis's second-in-command, Martin. He has used his mobile phone to call in reinforcements from *Pegasus V*, Walvis's state-of-the-art aircraft. Which is how the great man arrived in Munich. I know because I saw him coming to the shore with these.' He stooped, picked up a pair of field-glasses from the top step. 'You have come to make a purchase of something from me?' he asked casually after handing the glasses to Cardon.

'Yes, I have a shopping list. A hand gun, ammunition and stun grenades. I won't recognize anyone in that boat,' he said, handing back the glasses.

'Perhaps I will.' Hellmann focused the glasses. 'We are in trouble – or you are. All the heavy guns have been summoned to Munich. In that dinghy is a stocky fat man called Gulliver. He ranks with Martin.'

'Is this Martin a surname or a Christian?'

'No one seems to know.' The German lowered the glasses. 'He could be English. If you ever meet him and

147

he smiles at you reach for your pistol. Better still, escape his presence, if you can stay alive.'

'And why am I in trouble?' Philip asked as they descended the small staircase.

'Because Berg will be swarming with Walvis's men looking for you – the hunters directed by his two most ruthless subordinates – Martin and Gulliver. You still wish to cross the items off your shopping list?'

'As soon as we can . . .'

The spacious hall beyond the bungalow's front door was paved with teak woodblocks. Highly polished, they gleamed like glass. Hellmann took out a nail file from a leather holder, bent down, inserted it between two of the woodblocks near a closed door at the back. A single woodblock was lifted out, revealing a handle inside the deep hole below. Hellmann turned the handle and a trapdoor was revealed.

Still crouched, the German pressed a button and the secret door slid out of sight. He pressed a second button and a light came on in the underground room, illuminating a staircase.

'Follow me down,' Hellmann ordered.

As Philip reached the bottom step he saw the room was fitted with wall-to-wall carpet. Hellmann pressed one of a battery of switches in the stone wall, the trapdoor above them slid closed. He pressed another switch and a tilted screen in a corner was illuminated, showing the approach and front door of the bungalow.

'Useful in case someone calls while we're down here,' the German commented. 'The humming is the air-conditioning. Now, Mr Cardon, I can offer you anything you need in the way of hand guns. A Smith & Wesson .38 Special . . .'

'Not a revolver. I prefer an automatic,' Philip explained.

'Then we have what is popularly called the Luger, a .32 Browning, the 6.35mm Beretta, a 7.56mm Walther, capacity eight rounds . . .'

'I'd like a Walther.'

Hellmann took out a bunch of keys, opened a cupboard door flush with the wall, painted to merge with the stone, opened a drawer, put on a pair of surgical gloves and extracted a Walther which he handed to Philip.

'I would like to emphasize none of these weapons has been fired in circumstances where a police ballistics specialist could trace its origin . . .'

Philip was decisive. In ten minutes he had bought the Walther, spare magazines, five stun grenades, five grenades with explosive charges, a tear-gas pistol and a 6.35mm Beretta, only four and a half inches long, which he could tuck down inside his sock.

'Now we come to the sordid matter of money,' Hellmann remarked with a wry smile. 'Your armoury will cost you exactly twenty thousand marks. In cash, of course.'

Philip wondered whether he was expected to haggle. He had forgotten to raise this point with Marler. The German seemed to read his mind.

'We don't bargain here. I price my supplies carefully. I need a certain profit as danger money – to cover the risks I run. When you next see Mr Marler you will find I am telling the truth.'

Taking a fat envelope from an inside pocket Philip counted out forty 500-DM notes. He was intrigued by the fact that Hellmann wore surgical gloves. No danger of leaving his own fingerprints on the weapons he was selling.

Hellmann had skilfully arranged the weapons and ammo, protected with linen covers, inside a large back-pack with straps. He looked at Philip.

'The back-pack has become a standard item of travel, so it is the best way of transporting such items. And I

149

think you should take another precaution – when we get upstairs go outside and immediately park your BMW in a garage you will find at the back of the bungalow. Here are the keys for a grey Audi you will find in the same garage. They will be looking for that BMW.'

'The trouble is it belongs to someone else.'

'I hadn't finished. I will drive the BMW – if you will give me the key – to Munich late this afternoon. By then they will have given up the search for you. Where shall I park it?'

'Outside the side entrance to the main station. What time will you arrive?'

'I can be there at five o'clock precisely. I shall leave in good time to avoid the rush hour. There will, of course, be no extra charge. All part of the Austin Reed service, as Mr Marler used to say . . .'

After arranging to exchange cars so Hellmann drove away from the station in his Audi and Philip took back the BMW, they moved quickly. When Philip returned to the front door after getting out of Hellmann's Audi the German asked him to come back inside quickly.

'Up the staircase again,' he said as he closed the front door. 'A group of Walvis's men is prowling along the lakeside. Best if you see them . . .'

Philip, carrying the back-pack by one of the straps, was anxious to leave but he felt he must fall in with the wishes of his co-operative host. Hellmann had the field-glasses pressed to his eyes as Philip joined him at the top of the small staircase, leaving the back-pack in the hall.

'Yes, there are some villains down there,' the German reflected. 'The worst one of all is Lucien, a psychopath in my opinion.'

Lucien . . .

Philip froze inside. His mind flashed back to what he

150

had overheard while hiding in the cupboard at the HQ of International & Cosmopolitan. Throaty voice saying with a sneer—

Even if, Lucien, you were unsuccessful with Jean Cardon.

Philip had trouble speaking in a normal voice. He sucked in a deep breath before he spoke, trying not to sound urgent.

'Could I take a look at this Lucien – in case I come up against him? What does he look like?'

'He's the small wide-shouldered man who stoops most of the time. Reminds me of a hunchback. Black greasy hair and a similar moustache which curves down either side of his cruel mouth. It's rumoured even Walvis won't have Lucien near him. The one with the black windcheater . . .'

Philip exerted all his will-power to disguise his emotion as he took the glasses from Hellmann and aimed them at a group of three men walking slowly along the pavement and staring round frequently. Lucien's face came towards him clearly in the powerful glasses.

His hands gripped the binoculars like a vice as he continued staring at the man who had tortured – murdered – his wife. It was an evil face, totally devoid of any pity. As Philip watched, Lucien paused, put a cigarette between his slit-like lips, lit it, watched the match burn down until it almost reached his fingers, then he dropped it down the outside of the trouser leg of one of his companions. A much larger man, his companion jumped back, clenched his fist as though about to strike the culprit.

Lucien grinned. His right hand moved so quickly it was a blur as Philip watched. The hand held a flick-knife. The larger man shrugged, walked on, while behind him Lucien went on grinning. Philip handed the glasses back to Hellmann.

'Thank you. Now I'll know him . . .' He felt sick.

151

16

On the morning of the same day when Philip was visiting Berg, in London at Park Crescent Tweed was about to leave his office with Paula to catch their flight to Munich. Tweed had a habit of allowing plenty of time to reach an airport – he disliked a rush.

Newman had left earlier with Nield and Marler to board an earlier flight. It was Marler who had urged them to split up – causing Monica to make some hasty changes to bookings at Heathrow.

'We ought to assume,' he had pointed out, 'that at Munich Airport Walvis may have teams of watchers. Especially after Newman's encounter with Gulliver at Cleaver Hall and my little conversation with Mr Winter. They'll have reported to Munich. So, let's filter into Germany.'

'You are right,' Tweed had agreed. 'Should have thought of that myself. Proceed in that manner . . .'

Earlier he had received an urgent phone call from Butler, who had spent the night at the Penta Hotel at Heathrow.

'Speaking from a phone cubicle, Heathrow. Leo Kahn is about to board Flight LH4017 for Munich. I'll be on the same plane. Must go now . . .'

Tweed was standing up, clad in a sheepskin, about to lift his case off the floor, when the phone rang. He gazed skywards as Monica took the call. Cupping her hand over the mouthpiece, she looked at Tweed.

'You're not going to be best pleased. We have company

downstairs. Chief Inspector Buchanan and his sidekick, Sergeant Warden. Buchanan had the nerve to tell George he knows you're here – he saw you arrive earlier.'

'Wait a minute.' Removing his sheepskin, he hung it on the stand as Paula joined him with her fur-lined trench coat she had slipped out of.

'We'll have to see him, get it over with,' Tweed said grimly. 'But he'll have to be quick – and he mustn't know we're leaving for Germany . . .'

As he started speaking Paula had hefted up her case and Tweed's to put them back inside a cupboard. She tried to lighten the atmosphere.

'I'm doing a Jill Selborne – remember how she hid her case before she'd let Newman into her flat? And that was a case bound for Munich.'

'Tell George to send those two up immediately,' Tweed told Monica. 'And don't offer them coffee . . .'

He remained seated behind his desk as the door opened and Roy Buchanan led the way into the room followed by the wooden-faced Warden. Buchanan was six feet tall, in his forties, of slim build with brown hair and a moustache of the same colour. Lean and lanky, his approach was aggressive.

'Time you and I met.'

'Sit down, both of you,' ordered Tweed. 'I have a mountain of work so this will have to be brief. Very brief.'

'Really?' Buchanan sat in an armchair, stretched out his long legs, crossed them at the ankles as though ready for a prolonged visit. 'I am investigating a double murder case, so where have you hidden Philip Cardon?'

'I don't hide people,' Tweed snapped. 'Philip's wife has died under horrific circumstances, as you doubtless know. Understandably Philip is grief stricken, in a state of great shock. I gave him time off, so he could have gone anywhere.'

'I did say a double murder case.' Buchanan straightened

153

up, his grey eyes staring at Tweed. 'In the basement of his flat we discovered the dead body of an unknown motor cyclist – shot through the head. I must warn you that my number one suspect is Philip Cardon. We need him to help us with our enquiries. You're taking all this down, Warden?'

'Yes, sir.'

Warden, well built, in his thirties, wore a sombre dark suit in contrast to the light grey suit Buchanan was clad in. He had been sitting with a notebook in his lap as he wrote industriously. Tweed erupted.

'Tell that man to close his notebook or both of you can leave my office at once. I don't have to talk to you.'

Paula was surprised at Tweed's combative attitude. She was further surprised by Buchanan's meek reaction.

'Stop taking notes, Warden. Let's make this informal.'

'Let's get on with it,' Tweed growled, his manner hostile. 'I deeply resent your reference to Cardon as your number one suspect.' He leaned across his desk, his voice rising. 'For God's sake, are you suggesting Philip tortured and murdered his own wife? No, let me finish. Because if that is your belief you've gone off your rocker.'

'No,' Buchanan replied calmly, 'I don't for a moment think Cardon is responsible for that murder. But surely you can see I need to question him in my quest to find out who *did* murder Jean Cardon . . .'

'Your callous, cold-blooded approach to a grief-stricken man appals me. Perhaps there is something wrong with police methods these days.'

'That's not like you to say something like that,' Buchanan continued in the same quiet voice. 'This tragedy seems to have affected your judgement, if I may say so.'

'You just did,' Tweed rapped back. 'And at one time it would not have been like you to have no sympathy for a man whose wife has died under such terrible circumstances.'

'We do also need him to enquire into the mystery of the dead motor cyclist. He was found on Cardon's premises.'

'You said in the basement?' Tweed demanded.

'Yes, in the basement area outside the building . . .'

'So now are you suggesting Cardon owns the whole building?'

'No, of course not . . .'

'Then what are you drivelling on about? From your description this body was found in the basement area *outside* the building and therefore probably alongside the pavement . . .'

'That is correct,' Buchanan agreed equably.

'Then in Heaven's name why should Philip Cardon be involved? Other people have flats in that building. And isn't it more likely he was thrown down there by someone on the public pavement?'

'I think I should tell you we have searched Cardon's flat. We had a warrant, of course. But I thought I ought to inform you . . .'

'After the event!' Tweed stood up, towering with rage. 'That's it. This interview is terminated. You know how to find your own way out.'

'I must ask you not to leave the country without informing me,' Buchanan snapped with a flash of temper as he stood up. 'I shall be back later.'

'I won't put out the welcome mat. Just go. Don't forget to take Mr Plod with you . . .'

He waited until the two men had left, then smiled broadly at Paula. She stared, went to the window to watch the two men get into an unmarked car, turned to fetch the cases from the cupboard as she spoke.

'That wasn't like you at all – but you were putting on an act and you fooled me.'

'I had to fool them to shoehorn them out of the place.

I'm driving you to the airport now in the Escort. We can park it in the Long Stay area.'

'Maybe it will be a little less exciting in Munich than it has been here the past few minutes,' Paula commented, bringing his case across to him.

'Don't count on it,' Tweed warned. 'My sixth sense tells me Munich is a ticking time bomb.'

It was pure bad luck for Philip. By mischance he had come out on to the autobahn, returning to Munich, from the wrong exit. Minutes before, driving along a side road, he had passed a blue Audi parked at the kerb.

Inside the Audi Otto, his head bandaged, gazed straight at Philip as he headed for the nearby autobahn. The driver had kept his engine running on the instructions of Martin, who sat in the back.

'That's him!' Otto shouted.

'You're sure?' rapped out Martin, leaning forward.

'Certain. He must have changed cars, left the BMW some place. He's inside that grey Audi . . .'

'Then move, for God's sake!' Martin yelled at the driver. As the car started moving he turned to the man beside him in the back. 'Get ready to take him out, Karl.'

The thin-faced man with a duelling scar, in his mid-twenties, hauled out a 7.65mm Luger from his shoulder holster. He lowered the window on his side and sat with the gun in his lap. He was proud of his duelling scar. The illegal practice had sprung up again in certain German universities in secret: Karl had obtained his mark of pride at Freiburg.

Martin was excited as they turned on to the autobahn. Very little traffic at this time of day. He grinned and his face became even redder at the prospect of success.

'Pull this off and you all get a bonus,' he called out. 'The chief will be pleased with you. So will I,' he added.

156

Driving along the quiet autobahn Philip saw in his rear-view mirror the blue Audi racing after him. He lowered his own window. No point in trying to stay ahead of them – he'd be moving at a diabolical pace and, although the road ahead was still clear, he might run into traffic.

The blue Audi began to overtake him as he deliberately kept his speed down to a mere 65 k.p.h. – about 40 m.p.h. He could see now that one of the rear windows in the blue Audi was lowered. That was where the attack would come from.

'Come on, mate,' he said aloud. 'No other traffic about. I'm a sitting duck . . .'

The other Audi drew alongside him. The rear window came into view. He had a glimpse of a thin-faced thug with something in his hand, lifting it to aim at him point blank. Philip kept his left hand on the wheel. His right hand elevated, gripping the tear-gas pistol with its thick ugly barrel. He pulled the trigger. The tear-gas shell landed inside the rear of the blue Audi, exploded, filling the interior with its searing fumes.

Philip rammed his foot down, shot forward and away from the other vehicle like a rocket. Inside the blue Audi its occupants were choking. Karl had had no time to pull the trigger of his Luger, had dropped the weapon. Martin was swearing foully, both hands clutching his eyes. The driver was in an equally bad state, losing control.

In his mirror Philip saw the vehicle swinging and swaying crazily, as though the driver were drunk. The car smashed into the metal barrier, came to a sudden stop as the driver had the presence of mind to feel for the ignition key, switching off the engine before the car burst into flames. Then he bunched both his hands and pressed them against his own eyes, vision blurred, the pain starting.

'Pity Lucien hadn't been in that car,' Philip said to himself. 'I'd have come to an emergency stop, gone back and shot the bloody lot. Now, what's next on the menu?'

After the flight carrying Newman, Marler and Nield landed at Munich Airport they carried out the plan Newman had discussed with Marler on their way to Heathrow. Newman had driven them in his Mercedes, had parked it in Long Stay.

Marler was several passengers behind his two companions as they proceeded through Passport Control and Customs. He watched from a distance as they entered the exit concourse. Newman and Nield headed for a snack bar, ordered two glasses of beer and sat down.

'Marler was right,' Newman observed from behind his glass. 'Three thugs waiting by the doors leading to the outside world. Funny how they stand out when you're expecting them . . .'

Marler, having seen where the two men were sitting, moved fast. He took his own suitcase to a locker, inserted coins, pushed his case inside, locked the door. He then went into a shop selling Russian-style fur hats, tried several on, bought one which fitted and put it on his head.

He next walked to a public lavatory, locked himself inside a cubicle, took off his beige English-looking trench coat, turned it inside out and donned it again. It was now a dingy blue with small lapels. He doubted whether the watchers would recognize him as a passenger just off the flight. He didn't even look English when he went into the wash-room and checked his appearance in a mirror.

He then hurried to the car-hire counter where arrangements had been made prior to their departure from Park Crescent by Monica. He gave the hostess-style girl a broad smile and she responded with interest. Dealing with the paperwork, he gave her a large tip, asked her to

158

arrange for the hired Renault to be parked near the main exit.

Whistling, twirling the keys in his hand, he made his way to the canteen where Newman and Nield waited patiently. Buying himself a glass of beer, he timed his approach to the table carefully. As a waitress stood close to Newman he carried his glass towards an empty table.

The waitress saw him coming, realized she was in his way, quickly moved between other tables. At that moment Marler shook his hand, slopped beer on the floor, just missing Newman. He bent down.

'So sorry,' he whispered. 'Three heavies waiting for you by the exit doors. Get your cars, I'm ready . . .' He had spoken in English because the waitress was hurrying back with a cloth to wipe the beer off the floor. He raised his voice, speaking in fluent German. 'I apologize for my clumsiness. Has the beer stained your clothes? If it has . . .'

Newman shook his head, smiled briefly as if he wished the pest would go away. Marler moved on and sat at the distant table. The heavies hardly gave him a glance.

Ten minutes later Newman climbed in behind the wheel of a BMW waiting for him at the kerb while behind him Nield took possession of his small Mercedes. They left together, heading for the main highway into the city which was a good hour's drive away. The new airport was located in the open Bavarian countryside.

Close to the door Marler watched as the three Germans ran to a large black Mercedes. It had moved away when he ran to his Renault, unlocked the door, dived inside and drove after the big Mercedes. He could collect his bag from the locker later.

There was quite a lot of traffic on the highway as Marler skilfully overtook several cars and left behind honking horns. The fields on both sides spreading away were

159

covered with snow and the temperature had dropped suddenly in this part of Bavaria.

Marler waited his opportunity, saw much heavier traffic ahead, slid past the big Mercedes and took up a position just in front of it. The road surface had become icy, which suited his purpose admirably. He reduced speed, staying close to the big Mercedes, forcing it to slow down. There was no way the driver behind him could overtake – he was now blocked in by the solidity of the traffic.

Despite the fact that the car ahead of him was moving faster Marler maintained his slow speed. The driver behind him began honking his horn which, as far as Marler could recall, was now against the law. He reduced speed again.

A racing driver in his youth, Marler found it easy to perform the difficult manoeuvre, feeling the wheels on the verge of a skid. He stopped suddenly and the big Mercedes touched his rear bumper. A police patrol car appeared down a slip road – Marler had seen it coming. He climbed out of his car, waved his arms, then walked back to the driver behind him who had lowered the window.

'Cretin!' the man screamed at him in German. 'Get out of my way . . .'

'Get stuffed,' Marler snapped back in German. 'You rammed my car. You're one lousy driver.'

'I am! You crazy pig . . .'

A six-foot uniformed police officer who had just walked over from the patrol car arrived in time to hear the insult. Marler turned to the officer.

'The roads are like a skating rink – this idiot drives so badly he rammed my car. He should be arrested, his licence taken away,' he raved.

'Let's all calm down. You are both holding up a lot of traffic . . .'

The argument went on for five minutes – Marler was

160

pouring petrol on the flames. By the time he had agreed to go back to his car, that perhaps there was no damage to his car, Newman and Nield were well on their way to Munich.

Walvis was in an ugly mood. Padding slowly about his office at the headquarters on Maximilianstrasse he was listing his complaints to his confidante, Rosa. She sat in a chair, her legs crossed, wearing the black cap which concealed her hair, the black veil which masked her face.

'I have the foresight to send a team to watch for who is coming in from London at the airport and what happens? They lose them! The crap I have to employ.'

'Tell me about it,' Rosa said in her soothing voice.

'They are following two Englishmen coming in from the airport and they allow themselves to be stopped by a fool of a German driver who should have his licence withdrawn.'

'It is important, I gather?' she said tactfully.

'I have the strongest feeling that hostile forces are coming in to Munich. Gulliver, whom you have not so far met, is in an ante-room. He has just arrived from England with an interesting film taken at Cleaver Hall. I want you to watch this film, Rosa. You have a remarkable memory for faces – even if only seen in photos. See if you can identify anyone in this film. We will look at it in the projection room.'

Walvis was wearing a dark blue business suit and the jacket, closed over his huge body, had a strained look. He padded back to his desk, pressed a button on his intercom.

'Tell Gulliver he can come in now.'

A door opened and Gulliver, dressed in his smartest suit, walked in with a confident step, clutching a metal canister under his arm. Walvis extended a pudgy hand

161

and squeezed Gulliver's, then indicated Rosa.

'This is one of my closest associates, Rosa Brandt . . .'

The pear-shaped Gulliver looked very small standing close to Walvis, who towered over him. Cautiously, he gazed at the strange woman with the veil.

'This must be Walvis's fancy bit,' he said to himself. 'I had better play up to *her*.' Gulliver's coarse mind could not imagine that it was possible for a man to be very close to a woman without intimacy ever taking place. 'Wonder why she wears the veil?' he ruminated. 'Probably someone else's wife.'

Instead of voicing any of these thoughts Gulliver's manner became unctuous. He gave her a careful oily smile.

'Ma'am. A great pleasure to make your acquaintance. I am honoured to meet you.'

'Are you?' Rosa replied in the language he had addressed her – English. 'We have a job to do. I want to see that film you have brought. Bring it with you to the projection room. You can operate a camera?'

'Most certainly . . .'

'Then let's get on with it.'

A young voice, Gulliver noted as she stood up, moving very erectly and gracefully as she led them to a door, opened it, switched on a light and sat down. Gulliver blinked as he entered the room. It was like a modern cinema with rows of seats sloping down towards a large screen. One chair next to the aisle and alongside the seat Rosa had chosen was very large. On a platform at the back behind the seats was a projector perched on a heavy metal table.

Time I showed them I'm not just the floor-sweeper, Gulliver thought as he mounted the platform.

'I will call out when I am ready for you to view,' he said firmly.

Walvis closed the door, eased his bulk slowly into the

162

outsize leather-covered chair next to Rosa. Gulliver was trying to assert himself, he noted. A few minutes later the film was ready for projection and Gulliver called out again.

'This film was taken recently when a gang of men tried to photograph Cleaver Hall through the closed gates. Later you will realize other men had hidden inside a car behind the wall beyond the gates. Near the end of the film the car will come into view for a mere second as it speeds past . . .'

'We can do without the lecture,' Walvis growled. 'And if Rosa gives you an order you obey it immediately.'

'Understood,' replied a chastened Gulliver.

Walvis reached down beside his seat, pressed a switch and the lights went out. As Gulliver started the film running, the film taken by a man in a first-floor window at Cleaver Hall, Rosa leaned forward. The zoom lens showed clearly the gates and the far side of them.

A man appeared, holding a camera, photographing the Hall between two bars. He stood there quite confidently as a dog was released and leapt up against the inside of the gates. Two other men appeared suddenly.

'Stop the film,' Rosa called out. Gulliver obeyed her. 'That man holding the camera is the notorious foreign correspondent, Robert Newman . . .'

'We already knew that . . .' Gulliver began and immediately regretted having spoken.

'How very clever of you,' Walvis commented sarcastically. 'In fact, I also had recognized him. His picture has appeared often enough in magazines and newspapers.'

'I don't recognize either of the other two men,' Rosa went on, referring to Butler and Nield. 'Start the film rolling again . . .'

'May I suggest you watch the next part carefully,' Gulliver said in his most obsequious tone.

'I am watching it all carefully,' Rosa told him.

The three men disappeared to the left behind the wall. Shortly afterwards a car appeared driving past at high speed, a Ford Escort.

'Turn the film back and freeze that shot,' Rosa commanded. 'It is the two men who were with Newman, the two men I can't identify,' Rosa reported after a glance at the frozen shot. 'Proceed.'

A Mercedes sped past the gates, going in the direction the Escort had taken.

'Turn the film back and freeze that shot,' Rosa ordered, her voice sharp edged.

'Isn't it Newman driving that Mercedes?' queried Walvis.

'It is,' Rosa agreed. She called out again to Gulliver. 'This may be tricky. But I want you to do it. Freeze the shot so I can see the man in the back of the car.'

Gulliver pulled a face behind their backs. 'Don't want much, do you?' he said to himself. It took him all his limited store of patience to juggle the film until he had focused on the rear of the car. Then he waited as Rosa leaned forward, stood up and leant over the back of the chair in front.

Walvis was aware of tension in Rosa as she continued to stare at the profile of the man seated in the back with a blurred impression of a woman beyond him. Rosa sat down slowly.

'You're not going to like this,' Rosa said slowly.

'You have identified the man in the back, then?'

'Yes, I have. So far as I know there is only one photo of him in existence, a picture taken from a first-floor window in London after he had left his headquarters.'

'So who is he?' Walvis asked irritably.

'A man called Tweed. He is Deputy Director of the SIS.'

*   *   *

164

Walvis was thunderstruck by Rosa's identification. Hauling and heaving himself out of the chair he walked out of the cinema back into his office without saying a word. There he sagged into his swivel chair, his jowls working as though he was chewing something. His pale blue eyes were staring into the distance.

Rosa followed him, saw his expression, knew this was no time to speak. The intercom buzzed and Walvis automatically pressed down the switch.

'Martin has just returned,' a girl's voice said. 'He has some urgent news to give you . . .'

Walvis switched off the intercom without replying. Martin arrived, opened the door and came inside at the moment when Gulliver appeared with the film packed away inside the canister. Walvis exerted himself, sat upright and glared at Gulliver, his eyes twitching.

'Why the hell didn't you concentrate all your resources on eliminating this Tweed before you left England?'

Gulliver shifted from one foot to another and Martin suppressed a grin. There was no love lost between Walvis's two deputies and their chief delighted in playing one off against the other. He turned on Martin.

'And who the devil gave you permission to invade my office? You think now you can just walk in here any time you like? I'm beginning to get tired of your boring grinning face.'

Gulliver smiled maliciously. Nothing gave him greater pleasure than seeing Martin in the shit. Walvis suddenly shifted his gaze towards Gulliver.

'And you can wipe that smirk off your ugly mug. Now you can make yourself useful – for a change. I want fifty still pictures of everyone on that film run off and distributed to our soldiers. They are to scour Munich day and night to see if any of them have sneaked into this city.'

'It will be done at once, sir,' Gulliver assured him

165

hastily. 'I will deal with the problem personally.'

'Of course you will,' Walvis mocked him. 'I just told you to do so. Stand there until I tell you to leave.'

He swivelled in his chair and glared at Martin, who was not looking at Gulliver. Martin was carefully concealing his delight at seeing Gulliver taking a hammering.

'You are making a great effort to keep a straight face,' Walvis observed. 'What is this so-called urgent news?'

'Well, sir . . .' Martin swallowed. 'We ran up against bad luck this morning with Cardon . . .'

Walvis had leaned forward, was studying him. Martin fell silent, aware that Gulliver was taking all this in.

'Your eyes are puffy,' Walvis snapped. 'Drunk on duty?'

'Nothing like that. My eyes are still painful . . .'

'I'm not interested in your physical state. Just tell me the worst. You botched the job? Is that it?'

'We had bad luck,' Martin ploughed on. 'We followed Cardon very successfully to Berg. Then we were stopped by a patrol car officer who obviously wanted something to report to his superiors. He accused us of carrying a delivery of heroin. I convinced him this was nonsense, but by then Cardon had disappeared.'

'I think there's something more,' Walvis suggested with a threatening stare.

'I reacted to the situation immediately. Using a mobile phone I called up reinforcements from *Pegasus*.' He was sounding his usual confident self now. 'We set up ambushes at all the exits from Berg and it worked. The car I was in spotted Cardon leaving Berg. We followed him in hot pursuit.'

'So he's dead?' Walvis enquired, not believing it but increasing the pressure on his deputy.

'Well, no. We followed him down the autobahn back towards Munich. Karl was about to shoot him when out of the blue this cunning, sly rat Cardon fires a tear-gas shell

166

into our car. We smashed up against the barrier . . .'

'And you bloody well lost him!' Walvis roared. 'Out of the blue, you said. Cunning? Sly? He out-manoeuvred you.' His voice became soft. 'I wonder how much Cardon would want to act as your replacement,' he mused.

'You can't mean . . .'

Martin's face was red as a turkey cock. Fear mingled with anger. Fear won. He took out a handkerchief and dabbed at his eyes which still hurt.

'I'll make it my personal business to eliminate him.'

'No you won't,' Walvis rapped back. 'You'll do exactly what I tell you to do. I want you to collaborate with Gulliver . . .' He paused, saw the expressions on the faces of his two deputies, crashed his clenched fist down on the desk. 'You will collaborate with each other or I'll finish both of you. Have you forgotten what is about to happen?'

'Sorry, sir . . . I'm not sure what you're referring to,' Martin mumbled.

'Then I'll jog your memory.' Walvis's lizardlike eyes flashed between Martin and Gulliver. 'The largest consignment of arms we've ever handled is coming up the Danube by barge-train. It's about to dock at Passau in roughly two days from now ready for immediate distribution to our battle brigades. So I want Munich combed for any opposition – and when you find it crush it as you would a cockroach. That is the assignment for the two of you to direct. Don't forget to have those still photos made from that film, Gulliver. I want them in the hands of every member of our teams by four o'clock tomorrow morning. Now, both of you, get out of my sight . . .'

'Was that wise to talk to them quite like that?' asked Rosa when they were alone.

'Yes. You can rule men with affection or with fear. I

167

prefer fear. We're not dealing with angels. And they both value the enormous salaries I pay them. This Tweed worries me,' he said suddenly. 'I sense he is a most dangerous opponent.'

'He is probably still in London.'

'I think he could have arrived in Munich. That assault on Cleaver Hall was significant. Tweed was there – not sitting on his backside behind some desk miles away. He is a man who leads from the front. I admire that.'

'If he's here the photo Gulliver is distributing of him should track him down.'

'Then we have another job for Teardrop,' Walvis replied, and smiled at her.

Walvis was still at his desk at midnight when the phone rang. He listened to his informant. His mouth pouched and he repeated the name he had been given to make sure he had understood. Ending the call, he sat staring into space. So Captain David Sherwood, the partner of Parker who had sold out Reed & Roebuck to him, was in Munich.

He dialled another number, spoke to the go-between who dealt with lethal matters.

'An assignment for Teardrop. Most urgent. Her dining companion is a Captain David Sherwood, staying now at the Bayerischer Hof. The same fee as last time, I assume? One hundred thousand Deutschmarks? That is doubling the fee. The risk to her is growing? Well, I agree, but there is a time limit. She must carry out her assignment within forty-eight hours . . .'

After her conversation with Walvis, Rosa Brandt went up to the next floor to her private apartment in the office building. She locked the main door, made her way to a

168

large bathroom, again was careful to lock the door.

Over the marble wash-basin was a large glass shelf. It was crammed with expensive cosmetics and bottles containing certain other liquids. Taking off her black cap and veil she studied herself in the mirror. She spent some time tending to herself and then undressed, slipped on a mink-lined dressing gown and went into the bedroom, being careful to double-lock the door.

She was reading a contemporary novel when, half an hour after midnight, the phone rang. She picked up the receiver, identified herself, listened, asking only a few questions.

'I understand,' she said, still speaking in German. 'I will see you within the next two days . . .'

17

Tweed and Paula arrived at Munich Airport late in the afternoon. He had suddenly changed his mind when they reached Heathrow, a habit Paula was accustomed to.

They had a long leisurely lunch at the best restaurant and he ordered a half-bottle of Riesling from Alsace. Paula looked puzzled after the waiter had gone.

'What made you re-book us on a later flight?' she asked.

'It occurred to me there may well be watchers at Munich Airport. That's what I would do if I were Walvis. Now we'll arrive at the height of rush hour and take a taxi. Rush hour will make it difficult for us to be followed.'

'And the wine? You rarely drink anything.'

'It's my way of celebrating.' Tweed was in a buoyant

mood. 'First we're about to get to grips with Walvis. I want to upset his apple cart.'

'We don't know he's anywhere near Munich,' she objected.

'When I got back to my flat last night, no, early this morning, I called my old friend, Chief Inspector Otto Kuhlmann of the Kriminalpolizei in Wiesbaden. He never goes to sleep. He phoned me back after checking with a colleague in Munich. Walvis's Disney plane, *Pegasus*, landed yesterday on the Starnberger See south of the city. The local police in a place called Berg confirmed Walvis's limo with tinted glass was waiting.'

'I see. You didn't get much sleep yourself, yet you're bright as paint. What was the second reason why we're celebrating – apart from your thirst for action?'

'Getting away from Buchanan and his endless questions. That I can do without . . .'

At Munich Airport Tweed chose his cab driver carefully, standing back until he saw a lean-faced man who had his radio on and was waving his hands in time with the tune. He darted forward, carrying his case.

Tweed's prediction about the traffic had been right. The route into the distant city was solid with cars. Paula glanced back through the rear window several times but Tweed looked only once and briefly.

'We are being followed,' she whispered. 'A green Peugeot.'

'I know,' Tweed replied in a low voice. 'There were four unpleasant-looking gentlemen taking a great interest in us. They ran back to the Peugeot as we were getting into this taxi. Wait until we're entering Munich . . .'

They later had passed through the suburbs and tall white buildings – office blocks – loomed all round them. It was at this moment when Tweed called out to the driver in German.

'Don't look round. We've been followed from the

170

airport by a green Peugeot. It has business competitors inside and I don't want them to know where we're staying. An extra twenty-mark tip if you can elude them.'

'Green Peugeot.' The driver had glanced in his mirror. 'Got it. I'll take a roundabout route before I drop you at the Four Seasons. Hold on tight . . .'

He turned down a side street, rammed his foot on the accelerator, hurtled round a corner, swung right round a second corner along quiet streets. A driver of a Mercedes emerging from a drive blared his horn as the cab driver snaked round his bonnet with centimetres to spare. He kept this up round the back streets for several minutes. Paula glanced back as he slowed – no sign of the Peugeot.

'He just couldn't cut it,' the cab driver called out with satisfaction. 'Round the next corner and we're pulling in to the Four Seasons . . .'

Tweed registered at the long reception counter the two rooms booked by Monica for himself and Paula, asked a porter to keep the bags until they returned.

'You can wait to go to the powder room, I'm sure,' Tweed said. It wasn't a request.

'Yes. But where in Heaven's name are we off to now?'

'To the Bayerischer Hof by cab. I'm hoping we'll catch Captain David Sherwood in the hotel. I need to talk to him. He was Military Intelligence, so he knows how to ferret out information. I suspect he knows more than he has told us . . .'

'We'd better ask at the desk,' Paula suggested as they entered the luxury hotel. 'He could be anywhere.'

'I don't want to draw attention to us at this stage. I think we might just find Sherwood in the bar, from my impression of him.'

Again Tweed had guessed right. As they walked in a tall figure turned away from the bar, holding a drink

171

which looked like whisky to Paula. Sherwood's hooked nose seemed even more prominent and he stood quite still as he spotted Tweed and Paula approaching him. His alert eyes swept over Paula with admiration.

'Good Lord!' he barked. 'Of all the people I might have hoped to meet you were the last. Just arrived? Have a drink. Do. I'm a double whisky.'

'Thank you,' said Paula, amused at the way he was eyeing her. 'I think I'd like a glass of French dry white wine.'

'Mineral water for me. Fizzy,' said Tweed. 'We'll go grab that corner table.'

'Grab?' Sherwood chuckled. 'The place is empty. And that reminds me of a restaurant back home where I asked the Colombian waiter if he expected a busy evening. He said they were fully empty. Sit yourselves down and I'll bring the drinks.'

'I think he's rather fun,' Paula observed as they settled themselves at the table after taking off their coats. 'And he's quite good looking.'

'I'm not asking you to seduce him,' Tweed said in a mock growl.

'Pity. I wonder if he's found out anything about what happened to his partner, Parker?'

'We'll ask him.'

Tweed had chosen the chair in the corner where he could survey the whole bar with his back to the wall. He was still in a jovial, almost rampant mood. He waited until Sherwood arrived with the drinks and they had sampled them.

'Down the proverbial hatch,' Sherwood encouraged. 'Then we can have another round. On me, please.'

'Any news of Parker?' Tweed enquired.

Sherwood's expression changed, became grim. He put down his glass carefully and was silent for a moment, watching Tweed.

172

'I can tell you, I think,' he said eventually. 'I brought with me a photo of Parker I'd borrowed from his wife. I began showing it to the staff here. Didn't get far until by chance I scored a bull's-eye. Showed it to a waiter who had just come on duty. Six days ago he was standing outside, having a quick puff. He saw Parker come out with a man, then two more men helped to grab him, bundle him into a car. They were laughing as though it were a great joke – probably for the waiter's benefit. Car shot away from the kerb and he hasn't been seen since. Got a good description of the man who'd lured him out. Small, wide-shouldered, bent over all the time. Waiter said he looked like a hunchback. Had dark greasy hair and one of those 'taches which come down either side of the mouth. Like this.'

He used his index finger to describe an arc on either side of his own mouth. Tweed was staring at the entrance where a man stood remarkably like the description Sherwood had just given. He wore a black suit that was ill fitting. His eyes swept over their corner table, passed over Paula, stopped as they reached Tweed.

'Sherwood,' Tweed said quietly, 'look round at the entrance quickly . . .'

Sherwood lifted his glass as though about to drink, eased his chair back, placed the glass on the table and swivelled. He was out of the chair in a flash. The stooped figure by the door vanished. Sherwood ran, also vanished.

'That I call a weird coincidence,' Paula observed.

'It's the sort of thing that occasionally happens if you're on the alert.'

'Which you are,' she said. 'I noticed that he took no interest in me at all but he stared hard at you.'

'Yes, he did. Which suggests he recognized me but not you.'

'How could he?'

'Think back to that evening at Cleaver Hall. I wonder

173

whether that man with the camera at the first-floor window was still filming when we drove away past the gates.'

'The car moved pretty fast . . .'

'Not so fast when we had just started, which was when we passed the gates.'

'But I was in the car with you,' she protested.

'On the far side, away from the house and masked by me,' he pointed out. 'Careful, our friend is coming back. Any luck?' he asked Sherwood as the tall man sat down.

'No. Pure bad luck, but a whole crowd in dinner dress was coming in, probably for some reception. I lost him in the crowd, eventually pushed my way to the street. Not a sign of him.'

'Maybe you've discovered something else since you arrived?'

'When I was in Military Intelligence I was stationed with the Army here in Germany. I made a lot of contacts. I phoned a number of them from the post office – to be sure I was speaking on a secure line. They did come up with something. Ever heard of Project Tidal Wave?'

'Sounds pretty frightening,' Paula commented while they were on their own.

Sherwood had insisted on buying more drinks. He was standing by the bar when Newman appeared at the entrance, gazed round, walked quickly to Tweed's table, sat down.

'I've been roaming round Munich, going into the hotels, trying to find Philip Cardon. I tried the place where he called from first. He wasn't there. I checked the other hotel he'd visited, but still no luck. He wasn't there either. There was a weird incident outside here when that chap Sherwood rushed out through a crowd all togged up in evening dress . . .'

174

'What weird incident was that?' a voice behind Newman enquired.

It was Sherwood who had moved silently, returning
from the bar with a tray of drinks. Tweed made introductions. Sherwood offered to buy Newman a drink but
his suggestion was refused politely.

'So what weird incident?' Sherwood repeated. 'I was
running after a peculiar hunchback-like creature.'

'At least I can tell you his name,' Newman said,
staring at Sherwood. 'He had a car, engine running, and
two friends – heavy-looking types – waiting for him.
When Hunchback dashed out they called out to him in
German: "Get in quick, Lucien." The car sped off just
before you got outside.'

'Lucien,' Tweed said thoughtfully. 'Well, at least we
have another name.' He turned to Paula. 'Could you try
to phone Philip? He might have got back. Bob can give
you his number. Tell him I have more data, that I will
meet him anywhere of his own choosing, preferably this
evening. You may be more persuasive than I could be.'

Newman had already written down the number on a
sheet of paper. He tore it off his pad, folded it, handed it
to Paula, who left immediately.

'Now,' Tweed said to Sherwood. 'Tell us what you
found out concerning this Project Tidal Wave.'

Walvis sat behind his desk in his office with an expression of distaste. Rosa sat in a corner ready to take notes
with a pad on her lap, wearing her black cap and veil.
The object of distaste stood on the far side of Walvis's
desk. The people I have to employ, he thought to
himself.

Lucien, standing up on the far side of the desk,
stooped with his head thrust forward. He had just
arrived and was in an obvious state of excitement.

175

'Well, what is this urgent news – so called – which you have to tell me immediately?'

'I have located two of the targets. The man, Tweed, and Robert Newman. I raced back in a car to tell you before they leave . . .'

'Leave where? Get to it,' snapped Walvis.

'They are sitting at a corner table in the bar of the Bayerischer Hof talking to a man and a woman I didn't recognize . . .'

'Are you sure?'

'Here are their photographs,' Lucien said with an evil air of triumph . . .

Gulliver, anxious to improve his standing, had moved with great speed to produce the still photos from the film taken of events outside Cleaver Hall. He had further distributed them to Walvis's soldiers with extraordinary rapidity. Lucien pointed with a long talonlike finger at one photo.

'That's Tweed . . .'

'You have amazing eyesight,' Walvis commented drily.

'And this one is Newman . . .'

'Take back the photos and continue the search for the other two men. Leave the room now . . .'

As soon as they were alone Walvis pressed a button on his intercom. He nodded his satisfaction to Rosa.

'Send in Kahn,' he ordered.

Another door opened and Leo Kahn walked in. He stared at his chief with his usual bleak expression. Kahn's neck was still sore from his encounter with Marler near Cleaver Hall. He had replaced the bandage with the white collar of a clergyman. It transformed his appearance. Walvis glanced up at his subordinate, rapped out the order.

'If we are lucky Tweed and Newman – you have their photos – are at this moment in the bar at the Bayerischer Hof. I want both of them killed. How will you do it?'

176

'I will wait in a car outside the entrance to the hotel with an Uzi 9mm sub-machine-gun. They will both be liquidated . . .'

'You'd better hurry,' Walvis snapped.

He looked at Rosa when Kahn had dashed from the office. There was a grim smile on his face.

'The so-called Leo Kahn is really Nikita Kirov, a man the Russian Mafia have infiltrated into my organization. Teardrop shot the head of the Chechen Mafia in Moscow. He has been replaced by my own man.'

'You mean we control the notorious Chechen Mafia?' Rosa asked, unable to keep the surprise out of her voice.

'I mean exactly that.'

'But if Kahn's loyalty is to Moscow surely it is dangerous to keep him free?'

'It is much better to know who the spy is in your own backyard. He reports back to the Mafia's second-in-command – with misleading information I feed to him. Now we will wait to hear of the untimely demise of Tweed and Newman . . .'

Harry Butler possessed the patience of Job – and he had needed it after following Kahn to Munich aboard the same flight. One of the most skilled tails, he had tracked Kahn to Walvis's headquarters on Maximilianstrasse. He had parked the Citroën Monica had reserved for him at car-hire at the airport in a side street.

Later Kahn had emerged, disguised in his clerical collar, a disguise Butler penetrated immediately. He spotted Kahn's individual way of walking, taking quick short steps. Butler had been the top student in his class at the manor at Send in Surrey when the subject was body language.

All day Butler had followed Kahn, who drove a silver Audi. He noted that his quarry frequently consulted a

177

collection of photographs. Butler had a shrewd idea what Kahn was up to. When the little man went into a restaurant for a cup of coffee Butler slipped into a men's outfitter's, bought himself a dark blue German overcoat and a Tyrolean hat with a feather in the band, which struck him as comic. He also purchased from a shop near by a Swiss Army knife after testing its balance. When Kahn spent some time at a warehouse in a sleazy district on the outskirts of Munich Butler took the opportunity to wait a short distance away and practise throwing the knife at a thick wooden post. At Send he had been known as a weapons expert.

It was early evening when Butler, still without any food, found himself back at the headquarters building. Kahn had disappeared inside again and Butler was tempted to snatch a quick snack, but decided against it. He was carrying a litre bottle of mineral water purchased at the airport and he took another drink from it.

This time Kahn spent very little time inside the building. Seated behind the wheel of his Citroën, he saw Kahn rush out, carrying, of all things, a violin case. Three other men climbed into the Audi and this time, Butler noted, Kahn was no longer the driver. Instead he occupied one of the rear seats.

'Keep moving, little man,' Butler said to himself as he again began following the Audi.

'Project Tidal Wave,' Sherwood began in the bar of the Bayerischer Hof, 'is rumoured to be some kind of assault Walvis is planning against the West. No details. No idea of the timing or the nature of the assault. I was only able to pick up fragments.'

'Such as?' Tweed enquired.

'The river port of Passau on the Danube has been mentioned. Never liked Passau myself – something

178

strange about its atmosphere. It's where the cruises on the Danube start from. It's also a great centre for barges plying the river with their cargo – from as far away as the Black Sea. Don't know where it fits into the picture at all.'

'Any more fragments?' Newman enquired. 'It can be like a jigsaw – I found that as a foreign correspondent. You pick up a piece here, another piece there. Only when you have enough can you see the whole picture you mentioned.'

'Another fragment,' Sherwood continued. 'There are supposed to be training centres for refugees somewhere in the mountains of the Czech Republic. The rumour has it there's a selection system to find the most intelligent refugees flooding in from the East. Doesn't make sense.'

'Any more rumours?' Tweed enquired.

'Yes. Whoever is running Project Tidal Wave – if it exists – is killing off key business and political figures. A top man in the Chechen Mafia in Moscow is supposed to have been one of the targets. It's even reported someone has taken over the Chechen Mafia – the worst of the Mafia lot and the most powerful. Supposedly they've been promised backing for an independent and enlarged republic.'

'Chechenya, in the Caucasus,' Tweed mused. 'That does exist even though not recognized by the Russian government.'

'The Chechens are supposed to run these phantom training camps ruthlessly. Just another rumour, I suppose.'

'Any more fragments?' Newman asked.

'Yes. It's alleged a vast supply of sophisticated weapons is being smuggled into the West, including nuclear missiles. Bought partly from the enormous armoury the Russians sell for dollars – and the best the USA can supply from American arms dealers. It's all

179

supposed to be for the establishment of a new world order. Don't swallow that either.'

'Any mention of who is organizing this vast operation? Any reference to Walvis?' Tweed pressed.

'Not a whisper. Of course he does run his own huge outfit under conditions of great secrecy. Traitors just disappear, are found floating down the Danube.'

'The Danube again,' Tweed commented.

'I think that's all I can tell you,' Sherwood concluded.

'Well, well,' Newman remarked, 'look who has arrived – an interesting lady I met in London. And she's changed her hair style.'

He stood up as a woman in a dark blue jacket, a white blouse with ruffles at the neck and a mini-skirt came over to their table.

'May I introduce Jill Selborne, fashion consultant . . .'

When introductions had been made Jill sat down on the chair Newman had hastily fetched from another table. He grabbed the chair just ahead of Sherwood who had been starting out on the same mission. Now Sherwood sat down and smiled as he studied Jill.

Paula, remembering the way he had eyed her in the office at Park Crescent, was amused. Captain Sherwood was clearly a man who believed there was safety in numbers. The change in hair style which Newman had noticed was that now her jet-black hair was close to her well-shaped head, reminding Paula of a black helmet. After thanking Newman for the chair Jill spoke first to Paula.

'I hope I'm not intruding?'

'On the contrary,' Paula responded, giving her a warm smile, 'I was feeling out-gunned.'

'What would you like to drink?' Newman enquired, half out of his seat.

'A glass of dry white wine, preferably French, please.'

'My party,' boomed Sherwood. 'I'm dealing with the—'

'Not this time.' Newman placed a hand on Sherwood's muscular shoulder, forced him back into his seat.

'Such attention!' Jill exclaimed. 'I'm overwhelmed.'

No you're not, Paula thought. You're lapping it up. Like the cat that swallowed the cream. She smiled again as she started conversing with Jill as Sherwood opened his mouth to speak and then closed it again like a fish.

'You're a fashion consultant. That sounds an exciting occupation. Are there many shows on in Munich now?'

'Not a single one,' Jill answered, pushing back her chair and crossing her long legs. 'But that's the point. This city has oodles of money and some top-class women's shops. I shall be going around them to find out what's popular, and what isn't selling. Helps me to forecast trends for the future.'

'I like your suit,' Paula went on.

'Oh, it's nothing really. Cost a bomb, of course. That's the disadvantage of my profession. I have to spend a fortune on clothes to keep up appearances. It gets you into the inner sanctums if you look good.'

'Then here's to the success of penetrating inner sanctums,' Paula said, raising her glass.

Jill reached for her own glass, which Newman had just put before her, raised it in a toast. Newman tapped Sherwood on the shoulder.

'You've moved into my chair. Mind shifting back to where you were before Jill arrived?'

'Do mind, but suppose I must oblige you. Monopolize all the attractive females, you do.'

'I got there first.' Newman joshed Sherwood as he sat in his own chair. 'I met Jill in London.'

'Care to let me know where you hide yourself in London?' Sherwood asked Jill, twisting his chair so he could look straight at her.

181

'My hideyhole is a state secret,' Jill replied with a mischievous smile.

'When did you arrive in Munich?' Tweed asked suddenly.

Jill's playful manner changed. She became serious, looked directly at Tweed. She hesitated.

'I came in on an early flight this morning.' She checked her watch. 'And I'm afraid I must disappear now to change. I have a dinner date with a buyer.'

Newman caught her arm as she rose to go. She paused, gazed down at him.

'I'll see you again, won't I?'

'You know where to find me.'

She flapped her hand at everyone and walked briskly out of the bar. Sherwood stretched his long arms, stifled a yawn.

'It's a long soaking bath for me. Hope I've been of help,' he said to Tweed.

'More than perhaps you realize.'

He was alone with Paula and Newman when he looked at his own watch, then at Paula.

'Philip?' he asked her.

'Waiting to see you at the Four Seasons.'

'Then I think we'd better go. It should be quiet outside now. Easy to get a cab back to our hotel.'

18

As they emerged into the night-time street from the hotel a cab pulled up. Paula noticed a silver Audi was parked on the same side further along the pavement. Two women and two men, all in evening dress, began to get out of the cab.

'People take so long to alight from a vehicle,' Tweed remarked.

They were standing on the pavement, chatting, while one of the men fumbled for his wallet to pay the fare. Tweed moved forward, waited. The cab driver hadn't seen them and he didn't want to lose it.

Leo Kahn stepped out of a rear door of the Audi, holding an Uzi sub-machine-gun. He raised the muzzle, aimed it point blank at the crowd. Take them all and I'm bound to get Tweed and Newman, he was thinking. His finger tightened on the trigger.

'Look out! Down!' roared Newman, knowing he was too late.

A blade of steel flashed through the cold night air, for a second the hurtling blade was illuminated by a street lamp. The knife plunged deep into its target, Kahn's shoulder. The assassin jerked forward, blood pouring from the wound. His movement caused the muzzle of the Uzi to point skywards. In a reflex action he pressed the trigger. A stuttering fusillade of bullets. Several hit the street lamp, extinguishing it in a scatter of glass.

Kahn, still clutching the Uzi, staggered backwards. A man in the back of the cab hauled him inside, then reached out to pick up the weapon Kahn had dropped.

'*Gott in Himmel!*' yelped one of the Germans standing by the cab.

Butler, after throwing the knife, had rushed back to his Citroën parked further down the street. Tweed reacted swiftly, calling out to his companions as he raced towards the car.

'Follow me . . .'

The Audi had started moving, careering all over the empty street before it straightened up and began to speed off into the night. Butler was behind the wheel of his

Citroën, cursing because the engine wouldn't start, when Tweed reached him, jumped into the front passenger seat. Paula opened the rear door, dived inside, followed by Newman. The engine fired.

Butler accelerated, determined to catch up with the Audi. It had vanished round a corner some distance away. When Butler arrived at the corner he found he was looking down a deserted street.

'Give it up,' Tweed ordered. 'Take us back to the Four Seasons. And thank you for saving our lives.'

'All in a day's work,' replied the phlegmatic Butler.

'I feel like a crass idiot,' Tweed complained. 'I've never before walked out into a street like that before assuming there could be trouble, without taking a look around.'

'We all make one mistake,' Paula said soothingly.

'One mistake can be your last,' Tweed insisted. 'I could have got both of you killed. These people really play for keeps.'

'So let's do the same thing,' said Butler.

The lounge area at the Four Seasons, which stretches in front of the visitor as soon as he arrives, is spacious and luxurious. Guests in evening clothes were seated in comfortable armchairs, sharing couches. Several German men were puffing Havana cigars. Tweed caught the faint aroma as he entered with Paula and Newman. Butler had insisted on parking the car himself.

Tweed's heart leapt with relief when he saw a figure seated in a chair by himself. Philip was clad in a navy blazer with gold buttons and navy-blue trousers. He had a nautical look and was dressed for a five-star hotel. His raincoat was carefully folded, almost concealing a large back-pack. An untouched drink sat on the table in front of him and his chair was in a corner where he could survey everyone in the lounge and – more important – anyone

184

who entered it. He didn't smile as Tweed walked over to him and there were signs of strain in his normally fresh-faced look.

'Hello, Philip,' Tweed said, remaining standing. 'It's pretty public here. We'll go up to my room – after I've had the bags sent up.'

'They will have been sent up,' Paula reminded him. 'Can I help you carry that pack?'

'No, thank you. Weighs a ton. Marler is keeping an eye on me. He's standing just inside the entrance to the bar. Up those steps.'

'So I'll give you a hand,' Newman said firmly. 'You do look a trifle weary.'

'Busy day,' Philip replied.

'I remember this marvellous place,' Paula said. 'It is so welcoming.'

She looked round as Tweed and Newman went to reception to collect their keys. The walls were panelled with wood to the ceiling which gave an atmosphere of a vast library. The elegant women guests were dressed in the height of fashion and dripping with gold necklaces and bracelets. A number had four or five bracelets round their wrists. Paula wondered how they mustered the strength to lift their hands to have a drink.

Butler returned as Tweed and Newman brought over the room keys. Dressed in his dark blue German overcoat and holding the Tyrolean hat in his hand Butler appeared more than respectable enough to enter a five-star hotel.

'Where is Pete?' he asked Newman, anxious about his partner.

'Nield must still be doing what he's been doing since we arrived – roaming round Munich in his small hired Mercedes. I'll tell you about something he told me over the phone earlier in the day. We have to stay under cover.'

'We all meet in my room in five minutes' time,' Tweed

185

decided, showing them his room number.

'I'll go to my room first to unpack or my clothes will be ruined,' Paula informed him. 'And I want to freshen up.'

'See you in about an hour, then,' Newman joked.

'Since when have I taken more than five minutes to make myself look decent?' Paula rapped back at him.

'I've ordered several bottles of champagne,' Tweed said casually.

'Champers! Goody-goody,' Paula enthused.

'Didn't know you liked the stuff,' Newman mocked her.

'Bet you knock back your ration,' Paula told him.

'We'll go upstairs now,' Tweed announced.

They walked into an empty elevator. The doors were closing when Marler slipped inside with them. He stubbed out a king-size.

'Things to warn you all about,' he said in a bored tone.

'Then come with me at once to my room.'

'They have photos of some of us,' Marler said quickly. 'A nasty little man pretending to be a police officer goes round the reception desks of all the hotels. His identity card must be forged. Par for the course.'

'I can tell you he hasn't got your picture,' Tweed remarked.

'Then I won't stay long with you. I'm more useful loitering by the bar, making eye contact with the girls while I check on who is entering this place. Munich is not the safest city on the Continent. By the by, I'd better collect a suitcase from my room.' He looked at Philip who stood with a grim, withdrawn expression. 'I hear you visited Manfred Hellmann down at Berg earlier today. I went to see Manfred later and made a few purchases. Cost me forty thousand marks but it was worth it.'

'Forty thousand!' Philip exclaimed. 'And I thought he had piled it on when he charged me half that.'

'Wait until you see the contents of my suitcase,' Marler said in an undertone. 'He gave you a discount . . .'

186

They had stepped out into a wide corridor carpeted from wall to wall and illuminated discreetly by wall sconces. The silence struck Tweed and the corridor was deserted. He followed the sign indicating the way to his double room with Marler by his side. Newman and Paula walked off in the opposite direction.

'Had a struggle to stop porters accompanying us,' said Tweed. 'But they say the bags are in our rooms.' He stopped as he came to the right number. Marler gave a little salute. 'Be back in a tick. I'll tap on your door like this . . .' He rapped an irregular tattoo and Tweed went into a room which was more like a suite.

At the Bayerischer Hof Captain David Sherwood was in a state of expectant anticipation. While in the bath he had had a phone call from a mysterious woman. Clutching the wall instrument, he listened with surprise and growing interest.

'Captain David Sherwood?' a soft feminine voice asked.

'Speaking . . .'

'I am Magda Franz,' she said in perfect English. 'If we could have dinner at your hotel tonight I can tell you something about what happened to your partner, Mr Parker.'

'It will be my great pleasure to have you as my guest,' Sherwood had agreed. 'And this evening I am free. Had I not been,' he had gone on, 'I would have cancelled any previous engagement to accommodate you.'

'That's very sweet of you,' the seductive voice had continued. 'May I arrive at nine thirty?'

'Nine thirty this evening,' Sherwood had said enthusiastically. 'I'll be waiting for you outside the main dining-room. I'll book a quiet table.'

'A secluded table would be nice. I look forward to a wonderful evening.'

187

'How will I recognize you?' Sherwood had thought to ask.

'I will be wearing a long black dress, and a black cap on my head with a veil.'

'Sounds intriguing,' he had responded. 'But will you recognize me? Maybe a description . . .'

'Oh, I will recognize you, Captain Sherwood . . .'

Their conversation had taken place almost an hour before. Sherwood, relieved he had had his bath, had chosen his smartest business suit, had applied after-shave lotion, checking his appearance in the bedroom mirror. I'm still not too old for a little adventure, he thought. He was so elated the purpose of the meeting – finding out something about Parker's disappearance – was taking second place in his thoughts.

Having booked the table by phone, he went down to the restaurant to check it. A corner table, it seemed perfect for an assignation. Magda Franz, clad as she had described, arrived on time and extended a slim hand to shake his.

She was of medium height and the black dress clinging to her suggested a good figure beneath its folds. The head waiter escorted them to the corner table and she insisted that Sherwood sat in the corner chair.

'I know this restaurant so it is only fair you have the good view.' She glanced at the silver bucket on its tripod cradling a bottle of Krug champagne.

'Are you hoping to get me drunk?' she asked as they settled at the table.

'Maybe hoping to get you just a bit tiddly,' Sherwood replied at his most jovial.

He wished he could see her face more clearly. He had the impression of well-defined features and hidden beauty. They ordered the meal and Sherwood told them not to hurry.

'We want to enjoy the champagne first,' he told the waiter.

188

He raised his glass when they were alone. The restaurant was filling up but was still only half-full. No one had sat near them so far.

'Here's to friendship,' he said breezily.

'Here's to a memorable evening – and long life,' she replied.

19

Paula was the first to arrive back in Tweed's room. She had unpacked, had a shower, changed into a pale blue dress with long sleeves and a mandarin collar. Round her slim waist was a wide deep blue belt with a lion's head buckle. She stared round at the room.

There was a large seating area with comfortable armchairs and couches. Beyond was a large bedroom with a king-size bed. The furnishings were opulent, the lighting discreet.

'This isn't a bedroom, it's a suite,' she told him.

'I thought we needed a spacious private place where we could all meet. Bearing in mind what is happening, I was right.'

He spoke as though his mind was only half on the words. He stood staring into space after greeting her.

'A penny for your thoughts,' she teased him. 'I might make it half a crown, going back to old money.'

'I am convinced Captain Sherwood knows far more than he has told us. He was studiously vague. Maybe there were too many people at the table. Tomorrow I'm going over to meet him on my own. I'll call to make an appointment later.'

'What he did say was pretty scary. I see Philip has left his back-pack here.'

'He returned just after you'd all gone. Said he thought it would be safer here. It will be interesting to see the contents. Did you notice the change in his manner?'

'You tell me your impression first,' she urged, sitting down on one of the couches, arranging a pile of cushions.

'A much grimmer, more remote Philip. I'm glad you were able to persuade him to come over here.'

'I had a job with him on the phone. He was reluctant to leave the Platzl. I told him he owed it to you to see you. I reminded him of how you had backed him up in the past in certain tricky situations. Eventually he said he would meet you.'

'You did well.'

At that moment there was a tattoo rapping on the door and Tweed again unlocked it. Marler walked in, carrying a heavy suitcase, followed by Newman. Butler arrived as Tweed was closing the door.

'The clan is gathered,' Paula said in a quiet voice, sensing Tweed's sombre mood.

'We need to be weaponed up,' Marler said crisply. He put the case on a squat stool. 'Too many heavies patrolling the city. Walvis has Munich in his pocket. Ladies first,' he went on as he unlocked the case, raised the lid, lifted out some clothes.

Underneath there were packages of various sizes wrapped in opaque cellophane bags. He lifted one out, handed it to Paula.

'Feel happier with this in that special pocket you sewed inside your shoulder-bag? A .32 Browning with spare mags. Courtesy of Manfred Hellmann. Well, the courtesy cost a packet . . .'

Paula was already taking the gun out of its wrapping,

190

checking to make sure it wasn't loaded, weighing its balance in her hand before inserting a magazine of bullets in the butt.

'Much happier. Thanks,' she said.

Marler had already handed another package to Newman who found inside his favourite weapon. A .38 Smith & Wesson revolver complete with hip holster and plenty of ammo. Butler received a 7.65mm Walther automatic, capacity eight rounds. He was checking the weapon when someone tapped on the door.

Newman waved the others back, hauled out his revolver, which he had already loaded, held it in his right hand and used his left hand to unlock the door quietly, leaving the chain on. He opened the door a few inches.

'That's what I call a warm welcome,' Nield said drily as he was let inside.

'Where the hell have you been all this time?' asked Butler.

'Doing a job of work while you loaf around.' Nield looked at Tweed. 'There's a lot of trouble waiting for us in this town. Ah, that makes me feel better,' he said, accepting the Walther, hip holster and ammo Marler gave him. He took off his coat and jacket, strapped on the holster, checked the Walther and slid it inside the holster. He grinned and winked at Paula. 'Now I feel properly dressed.'

'What kind of trouble?' Tweed enquired, double-checking Marler's earlier observation.

'There's a swarm of armed thugs prowling round Munich – looking for us, I'm sure.' He patted his hip. 'But now I reckon we will cope. There's going to be blood in the streets . . .'

While he was speaking there was another tap on the door and Newman let Philip into the room in time for him to hear the last remark. He sagged on to the couch beside Paula.

191

'There was almost blood down at Berg this morning . . .'

He described his encounter with the men in the blue Audi after leaving Hellmann. Tweed watched him closely while he listened to the episode. Philip was obviously bone weary but he sat erect and there was a chilling look in his eyes.

'We did have our own spot of excitement,' said Tweed when Philip had finished.

Concisely, to brief everyone, he recalled the interview with Sherwood, what the Englishman had told them, the surprise arrival of Jill Selborne.

'I wonder how Captain Sherwood is getting on,' he mused. 'I doubt if he's remained inactive this evening . . .'

Despite Sherwood's enthusiasm for his dinner guest his old training as a Military Intelligence officer had not disturbed his normal habit of noting everything down. They had finished the main course when she excused herself.

'I'm going to the powder room. I'll only be a few minutes.'

During her absence he took out his notebook, scribbled a few words. *Dinner with Magda Franz. A most intriguing lady. Speaks perfect idiomatic English. Wonder when I'll be able to see her in all her glory without the veil.* He added the December date, had slipped the notebook back in his pocket when she returned. Tears were dripping down her face below the veil and, as she sat down, she dabbed at them with a scrap of lace handkerchief.

'What's wrong?' he asked her.

'Nothing. Just the smoke. The cigars.'

'What a shame. Look, this is clean. Use it.'

He had taken a folded white handkerchief from his pocket, was leaning across the table to hand it to her when she lifted her napkin, aimed the pistol concealed inside the cloth, pulled the trigger of her silenced weapon. A cyanide-tipped bullet plunged into his chest. He dropped the handkerchief, gave an anguished cry, slumped forward.

She jumped up, still wearing the white gloves which had covered her hands during the dinner, ran over to the nearest waiter.

'Get a doctor. Quickly! My companion is having a heart attack . . .'

She had raised her voice and everything became confusion. Several men stood up from their tables, colliding with each other as they tried to reach the sprawled figure.

A head waiter began calling out in German at the top of his voice.

'A doctor! Please! If there is a doctor present will he come immediately . . .'

Several women stood up to get a better view of what had happened, then crowded forward. The ghoul instinct had taken over. By the time a doctor arrived, made a quick examination and whispered to the head waiter that the guest was dead, Magda Franz had disappeared.

'I'm going to phone up Captain Sherwood now to make an appointment to see him first thing tomorrow morning,' Tweed announced.

'I'll get the number of the Bayerischer Hof,' said Paula.

Tweed dialled the number himself. He spoke in German and the receptionist told him Captain Sherwood was not in his room. Perhaps he was in the dining-room – he would transfer the caller.

Tweed had to wait several minutes before the connection was made. An agitated voice came on the phone, speaking in a low tone. It was bad for business to have a body in the restaurant.

'I need to speak to Captain David Sherwood,' Tweed said calmly in German.

'You are a relative of Captain Sherwood?' the voice asked.

'Yes, his brother,' Tweed lied immediately, sensing there was some crisis.

'I am afraid I have very bad news for you, sir. Captain Sherwood is dead. He had a heart attack during his dinner.'

'Oh, Lord. Was he alone at the time?'

'No, sir. He had a dining companion, an elegant woman who wore a black cap and a veil. I have not been able to find her since the tragedy occurred . . . Are you still there, sir?'

Tweed was not still there. He had put down the receiver. He grunted, turned round to face his team, who had stopped talking.

'The tempo of murder is accelerating,' he announced. 'I have just been told that Captain Sherwood was having dinner at the Bayerischer Hof when he died of a heart attack. He had a woman as his dining companion. She has since vanished. She wore a black cap and a veil.'

'Teardrop has scored again,' Marler drawled.

20

Walvis was a man who worked far into the night. He was behind his desk, poring over a list of names of well-known European figures, putting a cross behind certain names, when the door opened.

'I hope I'm not disturbing you,' she said.

Walvis glared at her. She was clad in her usual clothes, a black dress, black cap and veil. She was breathing heavily as though she had been hurrying. She sank down into a chair.

'Where? Where have you been?' Walvis demanded in a rough tone.

'Please don't talk to me like that. I went out to buy a few things from an all-night chemist. I heard police sirens and stood back in a doorway. A convoy of patrol cars came down the street, was stopped by some stupid drivers crossing an intersection – the lights were green for them and they hadn't seen the police convoy.'

'I suppose that in due course,' Walvis said sarcastically, 'you will get to the point.'

'I'm coming to it. You need the background, you always say . . .'

'I've got the background. What about the foreground for a change?'

'I wish you'd calm down . . .'

'I am calm. I will be even calmer when you eventually get to the point.'

'One of the cars . . .' Rosa Brandt paused for breath. 'I saw one car was a Mercedes, black, with patrol cars in front and behind it. The Mercedes stopped in front of where I was waiting. You know I have a memory for faces – I recognized the man smoking a cigar sitting beside the driver. It was Chief Inspector Otto Kuhlmann from the Kriminalpolizei in Wiesbaden. So why is he in Munich?'

'Kuhlmann . . .'

Walvis's head tilted sideways on his huge shoulders. He hunched forward and his expression was not pleasant. His heavy eyelids were twitching, his thick lips twisted. He stared at Rosa with a blank expression, looking right through her. She knew he was greatly disturbed by her news. When he spoke his tone was very throaty.

'Just a moment. He was probably on his way to the

195

Bayerischer Hof. Leo Kahn botched the job of killing Tweed and Newman. Someone threw a knife at him as he was about to open fire . . .'

'Tweed must be well protected,' she ventured.

'Keep quiet, woman. I was talking. The damned fools with him brought Kahn back here – into my office. He could have dripped blood on to the carpet. I told them to take him to the warehouse. That idiot of a doctor phoned me just before you arrived. Kahn will be OK in a few days. The knife didn't penetrate an artery.'

'May I speak?' Rosa asked.

'Yes, if you must.'

'That doesn't explain Kuhlmann appearing in Munich. Not all the way from Wiesbaden. He must have been coming in any case for some other reason.'

'You read my mind,' he sneered. 'I had exactly the same thought. And we are so close to launching Project Tidal Wave—'

He broke off as the phone rang. His large hand grabbed the receiver, he was suddenly calm, even cold. He said: 'Who is it? Ah, proceed . . .' in German and listened.

'Are you certain?' he demanded after a short pause. 'I see. Now she has the other assignment. The journalist. Ziggy Palewski. How would I know where he is? For what I pay that is your job. Find him. Then tell her.'

'That will give something to distract Kuhlmann,' he said, his manner jovial. 'Captain Sherwood was shot dead at the Bayerischer Hof while having dinner with a lady. Once more Teardrop has proved to be an expert. Wouldn't it be interesting if we could meet her?'

Rosa was startled. She recovered, crossed her legs, shook her head.

'I would not like to be present on such an occasion. You have now arranged for her to kill Ziggy Palewski. Why?'

'That pestilential scribbler is getting too close to us. I

196

have heard of certain people he has interviewed. He must never live to learn about Tidal Wave.' He became buoyant, waving his pudgy hands in a fresh explosion of energy.

'We must become even more aggressive. I will phone Martin at the warehouse . . .'

He dialled a number. There was a delay before someone answered. Walvis raised his voice to a vicious command.

'Put Martin on immediately, which means *now*! I said Martin. He will know who is calling . . . Ah, Martin. You have been having a good sleep? Stop protesting and listen. I have decided a fresh attempt must be made to road-block our competitors. Tweed and Newman – and Cardon. I will give the same order to Gulliver and you will co-operate. No, I will tell him myself. Put him on the damned line.'

'Would you like something to drink?' Rosa suggested while he waited, anxious to soothe him down.

'Gulliver?' Walvis said quietly into the phone. 'Listen. I have given the same instruction to Martin. I also told him you must co-operate together – but in a crisis you take over. That last is between the two of us. Tweed, Newman and Cardon must all be road-blocked. Their competition is becoming too fierce. Maybe your special expertise will be the answer. That is all.'

Rosa knew that, speaking on an open line, 'road-block' meant 'kill'. But she was intrigued about the end of the conversation.

'I would be interested to know about Gulliver's special expertise.'

'I'm sure you would. Well, on this occasion I will satisfy your disgusting curiosity. Gulliver is an explosives expert. He started out in life blasting stone out of quarries. Making a car bomb is child's play to him. So far attacks against Tweed's men have been from a car – as in Berg –

197

and by a gunman – as was Kahn's outside the Bayerischer Hof. They will not expect a quite new menace. You said something about a drink. I think brandy would go down rather well as a celebration of my fresh plans.'

Walvis was in the best of moods. He had just ordered the killing of four people.

The fist hammered on Tweed's door as though determined to smash its way through the wood. Tweed, since Paula was one of the few unknown members of his team, nodded and she slipped into the bathroom, locking the door behind her.

Earlier Marler had slid the case containing his own arms under the bed. Philip had hidden his backpack – after displaying its contents – in a wardrobe behind a spare duvet.

It was Newman who approached the door, Smith & Wesson gripped in his right hand. He was even more cautious this time, standing by the wall to one side of the door while he unlocked it, opened it on the chain.

'About time, too. Now let me in before I break down the door,' a voice roared in English.

'It's Kuhlmann,' said Tweed.

Newman let the visitor in. Kuhlmann was a short, broad-shouldered man with a large head who always reminded Newman of Edward G. Robinson, an American actor who had played gangster roles in old films. He was clean shaven, had a wide aggressive mouth and presence. The type of man who attracted instant attention when he entered any room. He pointed his cigar at Tweed like a gun.

'There's been a murder in the dining-room of the Bayerischer Hof this evening – in full view of thirty-five guests.' His voice was a growl as he went on. 'A Captain Sherwood. And the head waiter tells me that late this afternoon the victim was talking to two men and a girl. He described one of the men – a quiet man, but there was something very strong about him, yet you could pass him in the street and not notice him. With the physical description I at once thought of you. And who do I find when I start checking the top hotels? *You!*'

'That was really quite clever of you,' Tweed remarked mildly to throw the policeman off balance.

'And,' Kuhlmann thundered on, sweeping his arm round the other people in the room, 'I find nearly your whole team with you.' He suddenly looked at the bathroom, the closed door. 'I wonder who you are concealing in there?' he demanded at the top of his voice.

Taking short rapid strides across the bedroom area he took hold of the handle, found the door was locked, pounded on it with his fist.

Inside the bathroom Paula had heard every word. She knew Tweed's tactic would be to disconcert the Chief Inspector. As the pounding went on she unzipped her dress, slipped out of it, now wearing only an opaque slip and her tights. She unlocked the door, opened it.

'Do you have to make such a racket?' she enquired sweetly.

Kuhlmann stared at her, stepped back, horribly embarrassed. He had known Paula for years. He hastily removed the cigar from his mouth.

'I'm sorry. I really am. But how was I to know . . .'

'Well, you know now,' she told him and shut the door in his face.

'Had you asked me I would have told you,' Tweed informed him. 'Now why don't you sit down, take a deep breath and we'll talk to each other like civilized people. We can offer you coffee.'

'And I remember you like it black.'

It was Paula who spoke, who had appeared from the bathroom fully dressed. She lifted a pot on a tray, poured

199

coffee into a cup, handed it to the German. He looked up at her from the armchair he had sunk into at Tweed's suggestion.

'Thank you, Paula. Again my apologies ...' He stopped when she smiled and waved a finger at him. 'The trouble is in the past twenty-four hours I've had not a wink of sleep – and now Tweed sets Munich alight almost the moment he's off the plane.'

'How do you make that out?' Paula asked, sitting opposite him. He did look haggard. 'Drink your coffee.'

'Well, Tweed was – again with Newman – apparently involved in some bizarre machine-gun attack outside the hotel although nobody was hurt. I've seen the street lamp, which was shattered by the gunfire. So what is going on?'

'Would you tell me first,' Tweed intervened, 'why you've suddenly turned up in Munich – before any of this had happened? At least you must have flown from Wiesbaden before these events took place.'

'I'll hear your version first, if you don't mind. We are in Germany . . .'

'You have a point.'

Tweed settled down in another armchair and gave Kuhlmann a carefully edited version of what had happened. He laid great emphasis on the tragedy that Philip was enduring and full details of what had happened to his now dead wife, Jean.

'That sounds grim.' Kuhlmann chewed on his cigar, looked at Philip. 'I'm not going to mouth the usual platitudes like so many people do. Do they help?'

'They do *not*,' Philip said, his expression tense. 'Most people say the wrong things. Because they haven't had an experience like that they haven't a clue what to say – they're awkward, embarrassed. Some of them are frightened, just want to get away from the subject of death. They want to get away from me. I understand their

200

reactions perfectly. Unless they've had the same experience they just can't cope.'

'I know what you mean,' Kuhlman said quietly. 'My own wife died ten years ago after a car crash. She wasn't killed outright. She was rushed to hospital. For four days she seemed OK, the doctor said she might be treatable. But he warned me at the outset . . .' Kuhlmann paused to relight his cigar, changed his mind, put it in an ashtray, '. . . warned me that he couldn't make any promises.'

Tweed stood watching Kuhlmann, as if hypnotized. He had never known Kuhlmann was once married. And now there seemed to be only two people in the room – Kuhlmann and Philip – as the German continued.

'For the first four days she was sitting up in bed and talking quite normally. On Saturday evening I stayed to have an evening meal with her. The hospital produced a bottle of brandy. You know something? We really enjoyed that meal and chat together. I didn't know that was to be the last time we'd eat together.' He paused again.

'Yes?' Philip said very quietly. His eyes were fixed on Kuhlmann's.

'Was breathing a problem with your wife?' the German asked.

'Yes, it was. Her lungs were crushed.' He swallowed. 'It was agony for her to try and get some breath into her lungs. She became very agitated.'

'The same with Helga,' Kuhlmann continued. 'The doctor told me they were filling up with carbon dioxide, which is normally expelled by all of us as we breathe. On the fifth day there was a rapid deterioration. The doctor didn't like her state of agitation. Neither did I – she was always a strong woman, a fighter – to see her struggling for breath half killed me. The doctor – a top-flight consultant – took me into another room and I remember that as one of the worst moments of my life.'

201

'What happened?' Philip asked very quietly, his eyes misted over.

'The consultant was genuinely moved as he gave me the alternatives. There were tears in his eyes, which amazed me. He said he wanted to put her on a stronger drug – she had had milder pain-killers earlier. Diamorphine.'

'The same thing happened with Jean,' Philip whispered.

'The consultant explained,' Kuhlmann went on in the same flat tone, 'that they would feed her with diamorphine intravenously . . .' He paused as Philip nodded. 'That with my permission they would gradually increase the dose. The alternative? To put her on a life-support machine. He said he could keep her alive indefinitely but she would not be aware of anything . . .' Philip nodded again '. . . so I had to take the decision,' Kuhlmann went on as though he was reliving the experience again. 'If they fed her with diamorphine it would deaden the pain, there would be no more agitation.'

'The consultant at the Nuffield told me he hoped she would never wake up. That went through me like a knife,' Philip whispered again.

'I know. Helga and I had been married many years. Afterwards, although I realized people knew we were close, I was amazed at the number of friends who wrote to me – often from distant countries – commenting on what a rare partnership we had enjoyed.' He cleared his throat. 'I knew that Helga, such an active and intelligent woman, would have hated being kept alive as a vegetable. I agreed to the diamorphine, knowing that when the dose was regularly increased there would come a moment when her heart would stop beating. I gave permission to use diamorphine. I felt like her executioner.'

'So did I,' said Philip, still whispering. 'And then . . .'

'You probably know. The death watch. You sit in the room watching her – and watching something else.

202

Besides the intravenous drip for the diamorphine they have linked her to a machine which registers the rate of her pulse beat. Ninety to the minute is the rate our pulses are beating at. The machine's face registered ninety. Helga was in a deep sleep. The pulse rate dropped to eighty-five, then to eighty. I was alarmed. The sister watching over her with me smiled, said it would go back to ninety. It did. That went on for many hours.'

'I know. The death watch,' Philip said almost to himself.

'I was dog-tired,' Kuhlmann went on. 'They had given me a bed at the hospital in another private room . . .'

'The same with me,' Philip said.

'I didn't spend much time in my room. I had to get back to watch over Helga. Then in the evening the number on the machine dropped to forty. The sister glanced at me, no longer gave reassurance. Suddenly I was staring at the machine and the face went blank. She had died.'

'I greatly . . . appreciate . . . knowing someone who really understands,' mumbled Philip.

'Have you been back to your flat or house?' Kuhlmann asked.

'Not to the house she loved. Not yet.'

'Your ordeal has just begun. There is no one else in the house? I see. It was like that with me. I dreaded returning to what had been our home for so many years. It seemed like a tomb – so horribly empty. You will find you crucify yourself every time you go back for such a long time. In the privacy of that empty home you will cry alone many times. I can offer you no comfort – none at all.'

'Thank you for saying the right words.' Philip stood up slowly. 'I think I will go back to my room.' He fetched the backpack from the wardrobe.

203

Kuhlmann stared at it but said nothing, made no move to ask what was inside.

'I know who killed Jean,' he told Kuhlmann. 'I have seen him. I have a job to do . . .'

Tweed took a step forward towards Philip. Kuhlmann put out a hand, grasped Tweed's arm, stopped him as Philip left the room.

'Let him go,' said Kuhlmann. 'He desperately needs something to occupy his mind. The driver who involved Helga in the fatal car crash was never traced. If I ever locate him I will strangle him slowly with my bare hands.'

21

Newman had left the suite shortly after Kuhlmann made his grim promise. Marler, Nield and Butler had also left to go to their rooms, anxious to take showers and change their clothes. The conversation had made Newman feel restless.

He was recalling the time some years before, during the Cold War days, when his own wife had been murdered in a Baltic state, how he had set out to avenge her death in much the same way Philip was doing. The only difference – a big one – had been that his marriage, short and turbulent, had been on the verge of breaking up.

He went down into the lounge and headed for the main restaurant. There were very few people in the lounge and he was close to the restaurant entrance when a faint aroma of expensive perfume drifted across his nostrils, a hand touched his arm. He swung round.

'Well, I'll be damned.'

Lisa Trent, the attractive blonde he had met at the Bistro in Bosham, smiled at him. Financial analyst, detective and conwoman, as she had described herself. She wore a green form-fitting dress, high at the neck and with a thin gold belt round her slim waist.

'That's not quite the sort of greeting I had hoped for,' she said and made a moue.

'Pure surprise and pleasure,' he responded with a smile.

'I want to ask you a very big favour.' Carrying a green coat over her arm, she moved closer to him so her voice would not carry. 'I'm still after an interview with the great man. Walvis. And now I get asked to go over to see him at his headquarters. At this time of night. I feel a bit nervous. Would you come with me to hold my hand? I mean to act as an escort.'

'Just because you're nervous?' he probed.

'Well, that's not the whole story. As a foreign correspondent you must have interviewed just about every type – including some pretty powerful and tough men. You may have better luck at getting him to talk.'

'I'd have said I was the last man in the world Walvis would talk to.'

Newman was in two minds. The thought of her company was enticing, but there were too many coincidences. First Jill Selborne appearing at the Bayerischer Hof when they were talking to poor Captain Sherwood. Now Lisa Trent. Then he remembered she had told him she would be coming to Munich, would be staying at the Four Seasons.

'Please,' she coaxed, very close to him now. 'A lady in distress is asking for your help.'

'Well, put that way,' he said cynically, 'how can I not agree? But I must cancel a dinner engagement, leave a note at the reception desk . . .'

'All right.' She consulted a small diamond-encrusted

205

watch, a different one from the watch she had worn – also diamond-encrusted – in Bosham. 'We ought to leave soon. I don't think Walvis is a man who expects people to turn up late.'

'He'll just have to fume, then, won't he?'

Newman walked swiftly over to the reception counter, took a hotel pad, wrote a message on it.

Tweed, on my way to Walvis's HQ with Lisa Trent. We met her in Bosham. She's got an interview with our friend. Bob.

Tearing the note off the pad, he inserted it into an envelope, sealed it, put the rest of the pad in his pocket and told a receptionist to send the envelope up to Mr Tweed's suite immediately if not sooner.

Despite Lisa's impatience, he waited, saw the envelope handed to a messenger, watched him run to the bank of lifts, slip inside an empty one. As the doors shut Newman checked the number illuminated above it. Yes, it was the right floor. He walked back to Lisa.

'We'll have to get a move on,' she said. 'A porter is holding a cab outside. Oh, Lord, you haven't a coat. It's very cold outside.'

'Then I have two alternatives. To delay a little longer while I fetch my sheepskin from my room. Or freeze . . .'

'Let's run . . .'

She looped her arm over his and they ran into the night. It was well below zero and Newman was relieved to find the interior of the cab was heated. She gave the driver the destination, then snuggled up to Newman, again looping her arm inside his.

'Maybe I can help to keep you warm,' she whispered in her soft voice.

'Maybe . . .'

Newman was wondering what kind of a reception waited for them in Walvis's lair.

*   *   *

206

Kuhlmann, settled in his chair in Tweed's suite, was secretly relieved when most of Tweed's team left. Aside from himself and Tweed, Paula was the only person remaining in the suite. The German stared hard at Tweed before he spoke.

'And now,' he began, 'I need information. I have helped you in the past and you can return the favour. By telling me what you know about Sherwood, about the attack on yourself outside the hotel – about *everything*, please.'

Tweed nodded agreement, began talking. Paula listened, fascinated. Tweed, speaking rapidly, could impart more information, relating events in sequence, more concisely than any man she'd ever known. Finding Jean at Amber Cottage ... events at Bosham ... in London ... data gathered so far on Walvis. The only details he omitted were any reference to Ziggy Palewski and the trips to Berg by Cardon and Marler.

At an early stage in his recitation there had been a knock on the door. Paula, her .32 Browning in one hand, had answered the door, taken the envelope addressed to Tweed from the messenger.

She handed it to him, but he was in full swing, seeing in his mind's eye the events he was describing. He put the envelope in his pocket without stopping talking.

The taxi had gone when Newman pressed the bell at the side of the tall grille gates which were closed across the arcade entrance to the Walvis building. He put his frozen hands in his pockets, spoke to Lisa who stood by his side.

'If anyone does come, you do the talking. They're expecting you. I'm Wilson, your bodyguard at this late hour.'

'Got it. And someone is coming.'

Newman watched the dark-coated squat figure

207

approaching. He had already noticed the grille was protected with an alarm system.

'We are expected by Mr Walvis,' Lisa said through the grille in a confident tone. 'Lisa Trent for an interview. Now please open the damned gates – it's freezing out here.'

'You will come at this late hour,' the watchman grumbled in German as he stepped several paces back and pressed something in the wall. Deactivating the alarm, Newman observed. Lisa then exploded.

'This late hour was the suggestion of your boss, Mr Walvis. I shall complain to him about your atrocious manners . . .'

The watchman moved faster, closed the gates when they had entered, reactivated the alarm, escorted them to the end of the arcade and inside to a reception area with a bank of elevators. Lisa noticed he did not use the phone. Newman observed he paused briefly by the reception desk, pressed something under an overlapping ledge. A button to warn someone they were on their way.

Without saying a word the watchman led them into an open elevator, pushed his thumb against the tenth-floor light. Doors closed, they began to ascend. Lisa took hold of Newman's arm. She seemed genuinely nervous. When the door opened a tall, well-built man, clean shaven, in his forties and with a face as red as a sunset stood there.

'Welcome,' he said to Lisa. He looked at her companion and recognition showed in his eyes. He had grinned toothily at Lisa but now he glared at Newman and became pompous. 'The appointment was for Miss Trent alone. Who are you?'

'For starters,' Newman said aggressively as they stepped out of the elevator, 'who are you, mate?'

'I am Martin . . .'

'Martin who?' Newman rapped back.

'Martin is my surname. You are Robert Newman, the notorious foreign correspondent . . .'

'Then why play games and ask me who I am? Walvis makes an appointment late at night in an apparently empty office building . . .'

'*Mr* Walvis, if you please . . .'

'Lord Walvis. He doesn't mean a thing to me. But I am here as escort and bodyguard to Miss Trent. Now, take us to Walvis and stop wasting time. Our time. I don't give a fig for yours.'

Martin swallowed. Newman had already recognized this toad from Philip's description as the man who organized the attempt to kill him. Dressed in an expensive blue business suit with chalk stripes, Martin was obviously at a loss as to how to deal with a novel situation. He got a grip on himself, stood very upright, addressing Lisa.

'Mr Walvis sends you his apologies but a business crisis has cropped up and makes it impossible for him to meet you. So instead you will be interviewing Miss Rosa Brandt.'

'Oh, not again,' Lisa protested. 'This happened last time. I was sidetracked before to Miss Brandt.'

'A business crisis?' Newman enquired. 'Lost one of his satellites, has he?' He looked at Lisa. 'Might as well see the Brandt lady again. Saves a completely wasted visit. Lead on, Macduff.'

'The name is Martin,' their pompous escort snapped as he led them down a corridor.

'Never heard of Shakespeare,' Newman said to Lisa in a loud aside. 'The people they employ as flunkeys these days.'

'I am Mr Walvis's deputy,' Martin threw venomously over his shoulder.

'Oh? So where does Gulliver fit into this crooked set-up,' Newman taunted.

He saw Martin's shoulders stiffen, his hands clench. He did not look round and opened a door leading off the corridor which had no name on it.

'Miss Brandt, Miss Trent has arrived for the interview.'

'I'd mug up Shakespeare if I were you,' Newman said over his own shoulder as they entered the room. 'It might lift the tone of this place. Educate yourself, Martin.'

The door closed behind them and Newman had his first sight of Rosa Brandt.

'I am so regretful that Mr Walvis cannot see you, Miss Trent. He works all the hours and has very little sleep. I remember we once talked before.'

Newman said nothing as he studied the woman who had stood up behind her Chippendale desk. Everything about her clothes was black – from her high-necked dress with long puffed sleeves and the black cap which concealed her hair to the veil which masked her face.

He tried to see behind the veil but the mesh was so fine he could only discern a faint suggestion of well-moulded features. Only the shapely mouth – her lipstick was a tasteful pink – and her strong chin were exposed to view. She appeared to be slim, her movements elegant.

'Please sit down, both of you.' She indicated two hard-backed chairs in front of her desk. 'And it is an honour to meet you also, Mr Newman. I have read many of your articles and have always found them thought provoking. A pity you write so rarely these days. Now, Miss Trent, how can I help you?'

Newman and Lisa had sat down and Lisa crossed her legs to suggest she was there to stay for quite a long time. It was Newman who asked the question.

'It would be helpful if we knew what Mr Walvis looks like. A description would help Miss Trent to produce a readable profile.'

'I fear that is out of the question.' Rosa had also sat down and was very erect. 'Mr Walvis guards his privacy very jealously.'

'Why?' prodded Newman.

'He has so many important projects – can you imagine how much of his valuable time would be wasted if we became involved with the press? And so many foolish rumours are circulated about him . . .'

'The way to kill them,' Lisa suggested, taking over the interview, 'would be one long frank piece about what his objectives are – what he is trying to achieve.'

'His powers of concentration are unique,' Rosa remarked clasping her hands on the desk. 'He can recall word for word any conversation he will have with people.'

'Which could be a pretty limited number,' Newman pointed out. 'Considering how few people he ever meets.'

'I am meaning with deputies who run his empire, the personages like that,' Rosa replied with a trace of acid in her tone.

'My Memory Man. He could do a music hall turn.'

'Music hall?'

'Vaudeville, the Americans used to call it.'

'Vaudeville?' Rosa was showing signs of confusion. 'I do not understand.'

'Doesn't matter,' Newman went on. 'You mentioned his empire. So how much further can he expand his system? How much larger can he make his empire?' he explained as she still showed signs of not comprehending.

'Future plans? Is that what you ask me about?'

Lisa had left Newman to make the running. She was studying Rosa, her movements. There was a hint of Teutonic accent in the way she spoke. She used her hands frequently, pausing, as though careful what she said.

'Future plans, yes,' Newman continued, warming up. 'He has world communications in his pocket . . .'

'In his pocket?' Rosa queried.

211

'At his command, under his control. So where else can he go? How can he make his empire any bigger?'

A red light flashed on and off on a compact console Rosa had to one side of her desk. She stood up, checking with one hand to make sure her veil was in place. Her manner became hostile.

'I have to ask you to leave at this very moment. Mr Walvis wanted to see me when you arrived. I have the duties to perform . . .'

'Then I'll have to use my imagination when writing my piece for the *Washington Post*,' Lisa said, suddenly aggressive. 'I'm particularly intrigued by the change of name of his organization – to Danubex. Bob Newman thinks there is *the* major story.'

Newman showed no reaction but was startled. He had never said anything of the sort but Lisa's ploy was surprisingly effective.

The red light on the console flashed on and off twice and Rosa Brandt sat down again. Her whole body was rigid and he sensed she had become even more alert – with tension.

'You suggest you will make up the crazy story about Mr Walvis?' she enquired, her manner very feline, leaning forward closer to her interviewer.

'I didn't say that. I'm a financial analyst and someone supplied me with photocopies of certain documents showing how Mr Walvis operates.'

'Operates in what way?'

'Oh, the pressure he exerts on the owners of companies he wishes to acquire. Including one or two cases where an owner refused to sell and was killed shortly afterwards in a most convenient hit-and-run accident. I make no accusations,' Lisa went on in a genial manner, 'but I do my research before I conduct an interview . . .'

The console's red light flashed again. Just once as it had done the first time. Rosa stood up again, made a

212

dismissive gesture with her hand, her voice cold.

'You both know the way out. This interview is terminated. Please leave the very moment. Do not forget the libel law is the most powerful.'

'You know,' Newman began, standing up as he spoke to Lisa, 'something tells me we've outstayed our welcome. I think we should take the lady's kind suggestion . . .'

Rosa Brandt left the room by another door while they were still moving. Newman turned, waved a hand at a distant corner, called out.

'Goodbye, Mr Walvis. I am sorry if you didn't enjoy the conversation.'

'What on earth are you doing, Bob?' Lisa whispered as she grasped the handle of the door leading to the elevators.

'Oh, Walvis had a hidden camera recording us. I've no doubt he watched us on a screen in another room – and I faintly heard a tape machine recording every word. I'm sure Walvis also heard every word. Hence his signalling to Rosa with that red light on the console. You've put the wind up him . . .'

Lisa opened the door, stepped out into the wide corridor, followed by Newman. They both stopped suddenly. Newman slipped his hand inside his jacket to grip the butt of his Smith & Wesson.

'If I even see that gun, you're dead,' said Gulliver, who stood in front of the bank of elevators.

Pear Shape was holding a Luger by his side. Behind him Martin was standing and for once he wasn't smiling. Two more men, wearing dark overcoats, hands in their pockets, were flanking their bosses. Newman had the impression it was Gulliver who was in command in this situation.

'If it ever went public,' Gulliver continued in the same brutal voice, 'it was self-defence on our part. Your

213

fingerprints are on your weapon, the gun you have just let go of.'

'Miss Trent might tell a different story,' Newman snapped back.

'Miss Trent?' Gulliver's fat, fleshy face showed indifference. He rolled his eyes to heaven. 'What makes you think she will ever be seen again? Let alone that it will ever be known she arrived here?'

22

In the suite at the Four Seasons the exchange of information between Tweed and Kuhlmann had been going on for some time. At an early stage Tweed had asked Paula to order from room service.

'Plenty of good sandwiches – a variety – and two bottles of champagne.'

'Pushing the boat out, aren't we?' Kuhlmann had joked. 'Is that the correct phrase?' he had asked Paula.

The German prided himself on speaking idiomatic English and liked to use colloquialisms.

'Perfect,' she had assured him, and began giving the order over the phone.

At a later stage Kuhlmann described his arrival at the Bayerischer Hof to examine the body of Captain David Sherwood. He produced a notebook, kept it on his lap.

'I got there just before the pathologist. I like to do that so I can see for myself – as soon as he's checked the corpse he sends it off to the mortuary. I asked him what was the cause of death. Chap called Dunkel I'd met and disliked before—'

'That,' Paula interjected, after ordering the meal, 'is a

superb bit of English. Must remember it. "I'd met and disliked before." Love it. Do go on.'

'Dunkel is a smart-arse,' the German went on. 'He said to me, "Can't you see the bullet hole through his chest?" I said I had actually observed that but why was his face twisted in a rictus of agony?'

'Oh, here we go again,' Tweed commented.

'You've got it,' Kuhlmann agreed. 'The pathologist quack said he couldn't say anything definite until blah-blah-blah. But his first impression was cyanide was involved in the death. I'd already had the description of Sherwood's dinner companion. That, plus the murder technique, added up to one word.'

'Teardrop,' Paula said quietly.

'Exactly.' Kuhlmann looked at Tweed as two waiters arrived with trolley-loads of food when Paula answered their knock on the door. 'You might like to see this note Sherwood made in his notebook. There's no Magda Franz listed in the Munich directory. There wouldn't be, of course . . .'

He had dropped his voice until the waiters left. Handing the notebook to Tweed he gratefully took a ham sandwich off the plate Paula was holding. She poured champagne.

Tweed frowned as he studied Sherwood's note.

Dinner with Magda Franz. A most intriguing lady. Speaks perfect idiomatic English. Wonder when I'll be able to see her in all her glory without the veil.

'I find that *very* interesting,' he commented, handing the notebook back to Kuhlmann, who passed it to Paula.

'Well, doesn't seem to take us much further,' she remarked and gave it back to the German. 'So why do you find it so very interesting?' she asked Tweed.

'Cheers!' Tweed replied, raising his glass.

'All right, be secretive,' she rapped back, nettled.

'Switching the subject,' Tweed went on after consuming

215

a sandwich, 'I find two coincidences hard to accept at face value. One was the sudden arrival of Jill Selborne when we were talking to Sherwood.'

'And who is this Jill Selborne?' Kuhlmnn demanded, his manner suddenly very alert.

Tweed explained how Monica, researching Walvis, discovered that four years earlier he had been married to a Jill Selborne, that it wasn't known whether the marriage had been dissolved. 'So,' he went on, 'Monica found she had a London address and Newman went there on the off-chance of contacting her. He was lucky – she was at home, they had a chat. While she was out of the room Newman noticed she had concealed a suitcase under some piece of draped furniture. Label gave Munich as her destination, the Bayerischer Hof as her hotel.'

'So she turns up there. Don't see anything suspicious about that,' Kuhlmann commented.

'Then there is the case of Lisa Trent,' Tweed persisted. 'I told you how we met her at Bosham – another strange coincidence – and Newman later took her out to dinner. She works for the notoriously tough New York outfit of financial investigators, Aspen & Schneider Associates. She told Bob she also was flying to Munich, would be staying at this hotel.'

'Still doesn't excite me,' Kuhlmann said with the same lack of enthusiasm.

'I'm musing on the possible identity of Teardrop,' Tweed said vaguely.

'Fail to see any connection. What's the matter?'

Tweed had remembered the note Paula had handed him earlier. He read it once.

'Oh, my God! Newman must be mad. He's gone to see Walvis. And guess who with – Lisa Trent.'

He passed the note to the German, who scanned the message, jumped up and ran to the telephone.

*   *   *

216

No sirens were screaming, no red lights flashing as the convoy of three patrol cars raced down Maximilian-strasse. Kuhlmann was chewing on his cigar by the side of the driver of the first car. As the vehicle skidded to a halt on the ice outside the entrance to Walvis's headquarters Kuhlmann dived out, followed by other uniformed officers armed with automatic weapons. He pressed his thumb on the bell by the grille gates closing off the arcade and kept it there.

The night guard came clumping down the arcade, furious and shining his powerful torch on Kuhlmann. The German lowered his large head, held up his identity folder, bellowed as the guard began grumbling.

'Police! If these damned gates aren't opened up inside ten seconds my men will open them up – with their machine-pistols . . .'

'Hold on there . . .'

'Five of the ten seconds have gone.' He turned to one of his men. 'Norbert, I'm going to start counting . . .'

'I'm opening the gates,' the guard protested.

He had switched off the alarm as he passed it. As soon as he had unlocked one gate and was starting to open it Kuhlmann's large hand wrenched it aside, he waved the identity folder in the man's face.

'You can't come bursting in here—' the guard began.

Kuhlmann grabbed him by the collar, pushed him against the wall inside the arcade, his face close to the guard's.

'Listen, doorman . . .'

'I'm in charge of security . . .'

'I said *listen*, clod. Any attempt to warn your people inside that we're here and I'll put *you* inside for obstruction. A man and a woman arrived here within the last hour. Which floor did you take them to? Answer! This is an emergency!'

The guard made the mistake of waving his heavy

217

flashlight to stop Kuhlmann, half choking him. The flashlight grazed Kuhlmann's jaw.

'That's it!' Kuhlmann roared. 'I'm charging you with
aggravated assault of a police officer.' He loosened his
grip. 'Stop stalling. Take us immediately to the right
floor.'

'The tenth,' the guard mumbled.

'Hurry!' Kuhlmann growled.

Letting go of the guard, he grasped him again by the
scruff of the neck as the man turned round, frog-marched
him down the arcade to the double doors at the end. Ten
of his men followed him, all with weapons in their hands.

The guard had left one of the double doors unlocked
and he was hustled through into the lobby beyond. Still
holding him, Kuhlmann propelled him to the bank of
elevators where one stood open. The elevator was
spacious and Kuhlmann and his battle force crammed
inside it, Kuhlmann staying at the front, still holding the
guard.

'Tenth floor!' Kuhlmann snapped. 'And no warning of
our approach. If you're taking us to the wrong floor you'll
be inside a cell for the rest of your life. Probably as an
accessory to murder . . .'

The guard had pressed the indicator for the tenth floor.
The elevator climbed. Behind him Kuhlmann could feel
his men arranging themselves for an all-out onslaught as
the guard's morale collapsed.

'I took a man and a woman up to the tenth floor. They
said they had an appointment . . .'

'An appointment with death?' Kuhlmann enquired in a
soft voice which scared the guard even more.

'This is a business headquarters . . .'

'I know. Dirty business . . .'

Kuhlmann stopped as the elevator came to a halt, the
doors opened.

*   *   *

218

Gulliver stood with his back to the elevator as the doors opened behind him. He was raising the Luger in his right hand, aiming it at Newman. The Englishman had stepped in front of Lisa Trent, who stood frozen. Kuhlmann pressed the muzzle of his Walther against the nape of Gulliver's neck and thundered at the top of his voice.

'*Kriminalpolizei!* Everyone freeze!'

He had spoken in German. His men, members of the special anti-terrorist force, had leapt out of the elevator, moving round in a crouch, weapons held in clear view. Martin had had his right hand inside the jacket of his smart business suit. Two policemen reached him, each grabbing one arm of their target, forcing Martin's arms above his head and against the wall. The other two thugs endured similar treatment. The action took only seconds.

'OK! OK!' Gulliver called out in English, his pear shape quivering with shock.

'Not OK,' Kuhlmann said in his ear, reverting to English. 'Drop the flaming Luger.'

The weapon thudded on the floor. Kuhlmann moved into the centre of the wide lobby. Martin had been released by the two policemen who had relieved him of a Walther. In the process they had pulled out his silk shirt, torn it. Martin sucked in a deep breath, protested, trying to assert his authority before Gulliver recovered.

'This is an outrage. Look at what your men have done to my shirt.'

'Spoil your beauty sleep, will it?' Kuhlmann asked with a savage grin. 'Some business you operate – the staff carries guns.'

'I am the Deputy Managing Director,' Martin began huffily.

'So am I,' chimed in Gulliver.

'Both carrying guns,' Kuhlmann growled. 'You may face charges of kidnapping Mr Newman and Miss Trent – that's for starters,' he continued in English. 'Looked to

219

me like a murder was about to take place,' he accused Gulliver.

Newman moved close to Kuhlmann, whispered to the German who kept staring round.

'The second door along the corridor behind us is the office of a woman, Rosa Brandt, who fits perfectly the known description of Teardrop.'

'Right.' Kuhlmann's voice raised the roof as he glared at Gulliver and Martin. 'Come with me – both of you. Make with the feet . . .'

He strode down the corridor with Newman as the two men he had given the order to followed reluctantly. Reaching the door Newman had indicated, he hammered on it with his clenched fist. The door felt unusually solid. He turned on Gulliver and Martin after trying the handle.

'Open up this door. I mean yesterday.'

'Not possible,' Martin said smoothly, having regained his composure.

Kuhlmann stabbed at Martin's chest with his thick finger. Martin looked a mess, shirt half out of his trousers, the rips showing. He became less confident and it was Gulliver who replied.

'We can't. The main office doors, this one included, are on a time lock when they are closed by the occupant who is leaving for the night.'

'Then we'll have to smash it open.'

'You'll have great trouble,' Gulliver told him with a malicious smile. 'The doors are constructed of a special steel.'

'Wipe the smirk off your face!' the German shouted at him. 'Take me to Walvis's office.'

'I'm sorry' – Gulliver was conciliatory, taken aback by the ferocity of Kuhlmann's expression – 'but that door is also on a time lock. In any case, and I do wish to co-operate with you, Mr Walvis has left for his farm in the country.'

'I should warn you,' Martin began, determined to

reassert his authority now that Gulliver was crawling, 'Mr Walvis will undoubtedly be complaining to the Minister about your outrageous intrusion.'

'Erich,' Kuhlmann called to one of his men. 'Escort Mr Newman while he checks every door in this corridor.' He slowly lit his cigar while he studied Martin, who shifted his feet uneasily. 'Outrage?' He puffed on his cigar. 'And Mr Walvis will be complaining to the Bavarian Minister we know he has in his pocket?'

'I find that phrase . . .' Martin began.

'Insulting?' Kuhlmann enquired softly.

'Well, I don't remember using that word . . .'

'But you were about to!' Kuhlmann advanced on Martin who took several steps back until the wall stopped him. 'Outrageous!' he thundered. 'I arrive to find Gulliver pointing a gun at Newman, presumably about to shoot him . . .'

'I am in charge of security,' Gulliver protested. 'I was insisting these intruders left the building at once . . .'

'Crap,' said Newman, who had returned with Erich. 'All the doors are locked,' he informed Kuhlmann. 'Intruders, Gulliver said. We came here by appointment, we interviewed Rosa Brandt . . .'

'Prove it,' Gulliver sneered. 'And where is my Luger, my personal property – and I do have a permit?'

'One of my men,' Kuhlmann informed him mildly, 'has taken your gun, placed it in an evidence bag. It carries your fingerprints. You may well face a serious charge.' He looked back at Martin. 'As for a complaint to your Minister, I shall be phoning the Chancellor in Bonn in the morning. He will be interested to know how Walvis conducts his business.'

'I think I should apologize. Surely we can forget this whole unpleasant incident,' Martin went on. 'I apologize also to Mr Newman and Miss Trent for any inconvenience we may have caused them . . .'

221

'I may be prepared to accept your apology,' Lisa said, speaking for the first time, 'providing I have the apology in writing delivered to me by hand at the Four Seasons by tomorrow at the latest.'

'I'll see what I can do,' Martin mumbled, taken aback by her aggressiveness.

'No you won't,' Lisa snapped, her face grim, 'you'll just do it.'

'And,' Newman interjected, 'you can give us the address of Rosa Brandt.'

'Can't do that . . .' Martin began.

'Can't do that . . .' Gulliver said in unison.

'Tweedledum and Tweedledee,' Kuhlmann commented contemptuously.

'We want her address,' Newman insisted.

'We don't know where she lives,' Martin protested. 'Only Mr Walvis knows that.'

'What about my two guards' weapons?' Gulliver demanded. 'I saw your thugs taking them, putting them into those damn bags.'

'For evidence,' Kuhlmann informed him. 'For checking by Ballistics. Maybe they've been used to kill someone. We are now going,' he announced. 'I can't stand this bunch of clowns a moment longer . . .'

Kuhlmann took Newman and Lisa away in the lead patrol car, dropped them off at the Four Seasons. He explained he had machinery to set in motion.

Newman sat Lisa down in a chair in the lounge, ordered her a drink, went by himself to the phone, called Tweed in the suite, asked if it was convenient to bring Lisa up with him. Tweed agreed it was a good idea, told him to hurry.

Tweed and Paula were the only occupants of the suite when Newman and Lisa entered. Newman started to give

222

Tweed a concise account of what had happened when Tweed stopped him, jumped up.

'Paula, you know Lisa from Bosham. Entertain her until Bob and I get back . . .'

With Newman he hurried to Pete Nield's room. Inside he found Butler and Nield, the remnants of a meal for three on the table and – to his surprise – Philip.

'Thought you'd gone back to the Platzl,' he said.

'I decided I'd stay here and fill in Harry and Pete with my experiences today. We all need briefing up to the hilt on this one—'

'Splendid,' Tweed interrupted. 'Harry, Pete, I want you to take your hired cars immediately to the Walvis building. Philip will tell you how to find it. Maybe, Bob, you ought to join them.'

'Object of the exercise?' asked the laconic Butler.

'To follow anyone who leaves that building. I need to know the location of a farm in the country where Walvis is supposed to have gone.'

'Instead of Bob, I should go too,' Philip said firmly. 'I can identify Martin – I got a good look at him when they tried to kill me out at Berg. I caught a glimpse of him when I was almost caught in Walvis's office.'

'You must be tired,' Tweed said doubtfully.

'Not after the full-dress meal I've just had. I want to be in on this – I have a personal interest,' he added.

'I do really want to hear Bob's full account of what he experienced this evening,' Tweed ruminated. 'All right, Philip. The three of you had better get moving . . . And watch it. This could be dangerous . . .'

'You let Philip go to keep his mind occupied,' Newman suggested as they walked back to the suite.

'Yes, I did,' Tweed admitted. 'It's significant he went to Nield's room instead of back to the Platzl. He wanted to

223

be where the action might break. I can still see the pain in his eyes . . .'

He relocked the door after Paula had let them into the suite. There was a relaxed atmosphere when they entered – Paula and Lisa had been chattering away like magpies. Tweed got down to brass tacks the moment he was settled in his chair.

'Bob, you have total recall of a conversation. While it's fresh in your mind I want you to report every word of the conversation with Rosa Brandt, her expressions, her gestures.'

Newman, perching himself on the end of the couch where Lisa and Paula sat, began to recreate the scene and the words of the interview with Rosa Brandt. Paula watched Tweed who leaned back against a cushion, his eyes half closed as he took in every word, saw in his mind's eye what Newman was describing.

'That's about it,' he said eventually. He looked down at Lisa. 'Did I omit anything?'

'Bob, you didn't miss a trick.' Lisa looked up at him. 'I don't play up to men, but I could never have given such a complete record and I was there.'

'What was your impression of Rosa Brandt?' Tweed asked her.

'Cold as the ice outside. A really chilling woman.'

'Interesting comment.' Tweed looked again at Newman as he cleaned his glasses on his handkerchief. 'Are you confident that you relayed every single word of every phrase she used when talking to you? And I do mean every word – her manner of speaking when she was fencing with you?'

'Every single word.'

'Thank you.' Tweed replaced his glasses, clasped his hands together and gazed into the distance. 'I find what you told me of great significance.'

'In what way?' Paula asked.

224

'I won't elaborate now. I might just be wrong. Another important bonus – despite the fact that it must have been scary for you, Lisa – is Kuhlmann's assault on Walvis's staff. It will, I'm sure, rattle Mr Walvis when he hears about it. That might just lead to an event I'm anxious to bring about.'

'Which is?' Paula asked.

'Let's wait and see whether it happens. I wonder how Philip and the others are getting on? I set them a very tricky task. I hope nothing goes wrong . . .'

23

'That's Martin. He's my meat,' Philip said tersely.

He was parked some distance from the entrance to the Walvis building in the BMW loaned to him by Ziggy Palewski. By his side Pete Nield sat in the passenger seat. It had stopped snowing and Philip had been watching the exit from the building through night glasses.

Even though it was night and Martin was clad in a sheepskin and a fur hat Philip had a clear view of his red face as Martin passed under a street light before climbing behind the wheel of a blue Audi.

'Get out of the car,' Philip snapped. 'I'm going to lose him.'

'Get moving, then,' Nield snapped back. 'I'm staying with you. My car wouldn't start,' he lied.

'Jump out, damn you, and get into Harry's car . . .'

'No can do,' Nield replied in more soothing tones. 'I've arranged with Butler to wait in case Gulliver appears. Martin, we feel sure, is the number one target.'

225

'Blast you, I like to operate on my own . . .'

Philip started the BMW moving as Martin's car was on the verge of disappearing. He had no way of knowing Butler and Nield had arranged that Nield would stay with Philip. They both felt he was too emotionally involved to be left on his own.

'Sorry I swore at you,' Philip said as he drove on while he could still see where Martin was going. 'OK. We'll do it together.'

'But you're the boss,' Nield replied briefly.

'Is that tact?' Philip enquired.

'No, it sums up my attitude. Now I wonder, Martin, where you can be going at this time of night. You seem to be in one hell of a rush . . .'

He lapsed into silence, thankful that he had negotiated the awkward process of getting Philip to accept his company. Soon they were leaving the brooding city behind, driving along an autobahn into open country.

The moon was shining out of a clear sky and ice crystals glittered on the road surface. On either side flat countryside stretched away, the fields covered with a blanket of snow. There was more traffic on the autobahn than Nield would have expected and he commented on the fact.

'It's weird,' Philip replied. 'This is the autobahn to the airport. Surely Martin can't be flying off somewhere tonight.'

'Let's wait and see,' said Nield, who was studying his Kummerly & Frey map. 'At the moment we're on autobahn A9 – bound for the airport and Nuremberg and – eventually – Berlin.'

'So maybe it's going to be a long drive. One thing, their security is slipping, I'm pleased to note.'

'In what way?'

'Martin is driving the same blue Audi they used to try and kill me down at Berg. He should have changed cars . . .'

226

The traffic began to thin out. Philip let out a grunt of triumph. Nield grinned and spoke.

'This could be interesting. He's driven past the turn-off to the airport.'

'So I noticed. We could be on to a winner. And that BMW I'm staying well behind masks us beautifully. Somehow I don't think Martin has cottoned on to the idea he might be followed . . .'

'Now we're on autobahn A92,' Nield remarked. 'After a long stretch it leads to a place called Deggendorf.'

'I know,' said Philip, who had studied the map earlier. He omitted to mention that Grafenau and the Czech border lay to the east of Deggendorf. Philip was still struggling with his conscience – wanting to play his own hand and yet uncomfortable that he had not told Tweed what he had overheard in Walvis's office while hiding in the cupboard.

Grafenau – where Walvis exiled subordinates to as a punishment. The Czech border – where Sherwood had said training camps were located for some sinister purpose. Passau, which Walvis had also mentioned. The one thing he would never tell anyone was where Palewski was hiding out – in Salzburg.

'He's going a long way out into wild country,' commented Nield.

'We'll just keep after him . . .'

The autobahn stretched ahead in the moonlight. It had two lanes in each direction. Their two lanes were separated from the two coming in the opposite direction by a wide central island planted with snow-covered small trees and shrubs beyond the steel barrier.

Glancing out of his window every now and again Philip saw in the distance isolated villages. Snow had melted, exposing the steep red-tiled roofs of houses, the small red spire of a tiny church. Some people really did live in the wilderness, he thought.

227

'He's turning off the autobahn,' Nield said.

Martin's blue Audi had swung up a slip road and crossed a bridge over the autobahn. Philip followed at a discreet distance. Beyond the bridge they saw the blue Audi a long way off, travelling down a cart track into open country. Philip slowed down and the track became bumpy with hidden potholes. They felt the crackle of ice breaking under them. Despite having the heaters going full blast it was becoming cold inside the BMW. Philip had kept the wipers moving to keep the windscreen clear of a film of ice. The track dropped into a deep gulley.

'Can't see Martin's Audi now,' Philip remarked.

'But I caught a glimpse of a large farmhouse which could be where he's headed for. Looked like a very old and large farm complex. We may have hit pay dirt . . .'

Martin was frozen stiff as he approached the farmhouse. He wore heavy gloves, his sheepskin, his fur hat, but the white teeth he was proud of were chattering. He clenched them together, thankful he had almost reached his destination as the solid wooden gates came into view.

Earlier he had nervously checked to make sure he was not being followed but the BMW which had worried him had taken the turn-off to the airport. From that moment on he rarely glanced in his rear-view mirror.

The normally confident arrogant Martin was nervous for several reasons. Always he travelled with armed bodyguards, but Walvis's phone call summoning him into this bleak wasteland had emphasized he must come alone.

He was nervous because during their phone conversation he had started to give Walvis an account of that pig Kuhlmann and his raid on headquarters. Walvis had cut him off in mid-sentence.

'Not over the phone, idiot. Get your lazy backside out

228

here and then report to me. Come alone. You heard me? *Alone* . . .'

The connection had been broken before Martin could reply. Martin was nervous because he was very unsure of the reception he would meet when confronted by Walvis. As he bumped along over the infernal potholed track he recalled a mistake he had once made while talking to Walvis.

'That track out here is an obstacle course to drive over. Surely we could have a proper road laid . . .'

'Your head is a block of wood,' Walvis had replied.

'I don't understand . . .' Martin had begun.

'A normal state of affairs. I will explain to you in words of one syllable. That wreck of a track is an added defence for the farmhouse, my most important command post.'

Walvis was fond of using military terms. He often spoke like a general commanding a vast army poised to attack. Which, Martin had reflected, described coming events very well.

Now he paused as the track climbed out of the gully into flatland. With the Audi stationary, he opened a side window a centimetre. The icy night air flooded in, dispersing the fug which had built up. Martin wriggled in his seat, took in deep breaths to clear his head. He would need a clear head when he met Walvis.

After a minute he hastily closed the window, tried to turn up the heaters a little more but they were full on. The air had made him feel better, more able to cope. He drove on, cresting a rise which gave him an overall view of the farmhouse complex.

The main farmhouse building was massive, built of wood and with a wing projecting at either end, so the edifice enclosed a vast paved courtyard. Its steep roof, covered with snow, was like a ski run and had a series of dormer windows located on the first floor. Inside the ranch-style fence running a long distance round the

229

property were a number of large outbuildings, also constructed of wood. Some were linked to the farmhouse by wooden roofed corridors which reminded Martin of the famous covered bridge at Lucerne in Switzerland. Taking a deep breath, he pressed the horn three times and the right-hand gate opened to admit him.

Three minutes later he was ushered into the presence. Martin had hardly time to take off his outdoor clothes, check his appearance in a full-length mirror, stuffing the ruined shirt inside his trousers, adjust his tie, comb his thick black hair and apply eau-de-Cologne to his forehead.

'I could do with a quick shower,' he suggested to his master.

'Later. Sit.' A podgy finger indicated a hard-backed chair. 'Talk.'

The large, long sitting-room was luxuriously furnished with English chairs and couches and antiques which Walvis preferred to German. He was sitting in an outsize armchair to one side of a deep alcove where a wood fire crackled and flamed. Two shortened tree trunks threw out a fierce heat. The hard-backed chair was close to this inferno.

Walvis was clad in a velvet smoking jacket which just encompassed his huge bulk. He wore a white dinner shirt and a black tie with black trousers. He had spoken in a very quiet voice, which unnerved Martin. To one side of the room a door was half open. Martin began speaking.

'I think you had just left the building with Rosa by the rear exit when—'

'I had. Describe what happened.'

Martin was disconcerted by the fact that Walvis hadn't even glanced at him. He stared into the fire as Martin began with a sentence he had prepared.

'Kuhlmann burst out of the elevator with his storm troopers . . .'

230

'No dramatics, please. Just the facts. Newman and Lisa Trent were there. Proceed.'

Martin swallowed. He had intended to embroider his account, demonstrating how he had been in command of the situation. He decided it would be wiser to tell the truth, however humiliating his own role might seem, but leaving out how Kuhlmann had dominated him.

He spoke for five minutes, using as few words as possible. Walvis couldn't stand waffle. Martin was becoming physically more uncomfortable every second as the heat from the fire roasted him. His hands, frozen before, tingled painfully. He attempted at one stage to shift his chair away from the fire. The podgy finger pointed again.

'Sit still. Don't move your chair. Continue.'

Walvis was sipping a glass of champagne. By his side was a bottle in an ice bucket supported in a tripod. Walvis made no suggestion that Martin might like a glass as his subordinate went on explaining what had happened. He even refilled his glass, again without a glance in Martin's direction.

'Go on speaking,' he said at one stage.

Walvis had heaved himself out of the chair. The windows were masked by blinds and he had noticed one blind was not completely closed. He attended to it, padded back to his chair as Martin completed his account of the events at headquarters.

'You have left something out, haven't you?'

Walvis sighed, indicating infinite patience with a fool as he sagged back into the chair.

'I don't think so . . .'

'Your shirt is ruffled and ripped and torn.'

Martin inwardly cursed himself. He had left out the incident when Kuhlmann had grabbed hold of him, shoved him against a wall. He told Walvis about the incident.

'Was Tweed mentioned at any stage?' Walvis asked suddenly.

231

'No. Definitely not. Not a single mention.'

'Intriguing. Go to your quarters. I would recommend a long hot bath – not a shower. You are sweating like a bull. A reaction of your conscience, I expect. You have a conscience, haven't you, Martin? No need to reply. Just go.'

'I could do with something to eat . . .'

'Later. After the long hot bath. Go.'

Martin jumped up, left the room, relieved to get away from the silent inquisition, the disturbing quietness displayed by his chief. Walvis waited until he had closed the door, then called out.

'You can come in, Rosa, now. Tell me what you thought of Martin's account.'

Rosa Brandt, clad in her black dress, cap and veil, appeared from behind the half-open door. She sat in an armchair close to Walvis.

'I think he eventually told you the truth. He started, of course, by trying to save face.'

'Tweed organized this intrusion.'

'You are thinking that?'

'I am certain. The significance of that incident is that Tweed himself never appeared. We hardly know what Tweed looks like – except for the one photo of him in existence.'

'Perhaps he is rather like you,' Rosa suggested.

'A most profound observation. I sense Tweed is the cleverest and most dangerous adversary I have ever encountered. His presence disturbs me – with Tidal Wave being so close.'

'How close?' Rosa ventured.

'You know better than to ask questions like that, my dear. I even wonder whether I should arrange a clandestine meeting with Tweed. Just the two of us. So I can weigh him up for myself.'

'Would he trust you?'

232

'Not unless very elaborate security arrangements were agreed. Of course, he would then know what I look like.' Walvis's pouched eyelids were twitching and Rosa knew he was thinking furiously. He suddenly gave a great bellowing laugh. 'Going back over the years to the Cold War it would be like one of those old exchanges of captured agents at Checkpoint Charlie in Berlin. I would like to get his reaction to how I see the world and its future.'

'Think about it before you decide,' Rosa urged.

'I will do just that,' Walvis agreed.

Earlier, Philip had almost run into Martin's Audi and he thanked Heaven he had turned off his headlights, seeing his way by the light of the moon. He had climbed out of the gully to the crest and had seen the blue Audi entering the farmhouse courtyard, the gates closing behind it.

He thought quickly. In the cold night air the sound of the Audi's engine was loud and clear, which would hide the sound of his own engine. He drove forward, made a swift U-turn on the grass verge which had now appeared, drove back down into the gully, stopped.

'Might I ask what we – you – are doing?' Nield enquired.

'We're ready for a quick getaway back along the track. You stay here in the car. Get behind the wheel. If they get me drive like hell back to Munich so you can tell Tweed.'

'And what will you be up to?'

'I'm going to watch that farmhouse – you saw it?'

'Yes. A large place. You look down on it from that crest. You're taking a big chance.'

'Crouched down low, using my night-glasses to see what is going on down there, I should be OK. Keep the engine running – no one will hear it down here in the gully. And we have plenty of petrol.'

'Oh, I'll keep the engine running,' Nield assured him.

233

'You may freeze to death but I'm not going to . . .'

Philip got out of the car, closed the door quietly – the closing of a car door is a most distinctive sound, which carries a long way. He found a clump of frozen shrubs near the crest, crouched down behind them, buttoned his sheepskin up to his throat and began to scan the farmhouse complex with his glasses.

When the cold began to bother him he thought of his dead wife, Jean. He could feel tears forming behind his eyes and deliberately sucked in cold air. That quenched the rising emotion. He waited . . .

It seemed hours while he stayed crouched. He kept the glasses screwed to his eyes. Frequently he studied the blinds lowered over the windows of a room. Behind them brilliant lights blazed. One of the blinds was not completely lowered.

It happened without warning. He saw movement behind the blind only partially closed. He froze. But not with the cold. The silhouette of a huge shape appeared on the blind. It was a repeat performance of the massive silhouette he had seen appear against a glazed window when he was searching Walvis's study. The silhouette bent down, seemed even more massive. The blind was completely lowered, shutting off the thin band of light which had been present at the bottom.

Philip moved, still in a crouch, disappeared down inside the gully, straightened up. He wrenched open his door and Nield, startled, shifted to the passenger seat as Philip dived in behind the wheel, closing the door with care.

'They've spotted you?' Nield asked, his Walther in his hand.

'No!' There was grim triumph in Philip's tone. 'But we have discovered Walvis's secret hideaway. Walvis is actually there. Back to Munich and Tweed for us in double quick time . . .'

234

In the suite at the Four Seasons Tweed had suggested both Cardon and Nield should have a shower, a change of clothes, after they returned.

'Then you can tell me what you've discovered,' he said.

'That can wait,' Cardon replied.

'I'll hang in a bit longer, too,' Nield agreed.

Paula and Newman were sitting in the suite with Tweed and Paula said she'd get room service to bring up more bottles of champagne. Neither of the two arrivals objected to that.

'Have you heard from Butler?' Nield asked.

'Harry got back a while ago,' Tweed assured him. 'He's gone to bed. He was flaked out with lack of sleep. He had news but first let me hear how you got on . . .'

Nield let Philip tell the story of following Martin, finding the remote farmhouse. Tweed leaned forward when Philip described seeing the silhouette against the blind.

'You're confident that was Walvis?'

'Certain. He's huge, he moved in the same slow way as he did before he entered his office at Danubex head-quarters. It was Walvis all right,' Philip concluded, and sipped more of the champagne Paula had poured for him.

'We have made two mighty leaps forward tonight,' Tweed said almost to himself. 'Now, both of you, finish up your drinks, go to your rooms, have a shower and flop into bed. I have reserved a room for you, Philip.'

'Flop will be the word,' Nield said as the two men left the room.

'So what are the two mighty leaps forward?' enquired Paula.

'The first one is the experience Newman and Lisa Trent endured at the Walvis building. Kuhlmann's ferocious assault is the key. I feel sure that Martin was going out to that farmhouse to report to Walvis what had happened. I believe that Kuhlmann's invasion of Walvis's cage will have rattled our enemy. I expect he's still up, churning it over in his devious mind. It will have thrown him off balance and he will react. When he does he could make a huge mistake.'

'And the second leap?' Paula pressed.

'Philip and Pete finding Walvis's hideaway. Let's look at that map Philip marked the location on again.'

Paula unfolded the map Philip had left behind. She spread it out on a large table and the three of them gathered to study it. Tweed grunted with satisfaction.

'Interesting that it's on the way to the East. Let's sit down while I think for a few minutes. Finish up the rest of the champagne . . .'

Paula was marvelling at how fresh Tweed still seemed. He could get by on four hours' sleep a night. His stamina seemed limitless. She decided she felt like one of her rare cigarettes and asked Newman for one. He had just lit it when Tweed spoke and startled them.

'I need to know Walvis's psychology, what makes that man tick. The only way I can discover that is to meet him.'

'Which would be suicide,' Newman said promptly.

'I don't know. It might be arranged if we play our cards cleverly—'

He broke off as there was a tap on the door. When Newman checked it was Philip who walked in, dressed in

236

different clothes – a fawn polo-necked pullover and a pair of fawn slacks. Paula thought he looked grim.

'Hope you don't mind my coming back,' he said to Tweed. 'Had a shower, changed, found my brain was still in top gear.'

'Since you have come back,' Tweed mused, 'you might help with an idea I had. I know you have total visual recall of people and places. When you were hiding inside the cupboard you said the door wasn't closed properly, giving you a glimpse of the men who came into the room. Did you see enough of Walvis to describe him to Paula? She is very good at sketching Identikit pictures.'

Paula was already delving into her shoulder-bag. She took out the sketch block she always carried and a piece of charcoal.

'I could try,' Philip said uncertainly. 'Actually I will never forget the evil eyes, only half visible under his pouched lids, the huge head, the fat, fleshy face . . .'

'Stop!' Paula called out. 'Come and sit by me on the couch. I won't get it first time but don't be discouraged, I may have to make six sketches before you're satisfied I've got Walvis . . .'

Newman left the couch, went over to perch on the arm of Tweed's chair. They carried on a conversation in whispers so as not to distract Philip and Paula.

'Butler did well, following Gulliver when he came out of the building,' Newman recalled. 'I wonder what that huge old broken-down warehouse on the edge of Munich in a sleazy area contains.'

'Not as broken down as it looks,' Tweed reminded him. 'Butler prowled round the wall protecting it, found the alarm wire strung along the top. The gates, too, were guarded with a sophisticated alarm system. There's something inside that place Walvis doesn't want the outside world to know about.'

'Maybe we could get Kuhlmann to raid it?'

'Not yet. Let Walvis think the warehouse remains his secret. I think we've stirred him up enough for my purpose at the moment. Did you say you're having your breakfast with Lisa Trent?'

'Yes, tomorrow.' Newman checked his watch. 'No, today. You know, during that frightening interlude when Gulliver threatened us with his Luger she was as cold and calm as ice. She has a lot of guts. That I like.'

'You mean you like Lisa,' Paula called out. 'And a miracle has happened. Philip has described the subject so clearly I've got Walvis first time round – with a few minor adjustments.'

'Paula is very quick, a very good artist,' Philip commented.

'Well,' Tweed told them, 'since you're both so pleased with each other let's see the result.'

Paula brought over a small occasional table, placed the charcoal sketch in front of them. Newman stared at the sketch and winced.

'Lord! Is he really like that? Must be the ugliest man in the world.'

'You have just made a significant observation,' Tweed remarked. 'Which confirms what I have been thinking.'

'Which is?' Paula pounced.

'Just a theory. I'd have to meet Walvis to confirm it.'

'You keep talking about this mad idea of meeting Walvis,' Newman complained. 'I'd drop the whole thing if I were you.'

'But you're not me . . .'

Tweed was answering on automatic pilot. The greater part of his attention was on the sketch which he continued to stare at with intensity. Paula had produced a half-length portrait of Walvis down to his monstrous waist.

'His head is enormous,' Newman said. 'Heaven knows how much he weighs. And the face – its expression –

238

would curdle milk. No wonder he takes such pains to avoid being photographed. He's a massive evil hulk.'

'His appearance will have influenced his whole attitude to life and people,' Tweed said, thinking aloud. 'It could be that is one reason why his confidante is Rosa Brandt – and now I am wondering about her. If you feel the world has rejected you it might destroy for ever any remnants of humanity you once had.'

'But it's Walvis who looks so repellent,' Paula reminded him.

'That is true.'

He was still gazing at the sketch as though hypnotized by it. Leaning back, he studied it with his eyes half closed.

'Now you're being secretive again,' Paula accused. 'You haven't explained why Rosa should be the perfect companion and confidante for Walvis.'

'No, I haven't, have I? Paula, I would like to have this sketch framed so I can study it from time to time. The trouble is no one else must see the sketch.'

'Oh, I can solve that problem,' Paula assured him. 'I'll just make another sketch the same size – a sketch of an imaginary person who doesn't look a bit like Walvis. I can then take that to a frame-maker I found in a side street the last time we were here. They say they will frame a picture while you wait. Then I bring it back, take out the imaginary sketch and substitute Walvis.'

She jumped up, ran over to the telephone table, took a directory out of the drawer, found the page she was looking for, called out with a peal of triumph.

'Pfeiffer! I remembered the name because it's so unusual. For an English person, anyway. I can do the fake sketch now and take it to the frame maker in the morning. If you want me to?'

'Yes, please,' agreed Tweed.

'It is an excellent sketch,' Newman decided. 'Looking

239

at it you get the impression of a man who radiates immense power. Is it really a good likeness, Philip?'

'Frighteningly so.'

Newman was enjoying himself over breakfast at the Four Seasons in spite of having had very little sleep. His companion at the table was Lisa. She wore a polo-necked cashmere sweater, leopardskin ski pants tucked into knee-length boots and a diamond brooch on her left breast shaped like a cat.

'Do you mind if I have a cigarette?' she asked when she had finished her toast.

'I'll join you. How long ago would it be since you first interviewed Rosa Brandt? That is, unless you'd sooner not talk about last night.'

He had lit her cigarette, she blew a smoke ring, watched it float up and slowly disintegrate. She smiled as she shook her head.

'Don't mind a bit. Our little adventure with Messrs Martin and Gulliver is just one of those things. It goes with my territory.' She crinkled her smooth forehead. 'It would be about twelve months ago when I first tried to interview Walvis and got dumped with the charming Rosa.'

'Has she changed in any way since then?'

'Not one bit. I must stop repeating myself, using the same words too frequently. "Bit" is one of my favourites. No, it was the same Rosa, same voice, same mannerisms, even the same outfit. Just like a rerun of last time.' She glanced across the room. 'Oh, damnit, let's hope he hasn't seen me, although he's heading this way.'

'Who?'

'Ronald Weatherby . . .' She had adopted a woof-woof upper-class accent. 'He's one of the small British community in Munich. And a crashing great bore.'

240

'I think he has spotted you. What does he do – apart from being a bore?'

'A peculiar job. He acts as liaison agent between some of the world's biggest conglomerates. Soothes any dispute which arises between a couple of the giant corporations. Earns quite a packet, I gather. Brace yourself. Here it comes . . .'

'Ah, darling Lisa. The very sight of you is a wonderful way to start a grim day. I fear I intrude, but it is so long since we have met. Perhaps it would not be asking too much if I joined you for a cup of coffee.'

Weatherby was lean in build, servile in manner. He had an ingratiating smile, tufted eyebrows sandy in colour to match his untidy mop of sandy hair. His grey eyes flitted about, were never still and his face reminded Newman of a treacherous monkey. He kept licking his thin lips as he settled his lanky frame into a spare chair. Newman found him nauseating. Weatherby gazed at him.

'And of course here we have the most distinguished company. Mr Robert Newman, the most famous foreign correspondent in the whole world. How are you, Mr Newman?'

'I was fine a few moments ago, Weatherby.'

'Ronald. All my friends call me Ronnie. You are both staying at this magnificent hostelry?'

'Yes, Weatherby, we are.'

'Ronnie, please. Oh dear . . .' His expression became leeringly confidential. 'I do believe I have disturbed an intimate tête-à-tête.' His manner changed again as he addressed the waiter. 'Coffee. It must be freshly made. And bring a jug of hot milk. Have you got that, waiter?'

He turned away from the waiter who simply nodded with a blank expression.

'I must apologize if I appear to be not my normal self. Disturbing news from many quarters. At the moment I fear I cannot go public, as the Americans are always

241

saying. I belong to the old school, Mr Newman, and I am pleased to say I am a member of the small British community in this city. Some very refined people . . .'

'What's your job? How do you earn your living?' Newman suddenly threw at him.

'Well . . .' Weatherby sipped at the coffee which had appeared by return. He was obviously disconcerted by Newman's direct manner and Lisa suppressed a grin. 'Well, I suppose I could be called a negotiator . . .'

'Are you a negotiator? Either you are or you aren't,' Newman continued in the same aggressive tone.

'I suppose you're right. I do conduct negotiations between global organizations when there is an unfortunate clash of interests . . .'

'So is International & Cosmopolitan one of your customers?'

'Clients, Mr Newman, please. I, of course, know of Danubex and their remarkable president . . .'

'Then you've met Walvis?'

A receptionist appeared with a message for Newman inside an envelope. He opened the envelope, read the message without letting either of his dining companions see its contents.

Bob, please come and see me now. All hell is breaking loose. T.

'You have met Mr Walvis, then?' Newman repeated as he pushed back his chair, ready to leave.

'I do hope you won't mind my saying so,' Weatherby chattered on, 'but I find your manner almost that of an interrogator. Even intimidating.'

'I'm not over the moon about your manner either,' Newman shot back. He looked at Lisa. 'Have to go. Will be back as soon as I can.'

'Great,' said Lisa. 'Just great . . .'

She lifted a hand, pressed a wave of her blonde mane

242

over the side of her face to conceal it from Weatherby. Her expression spoke volumes. *You would go and leave me with this obnoxious little creep . . .*

'I suspect Walvis has launched the first phase of Project Tidal Wave.'

Tweed greeted Newman with this statement as soon as he was inside the suite. Tweed had spoken emphatically and was pacing round the suite like a caged tiger. Paula sat on the couch, watching him. By her side sat Philip. Against a wall Marler was leaning, smoking a king-size. He was the only person in the room who seemed unaffected by what Tweed had said. The others, Newman noticed, looked serious, almost grim.

'What has happened?' Newman asked. 'Your note spoke of all hell breaking loose.'

'Twenty-five key armaments factories – vital to the defence of the West – were blown to pieces in the early hours of this morning. Huge bombs had been smuggled into the factories. Most of the plants are write-offs.'

'You mean here in Germany? That's a lot of plants . . .'

'No. All over Western Europe – in France, Britain, Belgium, Germany, Sweden, Italy – and in five different states in America, including the Boeing plant in Seattle. I had a call from Monica who stopped Howard phoning me, thank heavens.'

'Many casualties?' Newman asked quietly.

'Very heavy when early morning work shifts had arrived. There is panic among all workers employed by other arms plants. They are refusing to go to work. In effect the arms industry of the West has been neutralized. I think I now know why Walvis retreated to his farmhouse hideaway last night.'

'Can any link be traced connecting Walvis with these atrocities?' Newman demanded.

243

'My first thought. I called Kuhlmann – who has returned to Bonn. The answer is no link. And Philip has told me certain information he gathered while hiding in that cupboard at Walvis's headquarters.'

'I'm sorry about that,' Philip said quietly. 'I planned to check on those places on my own. I thought one person might have a better chance of finding out what was going on rather than several.' He paused. 'That isn't really quite the truth. I wanted to do the job myself.'

'Where are these places?' Newman asked.

'Passau on the Danube,' Philip began. 'A very small town north of Passau and – close to the Czech border – Grafenau. Walvis mentioned both places while I was hidden in that cupboard.'

Philip fell silent. He was still wrestling with his conscience whether to let Tweed and the others know Ziggy Palewski was hiding out in Salzburg. In view of the catastrophic news Tweed had just heard he decided he had to say something. He looked at Newman.

'When I contacted Ziggy Palewski he told me how I could contact him. He's gone underground. I think the fewer people who know where he is the better. Salzburg.'

'Maybe they ought to be people still not known to the enemy,' Tweed suggested. 'The two we know who were not included in the photos which have been shown to hotel receptionists all over Munich. Marler and Paula.'

'I know Salzburg,' Paula volunteered.

'I also know the place well,' said Marler.

'But he will run if he doesn't see me,' Philip warned.

'Let me think how I am going to distribute our forces,' Tweed said crisply. 'Meantime, what happened during your breakfast, Bob? Anything interesting, significant?'

'Another player appeared on the scene,' Newman replied. 'Want to hear about him?'

*   *   *

244

Tweed wanted not only to hear about the conversation, word for word, with Ronald Weatherby – he wanted the same data on Lisa Trent.

As he had when recalling the interview with Rosa Brandt, Newman reported every detail of their conversations and their mannerisms. He rapidly painted a clear picture of Weatherby, careful to be factual and suppressing his dislike of the man. Tweed continued pacing, appeared to Paula to be fascinated by Newman's description of the new arrival, Weatherby.

'That's it,' Newman said after a few minutes. 'Now for my personal prejudice about Weatherby. My reaction reminds me of the old clubland saying in London I read about once. "Chap's a bounder, ought to be kicked all the way down the street."'

'That could be a very clever cover,' Tweed said. 'By his own admission he's a fixer – although I gather he never used that word. A fixer between global outfits. Some of the armaments plants which have been blown up are owned by global conglomerates.'

'That's a stab in the dark,' Newman objected.

'Here's another one,' said Tweed, suddenly cheerful. 'I have given a lot of thought as to how Teardrop may operate. Let's assume Walvis uses her – several of her targets have benefited his empire by being wiped out. So since she's so very careful to conceal her identity what is the obvious way she might drum up fresh business?'

'Not with you,' said Paula.

'By having a middle man – a fixer – to arrange a new transaction, which means a new assassination. Walvis knows who to phone – the fixer – but doesn't know, or want to know, the real identity of Teardrop. He gives the fixer the target's name, maybe his or her whereabouts, then sends the fee in cash to the fixer who, in turn, pays Teardrop.'

'You're not suggesting Ronald Weatherby could be this

245

go-between?' Marler interjected sceptically. 'From Bob's description Weatherby would run a mile before he got mixed up with anyone like Teardrop.'

'Tweed has just said,' Newman pointed out, 'that Weatherby, the apparent ultimate fool, could be using his manner as a very clever cover. I did get the impression he was a phoney. But he would be a quite different type of phoney from what I'd imagined.' He checked his watch. 'Lisa will skin me alive if I leave her alone with him any longer.'

He got up to return to the restaurant. Tweed used the trick he had used in the past to impress what he was going to say to someone. He waited until Newman had his hand on the handle while Paula unlocked it, then he called out.

'You're having lunch with Jill Selborne today. Make it an early one. And I had Monica double-checking certain people through the night. Including your Jill. Before she became a so-called fashion writer she spent two years working for Naval Intelligence. Have a good lunch . . .'

He waited until he was alone with Paula, Marler and Philip before he made his announcement.

'We'll all be leaving Munich today. I'm dividing you up into teams. More details later. Your objectives? Passau on the Danube, Grafenau near the Czech border – and Salzburg . . .'

25

'Jill, how long had you known Captain Sherwood *before* we met over drinks yesterday?'

Newman had timed asking the unexpected question

carefully while having lunch with Jill Selborne in the main restaurant at the Four Seasons. Earlier he had ordered a bottle of champagne, hoping to catch her off guard – although he suspected she had a head like a rock for alcohol.

They had chatted enjoyably over the starter and had finished the main course when he threw the question at her. She took her time over answering, pushed a curl of black hair behind a well-shaped ear, took another sip from her third glass of champagne, put down the glass, stared at him.

'That's a strange question.'

He could almost see inside her mind, trying to decide whether to bluff it out, pretending that occasion was the first time she had ever met Sherwood. Newman held her gaze, was no longer smiling.

'What makes you think I had known him earlier?' she enquired eventually.

'My sixth sense, plus information since received.'

It was the last four words which caused her luminous eyes to flicker briefly. She lowered them, took a further sip at her champagne, then drank the rest of the contents.

She straightened up in her smart navy-blue outfit, her right hand playing with the single strand of pearls resting on her dark blue jersey. A twin-set lady, Newman was thinking. You don't often see them nowadays – maybe they're coming back into fashion. The silence was now growing oppressive but Newman stayed quiet, relying on the long pause to compel her to speak.

'You are very clever, Bob,' she said eventually. 'I was playing along with what David had suggested. He said the situation was so dangerous it would be better for me if people thought I knew nothing about him.'

'What situation?'

'He was very vague. We'd met earlier soon after I

247

arrived here. He said he was expecting explosive developments.'

'What explosive developments?' Newman hammered on.

'He didn't specify. You *are* going on at me . . .'

'Because I think David was right. Explosive developments have already taken place all over the Western world. You know that overnight twenty-five armament plants vital to our defence have been blown up, totally destroyed? In various countries in Europe – as well as in America.'

'That sounds very dramatic . . .'

'You must have heard the news . . .'

'No!' Jill was getting annoyed. 'How would I? I don't read the papers unless they have fashion supplements. I don't listen to the blasted radio, let alone watch ruddy TV.'

'But your earlier meeting with Sherwood, both choosing to stay at the same hotel, was arranged.'

Newman was deliberately using a technique he had so often employed as a foreign correspondent. You don't ask people questions – inviting them to say no. You make statements as though you know the answer already.

'If you say so . . .'

'I'm waiting for *you* to say so . . .'

'You'll wait one hell of a long time.' Jill's eyes blazed, she launched into a counter-offensive against Newman. 'I was phoned by David after you left my apartment in Half Moon Street asking me to fly to see him in Munich urgently. He was once in Military Intelligence. He said he'd pay my fare, my hotel bill. He wanted information about Walvis – I only found this out when I got here.'

'What sort of information?'

'Information I didn't have. My marriage to Walvis was a fake. I don't think Walvis realized at the time. When I found out I walked.' She stood up. 'I'm walking now.

248

Thank you for the lunch, Mr Newman. I can't say it's been a pleasure. And unlike the meal, I haven't enjoyed our conversation. You'll excuse me. I have an article to write . . .'

Still in a flaming temper, she left. Newman watched her walk rapidly out of the restaurant. She had a very good carriage, held herself erect, walked with elegance. He called out to the waiter for the bill.

In the suite he found everyone assembled and the remnants of a lunch ordered from room service. Tweed again listened carefully to his account of the disaster lunch. Newman sighed as he finished speaking.

'And she lied. She said she'd been phoned by Sherwood *after* I left her apartment, the implication being that was why she was in Munich. But I found her packed case hidden away with a label marked up for the Munich flight and the Four Seasons hotel *before* I left her apartment.'

'You think she's playing some devious game?' Paula suggested.

'No doubt about it. I was suspicious from the moment she turned up out of the blue when we were talking to Sherwood. Too much of a coincidence.'

'And there I'd thought you fancied her,' Paula commented.

'I still like her, but I don't like her trickiness . . .'

Tweed didn't react to what he had heard. He stood up from his chair, faced everyone in the room.

'I have paid my bill, so has everyone else here. We're on the move. And I want us to move at top speed. Walvis has started Tidal Wave. It's going to be a race against time – to find out what Tidal Wave is and to stop Walvis in his tracks. If we can. I have decided how we will distribute our forces. Bob, I want you to go to Passau, find out what is the significance of those barge-trains on the Danube.'

He looked at Nield and Butler, as though reluctant to give the next order.

'You've drawn the black card. I want both of you to go to Grafenau. Harry, you were once a miner. I want those abandoned salt mines in the Czech mountains explored – I have a feeling they may be the key to Tidal Wave.'

'And the rest of us go where?' drawled Marler.

'You come with me, Paula and Philip to Salzburg. I must meet Ziggy Palewski, get him to tell me everything he knows. Which could be a lot. The four of us will travel to Salzburg by train. It should be safer than driving there.'

'Harry and I will take our cars,' Nield said.

'And I'll drive myself to Passau,' Newman remarked.

'Take as many weapons as you like,' Tweed went on. 'All these expeditions may be highly dangerous. Walvis will want to eliminate us now he's started whatever war he has planned – because I think it is some kind of war.'

'I'd be happier with some explosive and timers with detonators,' Butler said.

'I'm the quarter-master sergeant,' Marler told him. 'I brought back from Berg a large supply of Semtex, plus the other equipment you mentioned.'

'We should have back-packs to carry it,' mused Nield.

'Anything you request is at your disposal,' said Philip, standing up and going behind a couch.

He began producing a whole collection of back-packs of various shapes and sizes. He dumped a number in front of Butler and Nield.

Within ten minutes Semtex, timers and detonators had been distributed. Newman had paid his bill and Tweed looked at his watch.

'We'll leave the hotel in three separate groups – with an interval between each group departing. I'll leave first with my team otherwise we'll miss the Salzburg Express . . .'

The four of them – Tweed, Paula, Philip and Marler – were descending in the lift to the underground garage

250

where their cars were parked when Paula noticed how laden down Marler was.

'I can take something extra,' she said to him.

Marler gave her a polythene-wrapped instrument with a long handle. He told her not to bang the circular disc at the end of the handle against anything. The doors opened and Tweed, in a hurry, marched forward into the cavern illuminated by fluorescent strips to where Marler's Renault was parked.

'Don't you touch that car!' Marler shouted.

Startled, Tweed froze. Marler put down his various back-packs, including a large sausage-shaped container made of canvas. He took the long-handled package from Paula, stripped off the polythene, revealing a large mirror at the base of the handle which was telescopic. He extended it.

'I'm checking for a bomb,' he told Tweed. 'All of you, stay well away. I'm surprised at you, Tweed. You should be more cautious.'

'Sorry,' Tweed apologized. 'That was stupid of me.'

He had hardly finished speaking when a large black Mercedes came roaring down into the otherwise deserted car park. Only one man inside, the man behind the wheel. Gulliver. He skidded to a halt, climbed out, saw Paula aiming her Browning at him and beside her Philip held his Walther.

'Don't shoot!' Gulliver yelled. 'I'm unarmed. Don't get into that car. It could be laced with explosives.'

'It's Gulliver,' Paula whispered to Marler. 'So your cover is blown. And what in Heaven's name is going on?'

Tweed had disappeared before Gulliver could see him. It was Marler who called out to the pear-shaped brute.

'You can come over, I'll check you for weapons, then we'll examine the car together. All right?'

'All right,' Gulliver hastily agreed.

251

Paula then witnessed the extraordinary spectacle of Marler projecting the mirror under the Renault while Gulliver crouched beside him, staring into the mirror which gave them a clear view under the chassis.

'Something there that shouldn't be,' Gulliver said. 'If you hold the mirror I'll get under and take a closer look. I'm an explosives expert – used to be a quarry manager . . .'

'No, you stand back. Philip, come and hold the mirror and I'll explore . . .'

Before sliding under the car, Marler took a pair of pliers from a compact toolkit he always carried in his back pocket. He emerged, slithering backwards, in only a few minutes holding what appeared to Paula to be a slim metal canister in one hand and an object like a cartridge case in the other.

'Much obliged, Mr Gulliver,' he said genially. 'This would have blown everyone inside the car sky high. How come you guessed the situation?'

'We have contacts,' Gulliver said, reverting to his normal bombast. 'A gang of terrorists has entered Munich. Tell Mr Tweed when you see him that Mr Walvis was anxious nothing terrible should happen to him.'

'Will do. Now, you'll be on your way.'

There was an edge to his voice which made Gulliver back off, return to his car, get inside quickly and drive off out of the garage. Marler swiftly checked their other cars – the BMWs hired by Philip and Newman, the small red Mercedes driven by Nield and Butler's Citroën. He found nothing.

'What on earth is happening? Paula asked as Tweed appeared from behind a pillar. 'And we must have missed the Salzburg Express.'

'Not if we leave at once,' Tweed replied. 'You know I like to leave plenty of time to catch a train or plane . . .'

Marler was driving them to the main station and luckily

252

in mid-afternoon the traffic was light. Philip sat next to Marler while Paula and Tweed occupied the back. Exasperated, she tried again, turning to look at Tweed.

'I don't understand why Gulliver suddenly seemed to be on our side.'

'He isn't. I suspect he'd planted that bomb himself and was about to start on his deadly work with the other cars when he was ordered to report back in person. I noticed when he left his car door open he had a mobile phone. I think he'd acted on his own, Walvis heard about it later, and told him to go and remove the bomb Gulliver had already planted.'

'But *why*?' In her frustration Paula thumped Tweed gently on his arm with her fist. '*Why*?'

'Because Walvis has decided he wants to meet me. He'll just have to wait – if he lives long enough.'

Marler dropped the three of them at the station, Philip hurried to buy tickets, Tweed wandered inside to check the departure board. After helping Paula take her luggage out of the car Marler got back behind the wheel.

'Good luck,' he called out.

'But you're coming with us,' she protested. 'Tweed said you were.'

'We're using a little psychology where Bob Newman is concerned. You know Bob and I don't get along too well together – unless we're in a tight corner and then we back each other up to the hilt.'

'Yes, of course I know that. But you're supposed to be on the train coming with us to Salzburg.'

'That was a tactic Tweed and I arranged on the quiet. To avoid Newman blowing his top. I'm waiting until Bob has left Munich and then I'll be driving hell-for-leather to Passau. You see, Tweed thinks that will be the most dangerous assignment of all . . .'

26

Inside his remote farmhouse Walvis had his own office, a large austerely furnished room. His huge desk, most of the other furniture – chairs, tables, cabinets and bookcases lining the walls – was made of teak. Walvis liked teak. It represented *strength*.

He was dressed in working clothes: outsize corduroy trousers, a leather jacket, a check shirt open to expose his thick neck. Everything was tailor-made – Rosa Brandt took his clothes sizes to a Munich tailor and ordered three copies of any new garment.

It was ten o'clock in the morning – several hours before Tweed left for Salzburg – when the phone rang. Walvis had the day's newspapers spread out, reporting the wave of explosions at arms factories all over the West. His hamlike hand picked up the receiver.

'Yes.'

'This is Lucien. I have good news for you, sir . . .'

'Then spill it without more ado.'

'I have traced through contacts Ziggy Palewski. He is in Salzburg . . .'

'Where in Salzburg? Be precise for once.'

'I cannot tell you his exact whereabouts. I saw him for a minute in the Altstadt. Then he vanished. But it was him.'

'The Old Town? That sounds like Palewski. I will send someone to deal with him at once.'

'You want me to meet this person? Maybe at the station?'

'If you met her you would be dead. Keep trying to

locate where he is holed up. If you succeed leave a note at the ÖH addressed to Magda Franz . . .'

'The ÖH – the Hotel Österreicherischer Hof.'

'I see you know your Salzburg. Stop blathering and start searching for the target . . .'

Walvis put the phone down without a word of thanks. He then dialled a number, spoke to his usual contact for Teardrop, passed to him the information Lucien had provided.

'So,' he went on, 'Teardrop will be rushed off her feet. I want this deal concluded very quickly. Goodbye . . .'

He was replacing the receiver when he noticed a side door leading to Rosa's office was partly open. Frowning, he heaved himself out of his padded chair, walked quietly to the door, pushed it wide open.

Rosa Brandt was lying sprawled out on a couch against a wall, her head resting on a pillow. She remained still as he approached her.

'Did you hear what I said on the phone just now?'

'I did not hear anything,' she replied in the language Walvis had used – German. 'I am not feeling at all well. It is exhaustion, I think. I will drive to my small apartment in Munich and go to bed away from all interruptions. I need a good rest.'

'That apartment has no telephone. Suppose I wish to get in touch with you?'

'I will phone you at regular intervals. Please, no more. I have a splitting headache.'

'Go, then . . .'

Walvis walked back to his office in his huge reinforced leather slippers. He slammed the door shut. It always annoyed him when staff were ill. Still, he congratulated himself, rubbing his hands together, eliminating Palewski was a top priority – the journalist knew too much. Teardrop might well complete her task today.

*   *   *

255

Aboard the Salzburg Express Tweed, Paula and Philip had a first-class compartment to themselves. Walking up the platform at Munich to check who was on board just before it departed, Tweed had found the express was almost empty. The train had been moving at high speed when he made his unexpected observation.

'I wish we could identify Teardrop. Then we could hand her over to Kuhlmann.'

'I'd have no compunction in shooting her,' Paula said vehemently. 'She is an evil woman.'

'The female of the species is more deadly, et cetera,' said Philip, and he smiled at Paula.

It was the first time she had seen him smile since the tragedy of Jean's death. But it was a cold smile. Tweed was speaking again, with that far-away look Paula knew so well when he was concentrating furiously.

'Teardrop could be one of three people. Jill Selborne, Lisa Trent or Rosa Brandt.'

'Jill? Lisa?' Paula was taken aback. 'How can you suspect either of those two women?'

'Because I have given some thought to what sort of a life Teardrop must lead. She must be able to travel over long distances without arousing suspicion. Therefore she needs a job where travel seems natural. Lisa is a financial analyst. By her own account she does travel all over the world. Teardrop's targets have been killed in many different countries.'

'I find your theory hard to swallow as far as Lisa is concerned. And why Jill?'

'Same reason. She is a fashion journalist. Another job that involves travel abroad frequently. Also she is in Munich when there are no fashion shows, which I find odd.'

'And Rosa Brandt?' Paula queried. 'You think Walvis has Teardrop on his staff – conveniently available whenever someone gets in his way?'

256

'It is speculation on my part, but I do have the strongest feeling Walvis does not know the identity of Teardrop. Maybe he operates through a middleman, a fixer, I think he would prefer that method: then if Teardrop is ever apprehended no connection can ever be proved between her and Walvis.'

'Which wouldn't rule out Rosa Brandt, who looks like Teardrop.'

'Exactly,' Tweed agreed. 'Talking of fixers, Newman's favourite person is aboard this train, sitting by himself in the front coach. The delightful Ronald Weatherby. I recognized him from Newman's description.'

'You think he's going to Salzburg?' Philip asked.

'I wouldn't be in the least surprised if Salzburg were his destination. We are getting closer to that wonderful city. I can tell by the mountains . . .'

Paula, absorbed earlier by their conversation, gazed out of the window, fascinated. Across flat fields to the south in the distance loomed a vast range of snowbound jagged peaks silhouetted against a clear blue sky. They looked enormous and, as she watched, the Alps seemed to be moving closer to the train. She shivered.

'It must be Arctic up there.'

'Since this is December it will be pretty freezing in Salzburg. We shall need our sheepskins and the fur hats you had the presence of mind to buy in Maximilianstrasse this morning before breakfast.'

Paula nodded, only half hearing him. The savage summits were definitely approaching closer to the express. She stared at them as the train thundered on, then began to slow down. Tweed stood up, donned his sheepskin and fur hat.

'Better get ready, we'll soon be there. I wonder what delights Salzburg will hold for us. Why do I sense that this trip may also be dangerous?'

*   *   *

257

Nield and Butler had taken very seriously Tweed's warning of the climatic conditions they would face.

'I heard on the radio early this morning that temperatures in the Bayerischer Wald have dropped to −40°C,' Tweed had commented.

'That sounds a bit nippy to me,' Butler had said.

'And we really did draw the joker,' Nield had remarked humorously.

'Plus the fact,' Tweed had concluded, 'although it's stopped now, it was snowing heavily through the night. And the weather report said the heaviest falls were in the Bayerischer Wald area . . .'

'Wald is German for forest, isn't it?' Butler had asked as Nield drove them out of Munich.

'That's right. It's one of the most remote parts of Germany. Hardly any foreign tourists ever get there, but the locals ski there, mostly starting in January. It should be pretty quiet for us.'

'Let's not assume it will be too quiet for us,' Butler emphasized.

With Nield at the wheel, they were travelling in a hired Citroën, which was pale grey in colour – and therefore more likely to merge into the snow-blanketed countryside. They had deliberately left behind Nield's small red Mercedes.

After hearing Tweed's weather report they had dashed out to buy extra clothes. Now they were both muffled up like a couple of Michelin men. There was very little traffic when they had left Munich well behind, had turned on to the autobahn leading eventually to Deggendorf.

'Tweed was right about the heavy fall overnight,' Nield remarked an hour later. 'Thank Heaven we have a car equipped with snow tyres. And I think we're getting our first glimpse of the mountains along the Czech border.'

He had just obeyed a sign *Ausfahrt*, indicating the turn-off from the autobahn to Deggendorf. A few minutes earlier he had – to Butler's surprise – stopped the car by the side of the deserted autobahn.

'What's happening now?' Butler had asked.

'I haven't seen any sign that we're being followed. But if we wait here for a few minutes we'll be sure if no vehicle appears behind us. Meantime we can look at the Danube.'

Standing on the bank, Butler stared down at a fairly wide stretch of brownish water which was surging past at high speed. Slivers of ice like small floes kept appearing, floating past with the powerful current.

'That thing is the Danube?' Butler asked in a disbelieving tone.

'It is. We're fairly high up its course here—'

He had broken off as Butler raised a warning hand. The sound of the engine of a light aircraft was approaching fast. Nield jumped into the car. He had left the engine running and drove it a few yards forward until it nestled under the cover of a copse of fir trees, their branches sagging under the weight of frozen snow.

'Bleedin' freezing out there,' said Butler as he scuttled back inside the car. 'So I've seen the Danube and I'm not impressed. But what about that plane. Sounds to be searching for something. Us?'

'Could be, but I rather think it's a scout plane on a routine patrol. Maybe Walvis does have light aircraft checking anyone approaching where we're going. In which case he must have something pretty deadly hidden away in Grafenau or – more likely – in the mountains . . .'

They had waited until they heard the aircraft flying off, its engine sound dying away. Nield had then driven on to the turn-off. The countryside had been a series of rolling hills for some time but now they saw ahead mountains with a series of pointed summits, covered with snow which glittered in the sunlight.

'Immediately beyond those mountains is the Czech

259

Republic,' Nield observed. 'Some of them straddle the border. We'll soon be moving into enemy territory.'

They had been travelling on autobahn A92; they moved now on to A3, bypassing Deggendorf. A signpost carried the legend *Passau – Linz – Wien*. To their right Nield saw in the middle of nowhere the green onion-dome of a small church and a tight cluster of houses.

'I wouldn't like to live out there,' Nield remarked.

'I wouldn't like to live anywhere round here at all. Look ahead,' Butler replied.

The mountains had suddenly become much closer. On their lower slopes reared dense fir forests, again with their branches sagging under the weight of frozen snow sparkling in the sun. Then the weather changed in minutes, the sun vanished, low black clouds turned the world into a dark place.

Nield watched clouds like black smoke masking the summits, filtering down tree-crammed ravines. Why did the smokelike clouds remind him of poison gas, he wondered.

A small signpost pointed to the left – to the east – off the side road they had moved on to when a similar signpost had carried the same name. *Grafenau*. He entered a tunnel roofed over with trees, slowed, stopped and listened.

'I thought so. Another of those light aircraft prowling round. We're nicely under cover here. Now I'm pretty well convinced Walvis has a fleet of aircraft patrolling this whole area . . .'

Nield got out of the car for a moment. He was staring up as the plane flew low, zooming over the tunnel. It flew off again and he waited until he could no longer hear it before, frozen to the bone, he climbed back behind the wheel.

'It didn't see us,' he said.

'How can you be sure?' queried Butler.

'Because *I* couldn't see *it*. The atmosphere round here

is pretty eerie.' He picked up the map from Butler's lap, studied it briefly, tossed it back. 'I think the best thing is to avoid Grafenau. There's a Z-road which appears to lead to the mountains and across them into the Czech Republic.'

'What's a Z-road?' demanded Butler suspiciously.

'My name for what is probably little more than a farm track. We shouldn't run into anyone on that route on a day like this.'

'Don't say things like that,' Butler half joked. 'It's tempting fate . . .'

Leaving the tunnel of trees behind, the narrow road began to climb, became even narrower and steeper. Butler leaned forward as the whirling windscreen wipers fought a losing battle with ice forming. Another side road had joined the one they were driving along. Ahead in the snow there were wide deep ruts and already ice had formed in the ruts – they felt it breaking under their wheels. The temperature outside had to be arctic.

'Don't like this,' Butler said. 'A heavy vehicle has passed this way recently.'

'I know,' Nield said calmly, 'hence the wheel ruts and the wide gauge . . .'

He had just spoken when to their left they saw a large timbered building with huge closed doors. A notice was attached to the side of the barnlike structure. *Flugplatz. Grafenau. Elev: 4170ft. 48° 49' 24" N. 13° 22' 09" E.* Butler pulled a face.

'Why didn't I keep my big mouth shut about tempting fate? You know what this is?'

'A local airfield. Let's see if we can find somewhere we can wait and see if anything happens . . .'

Nield did find somewhere – a copse of fir trees perched on a knoll overlooking the small airfield. He parked the car, kept the engine running – hoping they were now far enough away for the sound not to be heard. He had a

261

nasty feeling that if he turned off the engine it would never start again. They forced themselves to get out of the car and wait.

Nield took up a position by the side of the airfield's hangar, the ancient wooden structure. Butler walked to a nearby copse of trees and stood where he could see between a gap in the tree trunks. Near by, at the top of a slope, was a stockpile of huge long stripped trunks, so straight Butler assumed they would be transported in due course for use as scaffolding. They were held together by thick hemp.

From Nield's vantage point he could see the absurdly short runway – a stretch of frozen grass cleared of the snow, presumably by a bulldozer that stood partially protected with a canvas cover. He tensed as he heard a light aircraft approaching.

The machine, a single-engined Piper, came in low, the pilot throttling back his engine. Nield estimated the crude runway couldn't be more than something over five hundred yards long. He waited for the plane to overshoot but the pilot was skilful, stopping the plane a few yards from the end of the strip. It had a freshly painted 'D' on the side of its fuselage.

'D for Danubex,' Nield said to himself. 'Walvis does have a fleet of planes patrolling this area.'

The moment the pilot switched off his engine Nield heard the sound of another engine. A fuel tanker was driving up the road they had followed. It stopped close to the plane, the driver got out, reeled out a long feed-pipe, attached it to the plane.

'Walvis is diabolically well organized,' Nield said to himself again. 'His aerial fleet can stay up all day with fuel laid on for it . . .'

The thought had just passed through his mind when a cold round metallic muzzle was pressed against the back of his exposed neck where his scarf had slipped. A voice spoke in German.

'Move a centimetre and I blow your head off. Now we will visit someone who will be most interested to meet you, stranger. A man you may not like meeting . . .'

Nield stood perfectly still, the freezing cold penetrating his thick gloves as he cursed himself for concentrating too much on what was happening below. It had to be his captor's right hand holding the gun because the left hand began feeling inside his sheepskin for weapons.

'Say something to me, dumb idiot,' the unseen man continued.

'I'm here on a skiing holiday,' Nield replied.

'And so are the wolves,' the unseen man sneered.

He had just finished his jeering remark when Butler's left arm wrapped itself round him from behind in a powerful bear hug. His left hand grasped the German's jaw, jerked it upwards. His right hand simultaneously fastened on the gun hand, forced it swiftly upwards so the muzzle was aimed at the man's throat.

Nield had jumped sideways. Butler was heavily built but the German was taller, wider shouldered. There was a brief struggle. The gun fired once as Butler forced the jaw back further and further. They both heard the unpleasant crack of his neck breaking and he sagged into the snow.

'Watch that lot down there,' Nield shouted.

He was gripping his Walther as the pilot hauled something out of his claustrophobic cabin. He aimed it up the slope and a hail of bullets rattled round the hangar.

'He's got an Uzi!' Nield warned, flat on his face, then realized Butler had disappeared.

Nield fired back, aiming for both pilot and driver, but the range was too great for a Walther to be effective. The pilot was reloading his Uzi. Only a matter of time before he advanced up the slope and slaughtered both of them. Where the hell was Butler?

263

The feed-pipe was still pumping fuel from the tanker into the aircraft. Butler had disappeared behind the stacked pile of tree trunks. He had a knife in his hand and was sawing away with great energy at the hemp wrapped round the left-hand end of the stockpile. He left a few fibres in position, ran to the other end, sawed furiously at the hemp holding the stockpile poised at the edge of the slope.

The pilot was advancing slowly up the slope, firing off another magazine, compelling Nield to remain sprawled behind a low ridge. The pilot was grinning, looking forward to a little sport. He rammed in a fresh magazine and there was a sudden sinister silence, broken only by the distant sound of the tanker pumping fuel while the driver watched in eager anticipation.

The silence was broken. The hemp binding the trees had given way. The massive tree trunks thundered down the slope, rolling over each other. Nield watched in amazement as the pilot screamed, turned to flee, was overwhelmed with the terrible avalanche of tree trunks, disappearing as they crushed him.

The driver looked up. For a moment he was frozen with horror. He also turned to run but the tree trunks had reached him. They crashed into the aircraft, reducing it to scrap metal. The feed-pipe was torn from the aircraft, spewed fuel over the tanker and its driver. Flame soared up from the wrecked vehicle, a deafening explosion echoed round the mountains as black smoke rose and the fire set light to the relic of the tanker.

Butler reappeared, rubbing his gloves together, brushing off snow.

'It will have to be well done,' Butler said grimly.

'What?' asked Nield.

'If you fancy hamburgers for lunch.'

'I fancy getting out of here and into the mountains before anyone arrives . . .'

27

The Salzburg Express slowed down as Paula, Tweed and Philip gathered their luggage together. The sky was an intense azure blue, close by to the south an alp loomed up massively. Tweed nodded towards the mountain Paula was staring at.

'That's further away than it seems.'

'What a glorious day to arrive in Salzburg,' enthused Paula.

'But perhaps not so good for Newman and Marler in Passau, let alone Butler and Nield in Grafenau.'

Paula switched her gaze to the north. A long distance away an army of low black clouds appeared to be so low they might be touching the ground. The train pulled up in Salzburg Hauptbahnhof.

'We're staying at the Hotel Österreicherischer Hof,' Tweed remarked as they alighted. 'You get a marvellous view of the great *Schloss* or castle. This station is rather unusual . . .'

Paula realized what he meant when they had to enter a lift which then went *down*. She then recalled that the street level was well below the platforms. Tweed let the first two taxis go and grabbed the third.

'No sign of Mr Ronald Weatherby,' he whispered as they were driven past ancient buildings and more modern edifices. 'I suspect he jumped off the moment the train had stopped . . .'

The Österreicherischer Hof was a magnificent four-storey building with stone walls painted white and flags of

265

many nations flying on its roof. Inside there was an atmosphere of peace and luxury and the interior was open to several floors above them with balcony walks along the side walls. This, Paula was thinking as Tweed registered, is so different from the rush and bustle of Munich.

Tweed invited them both to see his room when they had registered. Paula let out her breath as she surveyed its spaciousness and the french windows beyond. She ran to them, followed by Tweed and Philip, opened a door and stepped out on to a long low-walled balcony. This time she took in a deep breath as she surveyed the fantastic panorama.

On the fourth floor the balcony overlooked the Salzach River below, a green current with the sun reflecting off it in brilliant flashes. It was about sixty feet wide. But it was what lay across the river just to the south that fascinated her.

The immense bulk of a great grey stone castle, hundreds of years old, stood perched high up. Some distance behind it she saw the alp. Shoppers walked along the promenade on the far side of the river and below her was an arc-shaped footbridge, very modern, which spanned the river.

'Where is the Altstadt?' Philip asked, trying not to be too eager.

'You see the castle,' Tweed explained. 'The Old Town is below it on this side. Walk along that promenade and turn down any of the old arcades and you are inside it. Don't rush anything,' he warned.

'I think I'll take my things to my room,' Philip decided. 'Then I may go out for a breath of fresh air.'

'I want you back in thirty minutes,' Tweed said, checking his watch. 'We can then enjoy an early dinner together.'

They went back into the suite-like apartment and Paula waited until Philip had gone.

'You came here to keep an eye on Philip,' she stated.

'Not entirely. One of the keys to this mystery, I am sure, is Ziggy Palewski. I hope Philip can persuade him to meet me. Walvis is moving fast now and I need as much information as possible about what he is planning quickly.'

'I'll go to my room and freshen up,' she said. 'Then I'll come back here, if that's all right.'

'Yes. When you are ready come back and see me. I still wonder about the presence of Weatherby on the express . . .'

Philip checked his watch as soon as he reached his own room and dumped his back-pack in a large wardrobe. He had thirty minutes to find the Café Sigrist – the place where Ziggy Palewski had said he could meet him. It was too late today – Palewski had specified between ten and eleven in the morning – but Philip was anxious to locate the café.

He took the elevator down to the ground floor but he didn't leave the reception area at once. He wanted to make sure Paula wasn't going to follow him. She was quite capable of looking after herself but if she was near him he'd feel he had to watch out for her.

He lingered for a few minutes, studying some old framed prints on the wall. He had calculated he would have plenty of time to search for the Sigrist if he hurried over the pedestrian bridge. He glanced to his left as a motor cyclist clad in leather, holding his helmet in one hand, approached the desk. He could hear clearly what the cyclist said in German as he spoke to the receptionist.

'I believe you may have a message for Magda Franz.'

Philip stood still. Magda Franz, Tweed had told him, was the name the woman who had killed Captain Sherwood had used. The receptionist opened a drawer.

'Yes, there is a message for Madame Franz.'

267

He handed the cyclist a sealed envelope. Stuffing the envelope inside a pocket, the cyclist rushed out of the hotel, ramming his helmet on his head. Philip moved swiftly after him.

He cursed to himself as he saw the motor cyclist in the saddle of his machine, kick-starting it and speeding off. Philip looked round for a taxi but no taxi was anywhere to be seen. Why was it that when you desperately needed one there was nothing? Philip consoled himself with the thought that he doubted whether a taxi could have kept up with a motor cycle courier.

He went straight back to the elevators, stopped outside Tweed's suite, tapped on the door. Paula let him inside after checking.

'Grim news,' Philip said and told them.

'So Teardrop is now in Salzburg,' Tweed said thoughtfully. 'And I think I can guess her target. Ziggy Palewski.'

'At least I warned him about her.'

'Yes, but we are up against a very clever woman. Is there any way, Philip, you can contact Palewski?'

'Not until ten o'clock tomorrow morning at the Café Sigrist, as I told you.'

'Then we shall have to wait until then . . .'

'I'm not going to wait,' Philip said. 'I'll skip dinner, get a sandwich while I wander round the Altstadt. I might just get lucky and see Palewski. I'm leaving now . . .'

'You made no attempt to stop him,' Paula commented in surprise when they were alone.

'Deliberately. Philip needs something constantly to occupy his mind. He can take care of himself. I think you and I will now go down and have dinner.'

Philip, muffled in sheepskin, motoring gloves and a fur hat, walked rapidly across the pedestrian bridge over the Salzach. A bitter wind, blowing off the mountains, was

268

coming down the river and froze his exposed cheeks. He hardly noticed it, he was so intent on reaching the Altstadt. Walking along the now deserted promenade he had a strong sense of being followed.

He slowed his pace, trudging over the hard-packed snow as he reached the shops. He passed a modern arcadelike entrance which, inside, led nowhere except to a curving flight of steps leading upwards. The wide entrance was paved with marble. A notice read *Café Sigrist. Stock 1.* Palewski had said the café was on the first floor.

He walked on slowly past an expensive-looking pâtisserie, its window filled with triple-decker gâteaux. Plenty of chocolate and cream. Pausing, he turned as though to gaze at the view. Across the river the most prominent building was the Österreicherischer Hof. In the full glare of sunlight he now saw the walls he had thought were white in the shadows of the far side were, in fact, a delicate shade of pink.

Looking back he saw two women with shopping baskets and a man of medium height, wearing a fur cap, a leather coat, stooping slightly although he looked to be no older than in his mid-forties. He waited for the man to pretend to look in a shop window, the normal tactic of a follower when he might be spotted. The man continued to walk towards him.

Philip turned round, anxious to get out of the raw wind which had increased in strength. He turned down into a cobbled arcade, narrow and with ancient buildings on either side. He increased his pace, hurried along until he reached the end and entered an ancient street, the Getreidegasse.

A sign said *Café Mozart*. The street was long and very narrow and too empty for his liking. He climbed the staircase leading up to the Mozart, entered a spacious room with tall windows – each a pair with a space between them, the traditional form of double glazing over the centuries in Europe. The floor was laid with woodblocks, the tables marble topped. At the far end was a tall china cabinet displaying a variety of plates.

He sat at a table against the wall where he could see the entrance. He had ordered coffee when the man in the leather coat appeared, his hat in his hands, revealing sandy hair and tufted eyebrows. He walked to Philip's table and sat down, facing him.

Philip, having observed that they were the only two people in the café, reached inside his jacket. His sheepskin was draped over a spare chair. He took out a pack of cigarettes. He rarely smoked but the action had enabled him to feel the reassuring butt of his Walther.

'I do hope you will excuse my intrusion, sir,' the strange man said in English with an oily smile. 'But we are blessed with a mutual acquaintance. Mr Tweed . . .'

Soon after Philip had left, Tweed had escorted Paula to one of the dining-rooms. She was impressed as soon as they entered the room with windows overlooking the Salzach. The dining-room's walls were panelled in dark red wood, the ceiling was covered with the same wood carved into octagonal shapes, the floor was carpeted in a deep red colour. There was an immediate atmosphere of warmth and cheerfulness as they were shown by the head waiter to a wall table with a banquette.

'We are not too early for dinner, I hope,' Tweed enquired, glancing round the otherwise empty room.

'You have a whole evening to enjoy your meal,' the smiling *maître d'* assured him.

I'm not too sure about that, Tweed thought to himself.

'We'd like some wine,' Tweed said to Paula's surprise. He rarely drank. 'Chablis would go down rather well.'

'You are in Austria,' the waiter said. 'May I suggest a

very pleasant dry white Austrian wine, Grüner Vetliner?'

Oh, Lord, no, Paula thought, Austrian wine. The waiter sensed their indecision.

'May I suggest we bring two glasses for you to try? If you do not like it I will provide Chablis.'

The waiter was so enthusiastic Tweed agreed to sample a glass. They both sipped cautiously, looked at each other. Paula grinned at the waiter. It was a light dry white wine and the taste was excellent. She nodded to Tweed.

'We'll have a bottle – and thank you for the recom- mendation,' Tweed said.

'A whole bottle!' Paula whispered. 'Going it a bit?'

'Yes, but we have company.'

Paula looked up, froze inwardly. Jill Selborne strode across to their table, pressed her palms together in an attitude of prayer.

'May a lonely girl join you, or would you sooner dine by yourselves? Please be honest . . .'

Tweed's welcome was so enthusiastic Paula stared at him as their unexpected guest sat down. Paula also tried not to stare at Jill who had transformed her appearance. In place of the black helmet of hair sculpted close to her head – which she had sported during their meeting at the Bayeri- scher Hof in Munich – her hair now hung in thick dark glossy waves. Paula wished she'd had a chance to visit a hairdresser. Jill smiled warmly at Tweed.

'Before you ask what on earth I am doing in Salzburg I'll tell you. There's a concert here with a famous conduc- tor. He's agreed to give me an interview, which is a bit of a scoop.'

'I thought you were a fashion writer,' Paula said.

'I am.' She gave Paula a smile which was a shade too warm. 'But as a sideline I sometimes do profiles for top

271

magazines on distinguished people. It does pay very well. Better, actually, than my fashion articles. Are you here hunting?'

'Hunting?' Paula was taken aback.

'Yes, hunting.' Jill infuriated Paula by turning towards Tweed, giving him a ravishing smile as she sipped at the glass of wine he had poured for her. 'Thank you. This wine is glorious.'

'Hunting, you said,' Paula repeated with vehemence.

'I did, didn't I?' Jill turned to Paula and smiled coolly. 'You see, David – poor Captain Sherwood – told me that Tweed runs General & Cumbria Assurance, that he's Chief Claims Investigator and goes all over the world tracking down insurance swindlers who operate on a large scale.'

Bless Captain Sherwood, Paula thought. He covered for us and now he's dead. She smiled back at Jill.

'It's a confidential business, so if we were – hunting – I'm afraid we wouldn't admit it.'

'Of course, how very stupid of me. I can be rather thick at times.'

Thick my foot, Paula said to herself. You've got all your marbles and I'd like to know what *you* are up to.

'How long do you expect to be in Salzburg?' she asked. 'I presume you are staying at this hotel?'

'Best hotel in Salzburg, I think. When you can put your accommodation down to expenses why not go for the best? Don't you agree?'

She had again turned her attention to Tweed, then waited while they ordered their lunch. Tweed handed back the menu to the head waiter, clasped his hands and gazed at their guest.

'I do agree. I sense you are a lady who likes the good things in life. Smart clothes, good food, good wines.'

Jill was wearing an expensive beige woollen dress with long sleeves, open a discreet distance down the front

272

below a peaked collar. It fitted her closely and did not disguise the fact that she had a slim, well-formed figure. Her eyes held Tweed's and Paula was beginning to feel she did not exist.

'Yes, I do like the good things in life,' Jill said to Tweed. 'You missed out one item – jewellery.' She held out her right hand to him. Even in the half-light of the dining-room light flashed off a large sapphire ring and a diamond ring on another finger.

She continued to hold out her hand and Tweed took hold of it to look closer at the rings. Her hand was small, cool, and her fingers were long and elegant.

'I have a fortune in jewels in the hotel safe,' Jill remarked to Tweed.

Paula leapt in, seeing the opportunity to raise the subject.

'Was Walvis a very generous man when you were married to him?'

'Except that I wasn't truly married.' Tweed had released her hand and she gazed seriously at Paula. 'I thought I'd said it was a fake marriage, presided over by a pseudopriest in Slovenia. Walvis didn't realize this but I did.'

'You knew at the time the priest had no power to marry you?'

Paula let her incredulity show in her voice, pleased she had dragged Walvis into the conversation.

'Yes, I knew. It suited me not to be tied to him on a permanent basis. I wanted to find out what it was like to be married – to pretend to be – to a multibillionaire and the richest man in the world.'

'What was it like then?'

'Oh, he wanted to shower me with money, the best clothes, the most expensive jewels. I refused to let him spend money on me, and this intrigued him. Which wasn't my real motive. I knew I would walk sooner or later and I

273

didn't want to feel obligated to him. He adores women, trusts them in a way he never trusts men. He believes any man would betray him if it suited that man's book – so he watches them like a hawk and pays his deputies a huge salary, more than they would get anywhere else. I remember he once said to me that where men were concerned you bought their loyalty like buying any other commodity.'

She paused to drink more wine and Tweed, fascinated by this insight into his adversary, sensed she had not finished. She put down her glass and spoke directly to Paula.

'So, you may wonder, where did my jewels come from? I will tell you. I bought all of them myself over a period of time – from my earnings as a journalist writing fashion articles, but mainly from the profiles I write for American women's magazines on people who have refused to be interviewed before.'

'You must be very persuasive,' Paula suggested.

'I do my research very thoroughly. Before I approach a subject I know more about him – or her – than the people know about themselves. Now, Paula,' she said, challenging her, 'how have I stood up to your interrogation?'

'Dinner is here,' Tweed said quickly.

With half his mind he was wondering what was happening to Philip.

28

'But we are blessed with a mutual acquaintance. Mr Tweed . . .'

In the Café Mozart it was getting darker still when the stranger who had sat down at his table spoke these words and Philip remained silent. His uninvited visitor had a bony face and gave the impression the head had been subjected to great pressure, reducing its original size.

'Who did you say?' Philip asked abruptly.

A waiter appeared at that moment and the other man made a great ceremony about ordering something commonplace.

'I would like coffee – it must be freshly made. That I insist on. Also bring a jug of hot milk, piping hot. I shall send it back if it is not just right.'

The waiter nodded, glanced at Philip, went away. The monkeylike man leaned forward, his manner confidential.

'I said Mr Tweed. A most interesting personality, I should imagine.'

'You could be right – except I've never heard of him. I came in here for a quiet few minutes. Maybe you could move to another table – Heaven knows there are plenty of empty ones.'

Philip's manner was abrasive, verging on the aggressive. He drank more of his coffee as the man continued leaning closer to him.

'Mr Robert Newman could vouch for me. But I am forgetting my manners – I haven't introduced myself. I am Ronald Weatherby. My friends call me Ronnie . . .'

'I should imagine they are few and far between.'

'My dear sir, it is very lonely in Salzburg at this time of year. It can also be dangerous. Surely two Englishmen can have a polite conversation? I may even possess information which will prove valuable to you in your quest.'

'Quest? What the devil are you talking about?'

'I assume you are here looking for something. Or someone?'

'You assume wrongly. Look, Weatherby – that was your name, wasn't it? – you're a very vague man, a shadow. What do you do to earn a living? Assuming you do any work at all.'

'I saw three people alight from the Salzburg Express. One man who could have been Tweed, a most attractive young lady, and yourself. I saw the man who could have been Tweed with Newman and the same attractive lady having drinks in Munich at the Bayerischer Hof. Later, as I have said, I see the three people I have described – including yourself – disembarking from the express. I am not a complete fool.'

'I wouldn't bank on that.'

Philip was deliberately insulting the obnoxious Ronnie in the hope of getting under his skin, making him lose his temper. He had succeeded. Weatherby sat back in his chair and glared. His smooth unctuous manner and tone of voice vanished.

'I will warn you again. You should leave Salzburg by the next train or plane. Salzburg is dangerous . . .'

Philip stood up, grabbed hold of his sheepskin and walked away just as the waiter arrived with Weatherby's coffee. He didn't think the coffee was likely to meet with Ronnie's approval.

Philip walked slowly along the dark narrow canyon of the Getreidegasse, moving deeper into the Old Town. There were very few people about apart from the odd woman emerging from one of the many small shops lining the street. In places many footsteps had pressed away the snow, exposing icy cobbles beneath. It would be easy to slip and he still had the feeling he was being followed. Pretending to be interested in an antique bookshop he walked inside an alcove leading to the closed door. A hand grasped his sleeve. His right hand slid inside his sheepskin, gripped the Walther. A familiar voice spoke.

'You are in great danger – you are being followed by two men . . .'

Ziggy Palewski's warning was urgent. Philip stared at

the gnomelike figure, the strong face with a long straight nose, the thick eyebrows, the dark moustache and fringe beard. Palewski wore a padded windcheater, an old peaked cap. Philip took hold of him by the elbow.

'We're trapped in here – the shop is closed. We're going to walk out into the street together, heading away from where I've just come. Move but not too fast. You'll slip on the ice . . .'

As they emerged he glanced back, saw two men wearing leather jackets a dozen yards away, coming towards them. A third stood behind them. Lucien? Philip urged Palewski forward in the opposite direction. They were passing a narrow alley which seemed to lead somewhere and he pulled Palewski inside. He had noticed that parts of the Altstadt were laid with *pavé* stones and workmen had dug up part of the alley before going home. A large pile of triangular-shaped *pavé* stones stood against a wall.

'It is no good,' Palewski said, 'one of them is in the alley. That makes three . . .'

A stocky figure was advancing down the alley, grinning and with a long knife in his hand. Philip had once been a first-rate bowler, playing cricket when he was younger. His first thought had been to use the Walther, but that would cause a major fracas and Tweed wanted to conceal their presence in Salzburg.

'Stand against the other wall,' Philip ordered.

With his gloved hand he picked up a small slab of *pavé* with savage-looking edges. He hoisted his arm, hurled the *pavé* stone with all his strength. It hit the thug in the alley on the forehead. He groaned once, a muffled yelp, slumped into the snow, lay still.

Philip swung round, grabbed two more slabs, crouched behind the pile of stones. The two men had appeared from the main street. Each held a knife as he walked towards his target.

277

'There is a *polizei* post near by,' Palewski hissed.

Which told Philip why the thugs wanted quiet murders. He stood up suddenly. Startled, the two men paused, a fatal pause. Philip hurled a second slab of *pavé*, a larger piece. Its razorlike edge struck the left-hand man in the throat, ripping it open. He staggered, dropping his knife, grasped his throat, sprawled forward on the ground, lay there without moving. His companion rushed forward with his knife held in front of his body. He was closer when the third chunk of *pavé* smashed across the bridge of his nose, breaking the bone into deadly splinters. He stood quite still for seconds, arms spread wide, crashed to the ground.

'We're getting out of here fast,' Philip ordered.

Palewski had pressed his body against the wall and now he moved with Philip. Neither glanced down at the bodies lying in the alley. Philip grasped Palewski's arm again to stop him hurrying back into the street.

'Walk slowly, as though nothing had happened.'

'If I am not at the Sigrist tomorrow,' Palewski said, breathing heavily, 'I will leave a message with an address. Brodgasse 85. Please bring Tweed with you. I'm going now. Thank you for saving my life . . .'

'Wait a moment.' They had walked casually back into the main street. No one about anywhere. 'You also must be very careful,' Philip warned. 'Teardrop is in Salzburg.'

'Thank you for saving my life twice . . .'

Philip glanced back down the street behind them again in search of more thugs. It was deserted. The intense cold had driven even the inhabitants of Salzburg indoors. When he turned round the gnome had vanished. The man moved like magic but he was probably on home ground.

Philip shrugged, brushed snow from his gloves, walked on deeper into the Old Town. He wanted to know its layout like the back of his hand.

29

Newman's first impression of Passau was the same as his last. He didn't like the place one little bit. He had driven across the Danube over the Schanzl Bridge, turned left into the Old Town. He felt he was entering a large prison.

The buildings were ancient, the streets narrow, cobbled. Over the whole port loomed the Dom, the twin-towered cathedral with a round bulbous dome at the summit of each tower and a massive stone entrance between the towers.

In early afternoon the place seemed unnaturally deserted as though the inhabitants preferred to stay indoors. He didn't blame them. The geographical location of the Old Town was peculiar – crammed on a peninsula with the Danube to the north and the River Inn joining it to the south at the eastern tip, it gave him a feeling of isolation, of being hemmed in by the tall stone walls of the buildings.

He found a public car park near the Rathaus, the Town Hall, which was hardly an architectural masterpiece. He was not too happy that his BMW would be the only vehicle occupying the park and he left it under the lee of a wall while he explored on foot. What made this place important to Walvis?

The weather didn't help. The streets were layered with snow and overhead dark black clouds drifted so low they almost touched the towers of the Dom. He strolled down several alleyways and again saw not a soul. It was like a town abandoned by the inhabitants fleeing the plague.

The silence was beginning to get on his nerves.

Halfway down one alleyway he stopped to gaze at a new chrome plate attached alongside a worn stone staircase. It carried the legend *Danubex*. He had half a mind to visit Walvis's headquarters but decided he'd leave that until later. He was walking on when he heard the faint sound of footsteps behind him, footsteps which were clearly careful to make as little sound as possible. He reached inside his sheepskin, gripped the butt of his Smith & Wesson.

'No need to get nervous. You're like a cat on a hot tin roof, to coin a phrase from the late Mr Tennessee Williams,' a voice drawled behind him in English.

'I don't believe it. I just don't believe it. Passau – and now you.'

Newman had swung round as he spoke to Marler, standing a few feet behind him, muffled like himself to the eyebrows.

'Don't you like Passau, then?' Marler teased.

'I think it reminds me of a graveyard . . .'

'Let's hope it doesn't turn out to be ours.'

'Cheerful Charlie. Just what I needed. How the hell did you turn up here? You're supposed to be in Salzburg.'

'Tweed's specific orders. Thought you might need back-up. He seems to think Passau is a key to Tidal Wave.'

'You've just arrived?' Newman snapped.

'Lordy, no. I can drive faster than you. Remember when you stopped on the autobahn to drink some booze from that flask you carry? A ruddy great petrol tanker overtook you. I was overtaking the tanker – which masked me from you. I've been here some time.'

'Doing what?' Newman demanded.

'Getting the hang of this dump. I was here years ago and it hasn't changed a bit. Normally that's a plus – to find somewhere that hasn't changed over the years. Here it's one big minus.'

'So you don't like it either?'

'I think your use of the word graveyard was graphic. But I doubt if you've been looking in the right places.'

'So where are the right places?'

'Along the Danube waterfront. Incidentally, I saw your BMW parked all by itself. Which told me you'd just arrived. The bonnet was warm – even in this temperature. I drove my Renault from round the corner and parked it next to your jalopy. It looked too prominent – just one car parked by itself. Mine is pointed the same direction. I expect you parked yours in the same way and for the same reason – ready for a quick getaway across the Schanzl Bridge.'

'Let's get moving and see this spectacular sight. And you know I don't drink and drive – I was drinking coffee out of my Thermos.'

'Thought you'd rise to that one . . .'

Marler led the way through a labyrinth of narrow streets and alleys. Newman noticed that the walls of a number of buildings were plaster-covered and had, at some time, been painted in colours – yellow ochre, pale green – but the colours were fading. They passed arched openings leading to sinister-looking inner courtyards. Still no people.

'Something that will interest you is coming upriver,' Marler said. 'I saw it just before I came back and spotted your jalopy.'

'The jalopy is a BMW,' Newman pointed out. 'I don't think you'd be popular with the Germans . . .'

He stopped speaking as they suddenly emerged on to the open promenade lining the bank of the Danube. Here the view was more impressive – on the opposite bank the

281

ground rose steeply with old houses tucked into the hillside. The Danube flowed steadily, a grey porridge-like surge.

'So much for the Blue Danube,' Newman remarked.

'The cruises start from here,' Marler told him. 'Behind us several cruise ships are moored for the winter. What a bore it must be, drifting down to Vienna. Now you can see what I was talking about, what will interest our devious chief, Tweed.'

They had reached a point where the buildings ended near the tip of the peninsula and had a clear view down-river beyond where the Inn flowed into the Danube. Approaching Passau round a great bend in the river was an immense barge-train. Marler moved out of sight under cover of the wall of a building and Newman followed him.

The barges were deep in the water; the Danube was almost up to the top of the gunwales, Newman noticed. Marler was viewing them through a small pair of field-glasses he had taken from his coat pocket. He handed the glasses to Newman.

'Remember what we were told about Walvis bringing enormous supplies of sophisticated weapons up the Danube aboard barge-trains?'

'Yes. I think this could be one of them, and a major consignment.'

'I saw a security guard carrying an automatic weapon just before he disappeared below decks. If it's innocent cargo . . .'

'Why would they need armed security guards?' Newman agreed.

'So now it appears our visit might have some purpose.'

'Such as?' Newman queried.

'Waiting until that lot has berthed, then waiting until it gets dark before we board one of those barges.'

'Not a lot we can do if we do find the cargo is what we think it is,' Newman commented.

'That's because *you* didn't bring the right equipment.'

'So what did the man who thinks of everything bring with him?' Newman enquired ironically.

'A generous amount of Semtex, plus timers and detonators. We may have a very dangerous job to do tonight. It means hanging about in Passau for hours. That barge-train will berth further down from here.'

'I've got a better idea,' Newman said. 'There was a café on the far side I noticed when I was driving in. And just beyond it a restaurant. First, we linger over coffee, get in out of the cold, out of sight. Later, we go along to the restaurant and have a meal.'

'For once you score,' Marler admitted. 'We could be sitting right opposite where the barge-train berths, give us a good chance to weigh up the opposition.'

'And we're taking the cars – I don't like leaving them so we could be isolated on this peninsula when we want to run for our lives.'

'You score again. I wouldn't like to leave what's inside my Renault. It's a mobile bomb . . .'

Philip returned to Tweed's suite at the Österreicherischer Hof to find two worried people waiting for him. He dumped his sheepskin over the back of a chair and slumped into it.

'Sorry to be so long,' he said to Paula and Tweed. 'It was worth it, but it's like the North Pole outside. In an alley I saw a big wooden water butt which collects water draining off a roof. It was full and had a solid layer of ice on top . . .'

'I'll get coffee for you from room service,' said Paula.

'That would be welcome. Also some sandwiches. I couldn't face a full meal yet. It was cold as charity out there.'

'You found out something?' Tweed enquired.

'I think you'll agree my prowl round the Altstadt was worthwhile. There are things you should know. Maybe I should start with a most unpleasant character. A Mr Ronald Weatherby. "Call me Ronnie . . ."'

Philip later went on to recall his surprise meeting with Ziggy Palewski. Tweed, seated in a chair facing him, took in every word. Paula looked anxious while Philip was describing the violent encounter with three thugs.

'Were any – or all of them – dead when you left them?' Tweed enquired quietly.

'I've no idea.' Philip sounded indifferent to their fate. 'It was us or them. I did my best to make sure it was them.'

'You did well.' Tweed looked thoughtful. 'You may have done even better than you realize.'

'Why is that?' Paula asked.

'Because the news will rapidly reach Walvis. One of our men eliminating three of his will worry him, could stir him into further unbalanced action. I'm sure he has a massive ego. I want to disturb it, challenge it. But the most important event in Philip's exploitation of the Altstadt is his meeting with Palewski. Where is this Brodgasse?'

'I went out and bought a map,' said Paula.

She spread it out on a side table. Philip stood with them, pointed to the street.

'The Altstadt is very complex. I found Brodgasse after Palewski performed his disappearing act. At the far end of the street you walk into one of the many squares, the Residenzplatz. From there you walk on into another large square, the Domplatz . . .' His finger moved across the map. 'Then on and on until you come to where the funicular – the *Festungsbahn* – climbs steeply up to the castle. It's very isolated up there and you feel you are standing on a cloud as you look straight down on to the Altstadt labyrinth.'

'Many people up at the castle?' Tweed asked casually.

284

'No one except me. I was the only passenger on the funicular, going up and coming down later. From the platform you also get an incredible view of the Alps, but you feel very isolated and alone up there.'

'Might be just the place,' Tweed mused.

'Just the place for what?' asked Paula.

'I was thinking aloud. For what I have in mind I would be happier if I had Newman and Marler with us . . .'

The phone rang. Tweed picked it up quickly, almost anxiously, Paula thought.

'Yes?' he said.

'Bob speaking from you know where. And Nanny arrived some time ago to hold my hand. I can see him sitting at our table in a restaurant. What was reported might turn up *has* turned up – on a big scale. I can see it from where I am standing now. I think we should be leaving here this evening later after dark. So where do we head for next?'

'Where I'm staying now. Any idea when you both could get here? I'm not asking you to hurry.'

'Later tonight. Must go now. See you . . .'

For Tweed it seemed like an answer to a prayer. He put down the receiver, told Paula and Philip what Newman had said.

'It means a very large barge-train has arrive in Passau. Newman made it sound like an exceptional Walvis consignment of arms. Marler is with him.'

'They're not going to do something mad on their own, I hope,' Paula commented.

'We must leave it to their judgment—' He broke off as the phone rang again. 'That may be Nield or Butler reporting from Grafenau.' He picked up the phone again.

'Yes?'

'Good evening, Mr Tweed,' a deep throaty voice said. 'I have decided it might well be of mutual benefit if we could arrange a meeting. Walvis speaking. Just the two of

285

us. I think it might well be of advantage to both of us if we met at a quiet rendezvous. Precautions would have to be taken on both sides, of course.'

'Of course,' agreed Tweed.

'Then perhaps we can get down to brass tacks, as they used to say in London.'

'Not yet,' Tweed said firmly. 'I need a little more time. I agree the idea in principle. How can I contact you?'

'You can't. My dear sir, why should I reveal the cards in my hand when I know the cards in yours? At this moment you are staying at the Hotel Österreicherischer Hof in Salzburg. In Room 309. I compliment you on your taste. It is a most excellent hotel.'

'Then you'd better keep phoning me until I am ready. I would appreciate it if you don't bombard me with calls.'

'Have a care, Mr Tweed. Have a care. We live in dangerous times . . .'

Inside the spacious living-room in the farmhouse between Munich and Deggendorf Walvis slammed down the phone. As he stared at Gulliver and Martin his expression was one of manic fury. He chewed at his lips and then delivered his verbal onslaught.

'You two have made a bloody cock-up of it in Salzburg. Tweed has with him only a girl – doubtless of no account – and one other man. Lucien reported to me a few minutes ago from Salzburg. He sent in three men – I did say *three* – to finish off this man in the Old Town. More important still, Ziggy Palewski was with this man. What happens? Your three carefully selected soldiers end up dead! Palewski disappears and Tweed's man then calmly wanders all round the Altstadt.'

'What was Lucien doing?' Martin enquired and then wished he hadn't asked the question.

'Your Lucien,' Walvis said in a quiet voice Martin

found unnerving, 'your Lucien,' he repeated, 'was creeping round the Altstadt, after the massacre of his soldiers, following Tweed's man who did the job – but at a most discreet distance. He was scared stiff after what he had witnessed. I could tell that when he phoned the news and I cross-examined him.'

'He's not really my Lucien,' Martin protested feebly. I . . .'

'*You!*' Walvis thundered. 'You were in charge of the operation. Now Tweed is alerted. And on top of that Lucien had Ziggy Palewski in the palm of his crooked hand – and lost him! Why do I employ such trash?' His manner suddenly became mild. 'We have other things to think of.'

'Do you really propose to meet Tweed?' Gulliver enquired cautiously.

'Yes. I need to see this extraordinary man, to see what I am up against. I might even be able to convert him to my point of view. That would be a great coup, bearing in mind the prime objective of Tidal Wave is Britain.'

'Why Britain?' Gulliver asked, his confidence growing now that Martin was in disgrace.

'Really, Mr Gulliver, you should read history.' Walvis settled back in his chair, folded his thick arms across his chest. 'In two world wars American reinforcements have helped to save the West. Especially in the Second World War, when Britain was essential as a base for their troops. It will not be available this time. Gulliver, you have made all necessary preparations?'

'Yes, sir.' Gulliver glanced at his watch. 'At any time we shall hear news that three of the eleven Regional Controllers in Britain have been killed. Are you wise, if I may raise the subject, to meet Tweed?'

'I have decided to do so. At the moment he is keeping me dangling on a string as to where and when he will agree to meet me. I don't like that. But now I am most

287

concerned with the arrival of that huge and vital supply of arms at Passau. As you know, they are needed to equip the vast flood of refugees waiting to sweep into Germany across the Oder–Niesse line, into Austria and Italy, then on to France. Meantime we have Britain under our control, so Europe is trapped in a gigantic pincer movement.'

'Isn't there a danger the refugees will run amok?' queried Gulliver.

'No. They will be directed by the small army of leaders of different nations we have trained in the mountains on the Czech border. It is my genius to have foreseen the flood of refugees will come anyway – but to organize them for my own purpose. I shall go down in posterity as the man who changed the course of history . . .'

East of Grafenau, the town which they had avoided, Butler was driving his Citroën, with Nield alongside him, high up the track leading into the mountains.

'I hope those clouds don't come any lower,' Nield said, peering out of the window. 'If they do we shall be driving in a fog.'

'So let's hope we find out what's going on first . . .'

Butler had just spoken when Nield grasped his arm, pointing to the left where a sheer rock wall descended. An ancient iron truck, very like the type used in coal mines to transport coal underground, stood at the entrance to a cavern. Nearby a pair of rusting rails projected from inside the cavern.

'That we investigate,' Nield decided.

Butler parked the car behind a huge rock, covered the bonnet with a sheet of canvas he always carried, and hoisted a large pack on his back. He grinned briefly as Nield stared at the pack.

'That looks pretty heavy. Won't it restrict your movements?' Nield suggested.

288

'You've forgotten, Pete. I used to be a coal miner years ago. This lot is light as a feather.'

'And what is this lot?'

'Oh, little things that might come in useful. Mercury-tilt detonators, other types of detonators, timers and enough Semtex to blow up half this mountain. Marler was generous with the supplies he obtained from Berg.'

'Let's get moving, then . . .'

There was no sign of anyone within miles as they approached the rusting truck, the old railway which appeared to have entered the mountain. Nield frowned as they stood by the truck, which was open and empty.

'Something funny here. Look at those wheel ruts in the snow. They're recent and come right up to the entrance to the cavern.'

'Abandoned salt mine. We heard about them.'

Butler bent down, used his gloved hand to remove snow from the rails further inside the opening. Instead of rusting track he exposed clean new rails. He stood up.

'There is something phoney about this. Trucks have rolled over these rails during the past few days. You can see traces of wheel-marks. This mine is being used for something.'

'Then let's explore inside, but proceed cautiously – there could be guards . . .'

It was as ice cold inside as it had been outside – for a distance. Nield used his pencil torch to see their way after they had turned a corner into Stygian blackness. He moved the beam up the old rock wall, stopped as it reached the roof. Slung along the roof were a power line and a telephone wire. Which didn't suggest to him an abandoned salt mine. They carried on their conversation in whispers. Butler had seen the cable, the wire.

'Telephone communication with the outside world. Power – probably for heating and lighting. Think there's a Hilton inside here?'

289

'If there is I can't see it making a profit.'

'I'm used to mines, Pete. I recognize, can hear, noises a long way off. Think I should be in the lead.'

'I'll be close behind you.'

'Seems less cold,' Butler said as they progressed deeper along the tunnel.

'Warmer, I'd say,' Nield replied.

'So let's be even more cautious . . .'

Treading from tie to tie between the rails, which gleamed by the light of Nield's torch, they walked slowly deeper under the mountain. They had come to a corner when Butler, peering round it, put out a hand to cover the light from the torch, which Nield promptly switched off.

It was distinctly warmer and both men could hear a muted hum which reminded them of an air-conditioning system. Butler stepped back, gently pushed Nield away from the faint glow of light ahead round the corner.

'We've arrived,' he said. 'A ruddy great steel door with a wheel in the middle – like a bank-vault door – closes off the tunnel. Above it is a fluorescent strip. And under that is a guard with a machine-pistol.'

'Can we get close enough to take him?'

'We just might, but I don't know whether we'd ever open that door. We need a lucky break. It could be they change over guards regularly on a roster basis. In which case the door will be opened.'

'You take the guard you've seen and I'll tackle the one who arrives to replace him. If there's only one new guard, if we can do it silently, if a replacement does turn up. This is pretty "iffy",' Nield concluded, not his normal buoyant self.

'We could shoot them, do the job properly,' Butler said cheerfully. 'Tweed wants to know what's going on here.'

'We fire shots and others could come running, perhaps a whole battalion of them. How is the guard dressed?'

'Some kind of uniform. An army-type greatcoat and a

290

cap with the brim pulled well down over his forehead. And a pair of dark glasses like goggles. Funny thing, he's got a respirator dangling from his neck.'

'Sounds more and more intriguing, and more and more dangerous. Which means we *should* investigate . . .'

They seemed to wait for ever, not daring to sit down so they were ready for any eventuality. There came a moment when Butler couldn't resist peering round the corner of rock. He jerked his head back.

'Guard was looking at his watch. Maybe that's a good sign. You lose track of time in a mine shaft.'

'We've waited twenty minutes so far,' said Nield, who had been checking his own watch.

'Listen!' hissed Butler.

Both of them heard the faint sound of locks being shot into place. The door was being opened. Butler peered round the corner, suddenly leapt forward, followed by Nield gripping his Walther by the barrel. They saw the back of the guard, waiting to leave his post, his automatic weapon slung over his shoulder from a strap. Butler, hands bare, grasped the guard round the throat with one hand, placed the other over his mouth. He pulled the guard backwards. Instinctively the guard tried to jerk forward. Butler let go with both hands, took hold of the back of his head, slammed it forward against the rock face. He dragged the collapsing guard to one side.

It had all happened in seconds. In the same period of time Nield, standing to the open side of the door, back against the rock wall, saw another similarly uniformed guard walk out, pausing to light a cigarette, automatic weapon hung over his shoulder from the strap. Nield used his left hand to whip off the man's heavy cap, his right hand brought down the Walther's butt with all his force on top of the man's exposed skull. The vibration of the force of his blow travelled up his arm. The guard

291

made no sound as he sprawled forward, crashing on to the rails, lying still.

'We'll put on those greatcoats and caps,' Nield ordered. 'Then we'll explore inside. Shove the bodies into those rock alcoves. Carry your pack under your arm . . .'

'Come on! Come on! Hustle it up, you chaps. We've got a short class and a lot to get through. You'll be on your way to Sussex, the Midlands, Yorkshire, London before you can say knife . . .'

Nield and Butler, clad in greatcoats and peaked caps – pulled well down over their foreheads – stared in amazement. The voice was toffee nosed, the English spoken in a high-pitched tone sometimes adopted back home by the upper classes.

Turning a corner further along the woodblock-paved corridor – bisected down the middle by a sunken rail track – they saw a large group of men wearing English clothes filing down some stone steps into a large room. Over the entrance was the word *England*. Some wore casual clothes, others were clad in business suits.

'Wait here for me,' Nield said. 'I can join that lot.'

As though to confirm the plausibility that he would not be detected they heard the thin balding man with the plummy accent call out again.

'No time to count you in and out today. We're short of time,' hectored the lecturer, wearing a jersey and baggy trousers.

Nield always wore a business suit and underneath layers of clothes he stripped off, handing them to Butler, he wore a heavy grey business suit. He straightened his tie as Butler stared at him.

'You're mad . . .'

'I can merge in with that lot. I'll join you further down the tunnel towards the entrance. Hide that uniform and the rest of my clothes. Must find out what is going on – something very weird . . .'

He was just in time to join the last four people, two of them women, descending the staircase. He walked alongside a short plump woman wearing a Paisley sweater and a pleated skirt.

'Let's have a drink together later, get to know each other better. If we have the time. Tell you what – we will make the time.'

'Is that what men do with women in England?' she asked in a pukka accent.

'You'd be surprised what men do to girls in England, from what I hear . . .'

She giggled as they entered what appeared to Nield to be a public-school classroom with a raised platform at one end for the lecturer. He guided the woman to a couple of vacant seats at the back.

'You all know where you will be landed from the sea in England,' the lecturer began, perched on his platform. 'The majority in East Anglia at night, as you know, but others, as you also have been instructed, will land in Dorset on the south coast, where you will be met. Any questions so far?'

Nield saw a man starting to raise his arm and shot his own into the air. There were at least fifty people in the room and he was half hidden behind a very fat man as he asked his question.

'Supposing there's a cock-up and some of us are not met after we have landed. Can we lie low and use public transport in the morning? A local bus, something like that?'

'Ah,' the lecturer replied, 'we have someone here who shows great initiative. Certainly if your contact fails to meet you use any method to reach your destination. You have all been shown where to go to, the code word to be used. A local bus would be perfect, but I advise you

293

against stopping a motorist for a lift. There is so much crime in England today that people are afraid of stopping for strangers. They might even report you to the police. Next question . . .'

As the others asked questions Nield stared grimly at the large map of the British Isles hanging from the wall behind the lecturer. On it were marked major telephone exchanges, power stations, airfields and a square that appeared to indicate the position of a mansion. It was marked 'Regional Controllers' Secret HQ'.

'I am bringing this last meeting to a close with a word of warning,' the lecturer said eventually. 'When you leave here you will do so by the door at the end of the tunnel taking you out into Germany. That is now the only exit. The door at the other end of the tunnel you entered by from the Czech Republic has been sealed and cannot be opened. That is all. I know you will all help us to over-whelm the West. Remember this – NATO is equipped for conventional warfare. We shall be launching a guerrilla war, creating chaos. Something NATO will not be able to cope with . . .'

Nield was careful to mingle with the crowd as they made for the staircase, not among the first and not among the last to leave. At the top of the staircase he side-slipped away from the others heading in the opposite direction, into the tunnel.

'It's me. Don't jump.'

Nield *had* jumped as Butler appeared from inside an alcove, holding his companion's outer clothes. Nield talked quickly as he kicked off his slip-on heavy shoes with rubber studs on their soles. He slipped on a pullover, then another one, a pair of heavy trousers, a windcheater, his sheepskin.

'Remember we heard they were training leaders for the

294

Tidal Wave operation in these mountains? Well, they are, and a major contingent is aimed at Britain. Go into details later. We'd better get out of here . . .'

'I heard that fellow you were listening to bellowing away. Those smarmy accents carry and he'd left the door open. So I took action. Beyond that door behind me is their telephone HQ complete with switchboard. And an operator who will wake up with a headache, if he ever wakes up. The whole phone system is smashed up – no communication now with the outside world. You see my pack is a lot lighter? I've laced the tunnel with explosives and a timer set to start detonation in fifteen minutes. Plus a back-up timer. And the exit door is packed with a small amount – enough to jam it, although I don't think it matters. The roof above us will cave in. They probably have another exit at the other end . . .'

'They've sealed that off . . .'

'Then they're about to be entombed for ever. The air conditioning system will crack up too . . .'

'So maybe we'd better take our hasty departure . . .'

They carried the guards' caps and coats they had worn so as not to raise the alarm too early. Nield revolved the wheel on the inside of the steel exit door after Butler had warned him not to touch an almost invisible wire.

'They touch that, try to snip it and the small bomb explodes in their faces. But not powerful enough to blow open the door . . .'

The cold hit them the moment they were on the far side of the door even though earlier it had seemed warmer when they first arrived. Butler closed the door carefully and swung the control wheel until it was tight. He heard the faint sound of the many locks engaging.

'What are we going to do with these two?' Butler asked as he pointed to the two guards slumped inside a rock alcove.

'Just leave them. We've no time to waste.'

295

They threw the guards' coats and caps on top of them and Butler relieved them of their automatic weapons and the spare mags he found inside their pockets. They peered outside, pausing by the rusting miner's truck. Nield nodded at it.

'That's camouflage to keep up the fiction of an abandoned salt mine. Nobody about, let's hustle.'

They ran to the parked Citroën, Butler removed the canvas over the bonnet, which was stiff with the cold, dumping it in the back together with his pack which still contained a large quantity of deadly material. Nield was huddled in the front passenger seat as Butler jumped in, closed the door, inserted his ignition key. To his relief and surprise the engine started first time.

'Where to?' he asked.

'Earlier we passed a signpost to Passau, Linz and Vienna. Newman is in Passau. In case he's still there we'll head for Passau. Maybe we can lend a hand. The direct route from here is through Grafenau. We'll risk it . . .'

Grafenau was not what they expected. It was a small modern town with shops and supermarkets. They took a wrong turning and arrived in front of a luxury hotel, the Sonnenhof. Gleaming Mercedes were lined up outside and a German, smoking a cigar, came out holding a pair of skis over his shoulders. Checking the map, Nield guided Butler out of Grafenau and soon they reached the signpost.

'Passau, here we come,' said Nield cheerfully.

The car's heaters had warmed up and he was thawing out.

30

At his farmhouse Walvis was poring over a map in the living-room. It was a map of Britain and he was taking a particular interest in the coasts of East Anglia and Dorset. He did not look up as Martin came rushing into the room.

'Soon we shall return to England,' Walvis said. 'From my base at Cleaver Hall facing the beautiful village of Bosham I shall personally direct the takeover of Britain.' He looked up, irritated that his concentration had been disturbed.

'Never come rushing into this room again – or any other room for that matter. When you rush in life you make mistakes. Have you just made one?'

'No, sir . . .' The red-faced Martin was out of breath. 'I came to report that I cannot get through on the phone to the Grafenau complex in the mountains. The line seems dead.'

'Is that all? Have you forgotten this has happened before? They have heavy snow there. Maybe the line is down. Our people will repair it quickly.'

'They are due to depart on their vital mission,' Martin persisted, anxious to show how responsible he was. 'I would like permission to fly there in the helicopter to make sure they are on schedule.'

'Permission granted. Anything to get you out of my hair. Now, leave me alone.' He had been staring down at the map, taking no notice of his subordinate. 'Oh, one moment,' he continued as Martin was leaving. 'Have you

297

heard from Rosa Brandt? Not like her to be absent so long.'

'No, sir. Perhaps she has a bad cold. It is a nuisance she has no phone at her Munich apartment.'

'Depart, Martin. Depart . . .'

Tweed was sitting in his suite with Paula and Philip at the Österreicherischer Hof when the phone rang. Paula answered the phone, put her hand over the mouthpiece and pulled a face.

'You will not be best pleased. Howard is on the line.'

'Oh, hell,' said Tweed, who rarely swore even mildly. 'I suppose I shall have to listen to his blatherings.'

He took the phone and began speaking before Howard, his Director, could get a word in.

'I should warn you this call is passing through a hotel switchboard—'

'Devastating news. Absolutely devastating,' Howard interrupted, ignoring the warning. 'And we have no idea why it has happened, but it has such sinister undertones. I think you should come back at once.'

'I don't even know what has happened yet,' Tweed reminded him.

'Three of the Regional Controllers have been assassinated. All eliminated on the same day. The murders were synchronized. A car bomb. Another member rammed off the road into a deep gorge. The fool always used the same route from his home to work. The third was poisoned – we don't know how yet. Strychnine.'

'I see. Extra protection has been ordered for the other members, I presume?'

'Of course! I ordered it myself. Didn't go down very well with some of them. I only hope they obey orders. When can you fly home?'

'When I have finished the job I came out to do – which

may just be tied in with what you have told me.'

'I need your support in this unprecedented situation,' Howard bleated.

'I'm sure you can cope on your own. You'll have to.'

'I could order you to return home at once,' Howard said, with a feeble effort to sound commanding.

'You could,' Tweed agreed, 'the only thing is I wouldn't come back until I'm ready. But thank you, Howard – and I mean this – for giving me the information. It tells me more than you might ever imagine.'

'Well, I thought you ought to know,' said Howard, retreating. 'I'd appreciate it if you kept in touch. Is everyone all right – all our people?'

'So far as I know, yes. Goodbye . . .'

Tweed's expression was grim as he put down the phone. For a few minutes Paula said nothing, guessing that he was absorbing whatever bad news Howard had given him, sorting out in his complex mind how it fitted into a pattern he was building up.

'It was not good news, was it?' she ventured eventually.

'The worst possible. Three of the Regional Controllers have been murdered in Britain.'

'Regional Controller?' Philip queried. 'I've heard the phrase somewhere but I don't know what it means.'

'There are,' Tweed began, 'eleven Regional Controllers – at least there were before three were murdered on the same day. Most of the public has no idea they exist. They are tough able men whose job is to take over running Britain in case of a national catastrophe. By which I mean if the whole government could no longer function – maybe even wiped out by a bomb when a cabinet meeting was being held. A situation where all normal communications are out of action, people are bewildered, don't know what to do. The radio and TV systems knocked out. Chaos. Can you imagine the panic, the confusion?'

299

'So what happens? It sounds frightening,' Philip commented.

'It would be terrifying. That's when the eleven Regional Controllers are supposed to take over – take over the running of the entire country to try and keep things going. Secretly, Britain has been divided into eleven geographical areas. Each would have a Controller with dictatorial power. It's the last resort. I think Walvis has been fooling me.'

'How?' demanded Paula.

'By concentrating my attention on the Continental mainland. He probably thought I wouldn't detect the significance of these three assassinations. His prime objective is England. Hence that heavily guarded headquarters at Cleaver Hall – his base for Tidal Wave to submerge the island.'

'Shouldn't we go back there quickly, then?'

'No. What Walvis doesn't know is that thanks to Jean's . . .' He paused as he saw an expression of pain cross Philip's face, then vanish. 'Thanks to Jean's embroidery and Paula spotting those tiny crosses we'd be alerted to the significance of Munich, Grafenau and Passau. We'll wait until we've heard from Nield and Butler, from Newman and Marler. Later we may fly back to England.'

'Philip,' Paula said quietly, 'I hope you don't mind but I brought Jean's embroidery with me. I've taken great care of it.'

'Don't mind at all.' Philip's expression had changed, was now frozen in a grim look. 'I know you'll take great care of it – bearing in mind it was the last craft work she was engaged on.'

'I've even kept it folded in exactly the way she neatly folded it. I want another look at it over here. It's in my shoulder-bag.'

'Why another look?' Tweed asked.

300

'Because this time I'll use a magnifying glass to see if there's something I've missed.'

An ice-cold dark December night had fallen on Passau. In the restaurant perched above the river Newman again checked his watch. To give him an excuse for waiting longer he had recently ordered his third cup of coffee. He was worried about Marler.

An hour ago, after they had finished their meal, Marler had said he wouldn't bother with coffee. He insisted on going on what he called 'my recce' by himself.

'One man is far less likely to be seen than two,' he had argued. 'There's an outboard rubber dinghy moored to the shore below this restaurant. I'm going across in it to take a closer look at that lot.'

'It's so quiet down there any guards will hear the motor without any trouble,' Newman had objected.

'Which is why I hope it has a paddle . . .'

'That lot' was the train of immense barges that lay berthed on the opposite bank. Since Marler's departure Newman had seen single guards patrolling each of the huge craft, flashing torches along the decks. There had been no attempt to unload them and Newman assumed they were waiting for daylight. Eventually he could stand the waiting no longer. The bill had been paid but he left a large tip for the single waiter in a green apron who had disappeared some time before into the kitchen.

He had descended the steps to where his BMW and Marler's Renault were parked when he saw another guard walking along the nearest barge, flashing his torch. He ducked behind his car, cursed and again waited. He had just stood up as the guard vanished when a car's head-lights appeared from the direction of Munich. The car slowed as its headlights played over the BMW and New-man ducked out of sight for the second time, his Smith &

301

Wesson in his hand. The car stopped, a door opened.

'It's Bob's car,' a familiar voice said quietly. 'Now I wonder where the hell Bob has got to?'

'He's here,' said Newman, greeting Pete Nield and Harry Butler, who had alighted from their Citroën. 'What on earth brings you here?'

'Thought you might need the odd helping hand,' Nield said. 'Maybe even two odd helping hands . . .'

'We need all the help we can get,' said Marler, emerging from the gloom by the Danube river-bank. 'I've got a lot of explosive plus timers and detonators in my Renault, but we need more to send that cargo up in smoke.'

'What cargo?' Newman demanded.

'I levered open several hatches aboard three of the barges. Contents? Same in all of them. Explosives, Kalashnikov rifles, grenades and surface-to-air missile launchers – plus the missiles. A lot of the crates are stamped with the magic word: Danubex. I don't think Mr Walvis is planning a fireworks display for a charity ball . . .'

Butler and Marler, the top explosives experts, worked like Trojans and by feel most of the time inside the two cars, the Renault and the Citroën. Newman acted as lookout but Passau seemed even deader at night than it had appeared in daytime.

When they had carefully stored the assembled units inside back-packs Newman peered inside the Renault. Marler and Butler took no notice as they adjusted straps to ensure nothing inside moved.

'How do we get all this stuff across the fast-flowing Danube in one dinghy using only a paddle?'

'We don't,' Marler snapped. 'I found three dinghies, each with two paddles. And the reason my hands are blistered is I hauled them along the towpath higher up to another landing stage. Why? So we can let the three dinghies be carried out into midstream before we reach the barges, then use the paddles to guide the dinghies

302

alongside the first barge. From that one we can barge-hop to the others as we place the explosives in the holds. The barges are so heavily laden, so low in the water, we can climb aboard once we've moored the dinghies to their hulls.'

'But there are guards aboard and the four of us can't hope to avoid them all. OK, we can shoot them, but Lord knows what reinforcements that will bring.'

'So take this,' Marler said. 'Pete and Harry have several. And we do now have plenty of explosive, et cetera. Harry had a good supply in his Citroën. We even have some left.'

The object Marler had handed Newman was a canister of Mace, a gas that would disable a man with one squirt in the face, eliminating his ability to see and painful enough to put him out of action.

'So what are we waiting for?' asked Butler impatiently.

'Nothing,' said Newman, who decided he had raised enough objections. No operation could be planned without an element of risk.

Marler's calculations proved astonishingly exact. The three dinghies, looped together with ropes, their final stretch on the Siberian Danube aided with paddles, bumped silently against the stern of the first barge.

Newman left Marler to give instructions by hand signals after they had moored the dinghies to the propeller of the monster barge. They shinned up over the gunwale, packs on their backs, their feet landing silently on the solid deck. Marler led the way, met the first guard, who struggled to unloop his machine-pistol from his shoulder. While he was carrying out this exercise Marler aimed his canister, pressed the button. A jet of Mace hit the guard on the forehead, in the face. He had time to gurgle before Marler hit him with the stiffened side of his hand. The

303

guard toppled overboard, went into the water, began to drift swiftly downriver, making no noise. Marler, crouched low, hurried along the port side nearest the open river, reached a hatch. 'I've been down here earlier,' he whispered to Newman. 'I need that pack on your back. And Butler. You and Pete stay up on deck as lookouts . . .'

The two men disappeared down an iron-runged ladder into the depths of the dark hold. Newman pulled his watch down to check the time by its illuminated hands, shoved it back up his sleeve. After a brief conversation with Pete he took up a position on the port side while Nield moved to the starboard.

The only sounds in the arctic night were the sluggish swish of water against the hull, the occasional clank of a chain linking them to the next barge. There was no sign of a guard and Marler with Butler came back up the ladder surprisingly quickly. Marler spoke to Newman as he lowered the hatch into the closed position.

'Quicker than I'd hoped. That was due to Butler being with me – he's amazingly swift.'

'Piece of cake,' said Butler, 'when you once used explosives like I did in my old mining days. Next?'

They had thought the tricky part would be moving across the gap between barges – at least Newman had. Marler dismissed Newman's spoken anxiety.

'There's a plank – no rails – linking each barge with the next. Just don't look down . . .'

Marler had crossed the plank, had moved some distance in a crouch along the vast deck of the next barge, when a guard appeared out of nowhere behind him, silent as a ghost. He was unlooping his automatic weapon from his shoulder when Butler came up behind him, wrapped both arms round the guard in a bear hug, his normal tactic when possible. One gloved hand covered the guard's mouth, the other grasped his jaw, jerked it up and

304

backwards. What happened next was unpleasant and the guard ended up with a broken neck. Butler tossed guard and weapon over the side into the Danube.

Marler was already opening another hatch, his gloved hand easing up the iron ring, then hauling open the well-oiled hatch cover. He had noticed Butler's struggle with the guard but had continued with his work, confident that Butler would cope.

'This one is really important,' he said without explaining why.

He took from Newman the pack he had handed him on emerging from the previous hatch. Butler followed him down, Newman again checked his watch. He was taking up his lookout position on the port side when a torch glared in his eyes. Without a second's hesitation he lowered his head and charged the guard, head-butting him, sending him sprawling on the deck. Newman fell on top of him and only then realized he was wrestling with a tall heavyweight giant. The guard rolled sideways, sending Newman flat on his back on to the deck. The giant's large hands grasped his opponent's throat, began squeezing as he half lay on top of Newman. They struggled fiercely and Newman felt his consciousness slipping away. He clenched his right fist, swung it up and down on the bridge of the huge man's nose. The hands released the grip on his throat but the guard was still active. By the light of the torch lying on the deck Newman saw Nield had hold of the man's long hair, was pulling it upwards so the large head was tilted at an angle. Guessing what Nield wanted to do Newman forced the upper half of his body from under the guard's and slithered sideways. Nield suddenly used both hands to crash the man's skull down on the iron-hard deck. He then repeated the process and the guard lay still. Newman, still groggy, pulled the lower half of his body free of the guard's, made himself stand up.

'I hit him three times with the butt of my Walther,' Nield said, breathing heavily. 'He has a head of rock.'

'Thanks,' said Newman.

'Combined operation. It will take two of us to put him over the side . . .'

'Get rid of that lighted torch first . . .'

Nield picked up the torch, switched it off, threw it over the side. He turned and looked down at the huge guard.

'It *will* take two of us to heave him into the river. You look a bit under the weather. Take the legs, I'll take the upper half.'

Between them they lifted the guard, who still carried his automatic weapon looped over his shoulder. They began to swing him backwards and forwards and Newman, a strong man, thought the brute weighed a ton.

'Now!' whispered Nield.

They swung him outwards with all their strength, let go. The guard sailed out several yards beyond the hull, sank into the water and was caught up by the current, vanishing half submerged.

'I'd prefer not to meet another one like that,' Newman admitted.

'You took a big chance, charging him like that. He could have been aiming his weapon.'

'These guards are not very on the ball,' Newman explained. 'They patrol with their weapons looped over their shoulders. Fortunately for us. My Lord, they're coming up out of the hatch already.'

'We had a little trouble while you were enjoying yourselves down there,' Nield remarked.

Marler ignored the remark, concentrating on closing down the hatch, lowering the lifting ring into its original position. Then he spoke to Newman.

'This one is important – it is laden with launchers and their missiles. We deal with two more barges, which will make four out of six. With the amount of explosive we're

306

laying the last two barges will be sunk. Butler is setting the timers for ninety minutes from now. So let's hustle . . .'

They completed lacing the other two barges with explosives without incident. No sign of any guards. Newman theorized that they had pushed off for supper, relying on the guards they had encountered to protect the deadly cargo.

'How do we reach the cars?' Butler asked.

'First, we go back along the barges the way we came,' Marler said.

'What the hell for?' demanded Butler.

'To release the dinghies we left tied up. Something that I should have done when we arrived but I didn't know if we'd need them to escape.'

'Then what?' Butler persisted as they moved back towards the next barge, crouching low.

'We walk back along the waterfront, keeping in the shadows, to the bridge. I suggest, Newman, you take the lead since you have such excellent night sight. I'll follow with Butler and Nield can act as tail lookout . . .'

'Assuming we reach the cars, where to then?' Nield enquired.

'We drive straight to Salzburg,' Newman said firmly. 'I have an idea Tweed will welcome the reinforcements . . .'

Marler released the dinghies successfully and ten minutes later they were sitting in their three cars. Newman drove off first, followed by the others. They had left Passau behind when Newman checked his watch yet again. Ninety minutes was up.

In the distance there was the muffled boom of a series of explosions. In his rear-view mirror Newman could see the twin towers of the Dom at Passau. They were suddenly illuminated by a series of tremendous flashes which went on and on as the booming sound disappeared. The barge-train was at the bottom of the Danube.

31

Tweed, restless when no more news came through said to Paula and Philip he'd take them out for coffee. He was feeling he had to get out of the hotel to dispel the tension building up inside him. There had been no news from Grafenau, no further news from Passau.

'It will be bitterly cold out there,' Paula said, 'but I don't care with the prospect of a three-decker chocolate cream gâteau. My mouth's watering.'

'I could do with a cup of coffee and a pastry,' Philip agreed.

'Off we go, then,' Tweed decided. 'We'll make pigs of ourselves . . .'

'It's really amazing,' Paula recalled as they descended in the elevator, 'how a change of hair style transforms a woman's appearance, makes her almost unrecognizable.'

She saw Tweed's expression and frowned.

'Have I said something significant? I was thinking of Jill Selborne's new hairdo at dinner – a glorious long mane of thick hair compared with that black helmet style she'd adopted in Munich.'

'I think you may have said something highly significant,' said Tweed as he stepped out of the elevator and stopped. 'Speak of the devil,' he whispered.

Jill Selborne, clad in a sleek fur coat that Paula instantly recognized as sable, was just passing the elevator walking towards the exit. She had a small fur hat perched on top of her waves of dark hair and looked very fetching. She stopped.

'Hello there. I was just going out for a walk, feeling lonely.'

Philip was staring at her and Jill stared back, their eyes locked on each other. Tweed introduced them and Jill slipped her fur glove off her right hand to shake Philip's. It seemed to Paula they spent a long time holding on to each other.

'If you're feeling lonely,' Tweed suggested, 'why don't you join us? Two attractive women and two men,' he went on in his most gallant manner. 'We are looking for the best *pâtisserie* in Salzburg. Paula wants to stuff herself with cream cakes.'

'And I'd love to join Paula in the exercise,' Jill replied. 'If we go across the river to the Altstadt we'll get cut in two by the wind. I know the best *pâtisserie* in Salzburg, just round the corner.'

'Then take us there,' Tweed enthused.

They naturally divided into two couples – Philip and Jill leading the way while Tweed and Paula followed behind. Paula noticed Jill was taking a great interest in Philip, chattering away to him. He listened, looked at her, but said very little. The poor devil is going to take some thawing out emotionally, Paula thought, but it's far too early for that – so why is he studying her so closely?

The *pâtisserie* was still open but there were no other customers, Tweed noted thankfully. He wanted the others to talk animatedly while he ruminated, adding pieces to the jigsaw he was building up mentally.

'Have you managed to interview your famous conductor yet?' Paula asked Jill when she could get a word in edgeways.

'Not yet. He's playing hard to get.'

'And I shouldn't ask his name?' Paula chaffed her.

'Heavens no! Not yet. Not until I have persuaded him and completed the interview, if I ever do. Just look at those pastries,' she said as the waitress arrived with the coffee Tweed had ordered for everyone and a large double-decker stand with a variety of gâteaux and pastries was put on the table.

Paula noticed Philip was watching Jill. She had taken off her small fur hat and was using both hands to smooth down her waterfall of dark hair. He had a curious expression, as though he was observing someone he had seen before but could not place when it had been.

From the position he was seated in he could look out of the window next to them. He switched his gaze from Jill as a car approached, its headlights undimmed. The car was slowing down, had stopped.

'Down on the floor!' Philip roared.

As he called out he used one hand to pull a leg of Tweed's chair from under him, the other hand to unseat Paula. Jill reacted with great speed, not questioning his shout, impelled by the urgency in his voice, slid under the table. Tweed and Paula were sprawled on the floor as Philip joined them, jerking the Walther out of his hip holster. He had acted so quickly the mêlée had taken place in two or three seconds.

A rattle of automatic fire shattered the window they had been seated next to. Glass flew across the *pâtisserie*, bullets thudded into the walls, sprayed the empty tables in a murderous fusillade. The waitress had just vanished into the kitchen when the bombardment opened up.

'Lucien . . .!'

Philip's voice was cold and lethal. He jumped up as the car began to move on, ran out of the *pâtisserie* into the night. Near by a motor cyclist about to get on to his machine stood frozen as a waxwork.

Philip ran to the machine, jumped into the saddle, pressed the starter button and sped off before the owner

310

was able to react. He was just in time to see the car driven by Lucien turning over the bridge, racing at manic speed with no traffic to hinder him. Philip roared over the bridge and Lucien saw him coming in his rear-view mirror.

His long glance in the rear-view mirror was a mistake. As he looked forward again he saw a huge garbage truck turning on to the bridge and he was racing towards it. In a panic, he swung the wheel over, missed the truck by centimetres, rammed his foot on the brake as he saw the wall of a building sweeping towards him.

He had braked too hard. The car, a grey Audi, struck the edge of a stone wall at the entrance to an alley. There was a scream of tortured metal grinding against stonework. The car, caught in a skid over ice, was out of control. The bonnet slammed into a stone pillar, concertinaing the front part of the Audi, bursting open the driver's door.

Prepared for the shock, Lucien switched off the engine to avoid a fireball, shook his head, dived out of the open door and ran into the alley which he recognized.

Philip saw him leave the car, saw that the Audi had only partly blocked the entrance to the alley, slowed his machine, avoiding the ice patch, rode it round the rear end of the car and into the narrow alley. Lucien, wearing rubber-soled shoes with rubber prongs, was running down the alley over the snow- and ice-bound cobbles. Philip continued riding his machine slowly along the alley, which was deserted except for the distant fleeing figure.

'I'm going to get you this time,' Philip said aloud between gritted teeth.

He had left behind his sheepskin in the shattered *pâtisserie* but he was so intent on his prey he took no notice of the sub-zero temperature. The cobbles, exposed in places, slowed his progress. Ahead he saw the familiar small wide-shouldered figure who ran with a stoop, the

311

hunchbacklike man he had seen first through field-glasses from Manfred Hellmann's bungalow in Berg.

Lucien heard the motor cycle coming. He had almost run past when he noticed a large wooden barrel used for catching rain water from the rooftops. It was layered with ice. He took hold of it, realized from its weight it contained solid ice from top to bottom. He used his great strength to topple the barrel sideways, then started it rolling down the sloping alley. Philip saw it coming, knew there was no way he could avoid it, turned off his engine, jumped from the machine as the barrel crashed into it.

He began running close to the wall, the Walther now in his hand, but Lucien had disappeared to the left where the alley ended, entering a street. When he reached the exit, his own rubber-soled studded shoes helping his progress, he saw a tiny figure running at astonishing speed down the Getreidegasse in the direction of the labyrinth leading eventually to the castle.

He raised his Walther, lowered it immediately. The range was too great, a bullet too quick. He began running again down the otherwise deserted street.

At the *pâtisserie* Tweed helped Jill and Paula back on their feet. He warned them to be careful of glass, to check their clothes. Both women did as they were told but they had been lucky – neither of them found even a shard of glass on their clothing.

'What the hell was all that about?' Jill demanded in a tone which suggested they ought to know.

Still, better than a display of hysterics, Paula was thinking. Tweed had checked his own clothing. The pastries for their tea were scattered all over the shop, some decorated with bullet-holes.

'I presume,' Tweed said calmly, answering Jill's furious question, 'it was an attempt to kill one of us. Maybe all of

312

us.' He looked at Jill. 'You know anyone who would prefer you shot to pieces?'

'What do you think?' she snapped back at him.

'I was asking you,' Tweed reminded her. 'The most unlikely people have enemies. Maybe that mysterious conductor you are supposed to be interviewing doesn't want to meet you.'

'Why mysterious?' she blazed.

'Because I have checked with the concierge. At present no concert is taking place in Salzburg and no well-known conductor is in the city.'

'You're suggesting I made up the story?'

'I'm suggesting you have a lively imagination. Or perhaps you mistook the date. I wonder how Philip is getting on?'

Philip, slowing down to a fast walk, breathing heavily, beginning to feel the intense cold, had lost Lucien inside the maze which is the Altstadt. He was hungry, he was cold, but above all he was bitterly disappointed.

He was going to turn round to go back when a hand took hold of his arm. He was about to aim his Walther when he recalled the same incident, the same gentle grip on his arm, taking place when he had walked out of the Post Office in Munich.

'You have lost him in the rabbit warren, my friend.'

Again Ziggy Palewski, muffled in furs, had appeared out of nowhere. Philip gave a sigh of relief.

'Lost who?' he asked.

'I saw him run past here. A most recognizable gentleman. Lucien, the chief of Walvis's death squad. We will meet tomorrow, as planned. I advise you to take a taxi. You look very cold. Go down that alley and if you are lucky you may find a taxi.'

'A death squad, you said?'

313

'Oh, yes. Our Mr Walvis has a department to deal with all possible problems. Lucien is the most feared member among his organization . . .'

32

'Mr Tweed?' the stranger's voice had enquired when he had picked up the phone in his suite.

'Who is this?' Tweed snapped.

'Mr Tweed,' the voice persisted, 'I have a message for you from Mr Walvis. He is on his way to Salzburg to meet you tomorrow morning. He will call you himself tomorrow . . .'

Earlier, in the *pâtisserie*, Tweed had calmed down the proprietress who had emerged from the kitchen after the assault and Philip had left.

'Show us to another table away from this window – a blast of cold air is coming in. Then perhaps you would be good enough to serve us coffee and pastries again.'

His cool acceptance of the frightening incident had had the effect he was aiming for. Moving like a zombie the woman had escorted them to a distant corner table which was next to a radiator but nowhere near a window. None of the shattered glass had reached this corner and his two companions sat down with him.

'I can drink a lot of coffee but I don't think I can face a pastry,' Paula said.

'Me too,' Jill agreed.

She had recovered her poise, influenced by the matter-of-fact manner Tweed had adopted. Both women drank greedily their coffee which the woman had made afresh very swiftly. Tweed reached for the most succulent pastry oozing with cream and took a great bite. Both women watched him as he consumed it with evident enjoyment, wiped his mouth and reached for a wedge of chocolate gâteau.

'You know,' Paula said, 'I'm suddenly ravenous. I think I could manage one.'

'Me too,' Jill said again.

As each of them munched a pastry the proprietress was busy using a hand brush to sweep glass off tables and then using a long-handled brush to collect it in a dust pan. Both Paula and Jill reached for a wedge of gâteau. Tweed smiled to himself. Nothing like a full stomach to calm the nerves.

'I feel sure she will have phoned the police,' Tweed warned. 'When they arrive leave me to do the talking.'

'I'll be happy to do that,' said Paula.

'Me too,' Jill said for the third time.

'Now I think I could just manage an almond slice,' Paula said.

'And I'm going to join you,' Jill chimed in.

'Here come the police,' Tweed said as a car pulled up outside.

Three uniformed men with peaked caps rushed into the room. A tall heavily built man who appeared to be their superior went across to talk to the woman cleaning up glass. She spoke briefly, then pointed to the corner table.

'They don't look very bright,' Tweed commented. 'Which is all to the good.'

The tall policeman approached their table in an officious manner. He took out a notebook, stared at Tweed as he asked his question in German.

'I understand the gunmen fired at your table. Did you see any of them?'

'No, we didn't,' Tweed replied, not bothering to

315

correct his reference to a plural of attackers. 'We were too busy diving to the floor.'

'Have you any idea why this outrage should take place?'

'It could be the Chechen Mafia,' Tweed told him with an innocent expression. 'They are spreading across Europe, according to the papers. Perhaps they are planning to establish an extortion protection racket in Salzburg. So they wreck one shop to encourage the others to pay up.'

He could see the policeman didn't like this explanation one bit. He had stopped writing in his notebook, hitched up his belt.

'You have information, then – about this . . . Mafia?'

'None at all,' Tweed assured him. 'I'm only suggesting a theory based on what I've read in the papers.'

'Could I have your name and where you are staying?'

'We are not staying in Salzburg,' Tweed lied smoothly. 'We merely stopped here for coffee on our way home.'

'And where is home?' the policeman demanded.

'In London – that includes my companions.'

'You haven't given me your name,' the policeman said in a bullying tone.

'Mark Johnson,' Tweed said promptly. 'If you think we can help you in any way you are mistaken. We did not see who fired the shots, we did not see the car from which the shots were fired – so we can't identify the make.'

'I should like you to make a statement,' the policeman said pompously.

'Weren't you listening to me? I've just made one, letting you know we can't help you in any way, unfortunately. Why don't you ask the lady who runs this place all these questions . . .?' He raised his voice. 'Can we have the bill please, Fräulein? We are going to miss our train and we have to get home. We are late already.'

The woman made out the bill, hustled over and Tweed

316

paid her and left a generous tip. He stood up without looking at the policeman who seemed at a loss as to what to do next. The three of them walked out into the Siberian night after putting on coats and fastening them close to their necks. Tweed carried Philip's sheepskin.

'Thank you for the coffee,' Jill said with a wry smile as they entered the hotel. 'I'm heading straight for a long soaking bath. Could I come and see you later?'

'Give me an hour,' Tweed suggested. 'I have some phone calls to make.'

They had just entered his suite when the phone rang and the stranger gave Tweed the message about Walvis arriving in Salzburg. He relayed the message after replacing the phone.

'What do you think he's up to?' Paula asked immediately.

'I think for once he may mean what he says. That he does want to meet me and have a talk. Now I'm worried about Philip.'

He had enquired at the desk before they stepped into the lift and the receptionist, glancing at the key board, had told him Mr Cardon had not returned.

'Philip knows how to look after himself,' Paula said.

'That's true. But when he dashed out of the *pâtisserie* and the killer car took off I heard a motor cycle start up. I suspect Philip was in the saddle, chasing after the car. I also suspect Salzburg is crawling with Walvis's thugs – if Philip comes up against a gang of, say, five of them the odds will be loaded against him.'

He looked up as someone tapped on the door. Paula jumped up, slid the Browning automatic out of her shoulder-bag, went to the door, unlocked it on the chain, then opened it. She called out to Tweed over her shoulder. 'Guess who's arrived.'

Philip walked into the room. His clothes were torn in two places and his trousers were scuffed. He took off his

317

windcheater, laid it carefully over the back of a chair, his expression tough and bitter. He sat down.

'Coffee?' Paula asked. 'A drink? Scotch?'

'Later, thank you, Paula. The man who emptied that machine-pistol at us was Lucien.'

He pronounced the name in a vicious fashion. Then he went on to tell them what had happened afterwards before he had found a taxi to bring him to the hotel.

'So,' he concluded, 'I lost him in the Altstadt. The bastard moves like a greyhound. I can't wait to get my hands on him.'

'The Altstadt is the easiest place in the world to hide in,' Paula pointed out, trying to help his disappointment. 'He may even live somewhere inside it.'

'I'm beginning to think he does, so I'll be spending more time over there . . .'

He stopped speaking as there was a tattoo-rapping on the door. Paula was certain she knew who it was but even so she went to it with her Browning in one hand. When she opened the door, for the second time Tweed experienced a wave of relief.

Newman walked in first, carrying a pack, followed by Marler, Nield and Butler, who was also carrying a backpack. They all looked travel weary as they took off their coats and sank into different chairs.

'I think you should all go to your rooms,' Tweed said. 'Before you report have a bath and a change of clothes. When did you last eat?'

'The bath and the change of clothes can wait until later,' Newman said. 'A litre jug of coffee would help. But now you need to know what happened in the mountains on the Czech border and in Passau . . .'

Tweed listened to Newman without saying a word. Paula kept refilling cups with coffee. Nield had asked for

318

mineral water. Later everyone switched to mineral water while Nield gave his account of their experiences inside the mountain complex.

Tweed stood up when he had finished. He looked at each of the four men in turn – Newman and Marler, Butler and Nield.

'I find it difficult to express in words the magnitude of your achievements. In my highest expectations I had never imagined you would do what you have done. I thank you. And now, except for Philip and Newman, I suggest you go to your rooms and spend time freshening up. No hurry. We'll have drinks. But keep up the fiction that we don't know each other. So three different tables – one for Newman and Marler, another for Butler and Nield, and I will be with Philip and Paula.'

'It was just another job,' Butler said as he stood up.

'A mere sleight of hand in Passau,' drawled Marler.

'One moment – just before you go. Philip has not exactly been inactive. You will hear of his experiences soon.'

'Not until I've finished the job,' Philip said grimly.

Tweed waited until he was alone with Paula, Newman and Philip. He then told Newman about the stranger's phone call, the imminent meeting between himself and Walvis. Newman reacted strongly.

'Just a minute. I need to be in on this. There's an extension to the phone in this room. I want to listen in when Walvis – or whoever – calls. I'll pass scribbled notes to you. And from what I remember of Salzburg the last time I was here we avoid the Altstadt.'

'I know the Altstadt pretty well,' Philip said. 'From my being there more than once today. I could draw you a map.'

'Better if we consult a map together later,' Newman suggested.

'Jill Selborne had coffee with us this afternoon,'

Tweed told Newman with a wicked smile.

'Did she now?' Newman's expression was like stone. 'I get the impression too many coincidences are happening. We have Walvis on his way to Salzburg – if he really is coming. Now you tell me Jill Selborne has turned up. I have a bit of news for you I was keeping until we were on our own. Driving towards this hotel I saw someone in my headlights. I'm ninety-nine per cent sure it was Lisa Trent, of all people.'

'Lisa Trent? Here?' Tweed was briefly taken aback. 'How sure are you?'

'I told you. A woman dressed in ski pants with black knee leggings and a short black coat. She walked into this hotel. I can recognize her by the way she moves.'

'I've never heard you compliment staff so generously,' Paula said to Tweed when they were alone with Philip. 'That was quite a speech you made.'

'Yes. And no one realized just what I meant. They did bring off an amazing success in both areas. But the key element in my strategy is to throw Walvis into a panic. Imagine his reaction when he hears what has happened.'

'The end of Tidal Wave,' said Paula.

'Don't you believe it!' retorted Tweed. 'If I have any inkling of Walvis's character he will regard it as a temporary setback – but so long as he is alive he will press on with Tidal Wave. I'm bothered about something else.'

'Which is?' queried Paula. 'Or once again are we not going to be privy to your thoughts?'

'Teardrop,' said Tweed.

'What about her?'

'Philip has told us how he met Ziggy Palewski – who I'm sure knows more about Walvis than anyone else outside his organization. I'm convinced he is Teardrop's next target.'

320

'So?' Paula prompted.

'For various reasons which I won't list at the moment I'm sure one of three people is Teardrop. Lisa Trent, Jill Selborne, or Rosa Brandt. At least Brandt is not with us in Salzburg.'

'What does Rosa Brandt look like?' Philip asked.

'According to Newman – and Lisa Trent, who interviewed her twice – Rosa Brandt always wears a long black dress, and a black cap which covers her hair and has a black veil which conceals her face. Of medium height and slim build.'

'That's interesting,' Philip said. 'Just as I was getting into the taxi which brought me back here I saw a woman just as you have described her, but wearing a long black coat, disappearing into one of the alleys leading into the Altstadt.'

33

Inside his farmhouse Walvis was dressed for travelling when Martin came cautiously into the living-room. His welcome was not cordial.

'I am just leaving for Salzburg so I can't listen to any of your foolish chatter,' Walvis informed his deputy.

'But the weather is terrible.' Martin nodded towards the window where arc-lights illuminated the building. Outside snow was falling heavily. 'I should wait . . .'

'You would always wait. I am going by car – the armoured Mercedes, which will hold the road even in these conditions. What is it? Make it brief.'

'I still haven't been able to communicate by phone with

the training camp in the mountains. I couldn't leave earlier in the helicopter as planned. The stupid mechanics couldn't find the fault which had grounded the machine . . .'

'I know all this, idiot.'

'Please let me finish, sir. Now they have made the chopper airworthy the pilot says he can't fly in this snowstorm.'

'So you will have to stay here and act as housekeeper.'

Martin reddened an even deeper colour at this menial word. He decided to say no more and then Walvis suddenly swung round on him.

'Any news about Rosa Brandt? She has been away ages.'

'Same problem, sir. She has no phone so we can't contact her at the Munich apartment.'

'You could have sent a motor cycle courier. Too late now. Why do I have to think of everything myself? Any news of the barge-train arriving at Passau?'

'I'm afraid not. Apparently this exceptional weather has interfered with communications there, too. Shouldn't I accompany you to Salzburg in charge of your guard?'

'No.' Walvis smiled maliciously. 'Gulliver is in charge of protection. Think yourself lucky, Martin. There will be a Mercedes in front of me, another behind. Gulliver is travelling in the front car. Then if it skids into a barrier my driver will have ample warning.'

On this genial note Walvis began to walk towards the door, which had been specially widened so he could pass through without turning his massive bulk sideways.

'Maybe you would like a mobile phone,' Martin called out, hoping one suggestion would meet with approval.

'Are you mad? Or have you lost your memory? There will be no such rubbish in my motorcade – those instruments can too easily be intercepted, conversations

322

overheard, recorded. Do look after the shop and no more cock-ups.'

Outside the external door Gulliver, looking like a huge pear, muffled in a vicuña coat, used two hands to hold a massive umbrella over his chief. One of the armed guards was already standing by the rear door of the armoured Mercedes. He opened it as soon as Walvis arrived to avoid snow blowing inside. There was an awkward moment when Walvis turned himself sideways to enter the vehicle. The door was closed and Gulliver hurried to the front car which he would be driving himself, carrying three guards as passengers.

'I presume the brandy flask is full,' Walvis called out to his own driver who had settled behind the wheel.

'I checked it myself, sir.'

'Then I shall travel to Salzburg half sozzled – which is the only way to travel on a night like this. Do not drive too close to Gulliver. If anyone is to have an accident on the ice let it be my faithful deputy. That is why he is paid his exorbitant salary . . .'

Walvis closed the glass partition between himself and the driver, began to think about handling Tweed.

Tweed didn't go to bed that night. He sat up at a small desk, making notes, listing the multitude of events that had taken place, starting with finding Jean Cardon at Amber Cottage.

He was looking for the sequence of incidents which would give him a pattern as to what Walvis was planning. He kept coming back to Cleaver Hall.

Newman was also up early. He tapped lightly on Tweed's door in case he was still asleep. He stared in surprise when Tweed, fully dressed, opened the door.

'You're up with the birds too, then,' he said when he was inside and the door had been re-locked.

323

'I've been up all night. Don't let's waste time on that. I'm pretty sure this is going to be a decisive day. You couldn't sleep either?'

'Slept like a dog, a dog which sleeps well. Philip will be along in a minute. I want him to take me into the Altstadt so I know it as well as he does. If that's OK with you.'

'Why the Altstadt?'

'It could just be the best place for your rendezvous with Walvis. I changed my mind about that while I was getting to bed.'

'I'll leave it . . .'

He paused as Newman went to answer a tapping on the door. Philip, fully dressed and looking fresh and very determined, came in to join them.

'I'm glad to see you, Philip,' Tweed said. 'First, I'm happy about your acting as guide to Bob in the Altstadt. But two things I want to emphasize, Philip. First, if you should see Ziggy Palewski tell him I'm anxious to meet him urgently. Second – and mark this well – I'm fully aware of your feelings, but if we arrange a safe conduct for Walvis you keep out of the way. You might be tempted to kill him. I forbid it.'

'No need to worry,' Philip assured him, his voice cold. 'I could only shoot him if I had to. When the time comes I want it to be much slower.'

Tweed made no reply and they were leaving when Newman turned back.

'One vital point. If Walvis phones to arrange a meeting while I'm out stall him until I get back. I must listen in on that conversation to advise you.'

'I can think of a dozen reasons to make him call me back later . . .'

Tweed, who had earlier had a bath and shaved, was about to go down to breakfast when Paula arrived. She was wearing smart blue denims and a polo-necked sweater in a neutral tone.

324

Tweed told her where Newman and Philip had gone. She was staring at his notes on the desk.

'Have you had any sleep at all?'

'None. But you know that when I do that for the next day I'm even more alert.' He glanced at his notes and began gathering them up.

'You've been busy,' she commented. 'And I know you do not like me in denims but there are so many of them about it helps me to merge with the crowd. They should be OK for breakfast. What are the notes about?'

'Many things. One important subject is the identity of Teardrop. I know who she is.'

'And, of course, you won't tell me?'

'Too early in the day.'

'It always is, you secretive man.'

'I'm hungry,' Tweed replied. 'I could eat a very good breakfast. I wonder whether we shall eat alone?'

'It *would* make a change . . .'

They had settled themselves in the dining-room, had ordered a full English breakfast, when Jill Selborne entered.

'Ah, ah . . .' said Paula. 'If she comes over I'm going to concentrate on my meal. After the shock of the *pâtisserie* I have the appetite of a horse.'

'Best to eat when you can,' Tweed replied. 'On this trip you never know where the next meal is coming from – or when.'

He was staring at Jill as she walked close to their table. She paused and gave them a warm smile.

'Good morning. I'm going to leave the two of you on your own for once.'

'You're having breakfast with someone?' Tweed asked as he stood up.

'Well, actually no . . .'

'Then you'd be most welcome to join us.' He drew out a chair next to himself. 'Most welcome,' he repeated.

Paula tried not to show her surprise. First, at Tweed's pressing invitation. Second at Jill's hair-style. Instead of the long thick mane she had displayed the previous day she had reverted to her Munich coiffure. Her dark hair was close to her head like a black helmet.

'You look very smart,' Tweed said to her. 'And I like your different hairdo – like Joan of Arc preparing to go into battle.'

Jill, seated in her chair, glanced down at the menu, her eyes flickering briefly. Paula had the impression Tweed's remark had disconcerted her for some reason. Jill looked up quickly, gazed directly at Tweed and gave him a ravishing smile.

'Thank you. I appreciate the compliment. So very few men nowadays notice how a woman looks, and she may have taken ages to be at her best. Don't you agree, Paula?'

'I find it depends on the man,' Paula said briefly and started work on the steaming plate of bacon and eggs, which had arrived swiftly. Jill ordered coffee and said she only wanted rolls and a croissant. Then she concentrated her attention on Tweed.

'Any luck with your interview with the famous conductor?' he teased her.

'The one you didn't believe existed yesterday just before someone nearly blew us to kingdom come? Well, he isn't here to conduct because, as you rightly said, there are no concerts being performed. What you overlooked was the possibility that a conductor wanting a holiday might well choose Salzburg – which is such a beautiful city. And that he might be careful not to publicize the fact that he was here.'

'So would he welcome your intrusion, if I may use that word? And how did you find out he *is* here?'

'This is verging on an interrogation,' Jill mocked him. 'No, he wouldn't be too keen on giving an interview – but

326

I'm good at coaxing people. I have to be to earn my bread and butter.'

And your pearls, diamonds, sapphires and sable coat, Paula was thinking.

'And,' Jill went on, 'to answer your second question, I have to be good at locating people who don't always want to be located. You need the right contacts. Any more questions, Mr Tweed?'

'I'm just interested in your professional technique. I wasn't really probing.'

'Yes, you were,' Jill said with another smile. 'That is exactly what you were doing – probing. Polishing up your own professional techniques as a Chief Claims Investigator into insurance swindles. We do have quite a lot in common, you and I. We have to reach out to people. I'm right, aren't I?'

Paula was fuming. She had never known a woman wrestle so aggressively with Tweed. But she also had a sneaking admiration for Jill's manner of mingling persistence with a subtle charm that men would find disarming. The realization that Tweed was not disarmed came with his question.

'What made you think I was involved in insurance?'

'Oh, poor David, Captain Sherwood, was talking about you earlier in the day in Munich before that atrocious woman murdered him. He said he'd met you in London when he had visited your offices, General & Cumbria Assurance.'

'What atrocious woman are you referring to?' Tweed enquired.

'Well, I was staying at the Bayerischer Hof.' Jill sounded perplexed. 'The head waiter spent most of his time after the dreadful event describing in ghoulish detail what had happened.'

Tweed just nodded, then went on eating his bacon and eggs. There was an uncomfortable pause as no one spoke.

Jill ate her croissant and then Tweed spoke again in a quiet voice, leaning towards her.

'If you have any more information you should tell me now. Salzburg has become a dangerous place. For all we know you were the prime target of that assassin with the machine-pistol.'

'What?' Jill looked even more perplexed, almost bewildered. 'I don't know what you're talking about. And I can't think of any reason on earth why anyone would want to kill me. I'm just a journalist who writes fashion articles and the occasional profile.'

'Have you ever contemplated writing a profile on Gabriel March Walvis?'

'Why?' Jill slammed down her knife. 'What is going on here? I was looking forward to having some congenial conversation with my breakfast. You keep throwing these weird questions at me.'

'My profound apologies,' said Tweed, smiling for the first time in many minutes. 'Clearly I am talking to the wrong person. I was trying to protect you.'

'Protect me against who? Against what?'

'Possibly against a section of the Chechen Mafia operating in Salzburg . . .'

After leaving the hotel Philip had led Newman along to the road bridge over the Salzach, the route he had followed when pursuing Lucien. He told Newman in detail what had happened. His tone was hard and, for the most part, without emotion, except at one point where he gulped and fell silent for a minute or so. Newman pretended not to notice.

The morning was very cold and fresh, the temperature had dropped even lower overnight, and the sun shone brilliantly out of a clear blue sky. Reaching the alley leading to the Altstadt Philip pointed out where Lucien's

Audi had smashed a piece of the stonework. Someone, presumably the police, had removed the wrecked Audi.

'They won't be able to trace the owner,' Newman commented, 'at least not to Lucien. Ten-to-one he'd stolen it before he opened up on that *pâtisserie*.'

They walked out of the sunshine into the gloom of the ancient alley. Philip made his remark a few minutes later as they began to thread their way inside the Altstadt.

'It's possible – even probable – that Lucien is hiding up somewhere in this maze of streets and alleyways. If we see him don't shoot to kill. I want him alive. A bullet in the leg will be more than enough – then I'll take over and you push off. Hope you don't mind.'

Newman took Philip's arm, squeezed it briefly before he replied.

'I'm probably one of the few people who understands how you feel. My wife was murdered some years ago in the Baltic states. I went after the murderer – and the marriage was on the rocks. We were about to separate. But I felt I couldn't go on living until I'd found the bastard and killed him. Which, in due course, I did.'

'My marriage was made in heaven,' Philip said in the same hard voice. 'I know that sounds dreadfully corny . . .'

'Not to me it doesn't. So you'll feel even emptier than I did. Now, let's concentrate on our task so I'm as familiar with this rabbit warren as you are . . .'

They passed only a few shoppers hurrying along the stone canyons. Icicles like vicious daggers dripped from the guttering above their heads. There were treacherous patches of ice everywhere. It was distinctly colder than it had been since they arrived in Salzburg and the rays of the sun failed to penetrate the narrow streets below six-storey buildings which had stood there for centuries.

Newman banged his motoring gloves together to keep his circulation moving, glancing at old bookshops, shops

329

selling antiques as they moved deeper into the Old Town. They reached the entrance to Brodgasse, little more than a wide alley. On the wall was a stone plaque and Newman paused to read its German eulogy to some School Director. It was dated *7 Juni 1874*. They were walking further into the street when a fur-clad figure appeared at the entrance to one of the buildings. Newman had his hand on his Smith & Wesson when he recognized Ziggy Palewski.

Inside the journalist's austerely furnished room on the first floor a warm reunion took place between Palewski and Newman as they hugged each other in the Continental fashion.

'Welcome, my friend,' Palewski said in English. 'And Mr Cardon and I have made each other's acquaintance more than once. Coffee?'

'We haven't the time,' Newman said, 'but thank you.'

He was seated on a shabby couch with Philip while Palewski occupied an old rocking chair. Austere but neat and clean, Newman observed, glancing round the room.

'I saw you both coming from my window,' Palewski told them. 'Can I help you in any way?'

'Yes,' said Newman. 'So far we have seen no sign at all of Walvis's thugs, which I find surprising. I thought he was taking over Salzburg with them. From that window . . .'

'I also have seen not one of them. Which also surprises me. It is as though Walvis is planning something big – and has withdrawn his men from the city. Except for one man. Lucien . . .'

'Lucien?' Philip leaned forward. 'You have seen him today?'

'No. But last night – after you saved my life – I came back here. I had not switched any lights on and when I

330

looked out of the window I caught a glimpse of him under a street lantern. He was hurrying towards Domplatz, not looking round, like a rat returning to its lair. Because I am sure he does have a secret place he lives in while in Salzburg.'

'Any chance of seeing you at the Café Sigrist this morning?' Newman asked. 'Tweed very much wants to see you.'

'I shall be there between ten and eleven. I have things your Mr Tweed should know before his thugs kill me.'

'It may never happen,' Newman said as he stood up.

'Thank you, my friend. But my time is almost up. So the article for *Der Spiegel* I carry in my head will, I feel sure, never appear. Someone else must destroy this evil man, Walvis . . .'

Although Philip was the younger Newman almost walked him off his feet, exploring every street, square and alleyway, building up in his mind a complete picture of the whole area. Eventually they were close to the *Schloss*, the massive castle which loomed over the Altstadt like a menace.

'We'll go up there in the funicular now,' Newman decided.

Philip bought the tickets and they were the only two passengers as the single car ascended the steep rails, climbing higher and higher. There was the normal point midway where the rails curved in a loop with another pair of rails for a descending car which was empty.

Alighting from the car they were met by an icy blast and the cold seemed even worse. Newman was surprised at the height of the spacious platform which looked straight down on to the Altstadt, almost vertiginous. It was like staring down on a street plan of the complex area from a plane. The stone wall he peered over was thigh high, the drop sheer.

Newman turned back and walked to the foot of the castle. He was standing at the base of an immense tower. He looked up and its circular wall soared up above him like a vertical precipice.

'That's what they call the Reck Tower,' Philip said. 'I had a brief chat with the funicular driver when I came up here before.'

Newman glanced at the legend engraved in stone at the base. *Reckturm 1496*.

'It's stood here a few years,' he remarked. 'I think I've seen all I need to see.'

In the distance rose giant jagged mountain peaks, covered with snow and ice. It was one of the most forbidding views Newman had ever seen. When they boarded the car to return down to earth they were again the only passengers and Newman remarked on the fact to Philip.

'In December you won't get tourists,' Philip pointed out. 'And on a day as bitter as this the locals will stay indoors as much as they can. For the rest of the day you wouldn't meet a soul up here.'

'Which is exactly what I was looking for,' commented Newman.

34

'You gave Jill Selborne a pretty rough time,' Paula said as they settled down in the suite after breakfast.

'The interesting thing is she stood up to it brilliantly,' Tweed replied. 'I'm still not convinced as to why she is here, but she's clever, very clever. No doubt about that.'

'Where are the others? I haven't seen Marler, Nield or Butler this morning.'

'I told them to sleep in, have breakfast sent up to their rooms if they preferred. They had a very exhausting and tense time yesterday. They'll be along soon.' He looked at his watch. 'All three have insisted on accompanying us to the meeting at the Café Sigrist with Palewski.'

'Shouldn't we leave soon?' Paula had checked her own watch.

'In a few minutes. You and I – with Newman if he gets back in time – will go there by taxi. Our protectors will drive there independently in their cars. We are moving steadily towards a great climax.'

'And have you any idea where that will take place?'

'I *know* where it will take place.'

He turned to look out of the window. Paula pursed her lips in frustration. She jumped up and went to the door as someone rapped on it with a tattoo. It was Newman, followed by Nield and Butler.

'Where is Philip?' was Tweed's first question.

'Somewhere back in the Altstadt. I couldn't persuade him to come back with me. He's got it into his head he'll locate Lucien if he looks long enough. He's really got the bit between his teeth.'

'We'd better leave now for the Sigrist, hoping that—'

'Palewski *will* be there,' Newman assured him. 'We met him outside where he lives.' He deliberately didn't say where that was – there were too many people in the room and all were trustworthy but Newman felt he should keep Palewski's secret. They had been fellow journalists. 'Palewski is looking forward to meeting you,' he continued.

'Then let's go.'

'We're leaving on our own,' interjected Nield. 'You won't see us, but we'll be there.'

'What about Marler?' Tweed asked.

333

'Oh, Marler! He got up early, left ages ago. Said he wanted to check the lie of the land on his own.'

'Supposing Walvis does phone to arrange a meeting while we're absent,' Newman commented as Nield and Butler left the room, escorted to the door by Paula. 'There'll be nobody here to take the call.'

'So he'll have to try again later, won't he,' Tweed replied as he put on his sheepskin.

Newman told the cab driver to stop as soon as he had crossed the bridge over the Salzach. The three of them alighted at the entrance to the alley where Philip had pursued Lucien the previous evening.

'You two walk straight down this side of the promenade,' Newman said when he had paid off the driver. 'I'll loaf behind and appear to be window-shopping.'

There were few people about. They had missed rush hour and Newman guessed the intense cold – exceptional even for Salzburg, the hotel receptionist had told him – was keeping people indoors. He caught up with Tweed and Paula as they reached the interior semi-circle which led to the entrance to the Café Sigrist. He saw no sign of Marler, Butler or Nield but they had to be somewhere close by. Newman felt a little on edge – would Palewski feel it was too dangerous to keep the meeting?

Tweed led the way, following a sign which indicated the Sigrist was on the first floor. He ran agilely up a flight of marble steps curving round, walked into the spacious L-shaped room overlooking the river which was the Café Sigrist.

Close behind him, Paula had an immediate impression of spotless cleanliness. The walls were panelled halfway up and then they became brilliant white plasterwork. To her left as she walked in there was a service counter. There were marble-topped tables scattered round the

334

middle of the room and brown leather banquettes behind more tables against the walls. The atmosphere was light, cheerful and welcoming.

Ziggy Palewski sat on one of the banquettes with his back to the wall, away from the windows. He raised a hand in greeting as Newman entered. He appeared to be the only customer until Paula glanced into the stem of the L. At a table in the corner by himself sat Marler, a cup of coffee in front of him and a narrow duffle bag stretched out along the banquette beside him.

Oh, my Lord, Paula thought, he's brought his Armalite rifle with him.

Newman made introductions and the fringe-bearded Palewski stood up to shake hands with Tweed warmly. He suggested Tweed should sit alongside him.

'Coffee, everyone?' Palewski enquired.

A waitress wearing a white uniform as spotless as the premises had arrived. Everyone opted for coffee. As she sat down next to Newman, Paula glanced at Marler who was reading a newspaper and had taken no notice of them. He was wearing spectacles which, she knew, had plain lenses. They gave him a professorial look.

'This is possibly the most important meeting of my career, Mr Tweed,' Palewski began. 'I will tell you everything I know. Much you have doubtless found out for yourself, but not everything, I suspect. I hope you don't mind if I talk at length . . .' He glanced at Paula. 'I fear I may bore you stiff.'

'I think that's very unlikely.'

She smiled at him. Already she had taken a liking to Ziggy Palewski. Not only were his eyes shrewd and watchful, she sensed he was basically a very kind man.

'Then I will begin,' said Palewski. 'I have tracked Walvis for two years – in between doing other jobs to keep body and soul together. Walvis caught on quickly and he does not like my enquiries. He fears the highly detailed

335

profile I intend to publish in *Der Spiegel*. His idea is very simple and deadly – he plans to take over Western Europe by using guerrilla warfare against NATO, which is not equipped or trained to withstand such an onslaught.'

'What kind of guerrilla warfare?' asked Tweed.

'Quite diabolical. Can you imagine an army of tanks confronted with hundreds of thousands of refugees pouring across the Oder–Niesse river line from Poland into Germany, flooding across into Austria and Italy? How many people can trained soldiers slaughter in cold blood before they become sickened and give up?'

'Will the refugees be armed?' Tweed enquired.

'Yes. With automatic rifles, grenades, and he has special units which will use poison gas. But, Mr Tweed . . .' Palewski had turned to face him and now moved closer. 'Think of an endless horde, a vast multitude, advancing towards what he has told them will be a treasure house of food and gold – coming as they do from the misery of life in the East. Better be dead rather than go back to that. It will be like a surging flood of human beings. Hence the name – Project Tidal Wave.'

'Why is he doing this?' Tweed probed.

'For power over the world. The power to remould what we know as civilization into what he thinks should take its place.'

'And that is?'

'A stable world – in his sense of the phrase – with each country strictly controlled on a basis of iron discipline. That is, controlled by a governor appointed by himself.'

'Sounds like an impossible dream – or nightmare.'

'You think so?' Palewski lit a cheroot after obtaining consent from Paula. 'Think of Napoleon – he went further. He put members of his own family on the thrones of Europe. In some ways Gabriel March Walvis is a genius. Look how much he's achieved so far – and he came from nothing.'

336

'Where did he come from?' Tweed asked.

'That is one question my researches have never answered. He has spread so many rumours about being born in so many different countries the truth is lost in the shadows of history.'

'A strange man.'

'Also a dangerous one. I now come to the vital fact I have unearthed. He plans to govern Europe from your country. Britain he sees as an ideal base. And he has sent trained agents to America to destabilize the USA. Washington has no inkling of the inferno waiting to burst out with their different mixture of nationalities. Walvis plans chaos for them – to eliminate what he thinks is their destructive influence.'

'Have you any names and the locations of these agents in America?

'None. But I do have papers proving he organized the riots in Los Angeles. That he plans more, even more terrible riots in New York, Chicago, San Francisco and Miami. I think I have told you all I know.'

'It's more than enough,' Tweed commented. 'A nightmare scenario.'

'So he must be stopped – and quickly, before it is too late.' Palewski stared hard at Tweed. 'I have been watching you as I spoke. You are the first man I have met I believe could stop him. Under your quiet exterior I detect your determination, the necessary streak of steely ruthlessness, the willingness to go to any lengths to rid the world of this so talented – but evil – man.'

'I am certainly hostile to him,' Tweed said mildly. 'I know that in Munich Philip Cardon warned you that you are a target for Teardrop, this brilliant woman assassin who has killed so many who stood in Walvis's path.'

'It is supposed to be the age of equality.' Palewski was smiling. Such a pleasant smile, Paula thought, and such a nice man. 'So I imagine it is only fair and sensible to

337

expect some women will take up the profitable role of the assassin.' He looked at Paula. 'I hope I don't offend you,' he suggested with his usual courtesy.

'I think you are right,' Paula agreed.

'And also,' Palewski ruminated, 'I suspect the feminine mind with all its wiles, developed over the ages so women could survive against the dominant male – that type of mind may well be more adept at the profession of assassination than a male counterpart.'

'I think you're right again,' said Paula.

'We do know what Teardrop looks like,' Tweed emphasized to Palewski. 'She always wears black, a black cap which conceals the colour of her hair, a black veil masking most of her face, and a black dress or coat.'

'I shall avoid the lady like the plague if I ever encounter her,' Palewski assured Tweed.

'She's as bad as the plague,' Newman said, speaking for the first time since making introductions. 'Literally, bearing in mind her track record of victims all over Europe.'

'Thank you both for the warning.' Palewski turned his attention to Newman. 'It would be pleasant if we could meet while you are in Salzburg, so we could recall old times.' He looked quickly at Tweed and Paula. 'Both of you would be most welcome if you can stand our nostalgic reminiscences.'

'Dinner tonight at the ÖH, then,' said Newman, with a glance at Tweed for his approval. Tweed nodded agreement with enthusiasm. He also had taken a liking to the journalist. 'Eight o'clock. I'll be waiting for you in the lobby,' Newman said with a grin.

'Eight o'clock, then,' Palewski agreed. 'I will phone you fifteen minutes earlier to make sure it is still convenient,' he added, again with his eternal courtesy.

'We'd better be going now,' said Tweed, glancing at the time. 'I'm expecting an important phone call.'

338

'I will stay a little longer,' Palewski said. 'This is my only break from work and I will enjoy another cheroot before I depart.' He stood up, put out his hand to Paula who gave him hers. He bent down and his lips touched her hand. It seemed old-fashioned to her and she loved it.

'Take good care of Mr Tweed, my dear,' he urged her. 'I think only he can destroy the monster, Walvis . . .'

As they left the Sigrist, Marler folded his newspaper, took off his spectacles, and casually followed them out at a distance.

Palewski was enjoying his second cheroot, turning over in his mind what he had said to Tweed, what Tweed had said to him. An old friend of Newman's, he decided he found the company of Tweed and Paula Grey equally stimulating and pleasant.

He had ordered more coffee and was drinking it slowly, savouring the only part of the day when he could relax. He was particularly looking forward to having dinner with them in the evening.

'I must tell them some of the comical experiences I've had,' he said to himself. 'They should amuse Paula, who had to listen to some grim conversation. I shall insist that I am the host. It will involve a battle of wills, but I shall win and pick up the bill.'

He was still the only customer in the Sigrist when he heard the clack of feminine heels coming quickly up the marble staircase. A youngish and very attractive woman entered, paused to look round, then chose a table some distance from Palewski's.

Her hair was a blaze of titian red, falling to her shoulders. She wore a knee-length dark brown coat and a pair of kid gloves. Palewski noticed she had an excellent pair of legs and a slim figure. She wore over her shoulder a bag of a colour that exactly matched her coat and moved gracefully.

Sitting down, she used both hands to push the mane of titian hair back over her shoulders. Perched on her nose was a pair of tinted glasses. When the waitress came Palewski heard her ordering in an English voice.

'I would like the coffee, if I might, please. And if it should be possible, the toast. Is that a task you could manage, if you please?'

The waitress told her she could certainly have toast and she would personally make it herself. It would take only five minutes.

Palewski was puzzled. The accent was English, but the formation of the words suggested a non-English woman. He took another puff at his cheroot as the woman looked round at him, got up from her table and came over and sat opposite him. She had a cigarette in her left hand.

'Is it possible that you can give me the light, please?'

'Of course . . .'

Palewski produced his match-book, struck a light. The woman leaned forward, raised her right hand which was holding the gun she had taken from her shoulder-bag. She fired once and the silencer muffled the sound. The cyanide-tipped bullet entered Palewski's chest, his face twisted briefly in an expression of agony and he fell forward across the table. His cheroot rolled on to the floor.

The woman slipped her gun back inside her shoulder-bag, still wearing her gloves. The lighted match had sputtered out on the table. She was leaving the café when she met the waitress carrying a tray with coffee and toast. She pointed to the table.

'That man has just had a heart attack. I am going to bring a doctor. You had better phone for one yourself – or better still the emergency service . . .'

Then she was gone.

340

35

'*Am* I speaking to Mr Tweed?'

The throaty voice on the phone was arrogant, domineering. Tweed, holding the phone with one hand in his suite, made a gesture to Newman who then carefully lifted the extension phone from a table that also contained a scratch pad and a pen.

'That was a bad line,' said Tweed. 'It appears to have improved. Please repeat what you said. And who is this?'

'I . . . said . . .' The words were spaced out, the tone sarcastic. The same words were repeated slowly as though talking to a backward infant.

'Yes, you are,' Tweed replied briskly. 'And once again who is this?'

'The man you were expecting to call. Walvis. It is time we made arrangements to meet. Just the two of us. Today.'

'Agreed.'

'Now that is better, Mr Tweed. A positive approach. We both have security problems. I suggest we meet inside my stretch Mercedes which will be parked in an open field in the countryside after dark. There will be no one else near us for miles. Just myself, my driver and yourself with your driver . . .'

Newman was shaking his head furiously.

'That may solve your security problem. It certainly won't solve mine,' Tweed snapped. 'Try again.'

'Oh, dear me, I feared our negotiations would not be easy. You are a stubborn man, I have heard. Supposing then we meet aboard the Salzburg Express, at Salzburg. I will reserve a complete coach and arrange for it to be sealed off from the rest of the train.'

Newman again shook his head.

'Trains are not secure,' Tweed snapped again. 'I wouldn't consider the idea.'

Newman handed to Paula the sheet from the scratch pad he had been writing on. She stood midway between the two men and handed it to Tweed. He glanced at it, nodded to Newman to confirm he understood.

'Mr Tweed, I am getting bored. I have made two perfectly reasonable suggestions. You have rejected them both out of hand. Surely it is your turn to suggest a rendezvous?'

'You know where I am in Salzburg. There is only one place where I will meet you. At the castle above the Altstadt. We both meet at the entrance to the funicular. We both board the car together. We ride to the top and converse at the foot of the Reck Tower. There we will have privacy. You drive your own car with one man beside you. I will do the same thing. Our guards will check everyone for weapons before we board the car. I repeat, we will travel up to the tower together and on our own. When our discussion is ended we both then travel together in the same car down to where our cars will be waiting. We meet at the entrance to the funicular at noon today.'

'My, my, we do have it all worked out, don't we? I need a moment to think this over. I'm not at all sure I can get there by noon.'

'Yes, you can. You're much closer to Salzburg than you have let on. You have two minutes to decide . . .'

'Is that an ultimatum?' Walvis demanded.

'No, just a suggestion – and the only place and time I will meet you . . .'

Newman checked the time by the second hand on his

342

watch. He was smiling. He was confident Walvis was so anxious the meeting should take place that he would agree. This pause was while he consulted whoever was in charge of his security. Four minutes passed before Walvis came back on the line – a gesture to show he could not be rushed, Newman felt sure.

'I think we had better agree to the rendezvous you suggest, Mr Tweed.' Walvis had adopted a weary tone as though he was losing interest in the whole idea. 'You will understand if I arrive late?'

Newman was again shaking his head.

'I said noon,' Tweed emphasized. 'If you have not arrived by then I shall leave immediately. I look forward to hearing what you have to say.'

'Very well, Mr Tweed. They were right when they said you were a stubborn man.'

'Which is probably why I am still alive,' Tweed shot back, and he put down the phone.

Inside an old broken-down villa on the outskirts of Salzburg – and not thirty minutes' drive from the Altstadt – Walvis replaced the receiver. The building had the appearance from the outside that it was not inhabited. Closed shutters hung at drunken angles but effectively masked the interior.

The villa stood well back from the road, was surrounded by a crumbling wall – equipped with sophisticated alarm devices. The grounds had been neglected for years and a colony of tall weeds sprouted up from the gravel drive.

Inside wooden kennels sunk half into the ground, covered with moss, ferocious and hungry Dobermann dogs lay in wait, held inside their kennels by leashes which could be released electronically by remote control from inside the villa.

343

'Well, Gulliver, what do you think? At least I do know the *Schloss* – I once went up to the platform just to see the view. I remember this Reck Tower.'

'I'm not sure we should have agreed,' said Gulliver, determined to show how careful he was about guarding his chief. He also had been listening in on an extension phone, but unlike Newman he had not dared give advice while Walvis was speaking.

'But I take the decisions,' Walvis reminded him. 'And it was clear Tweed would not budge.'

He levered his bulk out of his chair, ambled over to the french windows giving a view over the neglected land at the rear of the villa. The shutters were open here – he could not be seen by anyone because the grounds were surrounded with dense evergreen trees. He stared out at the snow-encrusted firs as he spoke, his huge back to Gulliver.

'It confirms what I suspected some time ago. Tweed is a very strong man. So, if I cannot persuade him to my way of thinking he will have to go. He has chosen for the rendezvous a location where he will be untouchable.'

'If he doesn't agree with you . . .'

'Let us be more positive. If he agrees I might consider appointing him Governor of Britain.'

'But if he doesn't – when you are with him on the platform at the *Schloss* could we arrange for you to signal a negative result?'

'I expect I could, yes. But why?'

'Give me five minutes on the phone in my office here and I think I can arrange a method of eliminating Mr Tweed on the platform . . .'

'It will have to be foolproof,' Walvis warned.

'It will be foolproof,' Gulliver replied.

'Talking of fools, we haven't heard from Martin. He is probably spending time with a girl friend. Martin is idle . . .'

344

'I will go now and make the arrangement,' said Gulliver.

Martin was not idle. Inside the farmhouse so much further north than Salzburg, snow had continued to fall through the night, making it impossible for the helicopter to take off for Grafenau.

Frustrated, he had tried time and again to get through on the phone but the story was always the same. Communications had been cut by the storm. In the morning, when Tweed was meeting Palewski at the Sigrist, Martin was staring out of the window as the snow continued to fall heavily. The change in the weather came without warning.

The snow stopped, the sky cleared, and it was a sunny day. It was mid-morning when the Sikorsky flew a heavily muffled Martin to the small airstrip where Nield and Butler, on the previous day, had destroyed a plane and the petrol tanker.

'I don't like the look of that,' Martin observed to Hans, his assistant, who only replied when spoken to.

'What is that?' enquired Hans, a short stocky man with a Slavlike face.

'Look for yourself, damnit!'

As the machine was descending they saw the burnt-out relics of the plane and the tanker. Karl, the youngish good-looking man who was in charge of the Grafenau operation, was waiting for them. He had heard the machine approaching, had guessed who would be aboard.

Martin jumped out after the helicopter had landed, ducked to avoid the still whirling blades, started to run towards Karl to show how fit he was. He slipped on ice and sprawled forward in the deep snow. Karl began to help him up.

345

'Leave me alone,' snapped Martin, furious. 'What the devil is happening here?'

'The worst possible news, a catastrophe.' Karl never believed it paid to play up to your superior. 'The whole mountain complex has been destroyed. The men and women inside are dead.'

'Dead? What are you talking about? You must be mad – there are over a hundred people inside the complex!'

'Over a hundred corpses,' Karl corrected him. 'And I am perfectly sane. Do you want to hear what happened or don't you? If you do, please listen.'

In a state of shock Martin made no interruption as Karl explained. Two men had attacked the guards at the entrance to the complex. One guard was dead, the other had recovered consciousness before dawn. He had stumbled to a shed some distance from the complex's entrance where a car was parked. Although exhausted, he had managed to drive to Karl's villa on the outskirts of Grafenau.

'I immediately alerted a mixed team, including an ex-bank-vault robber with his equipment, and we drove up here. It took the man with the drill some time to open up the main door. An appalling stench met us. Briefly, the air-conditioning system had been wrecked, the phone wires cut. Without an air flow those inside had no chance to survive. The exit into the Czech Republic at the other end was sealed. We had brought breathing apparatus with us and I went inside. It was clear nothing could be done . . .'

'So what is the situation now?' Martin managed to ask.

'I realized it would be dangerous to Mr Walvis if what was inside was found. I sent for explosives and we created a minor landslide, blocking off – and hiding – for ever the entrance to the complex.'

'I do not know that Mr Walvis will like what you have

taken upon yourself to do,' said Martin at his most officious.

He felt it was necessary at once to shift the blame away from himself and on to Karl's shoulders. His tactic did not intimidate Karl, who saw what he was thinking.

'I take full responsibility for the decision. Further, I would prefer to tell Mr Walvis myself what happened and how I handled the situation. I don't want someone to give him a perverted version.'

'The implications of what you have just said I find grossly impertinent. You will regret that remark. So there is no danger now of the locals ever penetrating the complex?' he queried, contradicting what he had just said.

'None at all,' Karl replied in the same even tone. 'I've spread the rumour the storm caused a major landslide. It has happened before.'

'I can't waste any more time chattering to you. I must fly at once to Passau . . .'

As the helicopter neared Passau Martin was thinking he'd at least be able to give Walvis one piece of good news. That was important – to ease the shock of the catastrophe at Grafenau.

The pilot had radioed ahead for a limo to meet them. As the machine landed Martin waited, then carefully left the machine and walked slowly over the snow. Karma, the Finnish man in charge of the Passau operation, was inside the limo as Martin sat beside him and flashed his toothy smile.

Karma waited until they were driving into Passau before he told Martin what had happened. Martin again sank into a state of shock, couldn't speak for several minutes.

'You mean the whole barge-train is at the bottom of the Danube?' he said with an expression of incredulity.

347

'Yes. It will take ages to raise and all the equipment aboard will be ruined . . .'

Martin asked to be taken to the Danubex headquarters in the Old Town. He climbed the stairs like a zombie, asked to be left alone in Karma's office. It was five minutes before he could summon up the strength to phone Walvis at the old villa outside Salzburg.

'Mr Walvis is not here,' a voice told him in German after Martin had identified himself.

'What do you mean?' Martin shouted. 'Idiot, he has to be there.'

'He left for a meeting a few minutes ago. No, we have no idea where he went. No, he is not carrying a mobile phone in his car. He doesn't trust them.'

'When will he be back?'

'We have no idea . . .'

'You've no bloody ideas at all, have you . . .'

Martin slammed down the phone. He had thrown his sheepskin on the floor, had torn off a thick pullover before making the call. The room was like a hothouse. In an emergency he reached for the whisky flask he always carried. He reached for it now, unscrewed the cap, upended the flask and drank too much at once. He began choking and spluttering. When he recovered he looked down at his new suit, which had cost a fortune. It was stained with large patches of whisky. His language was unprintable, his hand holding the flask was shaking.

36

Tweed, for at least the seventh time, was studying the Identikit portrait in charcoal Paula had sketched of Walvis, guided by Philip. It was a quarter to twelve in the morning and Tweed was sitting alongside Newman, who was driving his BMW.

Before they had left the hotel Paula had begged him to let Nield and Butler take up hidden positions near the funicular to the *Schloss*.

'You need protection against that monster,' she had argued vehemently. 'You can't trust him.'

'The arrangement was we would each travel there by car and with only our drivers,' Tweed had said firmly. 'I stand by that agreement.'

He had even gone to the lengths of phoning both Nield and Butler and ordering them to stay in their rooms. No one seemed to know where Marler had disappeared to and Philip had not returned from the Altstadt.

Newman, who now knew the intricacies of the Old Town as well as Philip, had driven them there by the most direct route. It was five minutes to noon when Tweed climbed out of the car, went inside and bought two tickets from the office.

As he came out into the glare of the sunlight and the icy cold a black Mercedes with tinted windows glided to a halt. The rear door opened and Walvis eased his way out of the car slowly. He wore a black velvet cape lined with wool. The cape had a hood which flopped loosely on his immensely wide shoulders and the cape itself was

349

fastened at his thick neck with a gold chain.

His dense grey shaggy hair blew in the wind and
Tweed, despite having heard his description, stared at the
immense size of the man. Walvis removed a leather glove
from his right hand and extended the hand.

'Good morning, Mr Tweed. It is still morning by one
minute, I believe. So, at last we meet.'

His chauffeur, in blue livery, stood at attention by the
limo. Newman leaned against the driver's door of the
BMW, arms folded as he spoke.

'Surely we can dispense with this silly business of
checking each other for weapons.'

'It would hardly be a good omen for our talks,
indicating mistrust,' Walvis agreed, his eyes twitching as
he studied Newman.

'That's settled then,' Tweed said briskly, speaking for
the first time. 'I've got the tickets. Let's board the
coach . . .'

He waited on the funicular platform while Walvis
squeezed his body sideways into the coach. He followed
him and sat down. During the ascent neither man spoke a
word as Walvis fiddled with his cape, arranging it round
his girth. At the top they alighted and Tweed led the way
to the base of the Reck Tower. There was no one else on
the platform on that bitter morning.

'I'm a good listener,' Tweed told his companion. 'So I
am interested in your views.'

'Mr Tweed, you must agree the Western world is in a
state of chaos and anarchy. In every country there is no
real leadership, including your own. The politicians are
all corrupt. Decadence is the depth to which the West has
sunk. Women can no longer walk the streets alone in the
daytime – let alone at night – without fear of being horribly attacked and abused. Perverts, rapists – and murderers – if caught, receive absurdly short sentences in
prison by feeble-minded judges. Such men who commit

350

these dreadful crimes ought to be removed from society, should be shot so they cannot – when released – repeat their barbaric crimes. There is no discipline, no order, no stability. Democracy no longer works. The West is like the Roman Empire just before its collapse. Bread and circuses – that is what the politicians of all parties offer the people to buy their votes. The family, once the backbone of society in all these countries, is no longer respected. Women get divorced on a whim and put their children into crêches so they can continue to pursue their careers. Where was this system invented? In Soviet Russia. What was the ultimate outcome in Soviet Russia?'

'The Chechen Mafia,' said Tweed.

His eyes were fixed on Walvis's, trying to see what lay behind the pale irises. They held a magnetic concentration Tweed had rarely encountered. The face, incredibly ugly, radiated power and purpose.

'The Chechen Mafia,' Walvis continued, 'has been infiltrated and mastered. They still live under the delusion they are running their organization. They have been listed and when the time comes they will be shot. Returning to the West, their so-called governments are so weak they have sat back while the Chechens penetrated their society. They are operating in London. The police, enfeebled by the party system of government, do little or nothing to eliminate this plague. In due course I will direct the extermination of this vile force. But the decadence of the West runs far deeper.'

'In what way?' enquired Tweed.

'If children at a school were allowed to run wild they would act like savages. They are doing that in Britain. Adults – men and women – are terrorized by gangs of thugs who are still at school. The law, authorized by Parliament, can do nothing if they are under a certain age. The young thugs know this. If they can behave like that at this age what will they do when they grow up?

351

People no longer have a purpose in life. That strange man Adolf Hitler said life was struggle. There is no longer any struggle in people's early lives to strengthen their characters. Everything is handed to them on a golden platter. Bread and circuses again. America is sinking into anarchy. Crimes are committed – horrific crimes – and devious lawyers make a fortune out of portraying criminals as victims, to be sympathized with. What is the fashion in America today becomes the way of life in Europe tomorrow.'

'Assuming – only for the sake of argument – that you are right, what is the solution?' Tweed asked.

'There are precedents.' Walvis wrapped his cloak closer round his massive frame. 'Napoleon, for all his faults, ended the French Revolution, which was also in a state of anarchy. He then introduced strong discipline, gave the people a sense of purpose and patriotism. He even invented a new system of law, the Code Napoleon. That system is still the law of France, of Switzerland. His was a life of struggle – and the people had to struggle, but against a background of stability and law and order. Which is what the bewildered people of the West are crying out for.'

'Could you be more specific?' Tweed suggested.

'They want a world where their wives, their girl friends, can walk the streets in safety. By night as well as by day. The young are like loose cannons, charging about in search of they know not what. The older people wish to live their lives in peace. The so-called democratic parties are always changing, changing, changing everything. They feel they must offer a programme of something new, always something different – to justify their appeal to the voters. The system has crumbled, Mr Tweed. It lies in ruins. Someone strong has to take over.'

'Yourself, possibly?' Tweed asked.

'Do you see anyone else trying to save the West from

committing suicide as the mass of the people become more and more drug sodden? Traffickers in drugs should be shot. Only death will deter them from their greed in making huge profits. You could help me, Mr Tweed.'

'How?'

'By joining me in this great enterprise. You are an austere man who has lived a decent life.'

'If you say so.'

'What is your answer, then? I must have it now. Time is short. I have a position of great responsibility in mind for you. But it requires a strong man who has shown he is incorruptible. What is your answer?' Walvis repeated.

'I have understood you,' Tweed said quietly.

'You have . . .' The thick lips, the jowls tightened. The face became ugly in a different way, became menacing. 'You have just used General de Gaulle's words to the OAS in Algeria. Then he tricked them. You think you can trick me, Mr Tweed?'

Seldom had Tweed seen a man so consumed with rage. Walvis walked slowly across to the edge of the platform. Somewhere nearby in the sky a helicopter was circling. Tweed had heard the sound of its engine for several minutes.

He watched as Walvis stood by the wall above the Altstadt. Slowly and very deliberately he lifted the hood and wrapped it round his head. It was the signal Gulliver had suggested in case of need before Walvis had left the villa. The helicopter came closer and closer, the beat-beat of the engine a warning as Tweed stood alone at the base of Reck Tower.

In Tweed's hotel suite Paula was growing more and more worried. She had adopted Tweed's habit in a crisis – she was pacing back and forth across the room. She made up her mind suddenly. It would mean disobeying Tweed – or

353

would it? He had not specifically ordered her to remain behind.

She picked up the phone, dialled Nield's room number. He answered immediately.

'Paula here. Could you come to Tweed's suite urgently? Bring Butler with you and do not forget your equipment. It's an emergency . . .'

She let the two men into the room, relocked the door, swung round. As she spoke her manner was commanding, very confident.

'I've never said this before, but I out-rank you both. You appreciate that?'

'Of course we do,' Nield responded, and smiled. 'So how can we help?'

'I want Harry to drive you and me – armed – urgently to the Altstadt, to as near as we can get to the entrance to the funicular without being seen.'

'That would be going directly against Tweed's orders,' objected Butler.

'Oh, come on, Harry,' Nield told him cheerfully. 'Who is in charge when Tweed is absent? Paula. She takes her own decisions. So let's all get cracking . . .'

The helicopter flying closer to the platform below the *Schloss* was losing altitude. The pilot manoeuvred his machine so they had a good view of the whole platform. Beside him the man who had watched Walvis through field-glasses, who had seen the agreed signal – Walvis putting the hood over his head – had the window open.

He took hold of the swivel-mounted machine-gun. Tweed, at the base of the Reck Tower, was a tiny figure, his target. The pilot was nervous, issued a warning.

'Be very careful, Norbert. We don't want a bullet ricocheting and hitting Walvis. We'd be for the chop, the ultimate chop.'

354

'You worry too much,' said Norbert. 'Just keep the copter in a steady hover when I give the word. Leave me to do my job. I can empty half the belt into Tweed and he'll take all the bullets.'

'There's a crosswind,' the pilot snapped. 'I'll do my best but I can't guarantee anything.'

'Walvis said you were the top pilot in Austria. So now you can prove he was right. Won't be long now, just lose a little more altitude. Steady!' He had his finger on the trigger, his finger tightened.

Perched at the top of a flight of stone steps leading into the *Schloss* Marler had watched the approaching helicopter through his own field-glasses. After a brief talk with Newman on the quiet he had arrived half an hour earlier.

Through the lenses he had seen the passenger also watching through a pair of field-glasses. He had seen the appearance of the swivel-mounted machine-gun, had seen its muzzle lowering slowly, then remain stationary.

Marler had waited until he was sure the machine was hostile. The target could hardly be Walvis – and Tweed would never have arranged for the huge man to be assassinated after the arrangement he had agreed. Which made Tweed the target.

He had dropped the glasses looped round his neck, was aiming his Armalite rifle, which was loaded with a special high-explosive bullet. The best marksman in Europe peered through the crosshairs, centred them on the fuel tanks, pulled the trigger.

The chopper rocked madly. The pilot elevated the machine to gain height, flew away from the *Schloss*. Already black smoke was trailing from the Sikorsky as it headed towards the nearest alp, the pilot desperate to fly over it, to put it as a barrier between himself and the marksman.

From his eyrie Marler watched, his expression offhand.

355

'You're not going to make it, mate,' he said aloud.

His prediction came true. The pilot had not gained enough height. The alp rushed towards him as he fought for more altitude. His companion had slipped into a state of pure fear.

'Get the bloody thing up, for God's sake . . .'

As Marler watched the helicopter slammed into the alp just below the summit. It burst into flames, became a fireball. So intense was the heat Marler saw the deep snow and ice melted, the rock face exposed as the debris from the machine collapsed into an abyss.

The funicular car driver had heard the explosion of Marler's high-powered bullet. He came rushing out and stared in disbelief as the Sikorsky died. Tweed came towards him as he spoke.

'Statistics show more helicopters crash than any other type of plane. You couldn't get me aboard one for love or money,' he continued in German.

Walvis had left his place by the outer wall, padded with an uncertain step towards Tweed. His doughy face was set in a frozen expression.

'You'll be taking us down now,' Tweed told the driver of the funicular.

He waited until the man had, with a dazed look, vanished inside the shed which housed the car. He then looked at Walvis.

'So that was your idea of a safe conduct? Treachery is your middle name. We will travel down together just as we came up. You will leave the funicular first at the bottom.'

'Mr Tweed, I don't know what to say,' Walvis began in English. 'I shall hunt down whoever arranged that crime and he will be shot out of hand.'

'He probably will – for failing in his mission to kill me. No more talk, Walvis.'

356

'I have tried . . .' Walvis hesitated as he walked towards the funicular with Tweed beside him. 'So now it is war?'

'All-out war until you're dead and buried . . .'

It seemed to take much longer for the coach to descend than on their earlier journey. When it came to a halt Walvis alighted first, heaving himself slowly out of the door, walking on into the sunlight where their two cars waited.

Walvis gave the second signal, saluting his driver.

A second black Mercedes came skidding into the square below where Newman and the other driver stood by their cars. Two men holding pistols jumped out of the rear of the car. At the same moment a Citroën roared into the square, stopped abruptly. Paula jumped out, followed by Nield and Butler. It was all happening in seconds.

'*Achtung! Achtung!*' yelled Paula, both hands gripping her Browning aimed at the backs of the two men from the Mercedes. 'Drop your weapons or you're dead!' she continued in German.

The two men glanced over their shoulders, saw the three new arrivals aiming at them. Their pistols thudded into the hard snow. They raised their arms without being ordered to do so.

'Disable their car,' Paula ordered Butler. 'We'll cover you.'

It took Butler no time at all to raise the bonnet and wrench inside. He used the butt of his Walther to smash something, closed the bonnet, walked back and reported to Paula.

'It will take a skilled mechanic hours to put that car on the road again.'

From a distance Newman waved to Paula, who waved back at him, and then he opened the front passenger door of the BMW so Tweed could climb inside.

'Marler is still up at the *Schloss* . . .' Tweed began.

'No, he isn't,' Newman replied. 'He must have secretly

357

travelled down in the rear of the coach which brought you down. While you were staring at the square I saw him slip outside and vanish up an alleyway.'

'Thank heavens for that . . .'

'We can talk later. Top priority now is to get out of here and back to the hotel.'

He deliberately drove the BMW at the two gunmen who had emerged from the second Mercedes. They jumped out of the way, so startled they both sprawled heavily face down on the hard-packed snow, bruising themselves painfully. Tweed glanced back and saw the Citroën containing Paula and Nield, with Butler at the wheel, close behind.

'Bob, you arranged with Marler for him to go up there, I imagine,' Tweed said quietly.

'You imagine correctly.'

'Thank you for saving my life. Maybe I haven't had as much sleep as I should have had recently. My excuse for my terrible error of judgement. I had thought that in this case Walvis would take a pride in keeping his word.'

'So now you know what we're up against.'

'Oh, it's no holds barred from this moment on. But I understand now the psychology of Walvis. The frightening thing is he believes in what he's trying to do. No ordinary villain, this one. Probably the most dangerous man we have ever encountered. A man with a mission . . .'

Tweed waited until all his team were assembled in the hotel suite. Marler turned up last, still carrying the long canvas case containing the Armalite rifle as he took up his usual position, leaning against a wall. He lit a king-size. Only Philip had failed to return.

'Thank you, Marler,' Tweed said. 'The judgement – the actions – of all of you proved to be far sounder than my own on this occasion. My last words to Walvis were that it is "all-out war until you're dead and buried". I've never used such language before but I meant it.'

'What did he say to you?' asked Paula, her curiosity aroused.

Rapidly, and with total recall, Tweed repeated every word Walvis had spoken. Paula, seated on the couch, was leaning forward, drinking in the whole conversation as Tweed, standing, continued. She leaned back when he had finished, a thoughtful expression on her face.

'What a strange experience,' she commented. 'Some of the things he said are so true – about women not being able to walk about in the daytime safely any more, let alone at night. And some of the other things he said are true – and some are appalling.'

'He's a very complex individual,' Tweed agreed. 'But now we must look to the future. I was at least right when I suspected that Walvis's plan was to conduct his operation from Britain. I predict again that the final confrontation will take place amid that strange labyrinth of creeks south of Chichester, and at Cleaver Hall.'

'And the next step?' Newman asked impatiently.

'I am sure that what happened at the *Schloss* achieved one arm of my strategy. Walvis will return to wherever he is hiding out in a state of manic fury. And I am sure that when we met he had not heard about events near Grafenau and at Passau, for some reason. When he does hear that will add to his fury – and drive him into making a colossal blunder. We must all be armed at all times from now on. Having said that, I suggest a late lunch would be in order . . .'

359

37

'How did it go at the *Schloss*?'

Gulliver knew he had asked the wrong question the moment the words left his mouth. Walvis had just returned to the villa with the neglected grounds. He glared at his deputy, tore at the chain holding his cape across his neck, tore at it so viciously that the chain ripped the cloth and was left in his hand. He threw it across the room.

'You had it all worked out, Gulliver, didn't you? If I gave the agreed signal the machine-gunner aboard the chopper would cut down Tweed. Well, I gave the signal and it didn't work – your blasted chopper is scrap metal at the bottom of an alp. Tweed is alive and well and determined to smash me. That was the outcome of your brilliant planning.'

'I don't understand . . .'

'You don't understand anything,' Walvis stormed. He went to the french window, saw a helicopter standing amid the tall grasses, swung round. 'What is that thing doing out there?'

'It brought Martin, who has something to tell you,' replied Gulliver, hoping to divert Walvis's attention to another target.

'Martin! He was fool enough to let that machine land here? The locals will have seen it descend on to this property. This is supposed to be a secret hideaway. Am I surrounded with lunatics?'

Walvis hurled his torn cape across the room where it landed on a couch. He began pounding round the room, his large feet thudding on the woodblock floor, his hands clasped behind his back.

'The helicopter could be flown away at any moment,' Gulliver ventured.

'Then have it flown away – at *this* moment. Spread the rumour that it had to make a forced landing.'

'They might not be easily convinced – especially if they then realize this villa is occupied.'

'Oh, my Lord!' Walvis clapped a hand to his forehead. 'Do I have to think of every tiny detail myself? My dear Gulliver' – his voice became dangerously quiet – 'you send several men who speak German to buy something in different shops. While they are there they tell the story about the machine having engine trouble, that it had to land in the grounds of the abandoned villa. Shopkeepers gossip to their customers.'

'A good idea, sir . . .'

'I just wonder how long it will be before *you* get a good idea. If ever. Wait!' he commanded as Gulliver was hurrying from the room. 'Don't forget to order the pilot to take off immediately before you start the rumour.'

'Take off for where?'

'Anywhere, idiot! Just get it out of here. I presume Martin is here?'

'Yes, he is waiting in his room for you to summon him.'

'Tell him he is summoned! Tell him I want him here in thirty seconds . . .'

He heard the clatter of Martin's feet dashing down the treads of the ancient wooden staircase. There was a tumbling sound, then a heavy thud. Martin had fallen in his anxiety to obey the order. Walvis took one look at Martin, who was brushing dust off the new suit he had changed into after spilling brandy down the one he had worn in Passau. Martin always carried a spare suit.

'Stop trying to make yourself look like Heaven's gift to women,' Walvis shouted.

361

He was seated behind his desk. The chair creaked under his weight. He stared at Martin, who was trying to find the right words to break the news. He went towards a chair to sit down.

'Remain standing while you make your report,' Walvis ordered, his voice again soft.

'The heavy snow storm which continued all night prevented me from . . .'

Walvis sighed aloud. 'Get to the point. You are not about to tell me something has gone wrong?'

'Karl blundered at Grafenau. They were using explosives to widen the entrance tunnel . . .'

'Shall we start again, Martin? Or do you want me to call Karl to tell me what really happened?'

Martin took a deep breath, decided there was no way to avoid telling the truth. As he explained what had happened Walvis remained ominously silent, biting his thick lips. He sat back in his chair, which again creaked, his eyes never leaving Martin's.

'So,' Martin concluded, 'we were faced with a catastrophe.'

'That is putting it mildly. I ought to have you executed, buried in that land behind me. How long do you think it would be before anyone discovered the body?'

'I know it would be futile to offer an apology . . .'

'It would be quite futile. I have not yet heard whether the vital barge-train arrived at Passau.'

Martin had to wait, a wait which seemed an eternity. The helicopter in the grounds had been started up, the engine making an infernal row. It lifted off, vanished beyond the trees.

'You were saying?' Walvis enquired amiably.

'When I arrived at Passau I found another disaster,' said Martin, plunging in because his nerve had broken. 'The barge-train is at the bottom of the Danube, blown up by saboteurs who attacked the guards and used explosives.'

'Blown up by explosives?' Walvis smiled unpleasantly. 'I think you mean blown up by Tweed's men – as at Grafenau. *Tweed!*' he roared suddenly, standing up. He walked slowly round the room to quieten his emotions. 'He really should meet Teardrop.'

'Teardrop?' Martin repeated, puzzled.

'Yes. Maybe you also should meet Teardrop. It would be good for your health – good for mine, at any rate.' He began to speak calmly and so quietly Martin could hardly catch what he said.

'We have endured two major disasters.' Walvis was voicing his thoughts aloud and Martin was careful to say nothing. 'Such a situation tests a man's fibre – his depth of character. We shall simply have to change our plans, do the unexpected, make a major move which will take people's breath away by its sheer audacity – and by then it will be too late for anyone to stop me. I have decided what we are going to do . . .'

Tweed and the members of his team, still seated at separate tables, had enjoyed a lavish lunch when Tweed was handed a message by a receptionist. There was laughter and joking as the tension of the morning began to fade. Tweed's face was expressionless as he read the note; a shade too expressionless, Paula thought. The wording was brief.

Can we meet in your suite urgently? Philip.

Jill Selborne appeared, came across to his table as he was about to rise. A waiter followed her, carrying a tripod with a bottle of champagne. She sat down and gazed at Tweed after nodding to Paula.

'A peace offering. I really was rather abrasive at breakfast this morning. I do hope you both like a glass of champagne.'

Paula hesitated. She was waiting for Tweed's reaction,

wondering about the contents of the note. For a moment Tweed also seemed indecisive, then he sat up straight, smiled at Jill.

'What a nice gesture. And we like champagne . . .'

The waiter had placed glasses in front of them and now he opened the bottle. Tweed gazed at Jill, which was not difficult since she was making constant eye contact with him. He didn't believe for a moment that the only reason she had appeared was to drink champagne with him. She had, he was sure, some other motive.

They raised glasses, clinked them, drank. As she put her glass down Jill gave a flourish of her hand and spoke.

'My conductor is still playing hard to get but I don't care any more. I'm after bigger fish, much bigger fish.'

'Has the fish a name?' Tweed asked, as he was intended to do.

'I've heard strong rumours flying round Salzburg that Gabriel March Walvis is in town. Now that would be a real scoop – an interview with him. He has *never* been interviewed. No one even knows what he looks like. I know there are four different photographs in existence which have appeared in magazines and newspapers. They are all of different men.'

'How do you know all this?' Tweed asked her.

'Because I have been busy this morning.' She sipped more champagne. 'I have run up a huge phone bill, calling contacts in New York, London, Berlin and Vienna. That is when I was told about the fake photos.'

'In that case,' Tweed persisted, watching her closely, 'how can it have been rumoured he is in Salzburg? No one would recognize him even if he was here.'

'That's why I told you. I was hoping you would know the answer. Have *you* ever met him? You're the sort of man who does meet a whole variety of powerful and strange people.'

'If you say so.' Tweed still concentrated all his attention

364

on her. 'Don't you think you may be taking rather a serious risk?'

'Sorry. I don't understand.' Jill had drunk more champagne and was twiddling the stem of her glass. 'What kind of risk?'

'Well, I have heard that Walvis is well protected, that his bodyguards are not always gentle with people who try to get close to him.' He leaned towards her to emphasize what he was saying. 'Don't try it.' He shook his head. 'They say – only rumours – that the cemeteries of Europe are littered with people who tried to reach him.' Tweed had stood up as he was speaking. 'I'm afraid I must go. I have an urgent appointment.'

'Thank you for the warning.'

'Thank you for the champagne . . .'

'Teardrop,' said Philip.

He had rushed to the suite when Tweed, arriving back with Paula and Newman, had phoned his room.

'Who this time?' asked Tweed grimly.

'You're not going to like this. Ziggy Palewski. Shot and killed at the Café Sigrist this morning.'

'Dear God, no!' exclaimed Paula.

'That's not possible!' Tweed protested. 'He knew what she looked like, the fact that she always wore a black cap, a black veil which concealed her face.'

'Well, this time she didn't. She's a redhead. After she'd arrived at the Sigrist she went and sat at his table, asked him for a light for her cigarette, and shot him. The police weren't very efficient.' He took from his pocket a paper napkin with something inside it. When he unrolled the napkin Paula saw a cheroot, hardly smoked, with the tip burnt out.

'Could I keep that?' Paula asked. 'I really liked that man.'

365

Philip glanced at Tweed, who nodded, and then he rolled up the cheroot again in the napkin and handed it to her.

'How on earth do you know all this?' Tweed demanded.

'I had been wandering round the Altstadt for ages. Not a sign of Lucien. I was coming back here and felt thirsty. I saw uniformed policemen coming down the stairs leading up to the Sigrist. I went up and ordered a cup of coffee. It was mid-afternoon, about half an hour ago. The waitress was full of what had happened. The area where he had been sitting was roped off with police tapes.'

'I still don't follow this business about it being Teardrop and your saying she was a redhead,' Tweed pressed.

'Let me go on, then. The waitress knows English but I talked to her in German to make sure I understood her clearly. The police I'd seen leaving had returned to ask her a few more questions. The pathologist must have worked quickly because he'd told the police he had been puzzled by the expression of extreme agony on Palewski's face. He extracted the bullet easily, tested it, and found it was cyanide tipped.'

'I see,' said Tweed. 'And the waitress was able to give a description of the woman assassin?'

'Only a feeble one. She kept nattering on about how awful Palewski had looked – that would be the rictus brought on by the cyanide. As to the assassin, she simply said she was a redhead with a mane of very thick hair coming down over her shoulders. She thinks she was wearing a white coat. That was all.'

'So it was Teardrop,' Tweed commented.

'And she wore a wig,' said Paula.

'I'm sure you're right,' agreed Tweed. He looked at Philip. 'How did they know it was Ziggy Palewski?'

'I asked the waitress that. By the passport in his pocket. The police wanted to find out if the waitress knew the

366

name but she didn't. He was just a regular customer who often came in at the same time each morning for coffee.'

'There was probably only thirty minutes in it,' Tweed said in a tone of deep regret. 'At the outside thirty minutes – between the time we left him and Teardrop arrived. If we had stayed longer she would have gone away when she saw us with him. If he had left soon after we did he would probably still be alive.'

'Life is full of "ifs",' said Paula sympathetically.

She had rarely heard Tweed express such a viewpoint. He always dealt in realities, accepted what had happened, learned from it and pressed on. Perhaps he had sensed her thoughts.

'We must now take more action to disturb and upset Mr Walvis. Butler, in Munich you were watching Walvis's HQ with Nield. While Nield followed Martin with Philip, discovering the farmhouse, you later followed Gulliver to a large apparently derelict warehouse in a sleazy district on the city's outskirts. You told me you had marked its location on a map.'

'I did,' replied Butler.

He dived a hand inside his pocket, produced a folded map, spread it out on a table and pointed to a cross.

'That's the exact location of the warehouse.'

'Which, you said, in spite of its derelict exterior, was guarded with the most modern alarm devices.'

'Like a fortress.'

'And you,' Tweed said, turning to Philip, 'followed Martin to Walvis's remote farmhouse with Nield. One of you would have marked its location on a map.'

'Pete did,' Philip told him. 'But Pete and I were talking about that Siberian trip recently and he gave me the map. Here it is.'

He spread it out on another table and pointed to a small circle.

'Good,' Tweed said. 'Now this is what I propose to do

to strike another heavy blow at the enemy. I'm going to try and get hold of Kuhlmann. He's probably in Wiesbaden or Bonn. If I get hold of him I'll put you, Butler, on the phone and, later, you, Philip. Can you two – with the aid of those maps – give Kuhlmann the locations of both the warehouse and the farmhouse?'

'Yes,' said Butler, who had arrived a few minutes before.

'Easily,' said Philip.

'Later I want us to go over the sequence of recent events. I hope to find a clue to the identity of Teardrop . . .'

As Tweed sat down to phone Kriminalpolizei head-quarters in Wiesbaden Newman said he was going to take a stroll in the hotel downstairs. Tweed asked him why.

'To make sure the place isn't crawling with some of Mr Walvis's nice friends.'

'I'll come with you,' said Paula, jumping up. 'You may need protection,' she remarked and smiled wickedly at the expression on Newman's face.

Tweed had trouble getting through to the right person at Wiesbaden, Kuhlmann's trusted deputy. After he had identified himself the deputy said Kuhlmann wasn't there, that he had flown back to Munich earlier in the day, that he could be contacted at police headquarters. He gave Tweed the number.

After getting through to Munich he had to go through the same procedure all over again. It was a relief when a familiar voice came on the phone, a relief that it was Kuhlmann and that he was back in Munich. He warned the German that he was speaking from a hotel in Austria.

'This is the police commissioner,' Kuhlmann's powerful voice thundered in German. 'I think the operator at your end is listening in. If he – or she – is I'll put them behind bars within the hour . . .'

He waited, and Tweed, understanding the tactic, kept quiet. Kuhlmann was listening for a verbal reaction – or, more likely, the click of the operator tuning out. There was nothing and no click.

'OK,' Kuhlmann barked, reverting to English, 'what can I do for you?'

Tweed explained why he had called as concisely as possible. Kuhlmann listened without interruption. Then he barked again, full of energy, after a brief pause.

'Put each man on separately. I have a detailed map of Bavaria in front of me. Shoot . . .'

Tweed waited while Butler detailed the position of the warehouse, then nodded to Philip. It took Philip very little time to explain where the farmhouse was located. He handed the phone back to Tweed.

'He wants to speak to you.'

Tweed had to wait a couple of minutes. Kuhlmann then came back on the line.

'The delay was while I was arranging two teams of the special anti-terrorist force to stand by for immediate action. They'll be heading for both objectives within two minutes of this conversation ending.'

'How are you going to handle it?' Tweed asked. 'You'll need a good reason for both actions.'

'I've got one already. I'm investigating the murder of Captain Sherwood and the attack on you when you left the Hotel Bayerischer Hof. Give me your number and I may report back.'

Tweed gave him the phone number and Kuhlmann was gone. A few moments later there was the tattoo-rapping on the door and Newman returned with Paula. She seemed excited.

Walvis was putting on an outsize vicuña coat in the room at the back of the old villa on the outskirts of Salzburg.

369

He glared at Martin and Gulliver, who were also dressed for swift departure.

'The motorcade is ready, hidden in a nearby track, to drive to the front of the villa and pick us up when the coast is clear,' Gulliver reported, the soul of efficiency. 'All the cars have full tanks, as you ordered. But we don't know where we are going.'

'Of course you don't. You have spread the rumour that I am here all over Salzburg?'

'I had a team doing just that,' Gulliver replied with a smug smile. He was revelling in the fact he had been put in charge because of Martin's disgrace after the disasters at Grafenau and Passau. 'Hotel concierges are a perfect source for spreading wild stories. They love to be in the know, as they think.'

'I don't recall my asking you how you had done it – just that you had, for once, carried out my orders properly. Our destination,' he added casually, 'is Munich.'

'Munich?'

The word, expressed with great surprise, was out of Martin's mouth before he could stop himself. Walvis regarded him with contempt.

'Why, Martin, do you sound so startled?'

'I was just thinking . . .' Martin felt he had better finish now he had started. 'That Munich could be risky, bearing in mind the demise of the late Captain Sherwood and' – he glanced at Gulliver, who had been in charge of the operation, maliciously – 'the abortive attack on Tweed. Munich will be swarming with Kuhlmann's minions.'

'Will it?' Walvis smiled coldly. 'My best information is that Kuhlmann has returned to Wiesbaden and is still there. Martin, I gave you the job of cleaning up this villa so no trace that we have ever been here exists.'

'And I have arranged for a team to do just that,' Martin said, feeling more confident. 'There will not be one single fingerprint left when they have finished their work. But

370

what about Lucien? He is still in the Altstadt.'

'Lucien can stay there until Tweed and as many members of his team as possible have been killed. No one has asked me why we are returning to Munich.'

'I simply accepted the order,' Gulliver said unctuously.

'Wouldn't it be wiser if you knew the reason for the order? Wisdom, I fear, has never been your strongest point.'

'Why are we going to Munich?' Gulliver asked meekly.

'To move the vast armoury from the warehouse in Munich. To put it aboard my aircraft on the lake near Berg. That machine has greater carrying capacity than the largest American military cargo plane. I want those arms and equipment transferred to England. Later we will pay a quick visit to the farmhouse so I can collect certain papers concerning Tidal Wave. Gulliver! Summon the motorcade. We leave behind Mr Tweed thinking we are still in Salzburg. Hurry! We are about to make history.'

38

'You both look as though you have found the crock of gold,' Tweed commented.

Paula and Newman had returned to the suite after their excursion into the ground floor of the hotel. They glanced at each other.

'Who is going to tell him?' Newman asked Paula.

'It would be nice if someone would tell me,' Tweed grumbled.

'I was coming back into the reception area from the lounge,' he reported. 'I saw a familiar figure wearing a ski outfit complete with hood hurrying out of the main exit.'

'Go on,' Tweed coaxed, containing his impatience.

'It was Lisa Trent.'

Silence fell on the room. Philip looked at Butler, who shrugged. Tweed walked across to the window, stared out without seeing the storm clouds building up over the distant Alps. He turned round, looked at Newman.

'Are you quite sure?'

'I knew he was going to ask that,' Newman said to Paula. He looked back at Tweed. 'I am certain. Everything about her. Height, build.'

'And body language,' Paula added. 'The way she walks. I can remember that clearly even going back to when she first appeared at the Bistro in Bosham.'

'This is interesting,' said Tweed. 'I have three women on my list of suspects as Teardrop. Lisa Trent, Jill Selborne and Rosa Brandt. Now all three have been seen in Salzburg at the time when Ziggy Palewski was murdered. Philip, you are sure you saw Rosa Brandt disappearing into the Altstadt?'

'I saw a woman of medium height, wearing a black coat, a black cap – hid her hair – and a black veil, vanishing into an alley that night I was after Lucien when he'd sprayed us with his automatic weapon.'

'Are you sure you saw someone like that?' Tweed insisted.

'Certain. OK, I only caught a glimpse.' Philip glanced at the others. 'But that was a pretty unusual outfit she was wearing. Certain,' he repeated.

'So all three have appeared in Salzburg at the crucial time – when Ziggy Palewski was murdered.'

'Why would she change her appearance now?' Newman wondered. 'Paula thinks she wore a red wig.'

'Because,' Tweed replied, 'she's a very intelligent woman. She has to be – to have killed so many people and survived. I think she guessed she'd played the black card for long enough, that to go on dressing like that was

372

pushing her luck. It's further confirmation that I've detected her identity.'

'I'm not going to ask you who it is, so you don't have the satisfaction of saying it's too early to be sure,' Paula commented wrily.

'How perceptive of you. Now we come to the mystery of why Walvis is spreading these rumours that he is here in Salzburg. Because only Walvis could have triggered them off – and for a purpose.'

'I can't imagine why,' Newman said. 'So maybe you'll let your hair down and tell us?'

'Because he is *leaving* Salzburg – may have already left the city for another destination. We'll be doing the same thing within the next twenty-four hours.'

'Going where?' Paula asked. 'I must get packed.'

'To Munich for a brief stop before we move on. I want to talk to Kuhlmann face to face, not over a phone.'

'Then,' Philip interjected, 'I'll be going back to the Altstadt to search for Lucien. I may be there the rest of the day and all night.' He looked at Tweed. 'All right if I'm back by morning for breakfast?'

'Yes.'

'Want me to come with you as back-up?' Newman suggested.

'No. Thanks anyway. This is a job I have to do on my own. Lucien is the man who tortured Jean. I want to settle this myself. On my own . . .'

He turned away quickly and Paula thought he had tears in his eyes because the tragedy of Jean's death had flooded back into his mind.

Walvis, sitting in the rear of his armoured Mercedes, was fuming. His vehicle was again in the middle of the motorcade – with Gulliver driving the Mercedes ahead of them, carrying armed guards – while behind followed the

373

third Mercedes with Martin sitting beside the driver. More armed men sat in the back.

They had crossed the frontier from Austria into Germany, were moving along the autobahn to Munich. Walvis was fuming because the snow had fallen more heavily in this area, had frozen, forming treacherous patches of ice on the road surface. He reached forward, slid aside the glass partition separating him from the driver and the guard beside him.

'Can't you move faster than this?'

'Not if you want me to get you to Munich alive, sir,' the driver answered. 'The road is like a skating rink.'

'This is a heavy car,' Walvis snapped. 'It holds road surfaces better than other vehicles. Press your foot down and see what happens.'

'I know what will happen,' the driver persisted. 'At high speed we will end up smashing into the barrier – we might even smash through the barriers and end up in the east-bound lane. Look at the amount of traffic there is heading east.'

Walvis did look. There was a lot of traffic moving at high speed, far too fast for the weather conditions. Confirmation of this came a few minutes later when they passed a multiple pile-up on the east-bound route. The police were there in force, controlling single-line traffic. The pile-up was like a scrap-metal merchant's yard, a horror of what remained of cars twisted into distorted shapes. Ambulance men were threading their way among the havoc.

Walvis slammed the glass partition shut, sighed, sagged in his seat. It would be dark, early evening by the time they reached Munich in Lord knew how many hours' time.

Philip had spent ages trudging through the snow inside the Altstadt. Knowing it well now, he followed a definite route, gradually covering every street, every square, every alleyway.

He even contemplated taking the funicular up to the *Schloss* and then decided against it. Wherever Lucien was hiding out he wouldn't risk being trapped on that elevated platform. The storm which had earlier threatened to move over the city had gone away, the temperature dropped to even more Siberian levels as night approached.

Philip was hardly aware of the intense cold. There were so few people about he felt very alone and his thoughts wandered back to memories of Jean. He recalled the apparent accident when, over a year ago, she had nearly been killed by a hit-and-run driver in the Fulham Road, what she had said to him before she came out of hospital.

We are going to live a normal life.

At the time he had vaguely thought it was a strange thing for her to say, but he had been so busy, so relieved to be taking her home, he had pushed the query mark to the back of his mind.

Now he felt so guilty that he had not, when they had settled into everyday life, asked her what she had meant. Since then it had been quite clear to him – after her death – that she knew she had been living on borrowed time, that sooner rather than later she would die. He also knew she had deliberately not warned him, knowing the misery and anxiety which would overtake him if he'd been aware of the truth. She could have asked for protection, but she had been convinced the hand of Walvis would reach out to her however much protection she was given.

'What it comes to,' he said aloud quietly, 'is that she was a woman of the most extraordinary strength of character. Knowing she was under sentence of death she set out to conceal the fact from me so we could enjoy some last days of happiness. Oh, God! Why didn't I realize what was happening?'

But at the back of his mind he remembered there had

375

been a nagging fear that something was terribly wrong. He had, almost unconsciously, not raised the issue with her because he had known that was the way she had wanted it. A normal life for as long as she could last out, a normal life for *him*.

He stood for a short time against a wall while he wiped his eyes, blew his nose. He knew then that in the future there would be many times when, in the privacy of his house, he would cry for her, call out her name.

He took a deep breath of the cold air, forced himself out of the mood of deep, near overwhelming emotion. Seeing a café open, he walked inside, sat down and asked the woman who ran the tiny place for a cup of coffee. She began chattering as soon as she had served him – probably because he had ordered in German.

'Have you heard the rumours? The richest man in the world is staying somewhere in Salzburg. Someone called Walvis. I have never heard of the name. They say he is a multi-billionaire.'

'How did you hear this strange rumour?' Philip asked.

'The porter from a small hotel near by – one of my regulars – came in for a hot drink. The poor man was so cold his hand shook when he lifted his cup of coffee and he spilt it. I gave him a fresh cup, of course.'

Philip was now alert, his mind cleared, focused totally on his job.

'But how did the porter hear this?'

'I perhaps shouldn't talk about it, but there's a grape-vine that runs through all Salzburg – between concierges and porters. They love to tell each other when they have some very distinguished guest staying with them. Although this was slightly different.'

'Different in what way?' Philip enquired.

'Well, he said a man came in to ask for the tariff, wanted to know if they had a room for tomorrow night. They had, of course, at this time of year. The man told

376

the porter he would phone him if he needed the room. Then he asked whether the porter had heard that the richest man in the whole world was staying in Salzburg. A Gabriel March Walvis. I think that was the name.'

'So the porter asked where he was staying?' Philip suggested. Not that the woman needed any encouragement.

'That's exactly what he did ask this stranger. The man said he had no idea, that he had heard Walvis sometimes stayed at a five-star, but sometimes at quite a small hotel. I gather the porter was going back to phone all his contacts on the grapevine.'

'Thank you for the coffee. I must go now, so if you could tell me how much I owe you . . .'

Outside the cold hit him again but the warmth inside the café together with the hot coffee had provided good central heating. Philip felt he was ready for anything. Stopping at the small café had been informative. He now knew how Walvis had spread the rumour he was in Salzburg. He had used his thugs to tap into the hotel grapevine. And it had been clever to suggest Walvis used small hotels as well as the five-star de-luxe establishments. The news would be all over Salzburg by now.

Philip began trudging again down a main street. He pushed out of his mind the logical thought that Lucien would, in this weather, stay comfortably hidden away in his apartment, or whatever accommodation he occupied when staying in the Altstadt. I only need one lucky break, he told himself.

Tweed had packed his case as far as he could when Paula came back to find him alone in the suite. She looked at the case.

'Mine is packed, too, except for my night things and toiletries. I came to ask you something. I suppose it is the death of Ziggy Palewski which has enraged me. It's funny, but you can spend only a short while with someone and come to really like them. I suppose it was the kindness I sensed.'

'What were you going to ask me?'

'You say you know who Teardrop is. Do you think you'll ever prove a case against her?'

'I very much doubt it.'

'Then she goes free, the hideous greedy bitch.'

'Time will tell.'

'I wish you'd *tell* me who she is,' Paula coaxed. 'If it's Rosa Brandt I don't see how on earth you will locate her, let alone do anything about her.'

'There could be ways,' Tweed replied vaguely. 'Which is one reason why we're going to Munich. If Philip realizes his quest is hopeless and gets back on time I want to leave tonight aboard the evening express to Munich. I hope everyone has packed as far as they can.'

'They have. I called in on Newman, then Butler and Nield.' She paused. 'You're probably going to be mad about this. I couldn't find Marler. Pete told me he's gone after Philip in the Altstadt. He thinks Bob made the mistake of asking Philip if he could go with him.'

'Marler always plays a lone hand, doesn't he? The hired cars must be handed in to the local branch. I saw there was one when we were travelling in a taxi.'

'They've all assumed you'd want them to do that. They've handed in their transport.'

'Including Marler?' Tweed asked.

'I gather so. He left on foot for the Altstadt. What is the other reason we're going back to Munich for?'

'I'm betting that's where Walvis is headed for. Now, forget all about Teardrop.'

'Unless I catch her in the act,' Paula said grimly. 'If I do I'll shoot her down without a moment's compunction.'

*   *   *

378

Philip was dog tired. He had been on his feet for hours, still trudging round the deserted ice-cold streets and alleys in the Altstadt. He was walking back down the main street he had started out from after drinking coffee at the small café. It was closed as he passed it.

Earlier he had visited Ziggy Palewski's rooms in Brodgasse. He was passing the entrance by chance and took a quick decision. He wanted to pay his last respects to a talented and very human man. A sentimental act, he admitted to himself. No, a matter of sentiment, he thought as he mounted the worn stone staircase. He had stopped short when he reached the landing, whipping out his Walther. The door to Palewski's quarters was open – had been smashed open.

He had approached the interior cautiously, had found what he'd expected to find. No one about and the place brutally ransacked. Drawers pulled out, cupboards left wide open, their contents strewn across the floor. Palewski's books of reference, built up over the years, scattered like rubbish.

'Bastards,' he said under his breath.

But it was logical, another proof of the ruthless efficiency of Walvis's organization. They had undoubtedly taken away and destroyed the manuscript he had taken so long to prepare for his profile on Walvis to be published in *Der Spiegel*. It was a pathetic ending to a man's life.

He had left and resumed his wanderings. That experience had set the adrenalin moving again despite his fatigue. He walked slowly, glancing back frequently, looking from side to side at the closed antiquarian bookshops, the cake shops.

His rubber-soled shoes made no sound on the packed snow, the occasional stretch of exposed cobbles where he had to watch his footing – raw ice was exposed. He knew he was coming to the entrance to the alley where thugs

379

had attacked him while he was with Palewski, where he had used *pavé* stones to eliminate the attackers. He glanced down it and stopped dead.

Afterwards he realized it was the logical place to look for his quarry. Lucien had been there during the thugs' assault. So he probably had his hideaway near by. He had, after all, vanished during the fight.

Lucien was standing in the alley under a lantern. He grinned when he saw Philip, spat on the ground. By the light of the lantern he looked incredibly evil – his figure stooped in his hunchback fashion, the downward curve of his moustache round either side of his cruel mouth, the straggle of beard. He advanced towards Philip, both arms spread wide in a pacific gesture.

As he entered the alley, Philip felt soft loose snow under his feet, scuffed up by people hurrying down it earlier. Obviously it was used as a short cut. Lucien was walking past the large wooden barrel which collected rainwater, was close to Philip, when his right hand moved in an arc, so swiftly it seemed like an optical illusion. His right hand now held a flick-knife. There was a click in the heavy silence of the alley as a long blade appeared.

Philip stopped, as though frightened. His right foot moved back and then forwards in a movement as rapid as Lucien's. He kicked up a spray of cold snow which hit Lucien in the face, blinding him briefly. Philip was on top of him, grabbing his right arm, twisting it far behind his back. Lucien grunted with pain, dropped the knife.

Fury took hold of Philip, cold, lethal fury. As one hand grasped Lucien round the throat he scraped his shoe down the thug's shin, pressing it in hard. They struggled ferociously and Philip was surprised by the strength of the smaller man. Lowering his head, he rammed it into Lucien's chest, at the same time using his grip on his opponent's throat to turn his head sideways, to slam it into the rock wall.

Lucien, dazed, stood for several seconds leaning against the wall. In those few seconds Philip dropped into a crouch, seized Lucien by both his ankles, unbalanced him, lifted him high into the air and dropped him, still gripping the ankles, over the barrel. Lucien's skull smashed through the ice layer coating the water in the barrel, descended into the water below. Philip forced him in deeper as Lucien desperately grabbed hold of the barrel's rim with both hands.

Philip held him for a second by one ankle, crashed his fist down on both hands, which let go. Grasping the other ankle again, Philip thrust him deeper into the ice-cold water, then hauled him up, choking and spluttering with ice already forming on his moustache.

'I'm choking!' Lucien yelled. 'I can't breathe . . .'

I can't breathe.

The same words Jean had used when found at Amber Cottage. Philip had the expression of an executioner.

'My wife, Jean Cardon, couldn't breathe when you tortured her at Amber Cottage in England. Admit you did that and I might not finish you off,' he said in German.

'Yes, it was me,' Lucien gasped. 'I did it. But I was under orders . . .'

'Who gave you the order?'

'I dare not tell you that . . .'

Philip plunged him down again, deep into the ice-cold water. He was small, so his head had to be touching the bottom of the barrel. Under the surface the arms waved desperately. Philip held him under. The arms began to lose their vigour. He hauled him up again. Water dripping from his beard began to form into ice. Lucien was spewing out water, coughing, choking.

'Can't breathe,' he eventually gasped.

'Neither could Jean,' Philip said remorselessly. 'Who gave you the order personally to torture Jean Cardon? This is your last chance to survive.'

381

'I dare not . . .' Philip began slowly to push him under again. 'Stop!' Lucien screamed. 'I will tell you. It was Walvis . . .'

'Walvis who personally ordered you to do what you did?' Philip demanded ruthlessly.

'Yes. Walvis. It was Walvis. Walvis himself . . .'

'I thought so. But I had to know.'

Philip plunged him down again, plunged him in deep as he would go. The arms thrashed about again, Philip held on. The arms thrashed more feebly, then stopped. The disturbed water on the surface became calm. Bubbles of air rose to the surface, stopped rising. Philip thrust the booted feet under the surface. He took off his sodden gloves, wiped his hands dry on a large handkerchief, put on a spare pair of gloves. He would drop the sodden pair into the Salzach on his way back to the hotel.

He took one last look at the barrel before he left. Ice had formed on the surface again. Lucien was sealed in his tomb. Flaked out, incredibly tired, Philip left the alley, forcing his leaden feet to take him out of the Altstadt for ever.

39

'Walvis next.'

Philip sounded detached as he uttered the words in the hotel suite. The whole team was there – Marler, unable to find Philip, had just returned.

Tweed and the others had listened in silence while Philip, speaking almost like a robot, told them about his final encounter with Lucien. He left out the emotions which had assailed him at the time. Then he had uttered the two words and, still standing, fell silent.

'Thank you for telling me,' Tweed said quietly. 'We are leaving for Munich aboard the evening express. You'll want a bath. Can you be back here in fifteen minutes?'

'Easily.' Philip looked round the room, his eyes lingering on Paula before he spoke again. 'It was a horrific experience. But it had to be done.'

Paula felt relieved as he left the suite. His closing words had shown her he had not turned into a professional killer who enjoyed his work. He'd suffer a reaction later.

'Teardrop,' said Tweed. 'From now on you must all be on your guard. She's no longer recognizable from the weird outfit she wore for so long. She can appear in any type of guise. Beware of being approached by single women.'

'I'm always wary when I'm approached by a single woman,' Newman said with a smile.

'I'm not joking,' Tweed rebuked him.

'And I'm intrigued by Jill Selborne reverting to her earlier hairstyle,' Paula commented. 'The way she now wears her black hair like a helmet pasted to her head.'

'That's a highly interesting observation,' Tweed said with a strange smile.

Paula waited for him to go on, to explain the point of his remark. He said nothing more. I might have known, she thought in a mood of mild pique.

Fifteen minutes, their bills paid, they were all ready with their luggage in Tweed's suite to leave by taxi for the station. Tweed checked his watch, picked up his bag.

'We should just make the evening express. I wonder what developments we shall find in Munich . . .'

Ronnie, the creepy Ronald Weatherby, appeared while they were waiting on the Salzburg station platform. How strange, Paula thought – he appeared when we arrived at this station. Extending his limp hand, he came up to Tweed, wearing a leather coat and an Austrian hat with a feather in the band.

'A word in your shell-like ear while we are aboard the express,' he suggested. 'In private.'

Paula was surprised to note that when he shook Tweed's hand he gripped it firmly. Then the express glided in from Vienna. Tweed tugged at Paula's arm to indicate she should accompany him.

Inside the first-class coach Tweed chose four of the seats at the end. He frowned at Newman, shook his head slightly. Newman, who had been about to take up position as guard, nodded, opened the door and went outside to wait where he could see anyone who entered the coach.

Weatherby sat opposite Tweed who had Paula next to him. The rest of his team had separated into small groups, occupying seats at the other end of the coach.

'Weatherby,' Tweed began, 'Paula is my confidante and my right arm. You can say what you like in front of her.' He turned to Paula. 'Meet Ronald Weatherby, a member of Military Intelligence and chief security officer for the British forces in Germany.'

'I am pleased to meet you,' Weatherby said in a normal voice, his accent now crisp and clipped. 'I have heard from Mr Tweed some of the many ways you have helped him. We need more women like you.' He smiled warmly. 'I could do with one myself.'

Paula tried not to stare too hard at Weatherby. All his unctuousness and slyness had disappeared. He sat very erect and his previous cringing stance had vanished.

'I hope you don't mind my asking,' she said, 'but how do you manage it? You're a totally different person.'

'Ah, when I was very young I used to be an actor. I thought that was my vocation. But I didn't like most of the other people in the profession. Staring at yourself in a

384

mirror for hours, practising different expressions, is not my cup of tea. I took a mighty leap, joined the Army. They soon put me in the Intelligence Corps. I have known your Mr Tweed for a long time, but we always met in secret.'

'He is my secret weapon,' Tweed said quite seriously. 'Now, Ronald, I assume you have news?'

'Bad news, the worst possible. Hundreds of thousands of refugees from the East are being massed on the Oder–Niesse line separating Germany from Poland. The Polish authorities have tried to control them but sheer weight of numbers has overwhelmed them. The weather will help them, too.'

'In what way?' Tweed asked.

'The rivers they have to cross to flood into Western Europe are frozen solid. They will wait for Walvis's signal, then pour across the ice. We have found out he is in direct communication with trained leaders who arrived a week ago—'

'How does he communicate with them?' Tweed interjected.

Paula was fascinated by the conversation but every now and again she glanced across to the windows on the far side. The sky was clear, the moon had risen. By its light she saw the awesome mountains of the Alps, their fearsome jagged peaks silhouetted against the night sky, their lower slopes gleaming in the moonlight. They reminded her of a tidal wave – she shuddered as she thought of another tidal wave planned. The lights of small isolated villages glittered. What would happen to their peaceful lives when the hordes arrived? She had heard Weatherby answering Tweed's key question.

'Walvis has been very clever. He bought from American firms over two million portable radios with a long range. They were moved to Eastern Europe by Hercules transport planes. They have been distributed to the

385

leaders of the swarm of waiting refugees. When he judges the time is ripe he sends the signal and the flood sweeps over Europe from the Baltic to the Adriatic. Germany, Austria and Italy will be submerged.'

'What about NATO stopping them?'

'The NATO generals have admitted their troops and modern weapons will be useless against such a wave of primitive humanity. Walvis has even planned to take over GCHQ at Cheltenham.'

'What is the point of that?' Tweed probed. 'GCHQ has the task of monitoring signals all over the world – including satellite transmissions.'

'He has infiltrated his own men inside the organization. He will know what steps are being taken to counter the invasion.'

'That would be deadly,' Tweed agreed. 'But you said he will send signals to the trained leaders to order the advance. He can't do that from Cheltenham.'

'No. But we have heard he has a base in Britain which has the latest signalling equipment to send messages. The trouble is we cannot locate that base.'

Tweed sat silent for some time, absorbing what Weatherby had told him. Lights began to appear frequently as Paula peered out of her side of the window. The clusters moved closer together, became continuous. They were approaching Munich.

'I had an idea you'd turn up at the psychological moment.'

It was Otto Kuhlmann, in the middle of lighting his cigar, who greeted Tweed in this fashion at Munich police headquarters. He took the cigar out of his mouth, placed it in an ashtray, grinned cynically at Tweed to show there were no hard feelings. The local police had given him a spacious office with a very large desk. He

386

stood up and came round to meet Paula.

'You're a gutsy lady, working for this tough task-master.'

He clapped his hands round her shoulders and hugged her. She smiled at him as he took her suitcase, placed it by the side of the desk.

'You're a pretty tough guy yourself, Otto.'

Kuhlmann turned to Philip. 'Life has given you a rough ride, my friend, but maybe tonight we'll do a little to even up the score.' As he went on speaking in his growly voice he pulled out a comfortable swivel chair, gestured for Paula to sit down in it. He spoke over his shoulder to Tweed. 'You should be able to find somewhere to park the backside. Never stand when you can sit.'

'I feel like a spare wheel,' Newman said humorously as he remained standing near the closed door.

'You are a spare wheel,' the German told him, 'but maybe we can find something to occupy you. Park your case and sit.

'You look hungry,' he said to Paula. 'How about some of those long ham rolls? Coffee with milk, no sugar. Have I got it right?'

'Perfect. I could eat a horse.'

'Maybe you will.'

He walked rapidly back to his desk, leaned over the intercom. 'Coffee and ham rolls for everyone?' he enquired.

Heads nodded. Philip, still edgy from his experience with Lucien, perched himself on the edge of a smaller desk.

On arriving at Munich Hauptbahnhof Tweed had sent Marler, Nield and Butler to book rooms at the Four Seasons. Ronald Weatherby had accompanied them. Tweed had not been sure how Kuhlmann would react to his unexpected appearance and had been careful not to bring too many people with him.

Kuhlmann had pressed a button on the intercom, had picked up his cigar, gave the order with it in the corner of his wide mouth, speaking in German.

'Chief Inspector Kuhlmann. I want a feast of long ham rolls for five people. With plenty of coffee. Not the muck the canteen serves up. Send out for it now to that all-night place and get it here in five minutes. Move.'

He turned to Tweed. 'I have news.'

'Sounds like bad news,' Tweed said quietly.

'Bad news is in vogue these days,' Kuhlmann replied and looked at Tweed. 'You read my mind or – more probably – my tone of voice. Teardrop has been active.'

'Oh, my God, no!' Paula exclaimed.

'I'm afraid so. And she's changed her colours. The new murder took place about an hour ago. A busy lady, Teardrop. Must make a packet.'

Despite her impatience and anxiety to know who Teardrop had visited this time, Paula was amused at Kuhlmann's use of such colloquial English. She knew the police chief prided himself on his mastery of English slang.

'Who was the victim?' Tweed asked.

'Manfred Hellmann, dealer in arms to anyone who could pay his price – with the exception of terrorists, whom he despised. Manfred is – was – quite a ladies' man, so it must have been easy for Teardrop.'

'Why kill him?' enquired Paula.

'My guess is Walvis discovered he'd supplied weapons to certain people he regarded as a nuisance, a dangerous nuisance.' His eyes flickered in Philip's direction and away again. He obviously regretted looking at him because he went on, adding rapidly, 'A man who sounds remarkably like Marler was seen leaving Hellmann's villa the last time you were in Munich, Tweed. Who knows?'

'You said Teardrop had changed her colours,' Tweed reminded him.

388

'Yes, the lady who paid a call on Hellmann was a redhead. No black cap or veil this time. A glamorous redhead for a change. Wore a wig, I suspect.'

'You said the murder took place an hour ago,' Tweed recalled. 'So what makes you so sure it was Teardrop?'

'Pure chance. The Munich police pathologist, who is well paid and adds to his income with private work, lives in Berg. I had him at the villa within minutes of the discovery of the body. First the tortured rictus made him wonder if only the bullet had killed him. He then smelt an aroma of almonds on the corpse – which practically guarantees cyanide. We'll find the lady gave him a cyanide-tipped bullet. So again it was Teardrop.'

'That woman,' Paula said viciously, 'is a serial killer.'

'A good description,' Kuhlmann agreed. 'Now, while you eat these ham rolls I'll tell you how we hit Walvis in precisely one hour from now, hit him so hard he'll think the world has come to an end.'

'Could we come with you?' Tweed asked.

'Be my guests.' He looked at Philip. 'You can come in my car, ride shotgun alongside me.'

Walvis's motorcade had eventually reached Munich. In the rear of his armoured Mercedes Walvis was beside himself with impatience as they drove through the suburbs. They had to cross the city to reach the warehouse. He slid back the glass partition.

'Surely you can move faster now?' he shouted at the driver. 'The traffic is quiet, the streets are clear of ice.'

'That way we draw attention to ourselves,' the driver warned. 'Gulliver usually knows what he is doing and he is setting the pace.'

'I run this organization, not Gulliver,' Walvis shouted again.

'I can't signal to him in a way which will convey your

message. If I start flashing my lights he may think we want him to slow down, to proceed more cautiously.'

'Hell and damnation,' snapped Walvis and slammed the partition shut.

Fuming, he forced himself to sit back while he drummed his thick fingers on the arm of his seat. For once he wished he had a mobile phone he could use to communicate with Gulliver.

The motorcade proceeded at the same sedate pace. As it was approaching the warehouse, moving through an area which tourists never saw, if they were wise, Walvis's driver slowed, then stopped. Ahead Gulliver's car had also stopped, the driver's door opened and Gulliver stepped out to walk the last few hundred metres on foot.

'What is Gulliver playing at now?' Walvis demanded after again sliding back the partition.

'Normal procedure, sir. You must recall we have done this before – especially when you are with us. The top man in the lead car gets out a safe distance from our destination to go and check that everything is OK.'

Walvis cursed under his breath. The driver was correct and Walvis knew the procedure, but he was in one hell of a hurry. As he stirred restlessly he wondered vaguely what the red glow in the sky above the rooftops was. It increased in intensity as he watched it.

40

'There was a delay in getting hold of the anti-terrorist teams,' Kuhlmann explained, calling out to Tweed in the back of the Mercedes as he drove the car at a moderate speed behind the Mercedes in front. 'It turned out to be a hoax, but that's why I couldn't act as soon as Butler told me the warehouse's location over the phone.'

'How close are we?' asked Philip, seated next to Kuhlmann.

'Five minutes more and we're there.'

In the rear Tweed was squeezed next to Paula who had Newman pressing up against her right shoulder. Beyond Newman was a member of the anti-terrorist team, his head hooded. Two more members of the team faced them, seated on flap seats. Paula pointed to a long weapon with a wide ugly muzzle on the floor.

'What's that?' she asked in German. 'A bazooka?'

The young hooded man opposite her, who couldn't take his eyes off Paula, answered.

'An advanced rocket launcher. It fires incendiary shells as well as high explosives.'

'And then there's that big armoured-car vehicle behind us with a gun turret. You'd think we were on our way to attack a fortress.'

'We may be doing just that,' Kuhlmann called back to her. 'We sent out motor cycle scouts dressed like macho yobbos first to check out the whole area. They reported back that all the surrounding buildings are derelict, haven't been occupied for years. But Walvis's huge warehouse has every protective device ever invented. Yes, you're right, we could be assaulting a fortress, unless they come out meek as lambs.'

'Will they?' Newman asked.

'I'm assuming they won't. If that warehouse is one of Walvis's major armouries we can expect a dogfight . . .'

There were fewer street lights in the run-down district they were now moving through. Paula saw several men running into the shadows, disappearing altogether when the convoy approached.

'Do people live here?' she called out.

'That trash you've just seen giving us a wide berth are drug traffickers,' Kuhlmann replied. 'This is not exactly the Mayfair of Munich.'

'Is there anyone in front of that car ahead of us?' Tweed enquired.

He was talking to defuse the tension which filled the interior of the car like a gas. Yet the members of the anti-terrorist squad were holding their weapons lightly. One man even had an unlit cigarette which he rolled back and forth along his mouth.

'Yes, there are,' Kuhlmann said, replying to Tweed. 'We sent the scouts on motor cycles back ahead of us. They know the best route to approach this place – and we'll be there soon now. Tweed, with Paula and Newman, you stay in this car until I come back. That's an order...'

Paula was curious as to why Kuhlmann had not included Philip in his order for them to stay put. The reason became apparent when the car stopped beside the wall of a building as a motor cyclist returned. He spoke to Kuhlmann through the side window in German.

'No sign of life, sir. But there are people inside that warehouse, maybe a lot of them. I can sense it.'

'Then we'd better get on with it.' Kuhlmann looked at Philip. 'You're coming with me on one condition. You stay by my side. You obey any order I give you. And if I say duck, you hit the deck fast...'

More cars had appeared, had stopped near Kuhlmann's. Police with hoods over their heads and automatic weapons in their hands jumped out of the car that had stopped in front of Kuhlmann's, out of the other cars that had followed them. They fanned out, with plenty of space between each man so as not to present a massive target for any hostile reaction.

Kuhlmann had reached under his seat as he left the Mercedes and was carrying a megaphone as he warily neared the corner of the building. He peered round it, withdrew his head, looked at Philip.

'You can see the target. Don't blame me if you get your head shot off. And no heroics – this is a surgical operation if we have to launch it.'

Philip followed the German's example, took a quick glance round the corner. In the moonlight the warehouse, set back behind a high stone wall, was a mammoth building, its real size probably increased by the fact that the side he was looking at was in dark shadow. At different levels windows, some with broken glass, overlooked the approaches. Behind the wall was an open space of crumbling cobbles. Near the huge closed entrance gates he saw in the snow the ruts made by heavy vehicles. The width of the ruts gave away the size of the trucks which had passed through the gates recently. He jerked his head back, told Kuhlmann what he had seen.

'You're a pretty observant guy to pick up that much in so short a time,' Kuhlmann commented. 'Now, let's see if they're going to be sensible.'

He waved to the leader of the anti-terrorist team who was standing in a setback on the far side of the street. Philip had not even seen him dart across to the alcove. Kuhlmann raised the megaphone, pressing it close to his wide mouth, stood at the corner, peering round as he roared his message.

'Police here. You are surrounded. Come out one by one with your arms raised in the air. We know you are inside—'

He broke off. Under cover of the distraction of the bellowing megaphone one of the hooded policemen had darted forward to cross the open space to reach the cover of the wall. A fusillade of bullets from a window in the warehouse cut him down. He sprawled on the cobbles, his body jerked several times, he lay still.

'That's it,' Kuhlmann said after peering briefly round the corner. He took out a short-wave radio. Philip saw the unit leader in the alcove holding his own radio.

'The major assault begins now,' Kuhlmann said into the instrument. 'Phase One, Phase Two, then Phase Three – if you agree.'

'Agreed,' the group leader replied. 'We can't even send out a paramedic to attend to my man, who looks in a bad way.'

'I can try once more in the hope of saving your man,' Kuhlmann suggested. 'I'm going to do it.'

He raised the megaphone again, stood by the corner and began speaking.

'I am talking to the top man inside the warehouse. Can we send a paramedic out to help that seriously injured man on the—'

A second hail of bullets rattled out. Philip recognized again the sound of an automatic weapon, maybe an Uzi. This was going to be some siege. Kuhlmann threw the megaphone round the corner on to the cobbles.

'The bastards emptied another magazine into the chap lying on the cobbles. That really is it. No quarter for that lot inside – but don't ever quote me.' He spoke into his radio. 'A non-stop assault – I imagine you will agree now?'

'We're going in with everything we've got. Out.'

'And they've got a lot,' Kuhlmann said. 'You'll see it all from here. I just hope they have stored explosives inside. Again, don't quote me. And maybe we'd get a better view from the first floor of this place.'

He had noticed a shabby door in the building they were hiding behind. Standing back, he raised one foot and slammed it against the ancient door, his foot connecting just above the handle. The whole door came off its hinges, collapsed inwards. Kuhlmann, a Luger in his hand, used the other hand to push Philip back.

'I go first . . .'

'I've got a Walther . . .'

'Don't shoot me with it . . .'

They rushed up a shoddy wooden staircase littered with rubbish, Kuhlmann shining a powerful torch ahead of them. On the landing, where the smell was distinctly unsavoury, he opened two doors before walking into the second room. Bare floorboards, old newspapers, a smell of mice, not a stick of furniture. But the window at the back looked straight across to the warehouse.

'We each stand to one side of the window,' Kuhlmann ordered. 'We should have a bird's-eye view of the battle-field . . .'

The tragic news that one of their men had been shot down spread among the anti-terrorist team as though they were operating a bush telegraph. It was not the first shots that supercharged them – that went with their territory: it was the brutal second fusillade, hammering into the helpless man as he lay on the cobbles.

'It sounds as though they're kicking in the doors of every building in this block,' Philip said.

'They're doing just that,' Kuhlmann confirmed. 'Phase One – talking up positions where they can shoot point-blank into the warehouse windows.'

He had just spoken when blinding searchlights illuminated the shadowed side of the warehouse. One light was shot out by a defender and then a storm of bullets swept over the warehouse windows. Three defenders fell out of the second floor, plunging into the courtyard.

'The tactic of Erich, the unit's leader,' Kuhlmann explained during a brief pause in the bombardment.

'Entice them into shooting at the searchlights, they're exposed at the windows, take out as many as they can.'

He swung round, his Luger aimed, then lowered it. The hooded policeman who had sat opposite Paula had entered, carrying his launcher. He approached the window cautiously, crouched down.

'Both of you stay by the wall on either side of the window, please.'

He managed to give the instruction during a brief lull in the fighting. Kuhlmann, also crouching down, had run across below the window level to join Philip. Pressing his mouth close to Philip's ear, he spoke quickly.

'Phase Two. A volley of incendiary shells to set that place on fire . . .'

He had just spoken when the policeman held the launcher at shoulder height, aimed for a window in the centre of the warehouse, pulled the trigger.

Whoosh . . . !

The shell shot across the wall, disappeared through the warehouse window. Philip and Kuhlmann could not resist peering round the edge of the wall. Behind the target window flame flared, a vicious red flame. The same phenomenon appeared behind other windows as other policemen further along the block fired their shells.

Something heavy thudded into the building next to them. They felt the walls shudder, the floor tremble under the impact. Philip, who normally would have been terrified by the unexpected explosion, was ice cold, just hoping he would survive to confront Walvis. A sudden silence descended, the only sound the distant crackle of the warehouse beginning to burn.

'They have launchers over there,' Kuhlmann commented, chewing on his unlit cigar. 'That was a high-explosive shell which hit the building next to us. Phase Three is close. Erich likes to preserve the lives of his men as far as possible. Look at the gates. The spectacular is coming.'

Philip peered out again. It was getting difficult to see what was happening. Clouds of smoke, even more than he would have expected, were blotting out the courtyard between the gates and the warehouse. He saw hooded figures doing something at the base of the massive gates.

'They're laying an explosive charge along the gates,' Kuhlmann explained, peering over Philip's shoulder.

'There's a lot of smoke,' Philip observed.

'There should be. One section of Erich's unit has been firing smoke shells into the yard so the enemy can't see what's coming next. You will—'

Whatever he had been going to say was drowned by a deafening detonation. The policemen had retreated along the wall well away from the gates. The detonation of the charge lifted the gates off their hinges, hurling chunks of the gates into the courtyard. The entrance was wide open.

'Phase Three now,' Kuhlmann shouted.

The policeman with them fired his third incendiary shell. It disappeared through a window on the ground floor and more flames appeared, so bright they dispersed the smoke. Another sudden silence. Then Philip heard the sound of a very heavy vehicle trundling across the cobbles. The armoured car with the turret gun appeared, lumbered forward until it had taken up a position in the centre of the entrance. The large gun fired its first shell and the middle of the warehouse vanished. It fired a second shell.

The warehouse had become a vast fireball. Searing flame mingled with the smoke. The structure began to collapse. The roof gave way. Kuhlmann lit his cigar under cover of the wall. The fireball was exploding in all directions, creating a great glow in the night sky. Fragments of what remained of the warehouse soared into the night. Kuhlmann puffed at his cigar.

397

'Those explosions mean Walvis stored large quantities of ammunition in that warehouse.' He smiled drily. 'Which is illegal . . .'

Walvis, seeing the immense red glow, had ordered his chauffeur to drive a devious route through the back streets. Now he was parked at the end of a long street which gave a clear view of the rear of the warehouse.

He sat very still, staring at the raging inferno that had been his warehouse. The expanding glow seemed to hypnotize him. He watched as rocketlike flaming relics soared into the night. He was still sitting like a Buddha when Gulliver hurried to the car, opened the rear door.

'We ought to get out of here,' he said roughly.

'Two million dollars of sophisticated weaponry and ammunition have been lost in that funeral pyre,' Walvis said in a flat tone.

'I said we ought to get out of here,' Gulliver repeated.

'It's Tweed again,' Walvis went on in the same lifeless voice. 'He must die slowly, painfully.'

'OK, we can attend to that later. Wake up. We have to leave this area fast. *Now!*'

In desperation he took Walvis's right arm and shook it. Walvis slowly turned his head to gaze at Gulliver with the same dazed expression.

'Have you heard from Martin?' he asked. 'I sent him off in another car to fetch my important papers from the farmhouse. Have you heard from Martin?'

'Where do we go to next?' Gulliver demanded. 'We must leave Munich.'

'Of course we must,' Walvis replied, suddenly alert, his face contorted into an ugly expression. 'Unlike you, I can adapt to a crisis, change my strategy. I know exactly what we are going to do next. And we have immense supplies of munitions elsewhere.'

'We have,' Gulliver agreed impatiently, 'but where—'

'Do not ever interrupt me again. We are going to Berg where my plane, *Pegasus V*, is waiting on the Starnberger See. Tweed is a doomed man.'

41

Kuhlmann took Tweed, Paula, Newman and Philip to a restaurant off Maximilianstrasse. He was obviously known, by the way the proprietor greeted the Police Chief and escorted them to a private room. Their host settled Paula in a chair behind the table overlooking a small patio garden. Water in an elevated stone-walled pool was frozen, as was a vertical spear of water which was the fountain.

'It was good of you to take Philip with you,' remarked Paula.

'After what he's been through – is going through – I thought the experience might take his mind off thinking.' He changed the subject as Philip returned from the loo. 'Now, study this menu carefully – it's a good one.'

'I'd like to ask you a difficult, maybe impossible favour,' Tweed suggested.

'The possible is easy, boring – the impossible is a challenge. What can I do for you?'

'I'd like Rosa Brandt brought to London – under police escort if necessary.'

'Can do,' Kuhlmann replied promptly. 'She's a suspect in the murder of a British citizen, Captain Sherwood. I should first go through the extradition crap but I'll sort that out later. Just call me when you need her. She lives in an apartment on her own in the city – has no phone. Tell me when you're ready for her and she'll be aboard a plane.'

'Thank you very much.' Like the others Tweed was studying the menu as he spoke. 'How are things in Bonn?'

'You'll be surprised. Very good, from my point of view. The Chancellor is meeting the Austrian Chancellor and the Polish Defence Minister. They're so scared of that million mob of refugees waiting to cross the border I have practically been appointed Commander-in-Chief of the operation to stop them. Haven't a clue as to how I'll go about it.'

'Austerlitz,' said Tweed. 'The rivers are frozen, aren't they?'

'Frozen solid, so they can sweep over them at night. Why Austerlitz?'

'You know about Napoleon's great battle. He was facing a large Russian army. He lured them on to the lake, then fired his big guns, smashed the ice, drowned the whole Russian army.'

'I begin to see what you're driving at . . .'

There was a pause while they ordered. Kuhlmann asked the proprietor to bring them several bottles of white wine.

'Mobile artillery,' Tweed went on. 'Threaten to fire on the ice if the refugees attempt to cross.'

'You've given me a better idea,' Kuhlmann said, tasted the wine and nodded his approval. He waited until the proprietor had disappeared again. 'We'll use mobile artillery to get the heavy guns there fast. Then we'll wait until they *are* crossing, the advance horde, and open up a barrage. The others will see their comrades drown. Tough, I know, but there are Tartars from Russia among that mob and they don't fool around. Better than letting Europe go back to the Middle Ages. Drink up, Philip, this is good wine.'

'Any news of where Walvis is?' Philip asked.

400

'As a matter of fact, yes, there is. He's arrived with his gang of cut-throats in Berg. He has his big land–sea plane floating on the Starnberger See. And that's something else, which shows the clout he carries with a certain Minister he's bought in Munich.'

'And what is that?' Newman enquired.

'The locals – very rich – who have villas and palaces round the Starnberger See, had a law passed that no motorboats or any craft powered with engines could operate on the lake. Only yachts, sailing boats. Walvis informs the Minister his plane is coming and he is given full permission to land. They even issue a warning from the Minister's office to clear the lake of all craft.'

'Must be popular down there,' Tweed commented.

'Yes and no. Walvis gives the most lavish parties, invites top locals. He provides magnificent food, plenty of drink and attractive ladies. Some of them go for that. Others won't attend and send protests to Munich. Doesn't get them anywhere. Walvis never attends. Martin acts as host.'

'So he could be leaving Germany for an unknown destination?' Philip queried anxiously.

'I've alerted every airport controller in Europe to tell me where and when he lands. I'll let you know, Tweed.'

'That will be vital information for me,' Tweed replied.

'And this,' said Kuhlmann, ploughing into a heavy soup, 'is better than filling in a report on tonight's fireworks display. Erich is writing the report and I'll just counter-sign it. He is downcast at losing one man, but he did think he might lose more. Walvis has just lost a major ammunition and weapons dump.'

'I'm hoping it will throw him into a panic,' commented Tweed, 'but I'm not too hopeful. I don't think he'll give up until he reaches the end of the road.'

'And my bet is you'll be there when he does that,' responded Kuhlmann.

*　　*　　*

Kuhlmann sent them back to the Four Seasons in an unmarked car. Tweed had earlier phoned Marler, told him to have a long dinner with Butler and Nield. They had just entered the hotel when a woman jumped up from an armchair and came over to them with a warm smile and her arms stretched out in a welcoming greeting. Lisa Trent.

'I've been waiting for you,' she said, staring at Newman. 'I've had dinner, so you don't have to feed the wench – but I'd love some champagne.'

'Then the lady will have as much champagne as she can drink,' said Newman. 'Just let us dump our coats at the reception desk. Incidentally, how did you know we were coming here?'

'Asked at reception, didn't I? They told me you'd phoned and booked rooms. Hello, Mr Tweed. Lovely to see you again.' She darted forward, kissed him on the cheek. 'I have been frantically busy and need some amenable company. You fit the bill . . .'

Paula had been feeling tired but now she was curious to see what effect Lisa had on Newman. You're a little minx, Lisa, she said to herself, but an exciting one – especially for men.

When they had handed their outer clothing to the concierge and returned towards the bar Lisa was perched on the arm of a chair. Using a small pocket mirror she was smoothing down her waves of blonde hair, checking her lipstick. She snapped the mirror shut quickly, dropped it into her shoulder-bag when she saw them coming back.

'I could stay up all night,' she told Newman.

Oh, Lord, thought Paula. Better get the adrenalin pumping again if you want to find out what's going on. She quickly studied how Lisa was clad. She was wearing a black, form-fitting dress, calf length but with a slit slashed each side up to her thighs, exposing her good legs. The dress had a high collar but with a V-plunge revealing

402

smooth white skin. Newman is going to enjoy this, she thought as they mounted the steps into the bar.

'Another coincidence I find hard to swallow,' whispered Tweed to Paula.

'Champagne,' Newman ordered when a waiter came immediately to the table they sat at. 'I want it to rain champagne until dawn breaks.'

'I think that can be arranged, sir,' said the waiter and hurried off.

'A night to end all nights,' enthused Lisa. 'I'm so glad you're back.'

Her eyes switched between Newman and Tweed, then she looked at Paula as an afterthought. The champagne in an ice bucket arrived swiftly. Deftly, the waiter removed the seal, and the champagne popped as he detached the cork.

'Pop goes the weasel,' cried Lisa. 'Although I'd sooner have this than a weasel.'

As they began drinking Lisa played the old trick, linking the arm of the hand holding her glass round Newman's. He co-operated and they each drank out of the other's glass. Over the rim Lisa gazed at Tweed sensually, her eyes half closed.

Heavens above, thought Paula, which man are you after? Or do you want both of them in your pocket? Greedy-guts.

A slim-fingered feminine hand descended on Newman's shoulder. Jill Selborne bent down and brushed her lips over his cheek. Lisa smiled just a little too warmly.

'I suppose,' Jill said, 'that three women to two men would be a little too much?'

'The more the merrier,' Newman replied in an apparently jovial mood. He wrapped his free arm round Jill's slim waist, hauled her gently down into a spare chair between himself and Tweed, then introduced Jill to Lisa and Lisa to Jill. The two women gave each other their

403

best smiles. 'Waiter, one more glass,' Newman called out. 'We're painting Munich scarlet,' he said to Jill.

'Somebody got in before you,' she remarked. 'I was out for a breath of antarctic air when I saw a huge red glow in the distance. Can't imagine what it was.'

'We saw fire brigade vehicles racing off somewhere,' Tweed said quickly.

He was telling the truth. The fire brigade had arrived as Kuhlmann drove them away from the gutted warehouse.

Paula was discreetly studying Jill's outfit. She was wearing a dark blue dress with a high collar and no V-slit. A wide dark blue belt with a gold buckle encircled her waist and made her seem taller than her medium height. The full-length sleeves were puffed and Paula thought she looked very regal.

She raised the glass Newman had filled for her and she smiled in a mysterious way.

'Here's to a long life and a full life.'

'I'll drink to that,' said Lisa. She put down her glass and focused her attention on Tweed. 'Now, where did you all disappear to?'

'Salzburg. Do you know it?' he enquired, watching her closely.

'City of my dreams. Nowhere else like it in the world. Best to go there out of season.'

'I agree. We had an exciting time. Visiting all the sights. And we met some interesting people. You said earlier you had been frantically busy. Was all the activity worth it?'

'It was a secret mission.' Lisa put a finger to her full lips. 'Very hush-hush. But I will tell you. I was checking on the financial situation of the legendary and never seen Mr Walvis.'

'Walvis? Who is that?' asked Jill.

'Supposed to be the richest man in the world . . .'

404

' "Supposed to be"?' Tweed leapt on the phrase. 'Isn't he, then?'

'I've started on the subject, so I might as well finish. A client of the New York outfit I work for wanted me to check on his allegedly fabulous assets. The trail led ultimately to Liechtenstein.'

'The home of dud accounts,' Tweed remarked.

'Not in this case. His assets are enormous, a lot in cash. I'm talking too much. It's probably the champagne. Well, at least I haven't given away where I went or who I saw.'

'Couldn't that be a dangerous job at times?' Jill suggested. 'There must be people who don't like you making that sort of enquiry.'

'True enough.' Lisa drank some more champagne from the glass Newman had just refilled for the third time. 'I occasionally have to interview in his office an accountant I know is crooked. He doesn't know that I know he keeps two sets of books – one for the shareholders showing big profits, the other for the company's chairman showing just how close they are to going bust.'

'That must be dangerous,' Jill insisted.

'Oh, I mention at an early stage that I won't take up too much of his time – that my boy friend, who was in the SAS, is waiting for me in a coffee shop across the road. That ensures he'll behave.'

Tweed turned in his chair to talk to Jill. She swivelled round in her own chair immediately, her knees close to his.

'Are you glad to be back in Munich?'

'You mean,' she said with a pleasant smile, 'am I glad to be back from Salzburg?'

She had lowered her voice and Tweed had the impression she didn't want Lisa, who was now concentrating all her attention on Newman, to hear.

'I suppose I do,' Tweed admitted.

'There was something spooky about that place – I really

405

mean the Old Town, I guess. I saw a very strange woman when I was on my own in one of those claustrophobic streets. No one else was about and I thought she was very creepy. She wore a long black coat, a black cap with a black veil. She suddenly disappeared. I don't mind confessing I felt a sense of relief.'

'She does sound a weird type,' Tweed agreed. 'Did you get the interview you were after?'

'No.' She raised her eyes to the roof of the bar area in mock despair. 'You can't win them all.'

'You went there by train?'

'No. Which was another mistake. I hired a car here and drove there. A nightmare on the autobahn. I should have handed in the car and come back by train but I'm stubborn. I thought, if I can drive in these conditions I can drive in any climate.' She looked at Paula to bring her into the conversation. 'Do you like driving?'

'I love it,' Paula told her, grateful that she had taken notice of her. Newman and Lisa were lost in each other's company. 'Tweed tells me I drive too fast. He may be right.'

'And he may be wrong.' Jill squeezed Tweed's shoulder. 'You think she drives dangerously?'

'No, never.'

'Then let her be. I'll bet she's a terrific help to you. Paula strikes me as enormously capable.'

'She most certainly is. I'd be lost without her.'

'And what happened to Philip after he came in with you? I was sitting well back in the lounge when you all arrived.'

'Philip went up to take a bath. Talk of the devil. He's coming into the bar.'

'I thought he looked forlorn and lost.' Jill stood up as Philip approached them, hauled a chair from an empty table near by. 'Come and join us, Philip. You look like a glass of champagne.'

406

'In that case I must be a very peculiar shape.'

Jill laughed and Philip grinned at her as he sat down. Paula stared. It was the first time she had heard him crack a joke, grin like that, since the tragedy. Jill must have attracted him.

'The others are scattered round the lounge, drinking brandy,' he said. 'They look very relaxed and asked me to join them, but I thought it might be more fun in here. It will be,' he said, looking straight at Jill as he raised the glass she had poured for him.

It was his tactful way of reporting to Tweed that Marler and his companions were keeping a close eye on who was in the hotel.

'You look as though you could do with a bit of relaxation,' Jill said to him. 'I'll bet you have a hard taskmaster in Tweed. Enjoy yourself tonight. Learn to take the smooth with the tough. I'm the smooth.'

'And a very attractive woman,' said Philip, who had drained his glass.

'I recognize and appreciate a sincere compliment,' Jill responded as she first refilled his glass, then her own. 'Bottoms up.'

They were clinking glasses, drinking more champagne, looking at each other when a man in a dark business suit came up to the table. Tweed sensed he was a policeman in plain clothes, thought he'd seen him standing outside the restaurant Kuhlmann had taken them to.

'Mr Tweed!'

'Yes, I'm afraid.'

'An important message for you, sir.'

He handed Tweed a long plain white envelope with no name on it. The envelope felt thick. Tweed stood up.

'Please excuse me, everyone. I think this will require an answer.'

'Now don't slip away and abandon me,' piped up Lisa. 'I am looking forward to a cosy *tête-à-tête* with you this

407

evening.' She checked her watch. 'Make that this morning.'

'I'll look forward to that. Why should Newman have all the pleasure?'

He left the bar, saw Marler seated in an armchair where he could see everyone who entered the hotel. Tweed nodded, sat down in an isolated chair, opened the envelope, only to find a second sealed brown envelope inside with POLICE HEADQUARTERS stamped on it in German. He read the handwritten message and frowned.

Walvis has departed Berg in Pegasus. Flight plan indicates first destination is Lindau on Lake Constance. Police there report smaller seaplane waiting. Extra fuel tanks attached to seaplane suggest longer flight. Kuhlmann.

42

'Did I put on the performance you wanted down there in the bar?' Newman asked Tweed.

With Philip and Paula they had eventually broken free and gone up to Tweed's large room. Paula stared at Newman in disbelief.

'Performance?' she repeated. 'What *are* you talking about? You were having the time of your life with Lisa and Jill.'

'Tweed looked at me as we sat down and I nodded that I had understood him.'

'Understood what? Will someone please explain?'

'I will,' said Tweed. 'If you create a party atmosphere where anything goes and the champagne flows like water

408

people lose their inhibitions. It worked with both Jill and Lisa. At times they said more than they normally would have done. It's not a method I like – but we are faced with a desperate situation.'

'So,' accused Paula as she looked at Newman, 'you were acting the playboy, the more women the better?'

'I was doing just that. And they talked and talked and talked.'

'I did notice,' Paula recalled, 'that when Tweed was chatting to Jill, even though Lisa appeared to be absorbed by Newman she took in every word Jill said. It was interesting that Jill said she saw Rosa Brandt in the Altstadt.'

'*Said* is the operative word,' Tweed emphasized.

'You're implying she made that up, then?'

'I'm not implying anything,' he told her.

'But you don't believe her?'

'I don't remember saying that.'

'You are the most infuriating man,' she snapped at him.

'Also, at one point in the general conversation there was a significant evasion.'

'And you're not going to tell me what that was. You had a message while we were drinking and took it away to read it. I suppose we don't get to see that?'

Tweed smiled drily, took the envelope containing Kuhlmann's message out of his pocket, handed it to Paula and told her to show it to Newman when she'd read it.

There was a quiet knock on the door. Newman opened it and Marler peered in.

'Is this a private party or can anyone join in?' he enquired with a cynical smile. 'I've also got Nield and Butler with me.'

'Tell them all to come in,' Tweed ordered. 'There's a message you should all see so you're in the picture . . .'

He waited until they had all read the message. Paula was the first to react.

'Lake Constance? Now that must be . . .'

'Some distance to the south-west of Munich,' Tweed explained. 'It's a large and curious lake – the northern part is in Bavaria, the southern part belongs to Switzerland. I know the Bavarian island of Lindau. It's a beautiful place. When I say island it's linked to the mainland by a causeway which the train crosses to Lindau. I suppose, being in Bavaria, Walvis has contacted his Minister friend here to have the northern part cleared of wind-surfers. Some enthusiasts wind-surf even in winter.'

'It doesn't give us any idea of his ultimate destination,' Marler observed. 'I wonder why he plans to transfer to the smaller seaplane. Less noticeable? And what do we do next?'

'We exercise patience. We wait,' replied Tweed, 'wait for Kuhlmann's next message. Then we should know exactly where Walvis is heading for.' He turned to Paula. 'I think if you phoned the airport you could provisionally book us all on a morning flight to London.'

'I'll do that now,' Paula decided and went to sit down at the desk where the phone was perched.

'That means I'll have to dump all our weapons and the explosives Butler has left,' Marler said with a gesture of resignation.

'Maybe you could do that when we do know where we are going,' Tweed suggested.

'I'm going to bed,' Newman announced. 'Talking to two sexy ladies is exhausting.'

'Believe that and you'll believe anything,' called out Paula as she checked the directory.

'So you think he'll be flying direct to England?' queried Marler.

'I'm trying to read his mind, remembering that long conversation I had with him up at the *Schloss* in Salzburg.'

*   *   *

410

Kuhlmann did not send a second message. He arrived at the hotel himself, phoned Tweed, suggested they went for a walk. Tweed put on all his anti-winter clothes and hurried downstairs. Kuhlmann was waiting for him near the exit.

'Don't you ever sleep?' Tweed asked.

'Not when an operation is in progress. And look who's talking. Let's stroll along Maximilianstrasse. It's crawling with my men and I didn't want to send a second written message . . .'

They had walked along the apparently deserted street for several minutes in silence. Kuhlmann suddenly started talking.

'Walvis must be in a hurry. He must have radioed a signal to the seaplane pilot off Lindau. He's filed a provisional flight plan for the seaplane to fly to a place called Chichester Harbour. Take-off at ten in the morning.'

'Exactly what I expected. This is vital news.'

'That's why I needed this secure conversation with you. I'm suspicious. That monster plane, *Pegasus V*, has not taken off from the Starnberger See. Walvis is aboard but the plane just sits there. I think he's playing some trick.'

'What kind of trick?'

'My guess is he'll change his destination. So I suggest I phone you when I have more news. Even if it's in the middle of the night.'

'It's the middle of the night now,' Tweed pointed out.

'I know. I just wanted to warn you I might spoil your beauty sleep. I'll be in constant touch with Lindau.'

'Phone me as soon as you know.'

'Just in case anyone's listening in, I'll only give you the name of the changed destination – if he does change it.'

They were walking back to the hotel when Kuhlmann paused to light a fresh cigar. He made his comment as they resumed walking.

'Bearing in mind what you and I know, I think that idea

411

of a Partnership for Peace as they call it, is one of the craziest ideas ever to come out of Washington.'

'Which is just what Henry Kissinger said not long ago.'

Walvis sat in the darkness of his luxurious quarters aboard *Pegasus V*, staring out of a window to the shore where the lights of Berg sparkled in the ice-cold night. He found being in the dark, gazing at a scenic view, revved up his brain into high gear. He frowned as Gulliver entered after tapping on the door.

'Don't switch on any lights.' He pointed at the leather seat across the aisle – his own chair was much larger and he could swivel it in any direction.

'Sit!' he commanded. 'Why have you come to disturb my thinking?'

'I wondered what your plan was. Why we are waiting here on the lake. Martin has at long last come aboard, back from the farmhouse. Why are we eventually flying on to Lindau and transferring to the seaplane?'

Much tougher than Martin, Gulliver had no fear of voicing his impatience. If he got slapped down then he got slapped down. It wouldn't be the end of the world.

'So many questions, my dear Gulliver. Quite a barrage. I think we should ask Martin to join us, to report on how successful he was at the farmhouse in rescuing my papers. Relax, Gulliver, we have all just enjoyed the most excellent five-course dinner. Hans is the best chef in Europe – he should be, since I bought him from the Ritz. Martin does have good news, I expect?'

'Best let him make his own report. You always prefer it straight from the horse's mouth.'

Gulliver had no intention of giving even a hint of the news Martin had brought. Let him take his own flak.

Walvis pressed a button on the intercom attached to the seat well in front of his own.

412

'Martin, I gather you are anxious to show me the papers you brought from the farm. You may now attend the presence.'

Martin came in slowly with none of his normal air of supreme self-confidence. His usually immaculate suit, a navy-blue pinstripe, was smeared with dirt, the cloth split at the elbows of his jacket and the knees of his trousers. Walvis pressed one of a battery of switches on the arm of his chair. A ceiling spotlight came on, illuminated Martin like an actor on a stage. He moved to avoid its glare.

'Stand where you are,' Walvis said in a soft voice. 'I see your carefully maintained sartorial elegance is missing.'

'It was rough, very rough,' said Martin, his voice weary.

If he expected sympathy from Walvis he was disappointed.

'It could get rougher if you're here to report a cock-up. Are you here to report that?'

'I drove out to the farm.' Martin took a deep breath. 'As I got closer everything seemed OK. I was greeted by a guard, went inside immediately to gather up your papers. That was when all hell broke loose. One of the guards spotted them closing in, the idiot opened fire. Every window in the farmhouse was taken out with a hail of automatic fire. I realized they'd let me in through their cordon – an anti-terrorist group, men with hoods over their heads. They'd let me in so that I couldn't escape, but I did.'

'Perhaps that was a pity,' Walvis commented. 'Proceed.'

'All the guards inside went mad, firing back. The next thing they threw at us was incendiary shells. The farmhouse began to go up in flames . . .'

'My papers. Those relating to Tidal Wave. Where are they?'

'They'll be blackened ashes. I slipped out through a

413

window at the back where there's a gully across the fields. I crawled along it for miles on my belly until I reached the main road. I flagged down a motor cyclist. He saw the state I was in and took off his helmet to talk to me. I hit him over the head with the butt of my Luger, grabbed his machine and drove like the wind.'

'My, my. You seem to have had an exciting evening. Go on.'

'I drove back into Munich, saw a car park with a host of vehicles standing there. I must have checked a hundred before I found an Audi where some fool had left the key in the ignition. I drove it here . . .'

'What did you do with that car?' Walvis demanded. 'Will it lead them to Berg?'

'I shouldn't think so.' Briefly Martin recovered some of his self-confidence. He had reached the state where he didn't care any more. 'I took it to a quiet part of the lake to shove it in. It must be twenty feet under water now.'

'At least you did one sensible thing. Martin, your present appearance offends me. You have a new suit aboard?'

'Several in my cabin . . .'

'Then proceed to your cabin, have a long bath, put on a new suit. Only then come back here.'

Gulliver was hiding a malicious smile behind his hand as Martin left, dragging his feet. Walvis looked at him.

'Wipe that smirk off your face. Obviously they synchronized the attacks on the warehouse and the farm. Again I see the hand of Tweed behind all this. I will take my revenge in due course – and it will be unpleasant for him.'

'The papers – Tidal Wave papers – Martin was unable to retrieve,' Gulliver reminded him. 'Have you copies?'

'Why should we need copies?' Walvis tapped the dome of his forehead. 'All the details are up here. Tidal Wave will be launched as planned. From the communications base.'

414

'Then why are we waiting here? Why are we flying – when you decide to give the order – to Lindau? Why are we using the seaplane?'

'Your memory is going. You asked all these questions earlier. Perhaps you are tired and need a holiday.'

Gulliver quaked inside. Outwardly his expression was like stone. When Walvis had sent members of his staff on a 'holiday' in the past it had proved to be permanent and the victim was never heard of again.

'I do not feel tired and you know it.' He calculated the safest policy was to stand up to Walvis. 'Martin is the one who feels tired.'

'Then let us forget holidays. I will answer all your questions – up to a point. I have heard that Kuhlmann is back in Munich. He will be in touch with Tweed – I am sure of that. They monitor signals at police headquarters. The signals I send will be passed on to Mr Tweed. I am preparing the final trap to destroy him.'

Walvis sent Gulliver out of the cabin. When he was alone he picked up the phone. The underwater cable connecting the phone to the mainland system would have to be reeled in later before the plane took to the air.

He dialled a number. It rang for a number of times before the voice he now knew well – though still not the identity of the man he was speaking to – eventually answered.

'You know who is speaking?'

'Yes. How can I help you?'

'I have another assignment for Teardrop. She *must* make contact with Mr Tweed. At the moment I believe he is staying at the Four Seasons Hotel. He will be moving on but I am sure she has the talent to trace him. The price for this assignment – when completed – is a quarter of a million marks.'

415

'For that sum she will pursue him round the world to make contact. I will report when the assignment has been completed.'

43

'Philip, I think you ought to go to bed,' said Tweed when he returned to his room.

Paula was also still there, curled up on a couch like a cat. But her eyes looked alert as she rearranged the cushion behind her head. She was watching Philip as he replied to Tweed.

'Are you staying up?'

'Yes, I am,' admitted Tweed.

'Waiting for the next message from Kuhlmann?' Philip persisted.

'Yes, I am,' Tweed repeated. 'I'd like a bath but I hate handling the phone with my hands covered with soap. I can wait until he calls.'

'So can I,' Philip said grimly. 'I won't get any sleep until I know where Walvis is headed for next. Then we'll go after him, I presume?'

'You presume correctly.'

Paula thought she had never seen Philip look so frozen faced and determined.

'Philip, what are you thinking about?' she asked softly.

'Nothing much. Except about Walvis.'

'That I can understand. I think I'll stay up with the two of you, I'll order more coffee and some mineral water.'

'Mineral water would go down well,' Philip said automatically. 'I've got the thirst of the devil.'

416

He had lied. He was not thinking about Walvis. Memories were flooding back into his mind, memories of Jean. He could recall how she spoke, her voice with a deep timbre but soft. She was always so observant of people and had, on more than one occasion, warned him against people he had been prepared to trust. Always she had proved to be right. When he was working in London while she was at the house in Surrey she had worried if he was late, had been so relieved when she heard his key in the lock. He knew he would never meet her like again. It was a fact he felt he would never come to terms with.

'Mineral water, Philip,' said Paula, holding a glass.

He jumped, startled out of his heart-rending reverie. He looked up at her and she smiled down at him seeing the pain in his eyes.

'Thank you, Paula. I could drink a litre of it.'

'So isn't it fortunate they brought up three one-litre bottles.'

He drank the whole glassful at one long swallow and she refilled it for him. Then she perched on the arm of his chair and began talking.

'I have a feeling everything is going to explode into action soon,' she said in a low voice. 'We're going to have our hands full with this one.'

'Good. The sooner the better. I finished off Lucien and have no feelings of guilt. I can't wait to confront Walvis face to face.'

'Drink some more water. Go on. Tension, which I'm sure is affecting us all, dehydrates.'

'You're very good to me.' He drank the second glass and again she refilled it. He was beginning to feel better with the close proximity of a woman he liked and admired. There was nothing sensual in his reaction but he had always liked the company of intelligent women. He looked up at her and held out the glass of water.

'I'm damn sure you're thirsty too.'

417

'Actually, now you mention it, I am.' She took the glass, drank half, sighed with relief and drank the rest of the contents. She refilled it, put it on a table they could both reach.

'Let's see who goes for it first.'

She had just spoken when there was a heavy rapping on the door. Paula was about to jump up when Philip clapped a hand on her knee, stood up.

'I'll see who that is.'

He glanced over his shoulder as he went to unlock the door, his Walther in his hand. Tweed was sunk inside a deep armchair and appeared to be asleep, except that his eyes were wide open. He was deep in thought.

Surprised, Philip found it was Kuhlmann outside in the otherwise deserted corridor. The Police Chief nodded to Philip, strode into the room. Paula noticed he was freshly shaven.

'Could someone put on the radio – music,' he rumbled.

Paula darted across, switched on, swiftly found classical music. Tchaikovsky's '1812' overture. The thunder of the guns. Kuhlmann nodded his approval.

'Can we all go into the bathroom while I talk?'

He let Paula go in first, then walked straight in after her and turned on the bath taps. Tweed and Philip had joined them. There was a radio speaker in the bathroom, which was relaying the same music.

'You haven't had your suite flashed for bugs, I imagine,' Kuhlmann growled. 'No? I thought not.' He took out his cigar case, thought better of it inside the spacious bathroom, put the case away without taking out a cigar.

'I've just had Lindau on the phone. Walvis's seaplane pilot has filed a flight plan to fly tomorrow in the morning to England. His precise destination was also included. Aldeburgh, on the East Anglian coast.'

*   *   *

418

'The radio alone will scramble our conversation if anyone is listening in,' said Kuhlmann, leading the way back into the large bedroom.

Paula was amused when she saw the real reason for his decision. He lit up his cigar. She was watching Tweed as she absorbed the news. It seemed Tweed had guessed the final climax location correctly. So she was surprised at his reaction.

'Tell me, Otto, these signals you have monitored from Walvis. Did they have to be decoded?'

'No code was used. They were sent openly in English.'

'I find that strange,' Tweed said, frowning. 'Wouldn't Walvis, with all his resources, know you would monitor his signals?'

'I assume he would, yes.'

'And by now won't he also know you and I are working together?'

'Considering the way he has infiltrated Munich I would guess he knows that too. There are leaks inside police headquarters but I took that into account when I launched the raids on his warehouse and the farmhouse. The latter, incidentally, is burnt to the ground. _I_ coded those targets, so he wouldn't be warned in advance.'

'So,' Tweed summed up, 'he knows we're working with each other and he knows you monitor his signals, but he makes no effort to encode those signals.'

'What are you getting at?' the German demanded irritably.

They were now all sitting in a semicircle with Kuhlmann and Tweed facing them. Philip and Paula had arranged the chairs and sat listening to the two men.

'What I'm getting at,' said Tweed, 'is that something very strange is going on. When you said the seaplane at Lindau would take off tomorrow you meant today? It is already early morning.'

'When I said tomorrow, I meant tomorrow,' Kuhlmann

said with great emphasis. 'By which I mean the day after today – *tomorrow*. I thought I spoke pretty good English,' he grumbled.

The atmosphere in the room was becoming tense. At last the strain is showing, thought Paula. Tweed's manner was calm and amiable as he replied.

'I just wanted to make sure I understood you correctly. The timing is a crucial factor in my own decisions. And do you know where Walvis is now?'

'Yes. Still sitting inside that Walt Disney plane of his on the Starnberger See. No sign of movement.'

'Would it be possible to arrest him before he disappears?' asked Paula.

'No, I'm sure it wouldn't be possible.' It was Philip who had spoken, his expression hard, his tone vehement. 'We have no proof of any criminal activity that would stand up in any court.'

They all stared at Philip. It was Paula who caught on to the reason for Philip's forceful intervention. *He didn't want Walvis arrested.* He wanted to wait until he could face the man who had ordered the murder of his wife.

'Philip is right,' Kuhlmann admitted. 'I'd never get a warrant. He always covers his tracks so cleverly.'

'I'm really bothered about this,' Tweed commented. He stood up, began to pace round the room. 'I've met Walvis, listened to him talk at length. He's devious, cunning and very good at creating deceptive manoeuvres. So what is he up to now? Incidentally, Otto, I appreciate your coming to see us again instead of phoning.'

'I'm too alert to sleep tonight – but the main reason was I didn't think I could safely get all this across to you on the phone. Now you don't believe it.'

'I believe what you have told me. The man I don't trust or believe is Walvis. I think he is planning a diabolical trap.'

'What kind of trap?' Kuhlmann shot back.

420

'I only wish I knew. If you'd keep me informed about his movements – when he does move. We'll stay here. What I don't like is that puts the ball in his court.'

'I'll tell you when he plays it.' Kuhlmann stood up and stretched his short arms. 'I'm on my way back to police headquarters. You can get me there. If you must.' He grinned to take the sting out of the remark.

'Otto,' Tweed called out as Philip accompanied him to the door. 'You'll be able to put Rosa Brandt on a plane with an escort to London when I need her?'

'Whenever you want her, she's yours.'

'You said she lived at an apartment in Munich without a phone. Would it be a good idea to have that apartment watched?

'Hadn't thought of that – with all that's been going on. Will do, as soon as I get back. Sleep well. I will – tomorrow night. Something has to break soon . . .'

44

Kuhlmann had only left five minutes earlier when another tattoo-rapping came on the door. Philip again stopped Paula going to open it and unlocked it himself.

Newman, tousle-haired with a jacket on over his open-necked collar and rumpled trousers, came in, followed by Marler, immaculately dressed.

'Couldn't sleep,' Newman said apologetically. 'Neither could Marler, who comes armed for the fray.'

Marler was carrying a bottle of brandy and went over to the cabinet containing glasses. He took out a couple of bulbous glasses, looked at Paula and Philip.

421

'Join us in a snifter? Help to keep you awake. And we may have company.'

Paula and Philip both shook their heads and Marler poured two glasses. He handed one to Newman who had sagged into a chair.

'Thanks. Where is Tweed?' he asked Paula.

'Having a well-earned bath. I imagine he'll be in there for a while. When a problem's bothering him he finds a bath helps him to sort it out.'

'What problem?' Newman asked.

Marler was adopting his usual stance, leaning against a wall as he lit a king-size and then sipped at his brandy. How he could stand up for hours after a punishing day was beyond Paula.

She sat down next to Philip, drank some mineral water and gave a careful account of what had happened while Kuhlmann had been with them. Newman, freshly shaved, listened and did not interrupt her once.

Philip appeared to have slipped into a doze. In fact his brain was whirring. He remembered again how good Jean had been at warning him against people she mistrusted. How, he was wondering, would she have assessed Lisa Trent and Jill Selborne? She had been as shrewd at weighing up women as she had with men. God, I do need you, really need you for a thousand reasons, he thought. He felt depressed, lost, but another part of his brain imagined her reaction to Lisa and Jill. After a while it seemed obvious to him which woman she would have been very wary of.

Then he remembered the existence of Rosa Brandt. That threw all his thinking – Jean's thinking – back to zero. He came back to the real world as Paula, having finished her account of Kuhlmann's visit, poured him a fresh glass of mineral water.

'Marler,' she enquired, 'when you came in you said that we might have company. Who were you talking about?'

422

'Newman can tell you. It was his idea.'

'It was not!' Newman burst out. 'She invited herself. She knew we were coming along here . . .'

'Because you were careful to tell her that,' Marler teased him.

'Maybe someone would tell me who this mysterious she is?' Paula asked acidly.

There was a featherlike tapping on the door. Marler nodded to Newman.

'Your lovely kettle of fish. Better let her in. We may find out what she's after – because she's after something.'

When Newman opened the door Jill Selborne, still in her evening outfit, came into the room with her elegant walk. She smiled at Paula.

'I couldn't sleep. I had a shower, changed back into the same battle kit. If you're talking confidential I'm going straight back out of that door.'

'Nonsense. Do sit down,' Paula said.

What else could I have done? she thought. How many more of Newman's growing harem are going to turn up? Maybe we ought to evacuate and leave him to it. Except that Tweed is in the bath, the phone will ring, he'll have to answer it himself. He had once told her how he *had* dropped the phone in the bath. He never had known who was calling.

'Brandy?' Marler asked Jill.

'Just a small one, thank you. Or I'll get tiddly.'

'Like to see you tiddly,' Newman said roguishly.

He's deliberately acting the playboy again, Paula thought. More on the ball than I'd realized. Marler was not one of those men who gave women large drinks whatever they had asked for.

'That's perfect,' Jill said. 'Thank you.' She warmed the glass in both hands. 'I've heard a lot of strange rumours flying round Munich.'

423

Here we go, Marler mused. Now we'll find out why she really came here at this hour.

'What sort of rumours?' Newman enquired.

'That some deadly woman assassin is prowling round Bavaria shooting men. Another rumour is that David, Captain Sherwood, was one of her victims.'

'First I've heard of it,' Newman replied, and he sipped his brandy.

'Then apparently some warehouse full of explosives was blown up last night.'

'That does sound like a rumour,' Newman fenced.

'Going back to the woman assassin, I hope I'm not on her list. A creepy thought. Maybe I need protection.' She looked at Newman. 'Any offers as a protector?'

'Why should anyone want to kill someone like you?'

'You've evaded my request, you heartless man. I've made no secret of the fact that I would like to have an interview with Walvis, to write a profile on him. I'm wondering if that was a mistake, if it's set me up as a target.'

'Why should it?' Newman disagreed. 'All he has to do is to refuse to see you.'

'I suppose I'm imagining it.' She finished her brandy. 'I do know that at this hour you can't really think clearly, that your thoughts can be nightmarish. I think I'll go back to my room now and get some sleep. Oh, are you thinking of returning to London soon? If so, I'd love to be on the same flight.'

'Our future movements are uncertain. Our next destination unknown,' said a new voice.

It was Tweed who had emerged from the bathroom. He was wearing a new grey suit he had changed into after his bath. Paula thought he looked horribly fresh. Tweed was staring at Jill.

'Well, it was worth a try.' Jill flashed a smile at Newman, stood up. 'Good night everybody – no, good

424

morning. And thanks for putting up with my chatter. Maybe we'll meet again. Hope so.' She blew a kiss to Tweed and left.

'Tell me everything she said,' Tweed requested as he sat down, poured himself a glass of mineral water.

He listened until Newman had recalled the whole conversation. He then poured himself another glass of water, stared at the ceiling as he spoke.

'She came here to try and find out where we were going next. I wonder why? It's the old, old story. People talk too much and if you let them they give themselves away. I find her visit significant.'

'No use asking what you're thinking,' Paula remarked, 'so I won't ask. Anybody else feel the pressure building up? I'm getting positively edgy, as though the whole thing is closing in on us.'

'Philip,' Tweed said suddenly. 'What was your impression of Jill Selborne?'

'That she's a very clever lady, knows exactly what she's doing, and has some plan in mind.'

'Interesting. Paula, I'd like you to wait here a few minutes. The rest of you go back to your rooms and go to bed, whether you can sleep or not. That's an order . . .'

He waited until the three men had left and then turned to Paula.

'I want you to do something for me – and after that *you* go to bed. Call the airport and book provisional seats on a mid-morning flight to London, not only for today but also for tomorrow.'

'I'll get on with that right away . . .'

Tweed stood up, began walking slowly round the room, his glass in his hand. When Paula had made the reservations he thanked her, again told her to go to bed. She turned round as she reached the door.

'How about you getting some sleep too? Why put on a new suit if you are going to bed?'

'You know I never like a new suit the first time I put it on. Thought I'd get used to it before I got some rest. Sleep well. I know what's going on . . .'

Alone in the room, Tweed stood staring at the wall. The remark Paula had made about the pressure building up had been shrewd. Everyone except Marler had looked tense.

He had no intention of going to bed. He would stay up until the early morning, checking to make sure he had thought out correctly in the bath what the enemy's next move would be. He repeated mentally what the sequence of events had been, talking to himself inside his head.

'Walvis first sends a signal, not in code, so he knows Kuhlmann's monitors will pick it up, that it will reach me. He alerts the seaplane waiting at Lindau. His pilot there files a flight plan for Chichester Harbour. Now a gap. Then a second signal, again not in code, and a new flight plan is filed by the seaplane pilot. Destination: Aldeburgh, East Anglia. He'll know we're here in this hotel, being fed all this data in the middle of the early hours. Walvis . . .'

Tweed suddenly snapped his fingers.

'Got you!'

He hurried to the phone, called police headquarters, asked for Kuhlmann, who came on the line quickly.

'Don't you ever sleep?' grumbled the German.

'You're one to talk. Listen to me. Have you decoding experts where you are?'

'Yes, but they're home in bed . . .'

'Phone them now. Get them up and over to where you are. Are they top-flight decoders?'

426

'The best. They have all the computer equipment. They can break any code very quickly. Why?'

'Because there's going to be another signal soon from Berg. And this one *will* be in code.'

'I'll be popular, but I can get them here in thirty minutes. I'll send patrol cars. 'Bye.'

Tweed put down the phone. He strode across the room and poured himself another glass of water. Then back to the phone. He dialled Park Crescent, hoping to God Monica could contact Howard. She came on the line, he told her what he needed.

'Howard is here. He's worried stiff about you. He'll be on the line in a second . . .'

'Tweed, I have been up all night waiting . . .'

'This is very urgent, Howard. Thank Heaven you did wait. I recall you know someone in Aldeburgh well. Paula once met him when we were up against General de Forge. Now what was his name? I know – Brigadier Burgoyne. Are you still in touch with him?'

'Had a drink with him yesterday at the club before he went back to Aldeburgh. He's almost ninety but still has all his marbles . . .'

'How soon could you phone him?'

'Now, if necessary. He doesn't sleep much. Stays up all night and gets a bit of rest during the day . . .'

'Could you call him now? I want to know if the top man we're after – don't mention a name – has an estate there. A hall or a mansion – and this is important – equipped with sophisticated communications systems. That's it.'

'I'll be back to you soon as I can . . .'

'Take down this German hotel number, and my room number— Got it?'

'I'll come back to you . . .'

Tweed put down the phone, drank some more water and resumed his night watch. He found himself recalling the unexpected visit of Jill Selborne and what she had said. Like so many people she saved the question vital to her until the last moment, until she had been on the verge of leaving the room.

In his cabin aboard *Pegasus V* Walvis sat calmly playing the card game of patience. He placed one card on top of another and glanced at Gulliver, sitting opposite him. His deputy could hardly keep still, kept glancing at his watch. He had tried reading a newspaper and had given that up. Walvis could sense the vibrations of Gulliver's restlessness.

'Really,' Walvis said, 'when you are waiting you should try playing patience. It calms the nerves.'

'But what *are* we waiting for?' demanded Gulliver.

'The waiting to take effect on Tweed and his team locked up in that hotel, as your contact reported to you over an hour ago.'

'I don't understand what you hope to achieve.'

'I am letting the enemy sweat it out, probably sitting up all night wondering what I am going to do next. In short, my tactic is to break their nerves by masterly inactivity, as a historical figure once said. I would not like you to think I have just coined an original phrase. That really would be so dishonest of me, would it not?'

Martin, dressed in a new navy-blue suit, freshly shaved and showered, came in at that moment, came in hesitantly. Walvis greeted him cordially.

'Do come in and sit down, Martin. I have just explained to Gulliver we are engaged in an exercise of masterly inactivity against the enemy. Against Tweed.'

'Oh, yes,' said Martin, perching gingerly on the edge of a seat facing both men from a distance.

'Dear me,' commented Walvis, 'you also are deficient in a knowledge of history. You can learn a lot from how the great men of the past handled difficult situations.'

428

'I am sure you are right,' Martin agreed affably.

'If neither of you – witnessing me sitting here – have grasped my tactic then I am sure Mr Tweed must be going mad with frustration. I could do with some more fresh black coffee. The time for me to play my next card is fast approaching. I am not referring to patience.'

Martin jumped up, came back with the percolator, a Wedgwood cup and saucer and a gold spoon on a silver tray. Walvis waved him away, his tone caustic.

'I said fresh coffee. Take all that to the chef and come back with what I asked for. Don't hurry. If you do I'll send it back again.'

He waited until he was alone with Gulliver who sat with hands clasped to conceal his impatience.

'Has the telephone cable linking us with the shore been reeled in?' Walvis asked.

'I supervised the operation myself an hour ago, so the answer is yes.'

'And they are ready on the flight deck to take off at any time?'

'They are.'

'So we could leave at any time?'

'Yes. Sir.'

'Then take this to the wireless operator and ask him to transmit to Lindau immediately. Tell him I expect a one hundred per cent accurate transmission.'

Gulliver stood up, took the envelope Walvis handed him and walked quickly up the wide aisle to the flight deck. Once he had closed the first door behind him he extracted the sheet of folded paper inside, opened it. The message was in code.

429

45

It was seven in the morning and Tweed was about to go down for his early breakfast when Paula arrived. She looked as fresh as paint in her pale grey jacket and pleated skirt. At the neck of her white blouse flared a Liberty scarf.

'Did you get any sleep?' Tweed asked anxiously.

'Three hours and I feel great after my shower. Please be frank, would you sooner breakfast alone so you can think?'

'I'd much sooner have the company of an attractive woman and it looks as though I've struck lucky. I'll be the envy of every other man in the dining-room.'

'Thank you, kind sir,' she said and curtseyed gracefully. 'Have you heard from Kuhlmann?'

'Yes, he phoned some time ago. As I foresaw, Walvis sent a third signal – and this time in code. The trouble is his code experts are having difficulty in breaking it. So much for experts. I'm not going to let anything spoil my full English breakfast . . .'

They had alighted from the elevator and were crossing the lounge to the breakfast room when Paula stiffened. She whispered to Tweed.

'So much for our cosy breakfast together. Look who has appeared over there.'

'Take no notice,' Tweed snapped.

They had sat down at a table by the wall when Jill Selborne, wearing a beige suit, came into the room and paused by their table. No dark circles under her eyes, Paula thought, she's durable.

'Good morning. I'm not going to spoil your breakfast by gate-crashing.'

'But the gate is wide open for you,' Tweed said as he stood up and pulled out a chair for the new arrival. 'We haven't even ordered yet, so your timing is perfect. Did you sleep well? You must have been pretty late in bed.'

'That's nice of you, to put up with me.' She looked at Paula. 'I hope you don't mind, but I am fed up with the number of times on this trip I've dined alone.'

'You're very welcome,' Paula lied.

'I think you're being very nice about it.'

They were ordering breakfast when Paula looked up, pursed her lips briefly, said 'Damn!' to herself. Coming up to their table for four was Lisa Trent.

She pressed both her slim hands together in an attitude of prayer as she bent close to Tweed.

'Would three women be too much for one man? I fear you will be out-gunned.'

'I'm never out-gunned,' Tweed assured her, pulling out the fourth chair. 'And if Bob Newman appears he'll be furious. Will probably accuse me of monopolizing all the beautiful women in Munich. Why not order while the waiter is here?'

Lisa was clad in an expensive leather pant-suit with a green blouse, which went well with her blonde hair. The blouse had a mandarin collar and no revealing V-slit this morning. Paula had ordered and she watched the other two women as they studied the menu. Am I dining with Teardrop? she wondered.

She was puzzled by Tweed's affability and hospitality. Then she remembered his remark that if you let people talk enough sooner or later they give themselves away. He never stops working, she thought, although this is work most men would give their eye-teeth for.

'When are you leaving, Lisa?' Tweed asked her. 'Not for a while, I hope.'

431

'I don't know. I'm waiting for an important phone call. It could come today, could come tomorrow. I am always at the beck and call of my clients. There are times when I wonder whether it's worth it, then I remember the income it brings me in.' She looked at Jill. 'Are you a slave to money?'

'We all need money,' Jill said seriously. 'The great thing is not to let it become the major objective in your life. I suppose the trouble is we're all happy to get more.'

Paula was studying her coiffure, which was perfect. She was still wearing her dark hair close to her head like a black helmet. Tweed finished off his grapefruit, dabbed his mouth with his napkin, looked straight at Jill.

'And I hope you are not leaving Munich for a while. I was thinking of taking you to see the Nymphenburg Palace. It's the finest in Europe, far better than the over-rated Schönbrunn outside Vienna.'

'I'd love to come with you,' Jill said, her soft voice full of enthusiasm. 'Would it be impolite to suggest we keep in touch with each other? I have Lisa's problem – I'm expecting calls from two different fashion consultants who may agree to see me. One is in London, the other in Zurich. As soon as I hear I'll let you know.'

'Suits me,' Tweed agreed with a smile.

Don't understand this, Paula mused. Could it be he's falling for her? He'd better identify and lock up Teardrop first.

Tweed had just polished off his eggs and bacon when a waiter arrived with a message. Tweed read it and put the envelope with the folded note in his pocket.

'Could you excuse me? I'll be back soon . . .'

Kuhlmann was waiting for him in the lounge and his expression was grave. The lounge was deserted at that hour.

'At long last,' he told Tweed, 'they have cracked the code. The toughest one they've come up against for a long

432

time,' he explained apologetically. 'Hence the delay.'

'He is in the communications business,' Tweed commented. 'What does the signal tell us?'

'That he's a cunning, devious, two-timing bastard, but we knew that. Here is the decoded signal.'

Tweed read the few words, smiled without humour, read it again and handed it back. The signal was addressed to *Seahorse VIII*, presumably the name of the seaplane at Lindau.

Change flight plan. File new flight plan for destination Chichester Harbour, England. Walvis.

'This is a copy. You can keep it,' said Kuhlmann, handing back the envelope. 'And I have bad news for you.'

'Might as well get it all over with at once. Tell me.'

'Rosa Brandt has disappeared. She left the lights on in her apartment all night. She must have fled before my watchers arrived. I've put out an all-points, stressing it's a pursuit of a probable criminal. All airports, all train terminals, all frontier posts. With special attention on the routes to Lindau.'

'Thank you for everything, Otto. If you catch her – and I think you will – put her on the first plane to Heathrow and we'll have her met. If you could inform Park Crescent, I'd be grateful.'

'Consider it done.' Kuhlmann held out his large paw, shook Tweed's hand. 'You take care of yourself. You are dealing with a cobra. I assume you're leaving? Walvis flew from Berg to Lindau about an hour ago. I also assume you're leaving for London?'

'I am. This morning. I have thought for a long time the ultimate climax would take place in Britain.'

'So Walvis talked too much when and wherever you met him?'

'He did. One other favour. Would it be possible for you

433

to arrange for that plane to be tracked by radar?'

'I've already arranged for all main radar stations to track *Seahorse Eight*. I even got the co-operation of other European nations. I meant to tell you that. You will get a report of its position every hour phoned to Park Crescent.'

'So the fly has caught the spider in its own web . . .'

Tweed went straight back to the dining-room, stood in the entrance, brushed imaginary dust off his shoulder twice as he saw Paula watching him. She was leaving the table while he hurried to the lifts.

A minute later in the dining-room Newman and Marler also left their table. Newman was careful not to look across to where Lisa and Jill were sitting. Another minute later Nield and Butler casually got up from their table and strolled out of the dining-room.

They were all assembled in Tweed's room before he could haul his case out of the wardrobe and collect his things from the bathroom.

'Something has broken at last,' said Newman.

Tweed handed him the signal, told him to show it to the others. He went on completing his packing quickly.

'Chichester Harbour,' called out Paula. 'At least it is familiar territory.'

'Familiar to Walvis, too,' Tweed replied.

The phone rang. He swore under his breath and picked up the receiver.

'Yes, who is it?'

'Howard here. I'm frightfully sorry I couldn't phone you earlier . . .'

'Just give me the data,' Tweed said brusquely.

'I tried to get hold of Brigadier Burgoyne during the wee, small hours. Believe it or not, he was out playing bridge at that time of the morning. His housekeeper didn't

434

know who he had gone to see. I had to wait until he came back ages later. There is a large mansion several miles outside Aldeburgh owned by a multi-billionaire. No one has ever seen him. They don't even know his name . . .'

'That's Walvis. What next?'

'Burgoyne told me the mansion's roof was cluttered with satellite dishes and aerial masts. He's some kind of radio ham, Burgoyne thought . . .'

'*Thought?*'

'Please let me finish. I haven't exactly been idle and I knew you'd want to be sure. Something sounded phoney about the whole set-up, so I sent a helicopter pilot with a crew armed with high-powered cameras and field-glasses. It flew low over the mansion. The crew are communications experts. They say the whole apparatus is a front . . .'

'What kind of front?'

'They couldn't communicate with anybody with the stuff on that roof. Cables aren't attached for power. The satellite dishes are fixed, immovable. It's a front, Tweed, to give the impression of a communications base which doesn't exist. Now you can see why I took so long phoning you.'

'Yes, I can. Many thanks for taking so much trouble to check the place out. The last piece of the jigsaw has dropped into place.'

'What jigsaw? I'd appreciate knowing what's going on.'

'Later you will know all. Again, my thanks. Must go. I'm in a rush.'

He put down the phone. Philip, who had had breakfast in his room, arrived with his back-pack. All the others were present. Tweed stared at the back-pack.

'We're going by air. I hope you aren't carrying weapons of any sort.'

'He isn't,' Marler broke in. 'I personally collected all the weapons and explosives early this morning, including Paula's Browning. I drove to a quiet spot on the banks of the Salzach and dumped the lot in the river. Then I handed in the car.'

'We'll have to hurry or we'll miss the plane,' Tweed insisted.

'No we won't,' Paula told him firmly. 'We have bags of time. What was the phone call about? You have plenty of time to tell us.' She looked at Newman. 'Bob, maybe you could go downstairs and get the concierge to order transport. You can't always get him on the telephone.'

'Order three taxis,' Tweed said. 'One is for Paula, Philip and me. The second is for you and Marler – and the third for Nield and Butler. Now, about that phone call,' he went on as Newman left the room.

They listened as he rattled off the details of his conversation with Howard, glancing at his watch several times, which caused Paula to raise her eyes to the ceiling. When he had finished he looked at Marler.

'Fill in Bob on that while you're with him in the taxi.'

'He's a fiend,' said Philip. 'Walvis guessed you would check up on Aldeburgh. He thought the dummy apparatus would fool you. The sooner I meet Mr Walvis the better,' he said in a cold voice.

Paula, struck by his tone, looked at him. He was sitting bolt upright. She had never seen him with a grimmer expression. His mouth was closed tightly and the eyes spelt murder.

'Walvis is fiendishly clever,' Tweed remarked, seeing Philip's appearance. 'But I am confident I can out-manoeuvre him. Last night on my own I again studied that charcoal sketch you drew of him, Paula. Really it is an amazing likeness. Portrait of a study in evil. I wonder where he is now . . .'

Walvis was in a state of near manic rage. He was still aboard *Pegasus V* as the huge machine cruised above the

436

northern shores of Lake Constance. The co-pilot had reported to him a few minutes earlier.

'An unexpected delay, sir. The air controller says he has to check back with Munich to confirm that we do have permission to land . . .'

'Permission to land?' thundered Walvis. 'Of course we have. What is this crap? The Minister personally opened all doors to me.'

'This door is still only half open,' the co-pilot said.

He immediately regretted his witticism. Walvis glared at him, placed both hands on the arms of his swivel chair and began to stand up as though about to attack the pilot.

'Take it easy, sir,' advised Gulliver from the seat across the aisle. 'The co-pilot is keeping you well informed.'

'Giving me information I don't want to hear. Keep me in touch with the latest developments,' he hissed at the pilot. 'Send a signal to the Minister demanding immediate clearance.'

'At once, sir.'

The co-pilot returned to the flight deck, closed the door, sat down and told the pilot about Walvis's order. They both agreed they had no intention of sending a signal to the Minister. It was all in the hands of Munich Air Control now.

Walvis swivelled his chair so he could peer down out of the window. It was a beautiful day, the sky a clear blue, not a cloud in sight. Below the water was like azure glass as the machine approached Lindau again. Walvis could gaze down at the toylike seaplane resting at its mooring. So near and yet so far away. He looked across at Gulliver.

'At least we have sent Tweed & Co. on a wild-goose chase to Aldeburgh. Imagine his reaction when eventually he gains entrance to the mansion.'

Once more he stared down at the seaplane and sighed.

437

46

Paula went into action the moment they arrived at Munich Airport.

'Listen,' she said to Tweed, as they entered a fairly empty concourse, 'wait here with all the others. Watch me at the reservations desk. I'm going to collect the tickets, but there's an earlier flight leaving – they're calling it now. If I nod my head vigorously you all head for Departure Lounge Twelve.'

'But there may not be enough spare seats . . .'

'For Pete's sake, that's what I have to check – whether I can transfer us to the earlier flight. Don't argue. Just do it. We all have luggage we can take on board . . .'

'She's bossing you about,' said Philip, grinning, 'and making a good job of it. You said you were in a rush.'

Tweed, looking a little stunned, watched Paula at the desk. Newman arrived with Marler, followed by Nield and Butler. Philip explained the situation to them and it was Newman's turn to grin.

'Good for Paula. And as soon as you came in she must have glanced down that departure board over there giving the flights. You said you were in a rush, Tweed.'

'That's the second time someone has said that to me.' He was still watching Paula, who suddenly turned round and nodded her head up and down.

'She's got us on that flight,' Newman went on. 'Let's get moving, as you would say . . .'

They were the last passengers to file into Business

438

Class. Paula had arrived at the departure lounge check-point with the tickets and followed them aboard. To reach Business Class they passed through Economy and they were in such a hurry no one except Paula, bringing up the rear, glanced at the passengers who almost filled Economy. They were the only passengers in Business Class so they spread themselves. Tweed gave Paula the window seat and sat alongside her. He was still a little dazed by the way she had taken over control so decisively. He consoled himself with the fact that he'd had no sleep.

The jet had climbed to thirty-five thousand feet when Paula looked down out of the window. No cloud masked the snowbound fields, the small villages with steep roofs coated with white. She took a sip of the champagne Tweed had ordered. He even had a glass himself.

'What a saga it has been in Germany and Austria,' she remarked.

'The real saga is ahead of us,' Tweed reminded her.

'I have news for you,' she said. 'It will intrigue you.'

'Intrigue me.'

'In Economy Class there are two passengers sitting well apart from each other. Lisa Trent and Jill Selborne. Creepy to think we may well have Teardrop aboard.'

'That explains their conversation at breakfast. How vague both of them were as to when they would be leaving Munich. I was suspicious at the time.'

'Suspicions confirmed.'

'But don't forget Rosa Brandt has disappeared,' Tweed recalled. 'At least she isn't on board. I was rushing through to get to our seats but I'd have spotted her.'

'I wonder if Kuhlmann will ever find her?'

'If anyone can, Kuhlmann will. Then she'll be on her way to London. I'm certain now one of those three is Teardrop.'

'You think we'll ever identify her?' Paula mused.

439

'I'm sure I will eventually. Because I have no doubt at all that I'm her next target.'

At Lindau, Walvis with his deputies and some very unpleasant-looking characters had transferred from *Pegasus* to the seaplane. It was now flying along Lake Constance, the lake cleared temporarily of all craft by order of the Minister. The floats left the water, the machine climbed into the air, the pilot set course for southern England.

'You sent the coded message to Cleaver Hall?' demanded Walvis.

'It was transmitted half an hour ago,' Gulliver reported.

'I expect you'd love to know what was in that signal,' Walvis tantalized Gulliver and Martin.

'That's your affair, sir,' Martin replied with a smooth grin.

'What *was* in it?' Gulliver asked bluntly.

'You know Britain has eleven Regional Controllers?' Walvis enquired, staring at Martin.

'Yes, they're top secret,' Martin began, delighted to show his knowledge. 'Only a very few people over there know they exist. The whole island is divided up into eleven secret regions. In the event something happens that stops the government exerting any control over events – a sudden descent into chaos, for example – the eleven Regional Controllers immediately take over from concealed headquarters. Three have already been assassinated.'

'Very good, Martin,' commented Walvis slyly. 'My signal orders the execution of four more of these men. That makes seven out of eleven killed. The signal also activates the sabotage of all main communication centres. You used the right word. Chaos will reign.'

440

'And we take over Britain from our communications centre at Cleaver Hall,' Gulliver added. 'Project Tidal Wave.'

'Only the start,' Walvis corrected. 'We also signal the leaders of the vast refugee horde waiting to sweep over Western Europe – especially across the Oder–Niesse line. Meantime, Tweed will be stumbling round Aldeburgh until eventually he locates the mansion, which is a dummy. I have only one regret.'

'And what is that, sir?' Martin asked before Gulliver could speak.

'Rosa Brandt did not reach Lindau in time for us to take her on board. But she will find another way to reach Britain. A train to Zurich and she will fly to London. Everything is going according to plan.'

Aboard the jet Tweed appeared to have sunk into a reverie. His eyes were half closed, had been for some time. He stirred suddenly. There was often telepathy between Paula and Tweed and she hit the nail on the head when she spoke.

'Thinking yourself into Walvis's shoes? Trying to see what his next move will be?'

'You're right,' he admitted. 'I must send Howard the most urgent signal.'

Delving into his briefcase, he extracted a notepad, began to write out a long message, ending with his name. He called a stewardess after slipping the folded message into an envelope and sealing it.

'Could you give that to the pilot. It's actually for the radio op. Very urgent.'

She was back in a few minutes. She bent her head close to Tweed's, kept her voice low.

'The captain would like a word with you, sir.'

Tweed followed her on to the flight deck. The captain

441

had handed over control of the plane to his co-pilot. He stared hard at Tweed.

'This message is a most unusual one for us to transmit. I need to see some positive identification.'

'You can contact Chief Inspector Kuhlmann at Munich police headquarters and he will vouch for me.'

As he spoke he showed the captain his SIS identity card, which carried his photograph, a good one, unlike passport photos.

'Thank you, sir.' The captain handed back the card. 'We shall transmit your signal top priority at once.'

'You don't want to contact Kuhlmann?'

'Chief Inspector Kuhlmann has been in touch with me by radio. He has ordered me to obey any instructions you give me unless they endanger the safety of the aircraft.'

'Thank you,' said Tweed and left the flight deck.

He told Paula what had happened without saying anything about the contents of the message.

'Kuhlmann either had us followed to the airport or – more likely – had a team of men waiting there to see which aircraft we boarded. He's a good friend and a great police chief. That's a relief. The signal was to Howard.'

Paula refrained from asking what was in the message and stared down out of her window. They were crossing the Channel. White streaks against the intense blue of the sea showed where vessels were moving up and down the waterway. She looked back and saw Philip, occupying a seat on his own, his head back against the rest. He was fast asleep.

It was the first time in his life that Philip had fallen asleep aboard an aircraft. He was dreaming. He was walking with Jean along the streets of an old town. They

442

were chatting as they strolled, chatting happily as they so often did. They were never short of something to say to each other.

They had often noticed other married couples in restaurants and pubs who never exchanged a word. They had often remarked to each other on the phenomenon, something they had never experienced whenever they were together.

He could hear the deep, cool timbre of Jean's voice, the way she pronounced every word clearly. Life was normal, life was so pleasant – just the two of them together. They didn't need the world, they were enough for each other. They always had been.

There was a sudden bump. Philip was jerked wide awake. He realized it had only been a dream, that the bump was the aircraft's wheels touching down at Heathrow. He could remember the dream clearly and thought the town they had wandered through – which they had in the past – had been Chichester. Reality hit him like a sledgehammer blow. He grit his teeth to stop himself bursting into tears.

Walvis, damn you to eternity, he said under his breath.

47

'Welcome back. Thank heavens you're safe. Is everyone else all right? No casualties?' Monica greeted Tweed.

'No casualties. So far.'

Tweed sank back in his chair behind his desk and looked all round his office at Park Crescent. It was good to be home again. He jerked himself upright. Monica was standing with a sheaf of message forms.

'The others are downstairs, equipping themselves with every type of weapon and explosive. They'll be very much like an SAS team. Now what has been happening?' he asked her.

'Chief Inspector Kuhlmann has been my permanent caller. He specifically asked for me – not Howard.'

'Which confirms Howard is not his favourite person. Fire away.'

'Several messages about *Seahorse Eight* – whatever that may be – reporting its progress towards England. Latest was it has just crossed the French coast on course for Chichester Harbour.'

'So we beat Mr Walvis to it. *Seahorse Eight* is a sea-plane with Walvis aboard.'

'Next item – again from Kuhlmann. A Rosa Brandt was taken off a train bound for Lindau. She has been put aboard an executive jet under escort – here's the message giving its ETA at Heathrow.'

'Give that to Nield immediately,' he said after scanning the signal. 'Tell him to hurtle back to Heathrow so he can meet the plane and escort Rosa Brandt to the Dolphin and Anchor Hotel in Chichester. He should be armed. On arrival at Chichester he is to keep her confined to her room, by force if necessary. And warn Jim Corcoran, the Security Chief at Heathrow. If the jet arrives before Nield does I want Brandt held incommunicado until Nield does arrive. Tell Jim she faces criminal charges. Anything else?'

'I'd have thought that was enough for the moment. It is more than enough for me to deal with. I'll tell Nield to get cracking, then phone Heathrow . . .'

Tweed stood up as she left the room and Newman walked in with Paula. He went over to the large wall map of Western Europe, took a plastic ruler off the top of a cabinet, measured the distance from Le Touquet on the

444

French coast, which was where Kuhlmann had reported it crossing, to Chichester Harbour.

'Kuhlmann reported Walvis crossing at that point just a few minutes before I arrived. He's still being canny. From Le Touquet he could easily have turned north for Aldeburgh, but he won't have done . . .'

He told them the gist of everything Monica had told him. Returning to his desk, he chewed on the end of the ruler.

'Walvis will reach Chichester Harbour, then drive to Cleaver Hall. He'll get there before us but I doubt if he'll prepare for our assault. He'll assume we're lost in Aldeburgh.'

'I'll make coffee for us,' Paula suggested. 'Flying always dehydrates me.'

'Particularly if you're knocking back champagne,' Tweed teased her, leaning back in his chair.

'I had one glass,' she told him indignantly. 'If you don't treat me more respectfully I'll put sugar in your coffee.'

'A fate worse than death.'

Monica came back into the room as Paula left. She told Tweed Nield was on his way, that she had phoned Jim Corcoran from downstairs. The phone started to ring.

'It knew I was back,' she grumbled, picking it up. 'Who did you say?' she queried. 'Got it. Hang on a moment.' She looked at Tweed. 'It's Chief Inspector Buchanan with Sergeant Warden. Downstairs. They want to come up and see you. Buchanan knows you're here. Apparently he had the building watched for your return.'

'Did he now?' Tweed's tone was grim. 'Tell him yourself I can't see him now. Tell him when he says he's pursuing a murder inquiry that I'm investigating a serial killer. Under no circumstances have I the time to see him at the moment.'

He looked at Newman, who could see Tweed was close to boiling point. A very rare mood for Tweed.

'Bob, go outside that door. If they try to force their way

445

upstairs stop them. They're on SIS territory. He won't have a warrant so you needn't be polite.'

'I won't be . . .'

Monica was talking forcefully on the phone. Tweed realized she was talking to Buchanan himself. He must have grabbed the phone off George, their ex-Army guard. He didn't think George would like that.

Newman had hardly closed the door when he saw Buchanan slam down the phone. He started to come up the stairs, met Newman halfway, who blocked his progress up the narrow staircase. At the bottom George stood with his hands stretched out, grasping the banister rails to keep Warden in the hall.

'Be reasonable, Newman,' Buchanan said in his normal and calm manner. 'I need to have a few words with Tweed.'

'He hasn't the time to say good morning to you.'

'I'll have to insist . . .'

'Insist until the cows come home. You're not going to waste Tweed's time. You didn't even phone for an appointment. A gross breach of good manners.'

That caught Buchanan on the raw. He lost his temper, the first time Newman had known that happen.

'What's this bloody nonsense about Tweed hunting a serial killer? If it were true, which I doubt, that would be my job.'

'It is true,' Newman informed him. 'Since you doubt the fact call Chief Inspector Otto Kuhlmann at Munich police headquarters. And is it your job to hunt a serial killer all over Europe – and the mastermind behind Lord knows how many crimes?'

'You're trying to tell me it's out of my jurisdiction?'

'Why don't you see if you can get any co-operation from Kuhlmann? And I didn't know Europe came within your jurisdiction.'

'I have to see Philip Cardon,' Buchanan snapped, trying another tack. 'Where is he?'

446

'Could be anywhere between here and Tokyo. You know how this outfit operates.'

'I won't forget Tweed's lack of co-operation . . .'

'I don't think he'll forget your trying to force your way in here.'

'And,' Buchanan continued with less confidence, 'you are telling me you have no idea where Cardon is at this moment?'

'Didn't you hear what I said a moment ago? Warden is trying to push his way past our official guard. Stop him now. He's gone way beyond his legal limits.'

Buchanan glared at Newman, turned on the staircase. He looked down and called out.

'Sergeant Warden, I suggest you cease and desist. I have told you before never to put a foot wrong.'

Without another word Buchanan walked slowly down into the hall. George, free of Warden who had stepped back, went to unlock and open the front door.

'Let me show you out, gentlemen. Isn't it a lovely day for December?'

Newman went back into Tweed's office and reported what had happened. Tweed, still furious, listened in silence until Newman had finished.

'You did a good job seeing him off. Where is Philip, by the way?'

'In the basement assembling enough firepower to start a major war. He had a word with Marler and Butler before we left Heathrow. They told him what they wanted.' He grinned. 'Marler's last words were "Don't forget my Armalite." He'd be lost without that sniper-scope rifle. And while we're on the subject, where are Marler and Butler? I saw you having a quiet word with them while I was finding a taxi to come here.'

'Yes,' Paula chimed in, 'what are they up to? They did not come back with us.'

'Those two women on our plane.' Tweed's expression

447

was grave. 'You think that was a coincidence? Lisa Trent and Jill Selborne aboard our aircraft? If you do the moon is made of green cheese. Butler is shadowing Jill Selborne. Marler is doing the same with Lisa Trent. I want to know where both those women are at every moment.'

'You're thinking of Teardrop,' Paula suggested.

'Teardrop did cross my mind,' he admitted. He looked at Newman. 'Your Mercedes 280E is still parked in Long Stay at Heathrow, isn't it?'

'Yes, I left it there when I was flying out to Munich.'

'So, with you driving, keeping within the speed limit, we can reach Chichester in good time when I decide we go, which could be soon.'

'In record time,' Newman assured him. 'Keeping within the speed limit.'

'I'm surprised you're not all exhausted,' commented Monica from behind her desk.

'The sap is rising,' Newman told her, 'the adrenalin is flowing.'

'Well, I'm glad my name is not Walvis.'

Monica fed paper into her electric typewriter and began clacking away at top speed.

Paula had a sudden idea and dived into her shoulder-bag. She produced a small white folder and waved it aloft triumphantly.

'I thought I'd still got it.'

'Got what?' Newman asked.

'Wait a minute, contain that restless soul.' She turned to a page, ran her finger down columns of figures printed very small. 'I have news for you.'

'I suppose we'll hear what it is before dusk,' Newman remarked.

'This little folder gives the tide tables for Portsmouth and the amount of time you have to subtract to get the data for Bosham.' She checked her watch. 'That nice woman where we had a good lunch at The Berkeley Arms near Bosham gave me this folder.' She glanced up with a smile. 'It is now high tide at Bosham. Wouldn't Walvis need high tide to land on the water opposite Cleaver Hall? I'm sure he would . . .'

The seaplane, *Seahorse VIII*, flew in a smooth curve over Bosham Channel and descended. The locals rushed out to watch as its floats scudded across the smooth water up the creek, coming to rest on the opposite shore from Bosham.

A motorboat with a canopy concealing the interior cruised out from the shore near Cleaver Hall, slowing down as it approached the seaplane and bumped against a float. The clear sky was a brilliant blue and the temperature was close to zero. Walvis peered out from a window, then turned to speak to Gulliver and Martin.

'Home again. I always feel most at home in England. So isn't it fortunate we shall launch Tidal Wave from here, that we shall shortly take over this country and rule it with a rod of iron?'

'There's a lot to do yet,' Gulliver warned.

'Have faith, my friend.' Walvis was in a good humour. 'Imagine Tweed, in good time, plodding round the marshes of Aldeburgh to locate my communications base.'

'At least we don't have to worry about him turning up here,' said Martin, confident he had said the right thing and smiling broadly.

'The trouble with you, Martin,' Walvis rebuked him, 'is that you assume too much. I think you are right – but we must assume you are wrong. Gulliver, the first task as soon as we enter Cleaver Hall is to mount the most massive defences – lay land-mines, everything. Work on the opposite assumption to Martin's – prepare with the conviction that Tweed and his legions will arrive . . .'

Five minutes later, swaddled in a heavy sheepskin with

449

the hood pulled over his head, Walvis lowered his bulk down the metal staircase at the open door of the seaplane. He stepped carefully into the motorboat and sank into the huge seat brought on board for him.

A limo with tinted glass waited at the landing stage – although it was only a three-minute walk up the drive to the entrance to the mansion. During their brief time inside the limo Gulliver, ever practical, warned his chief.

'The seaplane will have to take off soon. Once the tide runs out it surges and leaves behind a quagmire. It can wait safely near the entrance to Chichester Harbour.'

'Just so long as it is there.'

Despite all his confidence Walvis had always made it a practice to have an escape route open. Leaving the car, which had arrived, he climbed the steps to the long terrace running the full width of the front of the great mansion. The tall double doors had been opened by a guard careful to carry his automatic weapon. Walvis was insistent that arms should be at the ready throughout the day and the night.

'We must test the roof,' he said to Gulliver.

He hurried across a spacious hall with thick woodblocks on the floor. For his size he moved swiftly up the wide curving staircase until he arrived at the top floor with Gulliver and Martin puffing behind him. On the top landing he opened a door in the panelling, a door which looked like just another panel. Inside were a series of switches. He pressed one and a large section of the ceiling opened, a staircase descended automatically. Walvis climbed it swiftly and arrived in a vast room immediately under the mansard roof. Illumination was provided by sconce lanterns attached to the walls.

'Now!'

Walvis hauled down a lever inserted into the wall. There was the sound of hydraulic machinery operating. The section of roof facing away from Bosham, looking towards a dense forest at the back of the grounds, slowly slid wide open, exposing the sky.

Inside the room a vast array of satellite dishes stared up at the sky. Vertical aerials, invisible to Bosham, elevated themselves. One of the most sophisticated communications systems in the world was ready for operation – and those locals in Bosham still scanning the mansion through field-glasses were unaware of its existence.

'When it is dark,' Walvis said, 'it will be darker still in Europe – they are one hour ahead of us. That is when I send the signal to the leaders in the East to order the advance across the continent.'

Walvis was gazing with pleasure at his communications equipment when he heard the approaching helicopter. He almost panicked. He shouted to Gulliver, who was nearest to the control lever.

'Get the damned roof closed! Hurry it up, for God's sake.'

Gulliver had already grasped the lever, pulled it down. The hydraulics hummed. With what seemed an agonizing slowness the roof began to slide shut. Like a statue Walvis stared up, dreading the appearance of the helicopter. The roof continued to close. The beat-beat of the helicopter's engine sounded dangerously close.

'Why does it take so long?' Walvis shouted.

'It's a heavy roof,' Gulliver reminded him. 'It always takes a time to open and close.'

'It's taking for ever.'

He was still craning his neck, gazing at the brilliance of the winter sky, certain the machine would come into view before the roof was shut. There was a loud click, the roof was in place again. Walvis mopped sweat off his forehead.

'I wouldn't worry, sir,' Gulliver assured him. 'There are a lot of choppers flying routine patrols. On the lookout

451

for drug traffickers. I heard the faint sound of that machine while we were coming ashore.'

'Then why the hell didn't you warn me?' Walvis thundered.

'Because I didn't know it would be coming this way,' Gulliver replied placidly. 'In any case it didn't come into sight while the roof was open. I think maybe you would like a tot of brandy after your long journey, sir.'

'Maybe a large tot?' suggested Martin, who had carefully kept quiet during the crisis.

'A very large tot,' Walvis said, throatily.

Aboard the Sikorsky the pilot, Haines, glanced over the shoulder of his co-pilot at the third man, Carson. In his hands Carson, an expert photographer, was holding a cine-camera with a zoom lens.

'Get it, Carson?' asked Haines through his mouthpiece.

'I'd say I have a complete record,' Carson said through his own mouthpiece attached to his headset. 'That is the most extraordinary subject I've ever shot. Looked like a full-blown communications centre hidden away in the roof, which slides back and forth.'

'You think they saw us?' queried Haines. 'We were told to remain invisible.'

'We did remain invisible,' Carson told him. 'Thanks to your clever navigation. I recorded at an extreme angle. It's my bet those people inside never even saw this chopper.'

'Then we'd better hike back fast to the landing pad at Battersea. Air Ministry said they wanted the results yesterday – and it was an air commodore speaking to me. That's a first – for me, at any rate . . .'

Monica's phone rang. She made a face before she picked up the receiver.

452

'That always happens when I'm typing great guns . . .'

She answered, looked startled, put her hand over the mouthpiece, stared at Tweed.

'Air Ministry. Air Commodore Standish for you . . .'

'Hello there. Tweed here. How goes it?'

'Rather well, I gather,' an upper-crust voice replied. 'Have just had a report from the chopper pilot on his way back to Battersea. Says they have marvellous pics. Apparently the roof of that mansion opens, was open when they took them. I gather inside – that is, inside the roof – is a major communications centre. You have a projection room?'

'We have.'

'Oh, the pilot also swears they were not spotted by the chaps inside. Got a police patrol car laid on to meet the chopper when it lands at Battersea. Courtesy of the Police Commissioner. You draw a lot of water! The patrol car will reach you quickly. Coming with sirens screaming and lights flashing.'

'Tell them to calm down before they get here. I don't want attention drawn to this building. And, Frank, many thanks. I owe you one.'

'I'll remember that. 'Bye . . .'

Tweed told Paula, Newman and Philip, who had just come into the room, what had happened.

'My Lord!' Newman clapped a hand to his forehead several times. 'The man never sleeps. When if I may ask, which I'm going to, did you arrange all that?'

'Don't you recall that after we'd arrived at Heathrow I said I had an urgent call to make? I phoned my contact at the MoD. I told him to instruct the pilot of the chopper to wait until not only the seaplane had landed, but also until the passengers had entered the mansion. I guessed that Walvis would want to test his system the moment he

453

arrived. It is so vital to him. It was a guess on my part, I admit.'

'But you guessed right,' said Paula.

'I'd like to add to our equipment,' said Philip in a determined tone. 'I'll need a chopper laying on as close to Bosham as possible.' He stood up. 'And I'd better collect that extra equipment from the basement.'

'I wonder what equipment he's talking about,' Paula mused. While talking she had carefully extracted something inside a plastic envelope from her shoulder-bag and was studying it through a magnifying glass. Tweed saw that it was the last piece of embroidery – of a map of Europe – Jean Cardon had been working on.

48

Walvis was drinking brandy, sitting in a high-backed Regency chair at the head of a long antique mahogany dining table in the Great Chamber at Cleaver Hall. He felt the chair, its position, the surroundings of panelled walls, suited his status. He looked at Gulliver and Martin, seated in chairs facing each other, three places down the table from their chief.

'Gulliver, have you yet traced that infamous Reynolds who I regard as a deserter? There is only one fate for deserters. They should be shot.'

Gulliver wrapped both hands round his glass of beer. For him there was only one worthwhile drink – beer washed down with a vodka chaser. He paused before replying.

Reynolds was a tricky topic. In Munich he had become

fed up with his lack of promotion. There had been a stormy interview with Walvis and Reynolds had ended the row by walking out and disappearing. Gulliver had been given the task of hunting him down and exterminating him.

'Through contacts I have a lot of data on Reynolds,' he said, approaching the subject warily. 'He has an English girl friend . . .'

'Name?' rasped Walvis.

'That's something I'm still working on.' He was talking quickly now, hoping to make a good impression. 'On top of all my other duties in Munich I did not forget the traitor Reynolds.'

'But you still haven't found him?'

'Not yet. I do know he flew back to London a few days ago, but I learned that too late.'

'You're not telling me he's still loose – with all the information he has in his head?'

'I have a team in London turning over the place. We'll find him soon. Then it will be curtains for Mr Reynolds.'

'Contact the leader of your team in London. Tell him he will receive ten thousand pounds when Reynolds is a corpse. You might even receive a bonus yourself, Gulliver. I did say "might".'

At Heathrow Airport Marler sat in the best restaurant as he devoured grilled sole. He had already paid the bill and left a generous tip on the table. He didn't know how long he'd have to linger there.

Lisa Trent, wearing outsize dark glasses, sat with her back to him at another table. She ate quickly and, like Marler, had already paid her bill. She kept glancing at her diamond-encrusted watch and Marler had the idea she was waiting for someone.

Miss Trent. A messenger had entered the restaurant

455

holding up a board with the name chalked on it. Lisa raised her arm. She tipped the messenger, tore open the envelope, read the typed message.

Cleaver Hall, Bosham, near Chichester is where you will find him. A.R.

The initials stood for Alfred Reynolds, the man who was dwelling under the illusion he was her boy friend. She stood up quickly, walked out of the restaurant and down the stairs into the main concourse. Marler, regretting he had not finished his Dover sole, strolled after her.

Lisa went straight to the car-hire desk, produced her papers, a concertina of credit cards, gazed at the girl waiting to serve her.

'I want a Jaguar now. Which means urgently. A cream Jag if at all possible. Use which card you prefer.'

Standing close by, Marler had bought a newspaper and was pretending to read it while he eavesdropped on the conversation. He had himself visited the same counter earlier, had hired a Rover which he had said he would collect later.

He waited until Lisa was escorted outside to pick up her Jaguar, then walked up to the counter. He showed the girl his form, handed her a twenty-pound note.

'That's for you – I need the Rover outside before you can say snap.'

It was his warm genial smile as much as the tip that did the trick. He was escorted outside to the Rover and saw Lisa driving off. She had been studying a map after getting behind the wheel.

'Bet you spot me, darling Lisa,' he said as he followed her through the tunnel, 'but you're in the devil of a hurry so you'll keep going. I wonder where you're heading for?'

*   *   *

456

Butler, also waiting at Heathrow, keeping an eye on Jill Selborne, was having a more difficult time. She had gone into the cafeteria after disembarking from the Munich flight.

She kept glancing round as though she expected to be followed. When she carried her luggage and a cup of coffee to a table she took a long time deciding where to sit. Butler stayed at the counter, pretending he couldn't make up his mind what he wanted, ushering other people ahead of him. The one factor in his favour was the fact that the cafeteria was crowded.

When Jill sat down at a small table by herself he also ordered coffee. He managed to sit at a table near the exit which she must pass when she left. 'Do make up your mind, lady,' he said to himself. He then made the mistake of sipping his coffee, pulled a face, decided he wasn't that thirsty.

Jill, whom he couldn't see, suddenly walked past him, her long legs striding out. Butler followed her at a distance. She went to the car-hire desk, spoke at length to the receptionist. Like Marler, Butler had hired a car while Jill, after coming through Customs, had spent some time pretending to glance at paperbacks as she looked round to make sure she was alone.

Butler took a chance. He went up to another receptionist who had appeared, showed his form, asked for the Ford Sierra he had booked. Jill had hired a Vauxhall Cavalier.

On a brilliant December afternoon with the sun glowing out of a turquoise sky there was very little traffic. So Butler was able to take over his Ford and sit behind the wheel without being moved on. He studied a map of London, which he knew backwards.

In his rear-view mirror he watched Jill climbing into her Vauxhall. She drove on past him and, waiting a few moments longer, he then followed her.

457

'Now where are you going?' he said to himself, echoing the words Marler had uttered earlier.

Tweed, Newman and Philip were animatedly discussing Cleaver Hall and arguing about the details of an assault. Paula sat listening behind her desk as Tweed paced the Park Crescent office while the others were seated.

'I'm beginning to have my doubts about using a chopper,' Philip said. 'They'll hear it coming and I think it should be a silent onslaught – to start with anyway.'

'You were going to use the chopper to attack the communications centre when they open the roof,' Newman reminded him.

'I know, but I've changed my mind . . .' Paula thought she had never seen him in such a commanding mood. 'I've remembered,' he went on, 'how Kuhlmann handled the attack on Walvis's warehouse. He used rocket launchers with incendiary shells. From the grounds at the back of Cleaver Hall we could see when the roof was opened and send a barrage of incendiary shells into it.'

'Assuming we can get into those grounds, assuming we'd be able to see from ground level when the roof had opened,' Newman objected.

'Look at these photos.'

Philip picked up several large prints from the collection produced at top speed in the basement. Earlier they had all watched the running film in the projection room and Philip had kept calling out.

'Freeze!'

It was the pictures he had selected which had been converted into glossy prints. After the helicopter had landed at the Battersea helipad a patrol car had rushed the film to Park Crescent.

Tweed had been surprised to find the photographer

458

aboard the chopper had filmed more than the interior below the open roof of Cleaver Hall. He had also filmed the large estate surrounding the mansion. It was one of these pics Philip had picked up and then several more, spreading them out on Tweed's desk.

They all gathered round the desk to study them. It was Tweed who took the decision after examining the prints.

'Philip is right. Damn it, the team we're taking is agile enough. Two or three could shin up those tall trees at the back with launchers looped over their backs. Then they'd have a bird's-eye view inside that open roof.'

'You are right,' Newman admitted. 'And I agree Philip's idea of a silent approach is sound.'

The phone rang and Monica, who had joined them, rushed to answer it.

'Butler has arrived,' she told Tweed.

'So soon? Ask him to come up . . .'

'You're just not going to believe this,' were Butler's first words. 'You are simply not going to believe it.'

'Try me,' said Tweed.

'As ordered, I stayed close to Jill Selborne at Heathrow. She doesn't know I tailed her. But she was looking for a tail. She fooled around in the cafeteria for a while, then hired a red Vauxhall Cavalier. I'd already hired a Ford Sierra, which is parked outside.'

'Outside here?' Tweed exclaimed. 'You mean you lost her?'

'Have more faith in Harry,' Paula advised.

'Thank you, Paula,' Butler said gratefully. 'So I follow her when she leaves the airport. You'll never guess where she went to.'

'Don't like guessing games,' Tweed snapped.

'She is, at this moment, sitting at the wheel of her Cavalier, parked round the corner from here in Maryle-

459

bone Road. Obviously waiting to follow you.'

'She can't be,' Paula protested. 'How would she know this address?'

'She would know it,' Tweed explained, 'because for two years she was in Naval Intelligence. And we are frequently in touch with Naval Intelligence.'

'The devil!' Paula stood up, fuming. 'I'm going out to take her to pieces.'

'You are doing nothing of the sort,' Tweed ordered. 'So sit down behind your desk. I *want* her to follow us when we leave for Chichester. Everything is working out far better than I could have hoped.' He looked at the wall clock. 'We must time it so we arrive in Chichester before dark. Monica, were you able to reserve rooms for the whole team at the Dolphin and Anchor?'

'At this time of year it was easy,' Monica informed him. 'Everyone has a room.'

'We still have a little time before we leave,' Tweed remarked. 'I'd like to hear from both Marler and Pete Nield before we go. If possible.'

'The executive jet from Munich has arrived,' Corcoran, Security Chief at Heathrow, told Nield. 'It's just been given permission to land. There was a bomb hoax at Munich Airport which delayed its take-off.'

'Well, at least the lady has at long last arrived. I don't think I could drink any more coffee, good as it is.'

Nield was sitting in a hard wooden chair in Corcoran's private office. The chair had seemed to grow harder and harder while he had waited. Corcoran, an athletic man in his early forties, clean shaven and with an outdoor complexion, had apologized.

'The chairs here are deliberately uncomfortable. They help me when I'm questioning a suspect.'

'You sit in the same type,' Nield remarked.

'I feel I should – and it makes our tactics less obvious.' The intercom on his desk crackled and someone said something Nield didn't catch. 'The jet has landed. Rosa Brandt will be brought to this office in a car with security guards. I hand her over to you and then she's all yours. At least you'll bypass Passport Control and Customs.'

'Many thanks for your co-operation,' Nield said. 'And I'd like to phone Tweed.'

'Be my guest.'

Corcoran stood up, took long steps to the locked door of his office. He looked round as he inserted a key.

'I'm meeting the car while you make your call. This Brandt, has she killed a lot of people?' he joked.

'That,' Nield said seriously, 'is what we have to find out . . .'

At Park Crescent Tweed put down the phone and looked at Paula and Newman.

'That was Pete Nield, calling from Corcoran's office. Rosa Brandt has arrived, so Kuhlmann was as good as his word. Nield will very shortly be driving Brandt to the Dolphin and Anchor and holding her there until we arrive.'

'I hope he watches his step with that woman,' commented Paula.

'Pete is nice, but tough and realistic,' Newman assured her. 'He won't handle her with kid gloves. You don't fool around with cobras.'

'If she is the cobra,' Tweed reminded him.

'But it was significant Kuhlmann took her off a train bound for Lindau,' Paula pointed out. 'It suggests she was on her way to board the seaplane with Walvis.'

'Which is something I had not overlooked,' said Tweed. 'And I hope Marler hasn't lost Lisa Trent.'

'Can you really imagine Marler ever losing a really attractive woman?' Newman said with a smile. 'He's

461

probably having the time of his life. I should have been given that job.'

'I'll still be glad when we hear from him,' Tweed insisted. 'And he has got a mobile phone . . .'

Marler *was* having the time of his life, but not quite in the way Newman had meant. As soon as the two cars had left London well behind Lisa was giving Marler a run for his money, ramming her foot down, racing the Jag like mad, roaring round corners on two wheels, or so it seemed as Marler followed her in his Rover.

'You are a fast little filly,' Marler said to himself. 'And I mean fast in every sense of the word.'

Earlier, in heavy traffic in the suburbs, Lisa had apparently made an effort to disguise herself. For a few minutes Marler lost her, then he had seen the cream Jaguar ahead. Lisa now wore dark tinted glasses and had wrapped a green scarf round her blonde hair.

Later, she made no attempt to avoid him but set a frantic pace. They were approaching a corner beyond Petworth, the wave-like curves of the South Downs were in view, silhouetted against a clear blue sky, when she increased her speed suddenly.

Marler accelerated, rounded the corner to find himself alongside her. Out of sight for seconds she had braked and was cruising. Ahead stretched a ruler-straight road for miles and rushing towards them was a juggernaut.

He had two options. One to jam on his brakes, to drop back behind her fast. The other was to accelerate even more, to get ahead of the Jag before the juggernaut reached him. The road was not wide enough to take the three vehicles.

Lisa gestured to encourage Marler to move ahead and gave him a sarcastic smile. He nodded without returning the smile, pressed his foot down, praying she would not be crazy enough to do the same. She maintained her cruising pace and he slipped ahead of her just before the juggernaut thundered past. The driver made a rude gesture at Marler.

'Ruddy truckers,' Marler said aloud. 'Because they're bigger they think they're king of the road.'

The next thing he knew was the Jaguar was storming past him, Lisa's scarf trailing behind her like a slipstream. She waved without looking back. They were leap-frogging each other all the way to Chichester when the road ahead was clear.

Reaching the hotel, she swung in ahead of him and took the last slot under cover. He swore colourfully to himself. As she jumped out of her car, carrying her small case and her bag, she waved again to him and called back over her shoulder before walking down the narrow cobbled alley leading to the entrance to the Dolphin and Anchor.

'See you in the bar. You owe me a double Scotch.'

49

'Marler's on the line,' Monica reported.

'You're the last one to report in,' Tweed began, not hiding his irritation as he took the call on his own phone. 'You do have a mobile phone.'

'No chance to use it,' Marler said tersely. 'Circumstances. Lisa Trent and I have arrived at the Dolphin.'

'She didn't spot you?' Tweed snapped.

'You have to be joking,' Marler snapped back. 'She's the brightest cookie I've wrestled with for some time.'

'That means she did spot you.'

'It means exactly that. Now I *have* reported in. See you all sometime . . .'

'You'll see us—' Tweed started to say forcefully, then realized the connection had been broken.

'He may have had a tough time of it,' Paula said soothingly.

'Marler?' Tweed exclaimed. 'With a woman?'

'Some women are tougher than others,' Paula reminded him.

Newman, who had gathered the gist of the phone exchange of pleasantries, was grinning when the door opened and Howard rushed in. Newman adopted a poker expression.

'Glad to see you back safely,' Howard said breathlessly.

He sank into an armchair. He was wearing yet another new Chester Barrie suit from Harrods, a white shirt and another flashy tie. Paula thought that he looked tired.

'Just back from the MoD,' he told Tweed. 'I've been there for hours – in connection with your phone call from Munich about the safety of the surviving Regional Controllers. You wouldn't believe the battle I had with those bureaucrats to get the message across. I had to keep asking to see a more senior person. Then go all over it again. Lost my temper eventually. Said I was going straight to the Prime Minister. That did it.'

'Did what?'

'They put their skates on. Phoned each of the men concerned, ordered him to stay in his house. SAS men have been flown from Hereford to guard them. The commander of the SAS units has been given authority to move each Controller to a safer house if he thinks fit.'

'You mean this has just happened?' Tweed demanded. 'I said it was very urgent.'

'Don't panic.' A remark Paula thought was very funny

464

as Howard hauled out a flaring display handkerchief and mopped his sweating forehead. 'They phoned each man hours ago. I insisted on staying until I'd seen they dealt with everything – including instructing Hereford. I'd have you know I've been there all day – with no sustenance except cups of filthy coffee.'

'Perhaps you'd now like some non-filthy coffee,' Monica suggested.

'Thank you, I would. And a Scotch. I really took your call very seriously, Tweed.'

'I'm relieved and grateful. Why don't you go to your office and relax completely? Monica will bring your drinks there.'

Howard's plump, well-fed face went a little redder. He stared round the room, then back at Tweed.

'You mean my presence is no longer required?' He stood up stiffly. 'Sometimes I think I'm surplus to requirements.'

'You are,' Paula whispered to herself.

'You'll find a sealed envelope on your desk,' Tweed called out as Howard reached the door. 'It gives you full details of the plan we finally hammered out for an assault on Cleaver Hall. You're being kept fully informed.'

'Appreciate that.' Howard paused. 'Any casualties while you were on the Continent?'

'None. So far.'

'Thank God for that. You'll be busy so I'm off now . . .'

'I could punch that man,' Paula said vehemently when Howard had gone.

'He is the Director,' Tweed replied. 'And he has done a very good job at the MoD. In a crisis Howard usually turns up trumps.'

'That's true,' Paula admitted. 'I wonder how Nield is getting on with Rosa Brandt?'

* * *

465

In the large library at Cleaver Hall Walvis sat nursing a brandy. He checked his watch, looked at Gulliver, pressed one of several buttons inset into the wide arms of his chair.

'Time for a news bulletin on the radio. There might be a vague item on the assassination of seven men in various parts of the country. They won't refer to them as Regional Controllers, of course . . .'

They listened to the news bulletin. There was no reference to any assassinations. Walvis, looking stormy, switched off.

'They should have killed them by now. It's an essential part of the plan.'

'I doubt they'd give out any news about it,' Gulliver replied. He took off the motoring gloves he had been wearing. 'We have laid all the land-mines in the grass and that was a job I was glad to finish supervising. They explode under the pressure of a human foot and have to be handled very carefully.'

'At both the front and the back?' asked Walvis.

'To be effective we have to lace the grass with them,' Gulliver lectured. 'We had a huge quantity, but by the time we had covered the front we had used them up.'

'But that leaves the rear grounds exposed.'

'Hardly. You seem to have forgotten the wall surrounding the grounds at the back is protected with two electric wires – plus an alarm system. No one is going to try to come that way when they see what's waiting for them.'

'Returning to the front,' Walvis persisted, 'I presume the gravel drive has no mines in it? I shall want to leave by car along that drive.'

Mines made Walvis nervous. He had once seen a film of a man treading on a buried mine. The result had been horrific. Gulliver clamped his lips together before replying. Give me strength, he thought.

466

'There are no mines laid in the drive,' he said. 'And, before you say that leaves the drive unprotected, I will recall to your memory that we have machine-guns on the first floor covering every inch of that drive. Have you any more queries?'

'Yes. Is there no way you can get in touch with that team sent to kill the Regional Controllers? No news is so often bad news.'

'There is no way to contact them.' Gulliver's patience was running out. 'They were specifically ordered *not* to take with them any means of communication. Mobile phones, radio sets. I banned the lot.'

'Why?'

'For God's sake, isn't it obvious? That operation is so important I couldn't risk a signal being intercepted. You do want it to succeed, don't you?'

'Yes,' Walvis said quietly, 'I do want it to succeed – and I also want you to stop lecturing me. I find at times I dislike your manner intensely – your lack of manners.'

'That's because I never had the benefit of your education,' Gulliver observed and walked out of the library.

Walvis was quite pleased with his reaction. Tension was steadily building up inside Cleaver Hall. Everywhere he went he could sense it as men worked to strengthen the defences. They dropped tools, they quarrelled with each other over the most trivial incidents. The atmosphere was exactly what Walvis desired – men under pressure were alert. The climax was approaching.

Nield had taken firm control of Rosa Brandt after escorting her from the Heathrow Security office. Holding her by the arm, he had guided her along the route Corcoran had led them to bypass all checkpoints.

Once he had her alongside him inside the Citroën he had hired, he had removed the bag from her shoulder.

467

'I don't make a habit of searching ladies' bags,' he told her, 'but you could be carrying a weapon.'

'Hardly,' she replied in English, 'after that pig Kuhlmann has me searched before we are put aboard the jet.'

She stared straight ahead as Nield returned the bag to her. Her case was in the back and he could search that when they reached the Dolphin. He had locked all the doors. From that moment on she said not one word to him as he left London behind, proceeded into the country, passed through Petworth and continued on to Chichester.

Occasionally he glanced at her but always she was staring straight ahead. Her only movements were to check the position of her veil, pulling it a little further down over her face. Nield found the silence uncanny – almost unnerving. There was something about her that was extremely disturbing.

'We are approaching Petworth,' he had said over his mobile phone to Tweed earlier.

'I appreciate your reporting in. Keep me posted . . .'

Tweed would like to have asked him a dozen questions. Had Rosa Brandt said anything? How was she bearing up under the strain? Was she still wearing the same clothes? He had desisted from asking a single question because he knew Nield could handle any situation.

'I'm impatient to get moving,' he said inside his head. 'To get the show on the road. And that's dangerous. It's the one lesson above all others I drum into new recruits. Never rush your fences – except to save your life.'

'The waiting can get a bit much,' said Paula.

She had been watching him as he stared out of the window, had guessed his thoughts. The view towards Regent's Park was beautiful. On a cold December day the air was clear, the sky was clear.

Newman was in the basement where he had gone to help Philip sort out more equipment. There had been a change of plan which involved the use of different weapons. As

468

Tweed remained standing, wrestling with his impatience, his doubts, his fears, the phone rang.

'It's Kuhlmann, speaking from eastern Germany,' Monica called out.

Tweed grabbed the phone off her, anxious for any kind of action.

'Yes, Otto.'

'I'm speaking from just this side of the river line – facing Poland. You can hear me clearly? Good. I'm talking over a line attached to a scrambler. I'm alone in a room at the top of a mobile tower that elevates. I can see across the frozen river. It's a frightening scene. The horde on the far side stretches back as far as the eye can see, waiting to cross.'

'You're getting full co-operation, I hope?'

'Your hope is not being fulfilled. I have the lot here in an HQ near by. General Reichenbach, the American Supreme Commander of NATO, with far too many staff officers – all putting in their five eggs, arguing the toss. At least the mobile artillery is in position, dug in all down the line.'

'What's the problem?'

'Reichenbach refuses point blank to follow my advice – to wait until they're crossing after dark, then to open fire on the ice and drown them, which would stop the others even attempting to come over when the ice freezes over again. It's well below zero here. I'm appealing direct to the Chancellor in Bonn. He's holding a Cabinet meeting to discuss the situation, for God's sake.'

'How will you handle it?'

'Fight on! Keep shouting at them, hoping they'll see sense in time. I'll keep in touch.'

'Speak to Monica if I'm not here. I know where Walvis is. Radar tracked his seaplane to his base.'

'Kill him. Then he can't give the order when darkness falls. Or darkness will fall all over Europe . . .'

*   *   *

469

'If only night would come,' Walvis fumed. 'Europe is one hour ahead of us but it's still daylight out there. Too early to send the signal.'

Walvis was padding restlessly round the library, unable to keep still. Gulliver was somewhere outside, perfecting the defences. Martin was the only other man in the book-lined room, wishing he were elsewhere.

'We don't have to wait too much longer,' he volunteered. 'Everything is prepared. It's only a matter of your sending the signals when the time comes.'

'Yes! That's all it is.' Walvis turned on Martin, waving his clenched fist. 'Do you realize how many years I have devoted to planning Tidal Wave? Don't answer! We are on the verge of tremendous success and I have a feeling something is going wrong.'

'Why do you feel like that?' Martin felt compelled to answer.

'Haven't you noticed? Of course you haven't. No one except me notices the *absence* of something. Normally the sky here frequently echoes to the sound of helicopters – checking for drug traffickers trying to slip in their cargoes. I have not heard the sound of one helicopter in over an hour. I regard that silence as deadly . . .'

'Air Commodore Standish phoned from the Ministry,' Monica informed Tweed as he returned, holding a plate of sandwiches, a bottle of mineral water. 'He gave me his message when I said you'd be back in a minute.'

'Well, what had Standish to say?'

'That he's put into operation the idea you suggested on the phone. All helicopters in the Chichester area and over the coast have been grounded.'

'Excellent!' Tweed's grave expression changed to one of satisfaction. 'This is a duel of nerves between Walvis and me. I'm sure he will have noticed the absence of the choppers. Which will make him wonder.'

He looked up as Philip, garbed in camouflage jacket and trousers, entered followed by Newman similarly dressed. It was Philip who spoke.

'We are ready to leave. Now. Newman has estimated we can reach Bosham before dark – providing the roads are clear.'

'They are,' said Tweed, putting down his plate. 'The Police Commissioner called back in response to my request while you were in the basement. All the roads on our route to Chichester have been cleared of traffic – with diversions and fake roadworks. Warn everyone driving us that if they see those horrible cones they ignore them. Drivers flash their lights four times when they approach them. At least I'm getting more co-operation than poor Kuhlmann. It may all be up to us,' he said as he slipped into his sheepskin.

Paula, who already had put on her own sheepskin, grabbed the plate of sandwiches Tweed had put down, wrapped them in thick paper napkins she took from a drawer, picked up the unopened bottle of mineral water. She nodded to Philip and Newman.

'Right,' said Philip, his manner still cold, 'we'll go, moving like the wind.'

50

Newman's Mercedes had been brought back from the Heathrow car park, so he was glad to use it for the drive to Chichester. The front passenger seat was vacant except for his loaded Smith & Wesson concealed beneath a cushion.

In the back Paula sat between Tweed and Philip with her shoulder-bag in her lap. They were driving through countryside with bare fields on either side of them, ploughed up for spring, and well beyond Petworth when she spoke.

She had taken out of her bag the folded embroidery of the map of Europe she had guarded so well. Again she studied it through a magnifying glass. Newman was driving the car very smoothly and it was still daylight when she put down the glass, having folded the map to show Chichester and the surrounding area.

'Well,' she said, 'Jean triggered everything off with her tiny crosses marking Cleaver Hall, Munich, Grafenau and Passau. How she dug out that information we'll never know – but she was researching the Walvis organization.'

She glanced at Philip. He had taken one quick look at the embroidery when she produced it and then stared ahead with the same cold, hard expression.

'I have to bring up this subject, Philip,' she said in a matter-of-fact tone, 'because I've found something else which may be vital tonight. I think she must have got hold of copies of the deeds of the thatched cottage next to Cleaver Hall.'

'That's quite some distance from the Hall,' Tweed commented. 'I remember noticing it when I was in the Bistro at Bosham, scanning the opposite shore through glasses.'

'That, I think, is the whole point,' Paula explained, 'the fact that it appears to have no connection with Cleaver Hall. But I think Walvis owns it and it is his escape route in case of an emergency.'

'How on earth do you make that out?' Tweed asked.

'Jean was a very skilled embroiderer,' Paula went on. 'I'm amazed at the fineness of the work . . .'

'She had good eyesight but she used a magnifying glass for the detail work,' Philip said in a terse voice. 'It hung looped from her neck so it was always handy.'

472

'She was still an expert,' Paula said. 'When I was looking at it again I concentrated on the Cleaver Hall area. She embroidered, very tiny, a dotted line running from what has to be Cleaver Hall to the cottage. And in really tiny letters she embroidered "esc. rt.". I'm sure that stands for escape route.'

'Let me see that,' Tweed requested, his interest aroused.

He took hold of the folded embroidery Paula handed him with great care, then the magnifying glass. Paula pointed with her finger as he stared through the glass. Tweed gave a sigh.

'She was incredible. But if that dotted line is an underground tunnel it must pass under Cleaver Hall's outer wall.'

'Which,' Paula pointed out, 'would make it a perfect escape route. When we were last in Chichester I slipped out to a bookshop and bought a history of Chichester and the Bosham area. I read it while we were in Munich. At one time there was a lot of smuggling in the district. The creeks made marvellous hideaways. And we know that smugglers were ingenious in building tunnels to escape the Customs and Excise.'

'May I look?' asked Philip.

He had his mouth closed tight, his teeth gritted as he studied the relevant area with the aid of the magnifying glass. He spent much longer looking at it than Tweed had, then handed it back to Paula. She slipped it back inside its plastic envelope, then inserted the envelope slowly back inside her bag.

'I think that is Walvis's escape route,' Philip decided. 'Of course, being Walvis, he would have one, wouldn't he? If humanly possible I'm going to look at that cottage as soon as we arrive.'

'There may not be much spare time,' Tweed warned.

'I'll make the time. I wish this car would go faster.'

'It can,' called back Newman, who had been listening

473

to the conversation. 'But you wouldn't have been able to study that embroidery – and the information Paula picked up could prove vital.'

'Your wife, Philip,' Tweed said quietly, 'may well prove to be the main element in bringing down the greatest villain we have ever confronted – an even greater menace to Europe than Hitler.'

Philip simply nodded, staring fixedly ahead.

Behind the Mercedes two Ford cars had followed them all the way from London. Each carried four heavily armed men Tweed had brought up from the training estate at Send in Surrey. And behind them two drivers followed in Land-Rovers, vehicles which had been specially adapted at top speed before leaving Send.

Arriving in Chichester, they quickly reached the Dolphin and Anchor. The four vehicles which had come behind them were parked temporarily in the council car park. All the drivers were equipped with mobile phones and carried maps showing the route to Bosham.

It was still daylight. Newman pulled in behind Marler's Rover but had to park in the open. Paula checked her watch.

'It will be low tide at Bosham in one hour's time – and that will coincide with night falling.'

'Exactly the conditions I had hoped for,' said Tweed, 'so let's get inside and find our rooms.'

Paula glanced into the bar while Tweed dealt with the receptionist, a girl who recognized him from their last visit. Paula strolled into the large lounge, which had the bar at the back. The place was empty except for two people at the bar with their backs to her. Marler and Lisa.

'Having fun, you two?' she enquired.

Lisa swung round, looked surprised, then flashed her a warm smile.

'Now I have a rival for Marler's affections.'

'The lady has a head for alcohol,' Marler pretended to grumble.

'You have to watch this man,' Lisa told Paula. 'I ask for a double Scotch and he secretly gets me a triple. I have suspicions of his intentions.'

'Won't get me anywhere,' Marler said, still mock-grumbling. 'She downed the lot in two long swallows. Now she's getting me tight.'

'Are you on your own?' Lisa asked.

Which told Paula she had not seen Tweed and Newman before they had gone up to their rooms. Nor Philip, come to that.

'Looks like it, doesn't it?' Paula answered.

'Then we could have a *ménage-à-trois*,' Lisa suggested with a wicked grin.

'I can only cope with one woman at a time,' Marler responded. 'Who do you think I am? Casanova?'

'It's when men talk like that you have to be on your guard,' Lisa riposted. 'Maybe we could all have dinner together? With oodles of champagne. We'll break his bank balance.'

'Sorry,' Marler said. 'It's a tempting idea, but I have a boring meeting outside with a lawyer.'

'I'm fixed up, too, I'm afraid,' Paula replied, trying to sound regretful. 'Maybe another night. Are you staying here for a few days? At this hotel, I mean?'

'Who can tell?' Lisa shrugged. 'You know my life. If New York phones and says board a plane for Tokyo urgently, I immediately contact Heathrow. That's my living. But if I am still here, let's have dinner, the three of us.'

'And you're staying at this hotel?' Paula persisted.

'No. The Ship Inn, down North Street. If they've got a room. On the other hand, I might just stay here. I'll leave a note for you, Paula – with the receptionist.'

'I must go now,' said Marler. 'See you.'

'And I must rush to a shop, if it's still open,' Paula said.

'We'll meet again. I know we will,' Lisa told both of them.

Paula waited until Lisa, who paused for several minutes at reception, had left the hotel. On her way out of the bar with Marler – he had picked up a magazine and appeared to have found something which caught his attention – she went to reception.

'Is a Lisa Trent staying here?' she asked.

'Yes,' the girl said, 'she booked a room by phone a few hours ago.'

'Lisa is tricky,' Marler whispered as they headed for the staircase.

'Miss Grey,' the receptionist called out, 'could you come back a moment. I almost forgot. Before she went a few minutes ago she left a message for you.'

Paula collected the message, read it, showed it to Marler as they went up the stairs to see Tweed. He had told them earlier he had the same room he had occupied during their previous visit.

Paula – it's been such a rush today. I am an idiot. I did book a room here by phone before I left London. Call me a muddlehead! Do let's meet as soon as poss. Love, Lisa.

Marler raised his eyebrows, handed back the message.

'So she isn't tricky. And that's typical Lisa. Shooting all over the place like a dragonfly. I wonder what Tweed has been up to.'

Tweed was just putting down the phone when they knocked on his door. He unlocked it after asking who it was. Paula knew the momentum was building up the

476

moment she saw him. He was in his shirt sleeves, his jacket carefully folded over the back of a chair.

'I have news for you,' he said before they could sit down. 'Jill Selborne is now occupying a room in this hotel.'

'This place is getting crowded,' Paula remarked. 'How on earth do you know that? We've just come from the bar.'

'After chatting to Lisa Trent. I saw you before I came up. As for Jill, I phoned reception, said I didn't want to disturb her but had she arrived yet. They said she had. Probably slipped in while you were hobnobbing in the bar.'

'What made you enquire?' Marler asked.

'I just had a call from the leader of the two cars and the Land-Rovers in the council car park. He reported they'd been followed all the way from London by a dark-haired girl – hair plastered close to her head – in a Vauxhall Cavalier. It's all working out rather well. Up to now.'

'What about Rosa Brandt?' Paula asked. 'Nield should have arrived with her . . .'

'He has, I've been along to the room where she is being kept confined. Cheviot has taken over.'

'Cheviot? The head of the training school at Send? He is here?'

'He came down in one of the cars behind us. He releases Nield, who I want badly in this operation.'

'How is Rosa Brandt reacting?'

'She isn't. She didn't exchange one single word while she was being driven down here by Nield. I had a brief word with her myself. All she said was she would like to see me later, just the two of us.'

'That could be dangerous. She has been searched, I hope.'

'Yes, by Nield. Shoulder-bag checked before he left

477

the airport. I searched her case in the room here. No sign of a weapon.'

'What about Jill Selborne arriving?' Paula asked. 'I think it was a colossal cheek on her part to follow us. I could use stronger language.'

'But I told you it was what I wanted. Now we have the three suspects for Teardrop in Chichester. I shall interrogate each one later.'

'I feel it's creepy – knowing that woman who killed so many people in cold blood is wandering around on the loose.'

'Brandt is under guard . . .'

'Lisa Trent and Jill Selborne are not under guard,' Paula reminded him vehemently.

'We must get moving. We have to be in place to launch the assault on Cleaver Hall just before dusk falls.'

'What are the Land-Rovers for? And how did the leader get in touch with you about Selborne?'

'The leader used his mobile phone to contact me here. The Land-Rovers are part of the totally revised assault plan – revised by Philip and Newman at Park Crescent. Wait and see those vehicles in action. I had insisted we needed a major deception plan. They gave it to me.'

Tweed put on his jacket, then his sheepskin.

'I said we must get *moving* . . .'

51

A convoy of seven vehicles turned into the car park near the creek that Bosham village faced. Newman, driving his Mercedes, arrived first, transporting Tweed and Paula.

Behind them followed the two Fords packed with reinforcements. The Land-Rovers drove in after them. Nield's Citroën came in next, with Marler's Rover close behind.

A deep purple painted the sky in the west, the advance guard of dusk coming. Paula again marvelled at the number of yachts hoisted up on cradles for winter inside the car park.

'Where is Butler?' she said suddenly.

'He's already here,' Tweed said brusquely. 'His Ford Sierra hired at Heathrow is over there. I sent him down in advance to spy out the land – and the creeks.'

As though on cue, a burly figure appeared out of the gloom. Butler spoke to Tweed as he stepped out of the Mercedes.

'There's a lot of activity at Cleaver Hall. That high wall creates a shadow behind it. Men with torches have been walking down the drive, shining their torches on the grass. But they don't walk on it.'

'But they *do* walk down the drive,' Philip questioned.

'Yes. A lot of them with automatic weapons patrol up and down that drive.'

'You haven't been able to check the grounds at the back, I imagine,' Philip suggested.

'Yes, I have. I used my telescopic ladder. I wanted to check the top of that wall. With the equipment I've brought I can neutralize the alarm system, cut the two electrified wires. One is concealed below the top one. Very cunning.'

'But no one is checking the grass at the back?' Philip persisted.

'No one.'

'You're sure you can take out the alarm system and cut those electrified wires safely?' Tweed asked Butler.

'With that kind of job no one can be sure until they've attempted it.'

479

'Butler,' Philip said urgently, 'I want to take a quick look at a thatched cottage beyond the wall and to the right, looking across from here. Can you drive me there quickly? Now?'

'The property next door to Cleaver Hall? Funny old cottage. Doesn't look as though it's been inhabited for years.'

'You haven't much time left,' Tweed warned.

'Then we'd better go now,' said Butler. 'Follow me . . .'

'When we were driving here along that country road to Bosham,' Paula said, 'I thought I saw the headlights of an eighth car behind the convoy.'

'A local returning home,' said Tweed.

He banged his gloves together as Butler's Ford left the car park. The temperature was dropping rapidly. Paula walked back down the drive from the car park towards the narrow road leading to the creek and to Bosham. Newman caught up with her.

'And where do you think you're going?'

'The headlights of that eighth car bother me . . .'

They reached the end of the drive. Paula glanced down the road to the creek in time to see Butler's Ford turning left, disappearing from view. He was driving without lights. She looked to her right and saw nothing coming.

'Probably your imagination,' Newman chaffed her.

'Famous last words.'

Butler drove at speed along the road round the end of the creek. As Paula had predicted, Philip noticed, the tide was out, leaving behind a quagmire of slimy ooze and areas of sinister green amid tufts of grass. Not a place to fall into.

Butler turned right at the end of the creek, slowed down as they approached the entrance to Cleaver Hall. Neither of them looked through the gates as Butler cruised past, slowed even more, stopping about ninety feet beyond the end of the high wall. He nodded his head.

Philip got out, followed by Butler, holding a heavy cosh. The ancient thatched cottage stood about twenty feet back from the road. Carefully opening a small wooden picket gate, Philip walked slowly up the path of moss. The garden was neglected, a riot of bramble bushes and weeds. He took out his pencil torch as they reached the wooden door under a thatched porch.

Butler waited several yards back, staring round, looking for trouble. Philip pushed at the door but it held firm. It was as old as the hills. He switched on his pencil torch, examined the door.

'Nothing here,' Butler said, coming up behind him. 'No one has been here for years.'

'No? Then why these?'

Butler peered over his shoulder as Philip directed his beam at two locks, both encrusted with mud. Using his gloved hand, he rubbed at the mud and it crumbled, exposed two bright new locks. A Banham and a Chubb.

'If no one has been here for years why these locks?' Philip asked.

'Does put a different complexion on this place,' Butler admitted. 'We'd better be getting back. Tweed will be doing his nut.'

They had closed the picket gate behind them when Philip walked to the edge of the creek. He didn't need the torch to see the large motorboat with its canopy, concealed in a mess of reeds. It was moored to a slipway alongside an ancient landing stage. The slipway slanted downwards to a large elongated pool of water left behind when the tide had receded.

Philip went back to where Butler was sitting behind the wheel of his car. Butler leaned out of the window, kept his voice down.

'This is where we part company. I can see across to the

481

other side and the convoy is on its way here. Newman has told me I'm in charge of the assault on the rear. I know exactly what's wanted. I looked round the outside of that cottage while you were checking the door. There's no one in that place, so I'll lead my team in here soon as they arrive.'

'Well, as I'm sure Bob told you, I'm in charge of the frontal assault – the deception plan to help you do your work. I'll wait here for my lot.'

'And I'm parking the car just a bit further along this road, then I'll walk back here to join up with my team.'

'I think the Cleaver Hall gang will spot those vehicles coming,' Philip commented, glancing across the creek where the convoy was driving along the same road they had taken.

'Doesn't matter if they do,' Butler assured him. 'They will stay inside their strong point, but they may react. See you . . .'

There had nearly been the most almighty row when Paula had returned to the car park, opened the rear door and climbed in beside Tweed.

'Get out. Now,' he snapped. 'You are not coming with us.'

'I damned well am.' She fastened her seat belt, took her Browning automatic from her shoulder-bag. 'So stop being so bossy.'

'I am asking you to get out of this car now,' Tweed said with an edge to his voice.

'And I'm telling you I'm staying in this car. I thought I had made the occasional contribution to the success of our excursion into the jungle of Europe.'

'You were a key player and I'm extremely grateful,' said Tweed in a softer tone.

'Then leave her alone and let her come,' Newman

called out from behind the wheel of the Mercedes. 'She is a vital asset . . .'

'I was thinking of her safety,' replied Tweed, backing down even more.

'I know,' said Paula. 'But if we survive, we survive. If we go down together, so be it.'

'We'd better get moving, then,' Tweed decided. 'The others must be nearly there and I just hope we're in time.'

'We're *on* time,' said Newman, switching on the engine. 'Dusk is beginning to fall. Walvis won't open that roof until nightfall . . .'

On the other side of the creek several cars had gone past the closed gates. Automatic fire from high windows in Cleaver Hall sent a hail of bullets through the bars of the wrought-iron gates. They all missed their targets.

As Newman parked his car under the lee of the wall before they reached the gates, Philip appeared. He pointed to the two Land-Rovers, one parked ahead of Newman, still this side of the gates, the other standing on the far side.

'I've just checked the time. I want to give Butler a few more minutes to get into position at the back with his team. They were all carrying their telescopic ladders. Zero hour is precisely five minutes from now. Keep close to the wall, they've started firing from inside at random. Get out of the car but stay there . . .'

Paula was intrigued by Philip's natural air of command, a quality she had never seen so strongly displayed before. She stepped out and a freezing current of air hit her. The ice-cold breeze was coming up the channel from the south-west. She recalled that the highest of tides were driven in from the sea by a sou'westerly.

'There's that car again,' she said to Tweed, who stood beside her.

'Which car?'

483

'The eighth car I warned you about earlier, following the convoy.'

The car was driving slowly along the road they had used to reach Cleaver Hall. Still on the far side of the creek, it was moving without any lights.

'You can't possibly teli,' Tweed objected.

'I think I can. It's a new silver Citroën. So was the eighth car – I saw it as it passed under a street lamp which had come on early.'

'The locals also drive cars,' Tweed said dismissively. He had checked his watch when Philip said zero hour was in five minutes' time. He checked it again.

'I hope Butler and his team have reached their objective. They only have three minutes left . . .'

Butler and Nield, with four men close behind them, were trampling down old bramble bushes at the base of the wall looming above them. Each of the six men carried a telescopic ladder in one hand, a large canvas bag in the other – containing rocket launchers and explosive shells.

Extending his ladder to its full length, Butler mounted it at a point he had surveyed earlier. Reaching the top, he peered over. No sign of life on the spacious lawn stretching away to the mansion. He took from his pocket a tube containing a substance perfected by the boffins in the basement at Park Crescent. He stood close to the master electrodes controlling the alarm system. Normally, if touched, all the alarm indicators inside Cleaver Hall would have registered the intrusion.

He squeezed a large quantity of a black thick substance the consistency of clotted cream over the electrodes. In the bitter air the substance froze immediately. Butler grunted with satisfaction. The alarm system was immobilized.

He capped the tube, shoved it in his pocket, took out a

484

pair of rubber-tipped pliers. He first cut the almost invisible lower wire where it passed through a ring circuit. Then he treated the upper wire in the same way.

He looked along the wall to Nield, who was perched at the top of his own ladder, his launcher unlooped from his shoulder, a shell inserted in the muzzle taken from a canvas bag hanging from his neck. Beyond him the other four men were in place at the top of their ladders with their launchers at the ready.

Butler raised an arm once, telling them the devices along the wall were out of action. He hauled his own launcher off his shoulder, fed it with a shell. Then he took out a mobile phone, dialled a number by the fading light, spoke in code to Philip at the front.

'The boat lands at high tide . . .'

Earlier, in the library overlooking the front, Walvis had grasped Gulliver so fiercely by the arm his deputy winced.

'What the hell is that firing? It's almost time to go up to the roof, to send the signals to the unit leaders in the East.'

Gulliver had been standing by the window, then had walked back to be grabbed by Walvis, who was still holding on to him.

'It has to be Tweed and Co.,' Gulliver replied. 'Clearly he was not fooled by the Aldeburgh manoeuvre . . .'

'Is it safe? Is it safe? Is it safe?' babbled Walvis in near incoherent rage. He squeezed his deputy's arm even tighter. 'Is it . . .'

'Is what safe?'

'The mansion. This mansion. Are you sure your defences are adequate?' Walvis demanded.

'First, let go of my arm. Thank you.' Gulliver resisted the temptation to rub it where it was sore with his chief's iron grip. 'I saw vehicles passing beyond the closed gates. They are going to mount a frontal assault. Our gunfire

485

will cut them to pieces. Should any of them scale the wall they will avoid the drive – the gunfire will be too intense. When they try to cross the grass the land-mines will blow off their legs, half their bodies. Tweed's attack will be a horrific disaster.'

'Are you sure?'

'I am sure,' Gulliver replied, cool in a crisis.

'I may have to call someone in Warsaw,' Walvis said in a soft voice. 'I shall lock the door so I cannot be disturbed – the door of my study on the ground floor.'

'Understood.'

Gulliver was not sure what Walvis was talking about. He asserted his authority.

'We must go up to the roof now. It is almost dark. The technicians who operate the satellites are with their machines. You are coming up, I presume?'

'I will follow you. Lead the way. You will give the orders since you know the technology. I will simply witness the end of Europe. Yes, we must go now – it is almost dark.'

'Why didn't we send the signals an hour earlier?' Gulliver asked as they climbed the staircase. 'The part of Europe that concerns Tidal Wave – the beginning of it – is one hour ahead of us.'

'Because, my dear Gulliver,' Walvis said smoothly, 'I am a good psychologist – and have a good memory.'

'Don't follow you.'

Gulliver was having trouble keeping up with Walvis despite his boss's huge size.

'Then I will explain. First, the psychology – the moon does not rise over the dark world for some time yet. So, imagine the frontier guards on this side of the frozen rivers suddenly seeing a human tidal wave sweeping towards them. They will be overwhelmed with terror before they are overwhelmed by the human sea in total darkness.'

486

'And the memory angle?' Gulliver asked, still toiling upwards.

'Very simple. I remember that helicopter, which appeared when we had the roof open before. I am still suspicious of that incident. If another one appears now it will see nothing.'

'Got a point. Two points . . .'

They had reached the top landing, the foot of the mobile staircase which had been lowered, which led to the roof.

'After you,' Walvis said. 'You will take command after I give you the initial order.'

Inside the cavern below the closed roof the wall lights were on, revealing the extraordinary scene. Men sat behind their screens and the satellite dishes above them. The dishes had already been revolved at varying angles, all facing east, all ready to send a signal in a specific direction. Gulliver walked round, checking the angle of each dish. He came back to Walvis, who stood near the exit down the mobile staircase.

'Everything is ready,' Gulliver reported.

'Then open the roof . . .'

52

Philip closed down the aerial of his mobile phone after Butler had reported they were in position. Paula watched, fascinated, as several of Philip's unit, all wearing camouflage jackets, got behind one of the Land-Rovers after Philip had slipped briefly into the front seat. It had earlier been moved down a slope facing the closed gates, hiding it from the watchers inside Cleaver Hall. They started to manhandle it towards the gates. A fusillade of bullets ricocheted off the front of the vehicle as it came into view.

'What *are* they doing?' Paula asked.

'That Land-Rover, like the other one, has been fitted with armour plating to protect the men moving it. As an additional protection you'll have noticed they're all now wearing metal helmets. You're looking at a mobile bomb of enormous explosive power,' Tweed explained.

'How do the two vehicles work?'

'They have a contact point on the reinforced rams at the front. When one of these rams hits the gates you'll see something memorable.'

'Get inside the car and watch from there,' ordered Philip who had returned to the lee of the wall.

They climbed into the front seats since Newman had disappeared. Behind the wheel, Tweed closed the door and waited.

'The steering wheel has been fixed so it will move straight forward under its own power when Philip, who is holding a radio transmitter, presses the button . . .'

The Land-Rover reached the level road facing the centre of the two high closed gates. The men who had manhandled it into position dropped flat, Philip pressed the button. The Land-Rover sailed forward under its own power. It slammed into the gates and there was a deafening roar.

Paula stared, hypnotized, as the gates disintegrated and pieces of rail hurtled into the air. A rain of iron fell down but nothing hit the roof of the car they were sitting in. The stone pillars which had stood on either side of the gates had collapsed and chunks of masonry were soaring through the air, landing in the creek. The Land-Rover had vanished, blown to pieces by the power of the bomb.

'The entrance is now wide open – which is a vital part of the deception plan I suggested,' Tweed told Paula. 'But the next move is spectacular and will convince the defenders the assault is coming from the front only.'

The second Land-Rover had been moved further down the slope facing the drive, had stood a few feet behind its destroyed twin. The men who had fallen flat were now behind the second vehicle, again manhandling it up the slope.

Philip darted towards them, crouched low to avoid the hail of gunfire now pouring from the mansion. He darted back shortly afterwards and reported to Tweed in the car.

'Only one casualty, minor, the medic said. One man was caught a glancing blow across the side of the head by a piece of railing. He'll be OK. So far, so good.'

He darted off again, running the gauntlet of the hail of bullets, which was continuous now. Paula was relieved when he reached the second Land-Rover safely.

'One thing puzzles me,' she said. 'If one of the bullets fired from the mansion had hit the detonator, wouldn't the detonator at the front have gone off prematurely?'

'No, because it's concentrated machine-gun fire they're aiming down the drive. If they'd fired a shell, that could have been a different matter.' He reached for the door handle as the second Land-Rover crested the rise. 'You stay here. This I must see . . .'

He got out, kept under the lee of the wall, waited. The Land-Rover paused briefly, pointed straight down the drive through the open entrance. Philip pressed the button, the manhandlers again dropped flat. The Land-Rover moved forward, passed through the open gateway as a bombardment of bullets bounced off the armoured plate.

Tweed peered cautiously round the corner of the ruined pillar, using a spyhole where the wall had partially remained intact. It was like watching through a small window. A hand lightly touched his shoulder and Paula spoke in a brief pause in the bombardment.

'It's only me.'

'I told you to stay in the car,' Tweed snapped.

'I'm getting quite insubordinate these days, aren't I?'

Tweed could think of no reply and if he had the bombardment had opened up again, a concentrated burst of many automatic weapons aimed at the oncoming vehicle. The Land-Rover continued trundling straight down the drive, increasing speed.

It reached the end of the drive, mounted the steps to the terrace, crossed the terrace and rammed full force into the main double doors under a wide porch. The detonation boomed out, again deafening. The doors disappeared, the stone porch which had stood for ages was thrown sideways and massive chunks landed on the grass, some hitting land-mines, causing fresh explosions. The way in to Cleaver Hall was wide open.

At the top of the mansion the roof had slid open ponderously. Gulliver watched the technicians, waiting for them to start tapping out the signals.

Perched on top of the rear wall, Butler stared in amazement as the roof had opened, then aimed his launcher. His first high-explosive shell landed just inside the exposed cavern, stunning Gulliver, wrecking two dishes.

Behind him Walvis quietly slipped away down the mobile staircase. He started to descend to the ground floor rapidly as the mansion shook with fresh explosions above.

He reached the ground floor, ran to his study, went inside, locked the door. The study was situated at the end of the mansion closest to the thatched cottage beyond the wall.

Walvis took out a key, inserted it into an almost invisible hole in the panelling, turned the key and pushed. The panel opened like a door. He reached inside,

490

switched on a light, descended the first two of a flight of ancient stone steps, turned round, closed and locked the panel door behind him.

He used a torch he had earlier pocketed to illuminate his way along well-worn paving which floored the tunnel, built Heaven knew how many centuries earlier. He felt better when he had passed a chalk mark he had scrawled on the dripping stone walls during an earlier visit. That showed he had passed under the outer wall of Cleaver Hall, that soon he would climb a flight of steps to the secret door leading into the thatched cottage.

Inside the cavern in the roof a second explosive shell had landed. It impacted at Gulliver's feet, and his remains were scattered over the wall. More shells landed. The interior became an inferno as fire took hold and all the equipment was wrecked. The bodies of the technicians lay on the floor at grotesque angles.

Still perched at the top of the rear wall, Butler gazed in awe as a red glow appeared, then flames danced above the open roof. He fired two more shells as Nield did the same.

'Just for luck,' Butler said to himself.

The cavern became a furnace, burning everything. No signals had been sent. The second shell Butler had fired fell straight through the opening above the mobile staircase. The mansion below the cavern began to burn, the flames spreading rapidly as they greedily ate up the mass of woodwork. The fire rapidly spread down the main staircase as Nield's second shell curved in an arc, travelled through the opening and plunged down the side of the banister rail, only stopping and exploding when it hit the ground floor. Fire soared up the wide staircase, swiftly merged with the flames on the upper floors. The whole mansion was ablaze.

*   *   *

491

The defenders began fleeing out of the broken entrance at the front, avoiding the white-hot remnants of the destroyed Land-Rover. Some came down the drive, throwing away their weapons, holding their hands in the air.

Others panicked, ran on to the grass. Land-mines blew up and the panic-stricken escapers became very dead men. Two, mingling with their fleeing comrades, carried ropes with grappling irons, their automatic weapons looped over their shoulders.

More determined than their comrades, they came close to the smashed exit on to the road, slipped sideways on to a narrow border of grass they knew was not seeded with the land-mines. Standing under the lee of the wall, they threw up the rubber-covered prongs of the grapples, saw they had caught on the top of the wall, silently shinned up the ropes, reached the top of the wall and peered over.

Below stood Newman, gloves worn to shreds where he had helped manhandle both Land-Rovers up the slope and into position. He had used all his strength to heave the Land-Rovers forward and stood wearily.

Paula happened to glance round to speak to him, caught movement at the top of the wall above him. Two men were aiming their weapons point-blank at Newman's back.

'Look out, Bob!' she screamed. 'Above you . . .'

She raised her Browning but knew she was too late as Tweed swung round. Two shots rang out. The men on the wall flopped over it, hung there, weapons slipping out of their hands as they lay inert. Paula was staggered. She hadn't fired a shot. Then she saw in the near distance behind Newman a black-clad figure.

The phantom-like figure vanished in the darkness which had now fallen, a pitch-black darkness. She turned to Tweed.

492

'Did you see someone? There had to be someone who shot those two men on the wall. Who could it be?'

'No idea,' said Tweed.

53

Walvis used the same key to unlock the door at the top of the steps he had used on the secret door inside his study. In his right hand he held a Luger he had snatched from a study drawer on his way out.

He had operated the switch by the side of the second door to switch off the tunnel lights, to accustom his eyes to the darkness. He pushed the door open, listened for any sound of life. A dead silence met him.

He had stepped into a large ancient cupboard built into the wall of the cottage, concealing the door he now closed. He opened one of the double doors leading inside the thatched cottage's kitchen. A musty, damp odour met him, caused by the cottage being empty a long time.

He had made no sound entering the kitchen – door hinges had been kept well oiled, a job he had performed himself. The floor was stone-flagged and in one corner stood an ancient iron range for cooking. He listened again. The shooting had stopped.

Taking two keys, a Banham and a Chubb, from the pocket of his jacket he padded towards the front door. He was already feeling the intense cold penetrating his jacket and trousers.

At least I have plenty of outdoor clothes aboard the motorboat, he thought.

Without making the slightest noise, he inserted the key

in the top lock, turned it, did the same with the lower lock. Again he had kept them well oiled.

Walvis had told not a single member of his team that the secret tunnel existed. 'Trust no one' was his favourite maxim. He wondered briefly what had happened to Martin. He now realized Martin had been conspicuous by his absence during the attack on the mansion.

He opened the heavy wooden front door, raised his Luger, prepared to fire. Philip was walking down the path.

He carried in his left hand a long rope, looped. Close to the cottage, he knew he couldn't reach the Browning in his hip holster in time. Paula had loaned it to him. It had given her a certain satisfaction to know Philip would kill Walvis with her weapon.

Walvis had not heard him coming because of the moss on the path Philip had walked down. But his reflexes were astonishingly swift. Hence the Luger in his hand, aimed point-blank, at a range of ten feet. He couldn't miss.

'I've been waiting to meet you, Walvis, for a long time,' Philip said, his voice hard as granite.

'Well, you've met me. And I'll be the last person you will see in your life.'

He pulled the trigger, at the same moment as Philip darted to one side, in what he knew was a futile attempt to escape the bullet. In the silence of the night, disturbed only by the crackling sound of wood burning furiously at Cleaver Hall, came another sound. A click. In his panic rush to escape Walvis had forgotten to load the gun.

Philip was on him in less than a second. Walvis tried to bring down the Luger's barrel on his enemy's forehead, failed as Philip slid round the back of his massive form. Walvis felt a rope wrapped round his waist, turned to struggle, felt the barrel of the Browning against his back. Philip prayed he wouldn't have to pull the trigger. Walvis froze.

'Now I'll tell you what we're going to do,' Philip whispered. 'We're going to walk to your motorboat, get on board, have a quiet talk. Make with the feet. And don't try to escape, I'm holding the end of the rope with a slip knot at your back.'

Walvis began to walk along the path. He foresaw a chance to outwit his adversary. The fool should have shot him on the spot. No guts. They passed beyond the wicket gate and Philip ordered his prisoner to crouch down, to move fast to the motorboat. To his right there were vague figures in the distance, but they were Tweed's men, standing with their backs to him as they searched captives, stared down the drive at the blazing mansion as the roof collapsed.

Philip followed Walvis, unseen by anyone else, to the motorboat, ordered him to step into it. Walvis obeyed and Philip tied the end of the rope to a stanchion, a small wooden post protruding from the gunwale.

With Walvis secured, he used all his remaining strength to push the boat down the slipway. It suddenly gained momentum, splashed into the large pool of water stretching away into the distance. Philip jumped aboard at the last moment. The boat continued moving across the dark water, slowed to a halt as it bumped against a bank of oozing mud.

'Walvis,' Philip began, 'I am Philip Cardon. Does the name conjure up memories?'

'I've never heard that name before . . .'

'Listen, you bastard, if you don't answer my questions honestly, I'll tip you overboard.'

'Not into that.' Horrified, Walvis stared at the ooze which was coated with green slime. 'For God's sake have mercy . . .'

'Mercy is not a word in your vocabulary. I'll try once

495

more. Do you recall the name Jean Cardon?'

There was a long pause. Walvis was trying to think of how best to reply to his grim captor. Could this man be her brother?

'Yes, I do believe one of my staff mentioned the name.'

'Lucien?' Philip hammered at him ruthlessly. 'The man who first tried to run down Jean Cardon in a fake hit-and-run accident in the Fulham Road? A year ago?'

'It was Lucien's idea. His instructions were to scare her . . .'

'You're lying. His instructions were to kill her.'

Philip felt a brief satisfaction. By bluffing Walvis he had discovered the identity of the hit-and-run driver. No one else to search for.

'She wasn't killed, may I remind you?'

Walvis had the impression that the longer he kept Cardon talking the more likely it was that the opportunity would arise to turn the tables on him.

'No. By chance she wasn't. Now an important question. You were the one who later gave orders to Lucien to torture Jean Cardon at Amber Cottage on the way to the Witterings. Yes? Don't forget my warning.'

Walvis glanced over the side again. He hesitated. He felt Cardon was boxing him in. Lying on a ledge close to his hand was an iron marlinspike.

'I have a world-shaking project I planned for years . . .'

'Stop that. You're evading my question. And we know all about Tidal Wave.'

'Can I take out a handkerchief to mop my forehead? I find sweat getting into my eyes.'

'Just take out the handkerchief carefully.'

Walvis produced a large handkerchief, mopped his forehead, dropped the handkerchief, stooped down with difficulty to pick it up with his left hand. His right hand grasped the heavy marlinspike as he stood up and he

496

hurled it at his opponent's head. Philip ducked. The marlinspike landed in the water beyond the stern of the boat.

Philip rushed forward, caught Walvis off balance, pushed him over the side. Walvis was calling out, his voice muffled with shock, sinking into the ooze when Philip unwrapped the rope end from the stanchion, held on to it. Walvis was even heavier than he had realized and he had to brace his feet against the deck to hold the rope taut. Walvis had already sunk into the ooze up to his waist. His mud-stained hands and arms flapped feebly but his sinking body had stabilized.

'Now,' Philip called out, 'I'm going to ask you again. If you answer truthfully I'll save your life. Did you give the order to torture Jean Cardon to Lucien?'

'I did. When you are engaged on a great project you have to do some dreadful things.'

'Which comes easily to you. Why did you do it?'

'That I can't remember . . .'

Philip let the rope go slack. Walvis sank steadily deeper into the quagmire with surprising speed. He caught Philip off guard when his head was submerged. Summoning up his last reserves, Philip hauled on the rope. Walvis's shaggy grey hair, plastered with mud, appeared first, then his head and shoulders. Walvis was spluttering out mouthfuls of the foul-smelling ooze. He went on coughing and choking as Philip repeated the question.

'Why did you do it?'

'She . . .'

'Say her name. She was no ordinary person, damn you.'

'Jean . . . Cardon . . . had investigated . . . certain of my . . . secret companies. She – Jean Cardon – had traced my secret bases . . . by investigating certain money payments. *Who* are you?'

'I was her husband.'

The statement hit Walvis like a hammer blow. Philip

497

saw the shock, the fear which contorted his flabby face.

'Oh, my God! She was a clever woman. No one else got near me.'

'Now I know everything,' said Philip in a voice he hardly recognized.

'You said if I answered your questions you would save me. I can't breathe . . .'

I can't breathe.

The very same terrified words Jean had used in her agony. Philip let the rope go slack.

'You said you'd save me,' screamed Walvis.

'I lied.'

Walvis sank deeper. The ooze rose to his chest, rose to his jowly jaw, rose to his mouth. He couldn't keep it shut any longer. He was swallowing great gouts of ooze as he sank deeper. Philip watched it reach his terror-stricken eyes, then they disappeared. His shaggy grey hair sank out of sight. The loose rope followed him. Its final length curled like a snake, then vanished. Walvis was entombed in the quagmire. Maybe for ever.

Returning to the wall in front of the mansion, which also had almost disappeared, Philip, looking tired, close to exhaustion, took Tweed and Paula aside. He handed back to Paula the Browning, told them in a flat tone what he had done. They listened in silence, then Paula laid a comforting hand on his arm.

'I got no satisfaction out of that horrific experience,' Philip ended in the same flat tone. 'But it was a job that had to be done. When can we get out of here?'

54

'I am determined to prove the real identity of Teardrop tonight,' Tweed announced. 'I want to clear up this whole business at one go.'

'And how are you going to do that?' asked Paula as she sipped at her glass of French dry white wine.

'I'd like to know, too,' said Newman.

The three of them had driven the short distance to The Berkeley Arms, where they had called in during the earlier visit before leaving for Europe. Tweed had left Philip in charge of all the men who had attacked Cleaver Hall.

'Take the prisoners – handcuffed to each other – and dump them inside that thatched cottage where you encountered Walvis trying to escape. Move them there and take our team back to London. You'll have to hustle before the Fire Brigade arrives, which will be any minute – the locals in Bosham can hardly have failed to see the conflagration that is consuming Cleaver Hall.' He had looked through the open entrance. 'Not much of it left now. That breeze coming up the channel has helped to finish it off.'

'I'd better put my skates on, then . . .' Philip said.

After giving his orders Tweed had been driven away with Paula by Newman in his Mercedes. The car was now parked out of sight in the area behind the pub.

'Why did you put Philip in sole charge – after all he has gone through?' Paula asked as she sipped more of her wine.

'To occupy his mind. To stop him thinking. And he has

proved himself to be a first-rate leader. That's why,' Tweed had told her. 'And if we hear a car pulling up outside it will be Pete Nield bringing his Citroën. I'll need that to reach Amber Cottage.'

'Amber Cottage!' Paula had exclaimed. 'Just what are you up to? It's something to do with Teardrop. Isn't it?'

'Yes, it is. You know when we arrived I said I wanted to call Howard from the box over the road? I didn't call him. Instead I called the three suspects, hoping they'd all be in their rooms. Brandt was, of course, guarded by Cheviot. I told Cheviot to release Brandt, to leave her alone with the key to the door—'

'That was a dangerous thing to do—' Newman began to protest.

'Please keep quiet until I've finished. Over the phone I told each of the three suspects – Brandt, Trent and Selborne – that I had found out who Teardrop was, but I needed them to tell me certain facts which would confirm my theory.'

'You're playing with dynamite,' Newman warned.

'I said, please keep quiet. I'm short of time. I invited each of the three women to meet me at Amber Cottage at different times – with a thirty-minute interval between each agreed appointment. One of them, I'm sure, will turn up early. Teardrop.'

'We're coming with you,' Newman said bluntly.

'No, I'm going alone. Butler has loaned me his Walther. I know Teardrop's tactics now. Her fake crying fit before she produces her gun and aims it, the one with the cyanide-tipped bullet. I will be ready for her.'

Paula glanced round the pub for the third time. They were still the only customers, at a corner table well away from the bar where the woman who ran the place was standing, polishing glasses.

'And how,' Paula enquired, 'will you gain entry into Amber Cottage? Break in?'

500

'Heavens, no. Butler not only gave me the gun, he also gave me his set of skeleton keys. He even showed me the one that opens the front door.'

'How would he know that?' Newman demanded.

'He left early, went straight to Amber Cottage as I had secretly instructed him . . .'

'It's pitch dark outside,' Newman pointed out. 'And the electricity at Amber Cottage will have been cut off – so no lighting.'

'Butler, as you may recall, is also a master electrician. He fixed it so the power was turned on again. The lights are now controlled by a time clock. As we speak Amber Cottage will be a blaze of lights.'

'You're mad as a hatter,' Paula snapped.

'I still think we should come with you,' Newman repeated.

'All right.' Tweed sat bolt upright. 'I'm giving both of you a direct order. You are to return to London as soon as Nield has brought me his Citroën. Philip will be waiting for him further down the road, ready to pick him up as soon as he's delivered the Citroën. Have you both got that? A direct *order*. Newman, you can drive Paula back.'

'I don't want to be thinking about you.' Paula stood up from the table. 'I've got a girl friend in Havant. I'm going to phone her now so I can spend the night chatting with her. If she's available then I'll phone for a taxi. It would be miles out of your way, Bob.'

She was gone. Newman threw up both hands in a gesture of despair.

'Better let her have her own way. Otherwise she'll have the heebie-jeebies over your crazy plan. She'll probably have them anyway.'

They looked up as Pete Nield came into the pub, walked to their table, put down car keys. He spoke quietly.

'The Citroën is parked out back next to Newman's

501

Merc. Plenty of petrol in the tank. I'd better get back to Philip. He's in no mood to hang around here. By the way, Tweed, we did as you suggested. Dumped all the captives handcuffed together in that cottage. Also we threw their weapons in with them, again as you suggested. We used gloves to handle them, gripped them by the barrels, so their fingerprints will be on them. Finally, we checked for a loaded weapon, in case some of them escaped. Not one was loaded. They must have emptied them before they came rushing down the drive, hands held up. I'm off now. Take care.'

'Very good work, Pete . . .'

Newman sat staring at his drink, pushed away the half-full glass. He switched his gaze to Tweed.

'I'm not in the least bit happy about this idea.'

'Nobody asked you to be happy.'

Paula returned shortly afterwards. She sat down, looked at Tweed, shook her head in disapproval.

'My girl friend was at home. So I'll spend the night at her place, then catch a train to London in the morning. A taxi is on the way to collect me.'

'I'm off, too,' said Newman. 'Good luck. You're going to need it. Best, Paula, if you wait in here until the cab arrives.'

'I'll do that,' she replied.

Newman left, got behind the wheel of his Mercedes, drove out and headed back for London. His expression was grim and he had to force his mind away from Tweed to concentrate on his driving.

He had one more order to carry out for Tweed – to phone Chichester police headquarters in the morning, to tell them the cottage next to the burnt-out Hall had a gang of drug traffickers inside the place. The call would be anonymous. He wondered if it would be the last order for Tweed he would ever carry out.

55

Tweed drove slowly as he approached Amber Cottage. The road to the Witterings and the coast was deserted of traffic in both directions. On a bitterly cold December night he had expected that. He started talking to himself, as he occasionally did on his own in a situation of maximum tension.

'Well, Harry Butler did a good job. Amber Cottage is lit up like a flaming Christmas tree. And the first candidate for Teardrop's mantle – or rather her veil – is due here in three-quarters of an hour. So is Lisa Trent already here with her cherished cyanide-tipped bullet?'

He drove the car on to the wide grass verge in front of the dwelling. Amber Cottage had no garage. But he did want his vehicle to be in full view as the women he had called arrived.

He left on the car lights, dimmed. Then he stood looking at the cottage standing well back from the highway. As instructed, Butler had closed all the curtains. He was watching for the hint of a shadow silhouetted inside the cottage. Nothing moved except the raw wind, which was increasing in strength.

Opening the picket gate, which squeaked on its rusted hinges, he walked slowly down the paved path leading to the front door under a small porch. In his right hand he held the Walther, in his left Butler's skeleton key.

Before opening the door he walked all round the cottage and found nothing indicating the presence of someone else. It gave him an eerie feeling to recall that it was inside this cottage Jean Cardon had been tortured almost to the point of death, her lungs crushed brutally by Lucien's fiendish instrument.

He completed his circular tour and arrived back at the front door. He inserted the key carefully, silently – because Butler had oiled the lock. He pushed open the front door, walked inside quickly because he knew he was silhouetted against the lights Butler had activated.

He switched off the lights closest to the door. He had walked straight into the living-room and Butler had removed dust sheets from the chintz-covered furniture. He paused before chintz curtains hanging from a side wall. Jerking them aside suddenly he stared into the alcove beyond.

'A good place for someone to hide,' he said aloud. 'I know I'm talking to myself but it's all right as long as you know you're doing it.'

He closed the curtains, explored cautiously the rest of the cottage. An ancient kitchen with a stone-flagged floor, a back door which was secured with two old bolts, a smaller sitting-room. That covered the ground floor. He slowly mounted the wooden stairs and they groaned under his tread.

Upstairs he found, again with the lights on, two small bedrooms, a storeroom and a bathroom with an iron bath with grotesque legs – the type which had for some incredible reason become fashionable again. The loo was in the bathroom.

He descended the stairs, went to the front door which he had left half open as an escape route. No, he told himself, I had a reason but now get your act together. He left the front door almost closed but not shut.

'This is where I'm going to wait for them,' he decided. 'Assuming they all come, assuming I'm still alive at the end of this great gamble. But how else could I have attempted to trap Teardrop?'

504

He took some trouble choosing where he was going to sit. Then he settled himself on a couch against the left-hand wall. It guaranteed his visitors would have to walk into the room before they saw him. He took a flask of brandy from his pocket, uncapped it, smeared his mouth with its contents, then splashed some of the liquid on the floor. It gave the impression he had been drinking to quiet his nerves.

He took an equal amount of time to select a hiding place for the Walther, somewhere out of sight but also somewhere he could reach it quickly. He chose a cushion, slipped the weapon underneath it with the butt nearest to his right hand. The aroma of brandy now filled the room. Tweed looked round the room, decided the stage was set. He had done all he could. Now he would have to endure the worst part. He would have to wait.

He never heard a car approaching the cottage. He never heard the front door being pushed wide open. But he felt the current of cold air flooding in and he tensed.

She came in slowly, the gun gripped professionally in both hands. A woman of medium height and slim build. A woman with a mane of flaming red hair, wearing a pair of large tinted glasses which concealed a large part of her face.

'Do come right inside,' Tweed said. He burped and had slurred the words. 'I assume you are Teardrop?'

'You have been a little too clever this time, Mr Tweed. I spoke to the receptionist at the Dolphin, made up a story, and she told me you had phoned two other women. You have been too clever by half – you have committed suicide.'

'So you are Teardrop?' he repeated.

'Yes, I am the notorious – and so successful – Teardrop. I think you will be my last assignment and then I shall retire. You can run out of luck if you go on too long.'

'You feel no compunction about all the men you killed – some with families?'

'The first was the most difficult. Then it became so easy. Men are such fools. An attractive woman can flatter them, twist them round her finger. And when you cry their defences collapse.'

'Excuse the aroma . . . Whoops!' He had burped again. 'I felt I needed a little sustenance before we at long last met.'

'You needed drink to control your fear before seeing me?' Her voice was filled with contempt. 'The formidable Mr Tweed has to get drunk before he meets Teardrop. Stop moving your right hand. Now do exactly what I tell you.'

The gun she was aiming point-blank at him was a Browning. Ironic, Tweed thought, it is Paula's favourite weapon.

'You will move in slow motion,' Teardrop ordered. 'You will lift up that cushion and drop it slowly on to the floor. Do it *now*!'

Tweed had no option but to obey. As he had foreseen, Teardrop had turned up very early, probably expecting to be inside the cottage waiting for him. He lifted the cushion slowly, dropped it on the floor, exposing the Walther.

'As I thought,' Teardrop commented in her hard voice. 'Now, again in slow motion, use your elbow to edge the gun on to the floor. *Now!*'

Tweed did as she had commanded. The weapon thudded on a worn rug, way out of his reach. He burped a third time, put a hand over his mouth.

'A drunken Tweed,' Teardrop sneered. 'The pathologist will include that in his report. What a dirty ending.'

'Exactly why are you shooting me?' Tweed asked.

506

'For money. For a lot of money. I saw other women flaunting their diamonds, their pearls, God knows what else – and all inherited. They never did a day's work in their life. They are paying me a fortune to kill you.'

'Which you will never get. Walvis is dead.'

'What has that to do with anything? I will get my fee, my fortune. I shall live a life of luxury. I deserve to. I am the best in my work. No one has ever been able to detect who I am. I shall be a millionairess – so say your last prayers . . .'

'I would appreciate it if you told me a few seconds before you press the trigger. To prepare myself.'

'Prepare yourself for a swift but agonizing death, Tweed. The bullet is tipped with cyanide. You have five seconds left of life . . .'

A shot rang out, a second shot, a third shot. Teardrop staggered, her body shook with shock, she was still holding the gun but it drooped in her hand. A fourth shot rang out. Five . . . six . . . seven . . . eight . . . nine. Paula, standing in the alcove, with the curtains pulled aside, had emptied the magazine into Teardrop who dropped like a stone, her body curling into a cat-like position on the floor.

'You emptied the magazine into her,' Tweed said with a note of wonderment.

'The lousy murdering bitch asked for it. I wanted her dead, very dead.'

'So I gathered. Let's see who she was. Wait a minute.' Tweed took out a notebook, scribbled a name on it, folded the sheet, gave it to Paula. 'Now let's see if I was right. She certainly disguised her voice.'

Standing over the corpse, he slowly removed the tinted glasses, then took hold of the mane of red hair and gently removed the wig. They both stared down at the face. Paula looked at the name he had written and he had been right.

Lisa Trent.

Epilogue

'I'm grateful for the way you kept me informed by talking out aloud,' said Paula as Tweed drove them back to the Dolphin.

'Well, you did find that concealed alcove to hide inside. I suppose you dashed into the cottage while I was upstairs.'

'That's exactly what I did. I stretched myself while we were waiting – I'd got cramped huddled in the back of your car while we travelled to the cottage from The Berkeley Arms. They're keeping up with us,' she said, glancing back.

After the death of Lisa Trent they had waited until Jill arrived in her silver Citroën, followed later by Rosa Brandt in a taxi. Tweed had met each woman at the door, told them it was all over, had asked Jill to wait in her car until someone else arrived.

'When we get back to the Dolphin I want a private word with Rosa Brandt. You can wait in my room until I have seen her,' Tweed said.

'Understood. Incidentally, how did you start suspecting Teardrop was Lisa Trent days ago?'

'It really was fairly obvious. As with Walvis, no one had seen Rosa Brandt, who kept very much under cover. Yet someone was going round dressed exactly like her each time they assassinated a target. Now only one person could do that – a woman who *had* seen her, had time to study her way of dressing, her mannerisms. And one person had. Lisa Trent told us she had interviewed

Brandt some time ago when she made her first attempt to interview Walvis. That was point one.'

'And point two?'

'Jill Selborne was very much on view in Salzburg – she even had lunch with us. But Lisa Trent never appeared, yet two people thought they had seen her, one being yourself. And poor Ziggy Palewski was murdered in that café. Circumstantial evidence but I felt it was so strong that Trent had to be Teardrop.'

'But what about Rosa Brandt? It could have been her.'

'I felt that was extremely unlikely as she was assistant to Walvis and spent so much time in his office. I'm sure a middleman told Trent about the next target, fixed the fee with Walvis. Walvis would have noticed if every time he ordered an assassination Brandt happened to be away. The clincher was Sherwood's note made when he had dinner with Teardrop. *Speaks perfect idiomatic English*. Newman confirmed that – he recalled how Brandt spoke during the interview with Trent. Not perfect idiomatic English at all. So I concentrated on Selborne and Trent.'

'Bob will be irked that I tricked him at The Berkeley Arms, saying I'd phoned a girl friend when I never made a call.'

'Leave me to handle Newman. And be ready to leave at the crack of dawn. Back to London.'

Tweed sat in one armchair in her bedroom while Rosa Brandt sat in another, facing him. His tone throughout the conversation was kindly and sympathetic.

'First, I fear I have to ask you to prepare yourself for a great shock.'

'About Walvis? You mean he's dead, don't you?'

'Yes. It was quick,' Tweed lied.

'Oh, my God. He was the only man who ever looked

509

after me.' Tears were rolling down her face below the veil. She took out a handkerchief, slid it under the veil and mopped her eyes. 'I'm sorry. He was a strange man – I suspect he did many dreadful things, but to me he was always like a loving brother. Occasionally he snapped at me, but he was still so kind.'

'I can understand and believe that.'

'I know from things I have heard that you must have suspected I was Teardrop. She dressed like me, didn't she? I thought so. Mr Tweed, only one man for many years has seen me without my veil in place. I think – because you have been so kind – you should see me without it.'

Tweed sat, relaxed, with a half-smile on his face. She removed the black cap and the attached veil. Her hair was dark. She stared at Tweed, studying his expression. He gazed back, still relaxed, still with the half-smile.

'I thought it was something like that. You must have suffered a great deal. May I ask how it happened?'

'A jealous woman who thought I was having an affair with her husband. She mistook me for the real culprit. She threw sulphuric acid in my face.'

'How vicious can you get? She must have been insane.'

'I don't know. What I do know is that, apart from Walvis, you are the only man who has seen me without showing great revulsion, without turning your head away. I sometimes thought the reason Walvis took pity on me was because he was such an ugly man and knew people would sooner not be in his presence. Maybe that affected his whole life.'

'In one way or another,' Tweed said, 'we all carry the scars of life.'

Tweed told Paula about Rosa Brandt as they approached London. He described in detail what had taken place.

'Poor woman,' Paula said when he had finished. 'To be

510

disfigured with a hideous scar – and on her face. No wonder she always wore that veil.'

'It was pretty hideous. I think I managed to sit and show no reaction when she took off her veil. What did help me was that I'd wondered if it was something like that which caused her always to wear the veil. Jill is bringing her back by car and driving her to Heathrow. I'll phone Kuhlmann and tell him all about it. He's a great policeman but also a great human being. He won't even question her.'

'We're going to arrive very early,' said Paula, glancing at her watch. 'When you said the crack of dawn you meant it. I expect all the others will still be fast asleep.'

After seeing to everything he had to attend to, Philip had gone back to his London apartment in the early hours. He felt bone weary and knew he would flake out as soon as he got into bed.

He dreamed during the night that he was walking with Jean in a strange English town by a seashore which curved in a bay. They strolled along the water's edge, chatting together.

Philip was watching some strange boats out at sea. He pointed them out to Jean who also thought they were weird. He woke up suddenly, realized it was daylight. Normally Jean was up before him, liked half an hour on her own to get her act together, then she would bring him a mug of tea.

He turned his head to nudge her awake. The pillow next to his was empty. The realization, seeing that empty pillow, again hit him a sledgehammer blow like the previous dream when he had been with her. He felt stunned with grief, got out of bed slowly, averting his eyes from the other pillow.

* * *

511

Newman arrived at Tweed's office in Park Crescent in midmorning. A few minutes earlier Kuhlmann had phoned.

'What happened on the river line, Otto?' was Tweed's first question. Kuhlmann checked he was on scrambler, then spoke.

'We got lucky. The top brass was still arguing the toss when the horde started to cross. They were halfway over, in midstream, so to speak, when they opened up with every weapon they were armed with. That did it – brought about what I'd been trying to achieve for hours. General Reichenbach, the American Supreme Commander, gave the order. All the hidden artillery down the Oder–Niesse line shelled the ice. It broke up, took down everyone trying to cross, drowned the lot. No more will try it.'

'I've seen, heard nothing about this news anywhere.'

'You wouldn't have done. Reichenbach had all reporters, all TV crews, moved back a hundred kilometres from the river lines two days ago. For their protection, he said. We've started circulating rumours that refugees tried to cross and their weight broke the ice under them.'

'That's very clever. Who had that idea?'

'I believe I thought of it. What about Walvis?'

Tweed told him about Walvis. He also told him about Rosa Brandt. Kuhlmann asked Tweed to notify him of her flight, said he'd have plainclothes policewomen to meet and escort her home. Then he told Tweed they'd raided Walvis's HQ, found a list of top Chechen Mafia names. When he checked the names Kuhlmann found they'd all been shot – by Walvis's men. Kuhlmann promised to keep in touch, said goodbye.

Paula was nervous about meeting Newman and buried her head in her files behind her desk when he walked in.

'Sit down, Bob,' Tweed greeted him breezily. 'Have some coffee. I've something to tell you . . .'

Newman listened in silence while Tweed told him about

512

the previous night's events at Amber Cottage. He told him the deception they had practised on him had been his own idea. When he had finished Newman stared at Paula.

'If I'd known I'd have insisted on coming with you.'

'Which,' Tweed told him, 'is why I arranged you shouldn't know. One person too many in the vicinity of Amber Cottage and Teardrop might have taken fright and gone away.'

'Also, Bob,' Paula said quietly, 'this is the age of equality. If women can become vicious assassins then another woman can shoot them down. I had a thing about Teardrop.'

'Which reminds me,' said Tweed. 'Buchanan has been told about Lisa Trent's body lying in the cottage – I called him several hours ago. He'll ask you, Paula, when he does turn up here, why you fired the whole magazine – all nine bullets – into her. The answer? She was still aiming her gun at me and you were worried she might pull the trigger at the last moment.'

'Well, I was worried, wasn't I?' Paula replied with a dry smile.

'That clears that up. There is something else. Jill Selborne impressed me with her coolness, her ability. Incidentally, she was secretly working for me – rather like Weatherby. Bob, she fired the shots at those men on the wall which saved your life.' He ignored Newman's stunned expression. 'Jill has asked if she can join us. Paula, would you show her the ropes, if I agree? I'll turn her down if you object.'

'But I don't object. I think it's a good idea. Yes, I will supervise her training. She'll have a tough ride – but I think she's good. Incidentally, remembering she was in Naval Intelligence for two years – and secretly working for you – why did you have her on your list of suspects?'

'Because you never know with another human being

513

when large sums of money are involved, the fees Walvis was paying Teardrop – not until that particular person has proved herself. So, we have a new recruit.'

Tweed, Newman, Paula and Monica were the only people in the office when Philip came in, holding a file. Paula looked at him and saw the pain in his eyes. That was going to take a long time to go away, if ever.

'I've completed my report on the Cleaver Hall firefight,' said Philip and laid the file on Tweed's desk. 'That's just about it, isn't it?'

'Thank you for all you have done. You have proved that you can operate on your own without any back-up – more than once. You have also proved you can lead a team on a major assault. Philip . . .' Tweed leaned back in his chair, stared out of the window. 'Permanent solitude in your private life is not something I would recommend to anyone. You won't believe me now, but over a period my words will come back to you time and again.'

He was still staring out of the window and Paula knew Tweed was thinking of his own wife, who had left him for a Greek shipping millionaire years before. He looked at Philip.

'You've had a tough time. You need some rest. Go home.'

Philip waved a vague hand at each person in the room and went to the door. He turned as he opened the door, on the verge of leaving.

'Home? Where is home now?'

A sombre silence descended on the room as he quietly shut the door.